PRAISE FOR THE WORK OF AUTHOR RICHARD C. WHITE

"Entertaining, old-school sword and sorcery, in the tradition of Fafhrd and the Gray Mouser."

—**Jim C. Hines**, author of the Magic ex Libris, Jig the Goblin, and The Princesses series, on *For a Few Gold Pieces More*

"What a fantastic ride! If you like sarcasm and snark reminiscent of Harry Dresden, good doses of magic, treachery, and myth, this is the book for you."

—**Goodreads**, on *For a Few Gold Pieces More*

"White's *Terra Incognito* is a solid introduction to the subject of world building. It succeeds in helping the apiring writer in creating a skeletal framework on which to hang the moving parts required of a believable fictional setting."

—**The Gaming Gang**, on *Terra Incognito: A Guide to Building the Worlds of Your Imagination*

"A very good spin on the tried and true 'good-guys-for-hire' formula. All in all, an enjoyable read that I would recommend to anyone."

—**Word of the Nerd**, on *Troubleshooters, Incorporated: Night Stalkings*

"An accurately dialogued epic set in a place and time of fantasy. If you like pirates or elves or fantasy adventure or pure swashbuckling, then pick it up."

—**Comic Genesis**, on *The Chronicles of the Sea Dragon Special*

CHASING DANGER

THE CASE FILES OF THERON CHASE

RICHARD C. WHITE

www.starwarpconcepts.com

new york

StarWarp Concepts

P.O. Box 4667

Sunnyside, NY 11104

Visit our website: **www.StarwarpConcepts.com**

Visit Richard C. White on the Web at:

www.richardcwhite.com

LOCC: 2019937982

ISBN: 978-0-9982361-6-2 (trade paperback)

ISBN: 978-0-9982361-7-9 (e-book)

First Print Edition: April 2019

10 9 8 7 6 5 4 3 2 1

Front cover photograph by StockSnap, courtesy Pixabay

https://pixabay.com

Back cover photograph by Michaela Wenzler, courtesy Pixabay

Edited by Steven Roman

Printed in the USA

This book is dedicated to Gerald Mohr (Phillip Marlowe), Jack Moyles (Rocky Jordan), Dick Kollmar (Boston Blackie), Howard Duff (Sam Spade), and Frank Lovejoy (Night Beat) for bringing me hours of entertainment as they brought their characters to life on the radio.

ACKNOWLEDGMENTS

Like any great project, there was no way I could have done this on my own. Here's a small measure of my thanks to the people who helped pull it together:

Tommy Hancock, for helping reignite my interest in pulps and noir again.

Elaine Witt, for not only being a great person, but also being the inspiration for the Sparkly Reaper.

Glen Cook, for showing that fantasy and noir fit together so well.

John G. Hartness and Natania Barron, for all the design work that went into turning a manuscript into a book.

Steve Roman, who not only is a fantastic editor and publisher, but also has put up with my quirks for 27 years now.

And finally, Joni M. White, who once again has put up with my foibles and ensconcing myself in the basement as I write these stories. None of this could have happened without your support.

CONTENTS

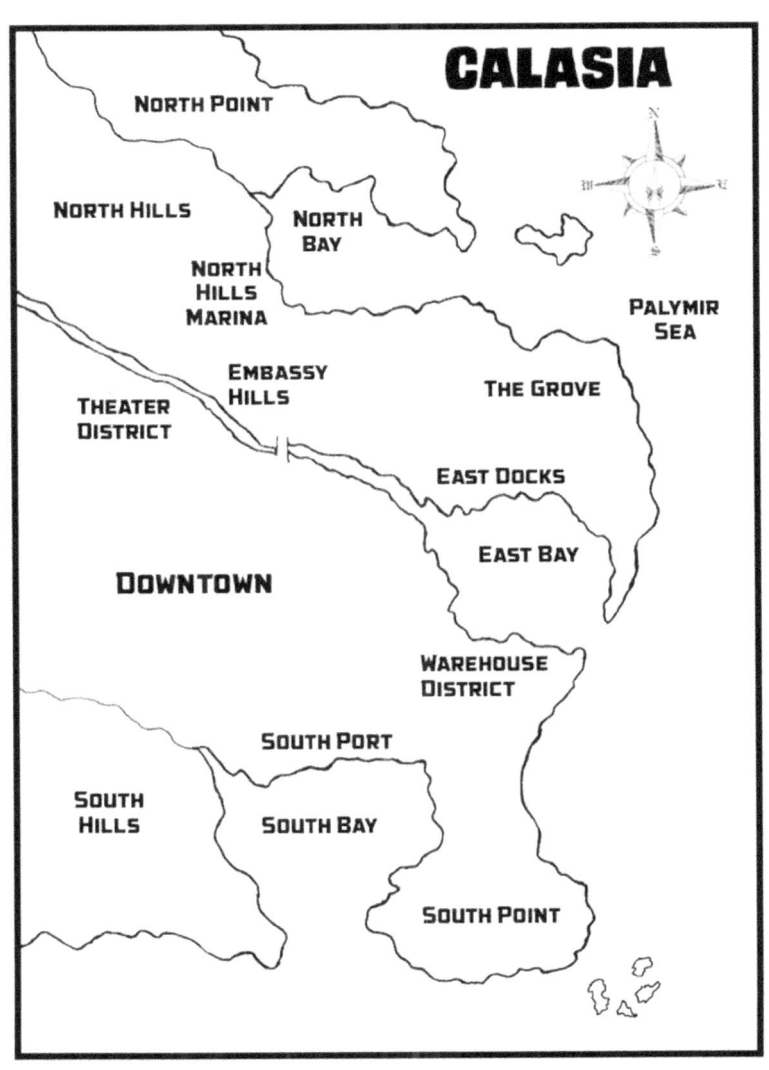

Case 1:
The
Full
Moon
Affair

THE FULL MOON AFFAIR

It was another Tuesday in Calasia. The cool breeze blowing in off the Palymir Sea brought a break in the unseasonably warm spring we'd been having and there was a hint of rain. I was doing what I normally do, sitting around my office waiting for the phone to ring, a message to appear on my desk, or more importantly, a client to wander into my office.

I glanced down at the book in my hands, realized I'd read the same paragraph four times already, and snapped it shut in disgust. Leaning back in my chair, I put my feet up on the desk, disturbing the pile of bills I was going to have to deal with sometime in the near future. Unfortunately, after settling the expenses from my last case, the accounts payable exceeded the accounts available by several factors.

The sound of the typewriter in the other room reminded me I was a very lucky man. My secretary, Kyra Sylvari, knew that I would make good on her back salary as soon as something came along. She also knew where I slept and had a couple of large cousins who'd be happy to remind me about what I owed her if I decided to skip.

Apparently, the warm weather had driven much of the crime in Calasia underground. No one seemed to have the energy to knock over a bank, rob a messenger, hex their rival or even jaywalk. It was a boon for the city, but it was murder for guys like me in the private detective business. No crime meant no pay. If not for my absolute hatred of time clocks and bosses, I might have been tempted to break down and get a real job.

Luckily, I hadn't fallen that far into the abyss when she came in.

Heels clacking on hardwood warned me Kyra was heading my way. I swung my feet to the floor and grabbed up a folder with some papers in it, attempting to look busy. Not that it would fool her; she knew the accounts payable amount better than I did. Still, there could be a client right behind her and better to look busy than bored. She slipped inside and pushed the door closed. When she turned back around, I saw a look of concern on her face.

"Theron, you've got a client waiting out here, a Miss Ze'eva Blackthorne."

"What's she like?"

Kyra pursed her lips before responding. "Young. Attractive. Well dressed but not too flashy. Seems like a good kid. Very worried about something."

"But you don't approve of her, Kyra?"

Kyra smoothed out her dress, something she typically did right before delivering bad news. She moved a little closer and spoke in a soft voice. "I believe she's in trouble and I believe she needs help. I also believe there's more to her than meets the eye. Just be careful with this one."

"Do I detect a hint of jealousy in your voice?"

Kyra blushed and laughed. "I know you. You fall in love five times a week. If you weren't such a good person, boss, I'd have been out of here years ago. Besides, it's not like you're hard to look at yourself . . . for a human."

Now, it was my turn to blush. "If you're bucking for a raise, you're on the right track. However, if you want a raise, I need to earn the money to pay you, so please show our client in."

"All right. Just be careful, Theron. You might lose more than your heart with this one."

"Always am, sweetheart."

She gave me "that" look as she pulled the door shut behind her. I should have known better—she sees the bills from the doctor before I get them. Hopefully, I'll make enough to pay Doc Griffin off sometime this century.

I cleaned off my desk as Kyra escorted the young lady in. I caught myself staring in spite of my best intentions. There was something almost unnatural about her presence. She was the kind of woman every other woman hated the second she walked into a room. I ushered her toward the only padded chair in the office and motioned for her to sit down. She adjusted her skirt and placed her well-made purse gently to the side.

"Mr. Chase, I'm looking to hire a detective to help me out of a situation. You come highly recommended for your efficiency and mostly for your discretion. I'm in need of both at the moment."

"If I take the case, it's twenty-five crowns a day plus expenses."

"If you take the case, it's worth that and more to me."

That caught my attention. Not that I would put the screws to her and jack up my price, but if a client was that desperate, what was I getting myself into . . . again? "Perhaps you should tell me about your problem and I'll see what I can do to help."

She reached into her purse and pulled out a small velvet sack. It jingled as she sat it down on the desktop. "That's two hundred and fifty crowns. That'll pay for five days' work plus a bonus for keeping this out of the public eye—"

"If I can," I broke in.

"If you can." She nodded her head and gave me a sad smile.

"I'm certain once you hear what I have to say, you'll understand my reasons for wanting to keep this private."

"Which you were getting to, I believe."

Her smile warmed. "Which I was getting to. Someone is trying to kill me, Mr. Chase. Several attempts have been made on my life and I need you to figure out who and why. Hopefully before they're successful."

"And because you're trying to keep this out of the public eye, you're coming to me instead of the constables."

"That, and the constables are basically inept."

"I like you better already, Miss Blackthorne. So, how have they attempted to kill you?"

She paused for a second and stared at me. I stared back, not that it was hard to do. Her dark hair fell forward, hiding her eyes for a moment; I could tell she was deciding on what to say, which meant my job suddenly got a lot harder. Some people think they can tell me "just enough." All that does is slow down the investigation, because I eventually find out what they're hiding. I just waste time tracking down leads to information they could have given me up front.

"This isn't easy to admit, Mr. Chase."

"If it was, you wouldn't be here, Miss Blackthorne. And please, call me Theron."

"As you wish, Theron. And it's Ze'eva, then. I'm a performer by profession. I sing at the Green Dragon currently."

"Tom Fitzgerald's place."

"Yes, Tom's booked me for the next two months. He's happy with the crowds and I'm happy for the opportunity. The trouble is, I can only work three weeks of the month. That's why I like working for Tom—he's found me a gig for that other week and it pays well."

I held up my hand to slow her down. "Okay, you're already losing me. You can only work three weeks a month, but he found you a job where you can work the other week that you can't normally work? So either you *are* working four weeks a month or I've suddenly lost the ability to count."

She paused and an honest smile spread across her face. "You are good. You actually listen when I talk instead of just watching me like most men. All right, Theron, I'll be honest with you. I'm a werewolf. I can't perform at a regular club during the full moon. Tom found a club that caters to were-creatures and he got me a booking last month."

"I can see why you don't want this getting around. Most people think weres should be killed on sight."

I saw her visibly relax when I didn't flinch away about her secret. "I've gone to great lengths to hide my affliction, Theron, but it's not easy dealing with the prejudice in this town. I wasn't sure I should take the job, but Tom assured me the clientele is very discreet. The club is dimly lit and the booths are shadowed; unless you want to be seen, you don't have to be. The attempts on my life started just after the first week I started working there. On my way home, three weeks ago, two men attacked me in the back alley. It happened right after moonset. Luckily, the doorman frightened them off."

"Are you sure that was an attempt on your life? No offense, but there are gangs who prey on beautiful women. There's been a rash of kidnappings lately in the theater district. You may have heard about it?"

"You're right and I assumed I might have been a random victim until three nights ago at the Green Dragon when their doorman was shot while walking me home. He was struck in the shoulder just a few inches above my head."

"Okay, that's pretty obvious, but couldn't they have been going after the doorman?"

"With a silver bullet?"

A low whistle escaped my lips. "So it appears not only was someone aiming at you, but they knew what it was going to take."

"Then last night, someone set fire to my apartment. It was only through chance I woke up. I barely reached a window before the smoke overcame me. One of the fire-brigade leaders found an empty fuel-oil bucket by the front door. He's the one who recommended I come to you."

"I'll have to make an extra contribution to the fire brigade for that favor. Now I'm going to ask the obligatory question, *why?*"

"That's why I'm hiring you, Theron. I don't have a clue. All I can think is it has something to do with my new job. No one seemed to pay attention to me before I started working there."

"I find that hard to believe, Ze'eva."

She blushed; it was a very attractive look for her. "Let me rephrase that. No one has ever *threatened* me before I started working at that club."

"Then perhaps I should check that club first. What's its name and address?"

She frowned and looked over my shoulder at the wall. "No, that won't work. They'd never let you in." She paused and then her face brightened. "However, I can escort you there. That way, you'll be around to protect me."

"Oh no. If someone is hunting you, then we need to get you into hiding before I do anything else."

"That's not possible. I still have to work. Tom understands up to a point, but if I miss my performance tonight, he'll find someone else and I'll be out on the street."

I paused and leaned back in my chair as a thought occurred to me. "Speaking of which, does Tom have any idea why these attacks are happening?"

"I don't know. I haven't seen him in a few days. Why? Do you think something has happened to him?"

"*Has* something happened to him?"

"Don't be cruel, Theron. How would I know? It feels like I'm in a nightmare and I can't wake up."

I stood up and reached for my hat. "Never mind. I think I'll see about hunting Tom down after I visit that club."

"You mean, *we'll* see about hunting Tom down." She leaned across the desk and stared into my eyes. "It looks like you've got a partner."

———

We argued but I knew she was going to win. First off, she was right about needing to escort me to the club. There'd been rumors about a place that catered to weres, and I knew of two other investigators who had tried to get inside. They found parts of one strewn around town. The other just disappeared. I tried not to think about where he wound up.

A quick cab ride later, I found myself standing in front of a dilapidated building down by King Street in the southern warehouse district. It looked no different from any of the others surrounding it except all the windows had dark tinting on them. The average person might not have noticed, but the tinting made the building stand out more than a neon sign would—even Calasia's constables weren't dumb enough to miss that. Someone with some pull had to be protecting this setup.

She led me to a side door and pulled a key from her purse. The lock opened noiselessly and she held the door open for me. It might have looked like a warehouse from the outside, but that's where the resemblance stopped. There was a long hall with well-worn but serviceable carpet leading to a pair of double doors. There were several doors on either side of the hall. We walked to the third door on the left and she paused, her hand resting on the latch.

"This is my dressing room."

"Do you work here under your real name or a stage name?"

"*No one* uses their real name here, Theron. People here know me as Lyssa Darkmane."

I noticed movement coming out of the darkness down the hall toward us. "It'll be a pleasure working for you, Lyssa."

She gave me a comforted smile before she looked up. "Good afternoon, Louie."

A large bald man with a voice that sounded like he chewed on boulders every day answered her. "Dis guy givin' you any troubles, Miss Lyssa?" He rubbed his hands together and I had the distinct feeling he was imagining my head between them.

Before I could get myself into trouble, she spoke up. "Oh no, Louie. This is Mr. Chase. He's my guest."

He gave me a dirty look and then looked back at her with an almost paternal gaze. "Aw right, Miss Lyssa. But, if you should need anything, you just give a yell. I'll be here in no time."

She smiled at him. "Thanks, Louie. I'm going to be showing Mr. Chase the stage and backstage. He's a fan of the theater. Is anything going on? We don't want to be a bother."

Louie thrust a thumb back over his shoulder. "Nah, the boss is gone and the band finished rehearsals about an hour ago. Are you performin' soon?"

"Yes, Louie. Mr. Tabor scheduled me for four performances."

"That's great, Miss Lyssa. The customers love it when you perform. Heck, I like hearin' you sing too. You got a great voice." To my surprise, Louie was blushing like a schoolboy. "Well, I gotta get back to cleanin'." He paused and gave me another dirty look. "I likes Miss Lyssa. Don't do nothin' to make her upset, udderwise then, I might get upset."

"Oh no. I'm a firm believer in getting along with everyone, Louie. I'll do my best to behave."

"Good." And with that, he clumped back down the hall and through the doors at the end.

She opened her dressing room door and ushered me inside. I noted the typical chaos of a changing area—costumes and dresses strewn about from obvious quick changes and a seemingly disorganized makeup table. She sat down and rummaged through a few things at the table. "I'm sorry, Theron. I just need to get something from here. It won't take a second."

"No problem, Lyssa. Tell me; is Mr. Tabor Tom's alias?"

"No. Mr. Tabor is the owner of this club. I assume it's not his real name, though. Like I said, no one uses their real name here." She paused and then put a hand up to her mouth. "Oh, you thought maybe Tom was a were?"

"The thought had crossed my mind."

She smiled. It was a sight I was beginning to enjoy. "No, Tom's a normal man. He just likes me and he wanted to help me out. I've never met Mr. Tabor. Tom handled all the arrangements about me working here and Louie brings me my schedule and my pay." She looked around the room. "I admit there are times I've thought about trying to find out more about him. Still, he's doing this as a favor to Tom, so I don't want to abuse the situation."

The room had two windows facing the alley behind the warehouse. I glanced outside and saw the alley was dingy and full of trash. I also noted there were no lights. It would be pitch black in the alley once the sun went down. I mentioned this to Ze'eva.

"That's the way the guests come in, Theron. It makes it easier for them to come and go at night without drawing attention. Don't worry, they can see well enough when the moon is full."

I decided against mentioning an attacker could get to her window in the darkness without being detected also. She seemed to be relaxing in the familiar surroundings, so there was no point in frightening her further. So, I changed the subject. "That Louie, I suspect he makes a pretty good bouncer."

"Oh, he's not the bouncer. He's the bartender. You should meet our bouncer, Tiny. It's quite a show when he has to eject an unruly customer." I was trying to imagine someone even bigger than Louie when she turned in her chair to face me. "Quint is the doorman at the Green Dragon, the one who got injured walking me home. They say he should be back at work in a week or so."

I was still thinking about the bartender. "So the crowd here can get a little rough at times?"

I could tell by the look she gave, she was questioning my judgment. "Theron, have you ever fought a lycanthrope before?"

"I can't say I have."

She leaned forward, making sure I was paying attention. It was not a hard task to accomplish. "Let me give you some friendly advice. Weres tend to be antisocial when they're sober. When they get drunk . . ."

". . . their inner animal comes out. Yeah, I should have thought of that."

She laughed at that comment. "You have a clever way with words, Theron. I think I'd like being around you even if I wasn't your client."

I thought I wouldn't mind that, either. I glanced out the window as she sat at the makeup table fixing her hair. A flash of light caught my attention and I leapt away from the window and grabbed her, pulling her down to the floor with me. A second later, there was the sound of shattering glass and a sickening *thunk* against the wall above me.

She started to scream, but I put a hand over her mouth. "Be still. Whoever's out there doesn't know if they got you or not. When I leave, crawl out the door and have Louie hide you somewhere. I'll be back in a bit."

I scurried to the door and inched it open. When I was certain no one was waiting in the hall to ambush us, I motioned for her to follow and then sent her running toward the main room. I let myself out the side door and circled around, slipping my revolver from my coat pocket. I reached the edge of the building and glanced down the alleyway, but as I'd suspected, it was empty. The sniper had cleared out as soon as he'd fired.

I went over to a pile of boxes and poked around. The

assassin had left his calling card, though; the casing for a silver bullet lay on the ground at my feet.

I t took almost ten minutes of arguing before Louie would tell me where he'd hidden my client. Once I was certain she was all right, we had another vigorous discussion with Louie to convince him it was safe for her to leave. I took her back to my office and had Kyra prepare the spare room. Ze'eva wasn't the first client of mine who'd needed to disappear for a bit. I'd taken over the office next door and modified it to contain a small room with a bed and a washbasin. If you didn't measure the outside and the inside of the room, it was virtually impossible to notice. I'd even used it once or twice to avoid the bill collectors who'd caught me before I could slip out the front door.

Once I was sure she was all right, I locked my automatic in my desk; where I had to go next, they wouldn't appreciate me packing a weapon. I had Kyra lock the front door to the office behind me, and I made it clear not to open it unless I said it was okay. I hated leaving her there but I knew Kyra could hold the fort if she had to. Despite her diminutive size, Kyra was a lot more resourceful than people gave her credit for—and dangerous if pushed too far.

I hit the streets; when no one took a shot at me, I decided it was safe enough to take a trip across the city. I made my way over the Great Arch Bridge, watched the traffic on the Calundash River for a while. When no one seemed to be paying attention to me, I kept going north until I reached the business section in North Point. A couple of turns later, I was standing in front of Blake Ferendel's brownstone.

Blake was a fixer—for a price there wasn't much he couldn't arrange. I didn't like Blake and he didn't like me, but we had a mutual respect for each other that came from butting heads too often. I knocked on the door, put up with being frisked three times by his boys, and finally was ushered into a small, darkened den in a rather sumptuous house.

An average-looking man in an average dark blue suit stared at me from behind an average-looking mahogany desk. That was his edge, everyone assumed he was *just* average. By the time they realized how wrong they were, it was usually too late. He motioned me to sit across from him. "Chase. Good to see you."

"Likewise, Blake. Seems business has been good lately."

"I can't complain. Always somebody doing something they shouldn't. You'd be surprised how much repeat business I get."

"I wouldn't say that. I've put away enough of your former clients. You really should cultivate a more upscale clientele."

"Who says I haven't? They tend to get into juicier scrapes than the common Joes. But you ain't here to talk about my thriving business . . . or are you?" A smile reminiscent of a shark eying his next meal spread over his face as he poured himself a drink from a crystal decanter.

I shook my head. "I hope not, Blake. I've got a new client and it seems someone has something against her. Keeps trying to put a bullet into her and, honestly, she's much too pretty for that. It'd be a crime against all creatures if that should happen."

Ferendel laughed but it rang hollow, given the dead expression in his eyes. "So, you want me to take care of her problem?"

"I appreciate the offer, Blake. No one has ever questioned the quality of your work. However, I'm more interested in finding out who's behind it and why. The sniper I can deal with, but if I don't find his boss, he or she will just send another one. Not that I mind spending time with my client, but it's not much of a life being used for target practice."

"You know, Chase, I'm not really known for my charity." I started to respond but he cut me off. "But, you've always been a stand-up guy. I appreciate that. Tell you what: come back here tomorrow, right after lunch. I'll see what I can come up with for you. Call it a professional courtesy.'"

I passed along the pertinent information, thanked him, and let myself out. From the looks on his boy's faces, someone had lost a bet I'd be leaving under my own power. I stepped out into the street—to find Captain Corvinus of the city's constables waiting for me.

"So, Chase, what have you gotten yourself into this time?"

"Good to see you too, Corvinus. To what do I owe the pleasure?"

"I'm afraid it's business, Chase. From the reports I've been getting, you've been a very busy guy today. Remember that warehouse off of King Street?"

"Sure, old run-down looking building . . . Hey, why'd you say 'remember it'?"

"Because it isn't there anymore, Chase. Apparently it burned down today shortly after you left with some unidentified young lady. I'm not so much worried about the fire, but you see, there's this matter of a corpse we'd like to ask you about."

"A corpse?"

"Come on, Chase. You were seen there. You must know something. We know it's a private club. No law against that. They kept to themselves and none of the neighbors ever complained. Not that there are many neighbors in a warehouse district."

"Get to the point, Corvinus; you said something about a corpse?"

"Yeah, yeah. Seems there was this big guy who worked there. Could have been a bouncer or a bartender. Wasn't a lot of the body left to identify. At first it looked like he'd gotten caught by the fire or the smoke."

"At first? Corvinus, you have the damnedest time getting to the point."

"Yeah, well here's the head scratcher, Chase. He had a big

knife wound in his back. Probably killed him instantly. But, what I can't figure out is, if he was there by himself, how'd he stab himself in the back? Want to shed some light on that?"

A sudden feeling of dread came over me. Before the captain could stop me, I rushed past him and caught a passing streetcar. I waved back at him. "Corvinus, if you want to ask me any questions, I'll be at my office. You can catch me there." He yelled something and a couple of his men started chasing after me, but they gave up after a couple of blocks. I knew they'd arrive at my office soon enough and Corvinus would *not* be happy with my disappearing act, but I needed to check something first.

I hopped off the streetcar once I was far enough away and flagged down a cab. That ride seemed to take forever and I tossed the driver my fare and jumped out once we pulled up in front of my building. I took the stairs two at a time, afraid of what I'd see at the top. I hit the landing just beneath my floor only to have my momentum halted by a large hand grabbing me by the shoulder and pinning me in place.

"Chase, I needs to talk to you right now."

I recognized the voice and spoke with a calm I did not feel. "Sure, Louie."

He let me go and started pacing around the small landing. "I was just up at your office, but your secretary wouldn't let me in. Chase, I need to know that Miss Lyssa is safe."

I leaned against the wall, massaging my shoulder. I was relieved to hear Kyra was all right, but Louie didn't need to know that. "She was safe the last time I saw her. But I heard there was a problem at the club right after we left."

The air seemed to come out of him and he slumped down on one of the steps in front of me. "Oh boy, you ain't kiddin', Chase. About a half hour after you left, these two guys show up. One's a big guy and the other's this little weasel. He's the one doin' all the talkin', though. I don't know how they got in 'cause I was certain I locked the door after you left."

"That's odd all right."

"That's what I thought. Anyway, this weasel guy, he starts askin' questions about Miss Lyssa. Says he's got somethin' important for her. But, I ain't buyin' it for a second. You know, Chase, maybe I ain't the brightest guy in the world, but I ain't no dummy. Peoples is always tryin' to get backstage and stuffs. But, I figures *this* guy knows somethin' about what happened earlier. Well, I guess I got mad, 'cause the next thing I know, I grabbed him and started shaking him. Figure I'll either scare it out of him or beat it out of him."

"But you forgot about his partner."

Louie looked up at me with a lopsided grin on his face. "Yeah, I kinda did. Well, the next thing you know, it's the three of us goin' 'round and 'round near the bar. Tables goin' one way; chairs the other. The little guy tries to pop me with a bottle of rotgut, but he misses. The bottle breaks near one of the lamps and the next thing you know, the whole area behind the bar is blazin'. We're still going toe-to-toe until the rest of the alcohol behind the bar catches on fire. What a mess! I take the opportunity to split out the back door. I got no idea what happened to them other two. Am I in trouble, Mr. Chase?"

"Louie, not yet, you're not. I need to know something first, though. Did you use a knife to defend yourself?"

"Why, no, Mr. Chase. I didn't want to really hurt no one. I just threw them around a bit and smacked them a few times. I think that little guy had one, but I knocked it out of his hands when I threw him into a table."

I let out a sigh of relief. "Louie, the constables found a body back at the club, only they think it's you. Let's keep it that way for a bit." I dug around in the pocket of my coat and came out with a key. "Here, this is the key to my house over on Butcher Street. It'll let you in the back door. Just wait there until I come for you. But, you might want to hurry; I suspect the constables will be here any moment."

It took a bit for Louie to grasp what I was saying but after some more discussion, he decided to trust me. "Okay, Mr. Chase. I'll wait for you. You takes good care of Miss Lyssa. I'm really worried about her."

"Me too, Louie. Me too."

I waited until I heard the door to the outside shut and then hurried on up to my office. I knocked and let Kyra know it was me. She opened the door and then warily glanced toward the stairwell. "You sure you're alone, Theron?"

"You mean Louie? Yeah, he just left a few minutes ago. We've been chatting one floor down. Lock the door behind me and grab your notebook, kid."

As Kyra relocked the door and moved a large chair to brace it again, I went to let Ze'eva out of the spare room. She seemed no worse the wear and was glad to have an opportunity to stretch her legs. Kyra took her usual seat behind her desk and I perched on the corner of it. I noted she kept glancing at the door.

"I take it Louie wasn't the only person who's shown up today?"

"No, there have been two others. Could have been more, but only two spoke. I can do a lot of things, Theron, but seeing through oak doors isn't one of them."

"Sweetheart, I'm disappointed. I thought there wasn't anything you couldn't do."

"Theron, you're a nice guy, but you've really got a few rocks loose in that skull of yours. Anyway, one guy was a real sweet talker, but the other guy was pretty brusque. Both demanded to be let in. Of course, that didn't happen. But the strangest thing was, the guy who was rude kept asking for a Lyssa Darkmane, whoever that is. The smooth-talking guy was asking for Ze'eva Blackthorne. I denied knowing anyone by either name."

Ze'eva's eyes got wide when she heard that last statement. "I never use the name Lyssa outside of the club."

Kyra's eyebrows arched in an unspoken question but I ignored it and turned to Ze'eva. "I've got some bad news. The club burned down about a half hour after we left. You heard I was talking to Louie? He said a couple of thugs showed up looking for a Lyssa Darkmane. Now, Louie only knows your stage name, so he knew who they wanted and he didn't take it very well. He's pretty protective of you. Have you ever told him not to call you that?"

"No, but then Louie lived at the club. Mr. Tabor paid him good money to stay there and watch the place. As far as I know, he's never leaves the building. In fact, Louie's one of the few people at the club who's seen me in my human form. I usually arrive before sundown on the nights I work and stay until all the customers go home."

Kyra's eyebrows rose even farther, trying to join her blond hair. "Your human form?"

Ze'eva looked at me. "You didn't tell her?"

"You seemed determined to not let people know. I've respected that wish."

"Thank you, Theron." She turned her attention to Kyra, who was gazing at her suspiciously. "I'm a werewolf, Kyra. Given the local prejudice, I try to keep that private. However, if we're going to be staying here together, I feel you have the right to know."

I could see the surprise in Kyra's body language, but she kept her voice steady. "Thank you for telling me. I knew there was something different about you, but I wasn't sure what."

Ze'eva laughed. "It's true. I'm not quite as obviously non-human as you are. I've always envied the fae for their wings."

Kyra laugh was a little forced, but she appeared to relax. "You say that now. You've never had to get a dress measured to accommodate them."

"No, but I have had to have stage costumes made with tail holes."

They enjoyed a laugh before my "harrumph" caught their attention. "Ladies, I'm certain you'll have all kinds of time to discuss your wardrobes later. However, I would like to get this in writing before Corvinus shows up. You see, there was this little matter of a corpse back at the club they think is Louie. I'm going to let them keep thinking that for a bit, but Corvinus has questions I don't have answers to, and I better get some quick. Honestly, I can't imagine why he hasn't shown up already."

Ze'eva turned pale at the news, but Kyra took it like a pro. Unfortunately, in my line of work, bodies seem to come with the territory. I admit some nights I don't sleep too well, but now was not the time to get maudlin.

I spent the next few minutes dictating a list of places I intended to visit that afternoon. If I failed to show up, Kyra was to take a hundred crowns from Ze'eva's payment and deliver that list and the money to Blake Ferendel with one instruction—"Find me." For a hundred crowns, I knew at least my body would be recovered. I also informed her Louie was staying at my house and to have Pinkie Rusentha, another private detective I knew, to stake it out. He was to let her know if *anything* happened there. She should take Pinkie's fee from the stack too.

I was beginning to think I wasn't going to make any money on this case, but I'd rather have all my bases covered. I got the last known address for Tom Fitzgerald from Ze'eva and motioned for her to return to the private room before I left.

That was a good move on my part because no sooner had she done so, than there was a knock at the office door. I motioned to Kyra to move back to my private office before I shifted the chair and opened the door. There, not to my delight but to my relief, was Captain Corvinus.

"Captain, you're a bit tardy. I was expecting you a while ago."

"Can the corny act, Chase, and let us in."

"By all means, Captain. I'm assuming by 'us,' you mean the three boys behind you." I opened the door and they came traipsing in. Two large men with their official and very effective looking sabers took a position on either side of the door. The other stood next to the door to my office, while Corvinus plopped down on my couch and helped himself to one of my single malts. I waited patiently, perched on the corner of Kyra's desk. After Corvinus made himself comfortable with my alcohol, he fixed his gaze on me.

"Like I was saying before you went running off, I heard you've been a very busy boy today, Chase. I'm surprised at you."

I blinked a couple of times in confusion. "I believe you're mistaking me with someone else, Corvinus. I've spent the majority of the day here in my office. I've only left twice: once with a client to visit that warehouse and the second time to visit Blake Ferendel, which you knew since you met me at his door. I'm assuming his men wouldn't let you enter since I found you waiting outside."

"Don't get smart with me, Chase. Now, who's your client?"

"Not at liberty to say."

"Look, Chase, I'm not here to play games. I've got two murders to solve and right now, you're looking pretty good for Suspect Number One."

That took me by surprise. "*Two* murders?"

"Did I stutter, Chase? We just got back from Tom Fitzgerald's place. His neighbor reported unusual noises last night. When we arrived, he'd been dead approximately twelve hours. Well, that's the best guess we had, given the state of the corpse. Someone dismembered it and poured acid on it to try and destroy the body."

I walked over and liberated my single malt before he poured himself another glass. He gave me a dirty look and rearranged his rumpled suit, which only made him look more disreputable. I poured myself a drink and put the bottle into a drawer in Kyra's desk before responding. "I fail to see how that makes me a suspect. I've only met the man socially a couple of times. We didn't exactly run in the same crowds. Besides, from what you just told me, there's no evidence it's Fitzgerald."

"Body is about the right height and weight. Besides, who else would be hanging out in Fitzgerald's place?"

"I don't know, Captain. Perhaps you should do your duty and prove whose corpse you've discovered. I'm certain Fitzgerald, if he's still alive, would appreciate knowing who was in his home. Besides, you still haven't told me how that makes me a suspect."

Corvinus stood up, grinning at me like I'd just given him the keys to a doughnut shop. "I'm glad you asked, Chase. I have an eyewitness who places you at the scene of the crime a few minutes before and after it went down last night."

I nearly spit out my single malt. "That's impossible. I wasn't anywhere near his place last night."

"And you have someone who can prove that?"

"Only if they were peeking in my windows last night while I was reading and sleeping."

"Well, then you must be killing people in your sleep because you were spotted at Fitzgerald's house last night. One of the neighbors came forward while we were removing the body. We were tipped to the incident right after you left Ferendel's. You already admitted you were at the warehouse right before we found the stiff there, so unless you can come up with an alibi for your whereabouts with regard to Fitzgerald, you're gonna have to come with us."

"I admitted nothing and I have no intention of going with you. If I get locked up, the real murderer is going to escape because you're going to be too busy making up evidence to prove it was me."

"Chase, you know we don't do stuff like that. If you're innocent, you'll be released by the magistrate."

"What? In six to eight months, if I'm lucky." I shook my head.

"Oh, no. That's not going to happen. I'm going to catch this person and clear myself."

"Can't let you do that. All right, boys, take Mr. Chase into..."

He froze in mid-sentence, a strange dreamy look coming over his face. As I watched, the other constables froze in place too, each one staring off into space. Then it dawned on me what was going on. Kyra was singing a spell from inside my office. Not being one to look a gift Sylph secretary in the mouth, if you'll pardon the mangled expression, I rushed inside and grabbed Ze'eva from the other room and we vacated my office. I didn't know how long Kyra could keep it up, but I wanted to get as far away as I could before they woke up.

We went down the back stairs to the alley and then I flagged down a cab. I told the cabbie to take us to Pyridan's Park and to step on it. I lowered and secured the window shades as the cab lurched forward, merging into traffic. I didn't like being unable to see out, but at this point, not being seen took precedence.

Ze'eva peeked through one of the curtains before turning to face me. "Theron, why are we going to the park?"

I slid the curtain back into place before answering. "Because it's busy and crowded. Probably the best place to lose ourselves for a bit. I still want to go to Fitzgerald's house and then I'm going to want to check his club. If he's not dead, I might be able to pick up his trail. If he *is* dead, then someone may be there trying to clean up the evidence."

"So, why aren't we heading there right now?"

"Because someone's been following us ever since you arrived at my office. I should have realized this earlier, but some days I'm a little slower than others. I don't know if there's a group or just one, but there have been too many coincidences today. We go to the club and someone takes a shot at you, then the club gets attacked, Fitzgerald turns up either missing or dead, and two stooges show up at my office looking for you—under both of *your* names. That tells me we're going to have to figure out some way to ditch our tail, and I know just the person to help."

She sat back, a sad expression on her face. "You don't think that I'm involved in this, do you?"

I admit I'd considered it, but I didn't think she was. Even realizing she was a performer, I didn't think she could play scared that well. "No, I don't think you're setting me up, but *someone's* going to a great deal of trouble to separate us. It would help if we knew why he was after you."

"Are you sure it's a he?"

I mulled it over for a moment before answering. "No, but this doesn't feel like a jealous lover or a worried wife. Most prefer to do the deed themselves. This feels like someone who's worried about being exposed. He's hiring people to do the job, probably through a middleman. He'll try to stay out of the footlights if possible."

She scooted over next to me in the carriage and rested her head on my shoulder. "All right, Theron, You know best." As we rode in silence, I felt the tension easing from her body as she fell asleep. I realized she probably hadn't relaxed in days and who could blame her? I know I hadn't since she'd walked into my office. I shifted to make her more comfortable. I occasionally peered past the drawn shades while the cab made its way south to Pyridan's Park.

It took a couple of tries to wake her up once we arrived but soon she was ready to go. I tipped the cabbie well and we set off through the throng. It might seem counterintuitive to go to a place like that, but I wasn't trying to hide from pursuers. I had a plan but it relied on the idea there were too many witnesses around. I had to hope they wouldn't try anything stupid or get too close.

As I had hoped, the park was filled with couples, which meant any pursuers would have to really work to keep us in view. Acting like every other couple, I cautiously reached for her hand and like the performer she was, she took my arm in hers and pressed up against me like we'd been in love for years. I almost wished it wasn't an act.

After a leisurely stroll through the grounds, I led her to a ramshackle building near the center of the park, indistinguishable from the others housing food vendors and games of chance to draw in the locals. We slipped inside, past the junk and trinkets set out to catch the eye of a potential customer, and made our way to the counter. A large woman appeared from the back room and got a big smile on her face when she recognized me.

"Theron, you old scamp. About time you came back around. Haven't seen you in forever."

"Good to see you too, Mama Belltre. You're looking lovely as always. How's business been?"

She gave me a dirty look and turned to Ze'eva. "If he's starting out with the flattery and compliments, I know he's up to no good. Honey, you'd be better off getting while the getting's good. This one's a royal pain when he gets like this."

"Mama, I'm hurt. Hurt to the core."

"Not yet you're not, but if you keep that up, I'll be happy to see what your core looks like."

I turned to Ze'eva with a wink. "You think you know someone and they turn on you. Ah, well, I guess we'll have to take our business elsewhere."

"Get over here, you goof, and introduce me to your client."

"How do you know she's a client?"

"'Cause she's too good looking to be hanging out with you otherwise."

Ze'eva blushed while I tried to look offended. "I'll introduce her to you, not because you deserve it, but I *do* need your services. Mama Belltre, this is Ze'eva Blackthorne. Ze'eva, Mama Belltre."

Mama's eyes grew wide and then narrowed again, giving me

that "we'll talk later" look. When she turned back to Ze'eva, her smile was in full force. "The singer?"

"I'm flattered you've heard of me, Mama."

"Don't sell yourself short, kiddo. Not only do you have a good set of pipes, but the guys around here are all big fans of yours. I get to hear them talk about you all day." Ze'eva blushed even more furiously, a trait I was beginning to enjoy. Mama Belltre turned to me. "And what exactly do you need me to do this time?"

"We seem to have picked up some unwanted interest."

"'Course you have. You're with a beautiful woman. Probably following you out of pure shock."

I harrumphed and continued. "Be that as it may. I need to lose them and I need to make use of your trapdoor."

"You still owe me for the last spell."

"I'm sure it's a clerical error. Kyra should have sent over that payment weeks ago."

"Pfeah. You probably tore up the bill as soon as you walked out the door." She nodded at Ze'eva. "But for her sake, I'll do it. She's got spunk. I expect you'll settle your account soon?"

The look she gave me would have frightened anyone with sense, but I pressed on because I had a bad feeling we were about to get company. "Mama, if you please?"

She turned and motioned to a curtain behind her. "Right on through here, Ze'eva, and bring that deadbeat with you."

Mama Belltre ignored my howls of protest and pointed to a couple of chairs in a room possibly even more cluttered than her shop. She ran her fingers along a row of dusty books on the wall and eventually settled on one. She flipped through the well-worn pages until she found what she was looking for, grabbed a couple of candles from who knows where, and a small black pot. She poured in some water, tossed in a few unidentifiable herbs, and lit the candles. I knew what was coming but Ze'eva's eyes were wide as she tried to figure out what was happening. Finally, Mama Belltre began speaking in a language I couldn't recognize and the candles grew brighter. A few seconds later, their flames went out and there stood two perfect replicas of Ze'eva and myself in front of Mama Belltre.

Mama leaned around them and fixed me with a glare. "All right, Theron, what do you want them to do? Remember, they're not too bright, so don't get cute."

"Have them stroll through the park and then head down toward the wharves to Kirian's and get a booth. Have them order a couple of cocktails and sit there and drink them. How long will this last?"

"No more than a couple of hours, Theron. I'm not that powerful a witch."

"Good enough, Mama. I'll send the money in a day or so. Just send the bill to Kyra."

"I've heard that before, Theron. If you weren't such a good kid, I'd have cut you off years ago."

"That's what I like about you, Mama. Now, that trapdoor?"

"Same place it was the last time you used it. Leave me be, so I can give these two their orders. Nice meeting you, Ze'eva. I'll have to come around and hear you sing sometime. See if these boys around here have a clue between them."

I didn't wait while Ze'eva and Mama made nice, just climbed over a few piles of gear and cleared enough junk to expose the trapdoor. As I opened it, I saw our doubles heading out through the curtain; seconds later the outside door opened and shut. Below me, an iron ladder led down into the darkness. I climbed down a couple of rungs and then grabbed one of the lamps hanging there. As Ze'eva joined me, I lit the lamp and led her down into the sewers. There was a good-sized walkway to either side, so we'd be dry as we made our way back across town.

"Are you *sure* this is a good idea, Theron?"

"No, but it beats any other I can think of. If we're lucky,

those doubles will keep our friends busy for a while. If we're incredibly lucky, they'll be assassinated and everyone will stop looking for us."

I felt her shudder. "It's hard to hope I'll get killed, but I see your point."

We walked in silence as we made our way toward Fitzgerald's place. In this business, it's amazing how well you get to know some parts of the city other people never give a second thought about. More business goes on in Calasia's sewers than aboveground. We took shelter a few times while groups of men or families made their way down the walkways. I didn't care if anyone saw me, but Ze'eva was not your average sewer rat. Her presence would have been noted and talked about.

After about an hour, we reached our destination. I let her catch her breath before we climbed up the ladder in front of us. I reached the top and blew out the lamp, securing it on the hook there for it. I listened and then eased the trapdoor open. The small storeroom in the Lord's Ladle was empty, so I helped Ze'eva up and we brushed off the sewer muck before closing the trapdoor. I looked out the window and guessed we had a couple of hours before it got dark.

"You sure you want to perform tonight? I recommend against it."

"You've heard 'the show must go on'? If I don't go on, I don't have a job. Unreliable performers do *not* get re-hired, Theron. Besides, I doubt anything will happen at the Dragon."

"You've got more faith in your patrons than I do. If we're going to get you there in time, we need to hurry. Come on."

I opened up the back door and we slipped down an alley to Fitzgerald's home. There were signs the constables had been around earlier but it seemed deserted. I jimmied the back door and we went in. It was a typical house for a typical bachelor; in other words, it looked a lot like my apartment.

While Ze'eva kept watch by the front curtains, I tossed the

place looking for anything that might shed some light on this mess. I saw where the murder must have happened. The body was gone but the stains on the floor told me all I needed to know. I examined Fitzgerald's office but turned up nothing. There was no evidence he was involved in anything—no racing slips or markers to show he owed money to anyone, no letters from ex-girlfriends, not even so much as a late notice for his rent. Apparently, based on what I could find, Tom Fitzgerald was an upstanding businessman in the community. He did not fit the profile of a murder victim, especially one murdered in such a brutal fashion. Then again, my client should not have been the subject of several attacks, either. The more I thought about it, the more my head hurt.

"Theron, someone is outside. They're just leaning against the gate. It looks like they're waiting for someone."

"That's our cue, Ze'eva. Let's get out of here."

I was heading toward the back door when something caught my attention. A long, thin knife rested on the floor beneath a table. I grabbed it and gingerly stuck it in my pocket for further examination. Reaching the door, I heard a couple of guys talking out back and knew we'd been cut off. I motioned for Ze'eva to be quiet and we made our way to the stairs. At the top, we found a couple of bedrooms and a library. I picked the room that didn't look like the one Fitzgerald slept in and pointed to one of the closets. Ze'eva went into it and left the door slightly ajar. I waited in the shadows at the top of the stairs to see what would happen.

I didn't have to wait long. There was a rustling at the back door and then the sound of footsteps walking across the floor. A couple of seconds later, I heard the front door open and more men come in. I wasn't sure how many there were, but I knew we were woefully outnumbered.

A raspy voice sounded from the living room. "You sure this is the right place, Leo?"

A squeaky voice replied sounding indignant. "Yeah, yeah, this is the place. I spent the last couple of days watching it. I still see it in my dreams."

The raspy voice did not sound sympathetic. "You got your orders, same as the rest of us." There was a pause and then Raspy continued. "All right boys, you know what we're looking for. Spread out and search."

I didn't know what they were looking for, but the fact they were going to search the house wasn't encouraging. They didn't seem like the kind of guys who'd want witnesses hanging around. I went over to the closet Ze'eva was hiding in. She'd arranged some boxes she'd found in the closet to make a hiding place. It was about as good as it was going to get. I returned to the stairs and watched. They were going through the downstairs and, from the sound of things, they weren't worried about making a mess.

I hoped they'd say something about what they were looking for, but they were pros. I spotted five figures moving around downstairs. I also was able to spot two more lookouts outside, so the idea of slipping out a window was pretty much shot. I checked my personal arsenal and found it lacking. I had a sap in my coat pocket, a dagger strapped to my belt, and that weird knife I'd picked up downstairs. My heavy artillery was back in my office. When Corvinus showed up at my office, there was no time to grab it from my desk.

That reminded me of something that had been gnawing at me. Hopefully, Kyra had made her escape before the boys woke up. She had taken an awful chance to spring me and if Corvinus had a clue what had happened, he'd throw the book at her. I was just getting good and worked up when I heard footsteps gathering at the bottom of the stairs.

"Any luck?"

"Nah."

"I guess he dropped it upstairs. Let's go take a look."

That was my cue to retreat to the closet. I opened the closet door, but no one was there. It was impossible, but Ze'eva had vanished. Then a small crack appeared in the back wall of the closet and slowly widened into a door. Ze'eva stuck her head out.

"Come on, Theron, there's a stairway to the attic here."

I was *not* going to argue with this stroke of luck. I eased the closet door shut and locked it. I felt my way up the stairwell to the attic trying not to make a sound. It was really more of a crawl space, but it looked like a palace to me. We lay down on the floor and waited.

It didn't take long for the boys to reach the bedroom below us. From the sound of things crashing and breaking, they were being thorough but not very careful. They tossed the boxes out of the closet we'd just been in, but no one seemed to notice the hidden panel. After a bit, the noise died down and faded away.

I rolled over on my side to look at her, not that that was an unpleasant chore. "How did you find this?"

"I *am* a werewolf, Theron. Even in my human form, I have a good sense of hearing and smell. I knew Tom had touched that particular section of wall a number of times. So, while you were watching them, I poked around and found the hidden lever. I was investigating up here when I heard you come back, then came down and got you."

"Pretty smart thinking. I didn't want to have to fight five guys in that little bedroom. Actually, I don't particularly want to fight five guys at the same time, no matter how much room I have."

"What now?"

"We wait until we're sure they're gone and then we get out of here. From the tone of their voices, I don't think they found what they were looking for. Could you make out what they were saying?"

"Only a bit, Theron. It sounded like they were afraid to tell their boss they couldn't find it. Seems he was pretty sure what-ever it was that he'd lost it here."

"Which tells me either they're working for Fitzgerald, since this is his house . . ." She started to interrupt me but I continued quickly to cut her off. ". . . or, their boss is the one who carved up whoever was killed downstairs and he dropped it while he was busy."

She glanced at her watch before responding. "We can't wait too long. I have to be at the theater in two hours."

"I can't talk you out of this?"

"I do like you, Theron, but I don't think you're ready to take care of me full-time unless you plan to marry me. The only other options I can think of are taking me on as your new partner or finding another club hiring singers. Especially now that Mr. Tabor's club burned down."

"Okay, Ze'eva, but you've got a new stagehand tonight. I need to make one stop and then we'll hit the Green Dragon."

"You're the boss, Boss."

I have to admit, the thought of having her stick around struck my fancy. She wasn't like a lot of my clients. Ze'eva was pretty darn resourceful, and she didn't buckle under the first sign of pressure. Still, I wasn't sure how Kyra would take it. There was nothing formal between us but we had passed that state of boss/secretary a long time ago. She still dated other guys and I certainly dated other women, but that was away from the office. I wasn't sure how she'd deal with having someone like Ze'eva around every day.

I shook my head to clear my thoughts. I'd worry about that later. Right now, I had to figure out how to keep both of us alive long enough to solve this case. Everything else could wait.

We arrived at the Green Dragon and she introduced me to

Pavel Orlovsky, the stage manager. I explained what I was going to do, and after a bit of grumbling on Pavel's part, he finally agreed. I inspected Ze'eva's dressing room before she went in, found nothing out of the ordinary, and then took up a position outside her door. There was the usual bustle that goes on backstage as they prepared for the night's entertainment. After about an hour, Pavel came by to let Ze'eva know she was on in five minutes for her first set. He agreed to wait and escort her to the stage and I went backstage and climbed up into the rafters.

I eased out onto a small landing and made sure the pistol I'd picked up en route was where I could reach it. I made myself as comfortable as possible and then pulled out the spy glass I'd also acquired and scanned the crowd. It seemed like a typical night at any club. I spotted some of the usual characters and noticed a few boys I knew Corvinus looked for on a regular basis, but no one seemed out of place here. In general, the Green Dragon catered to a higher clientele than the clubs near the docks. I recognized a few nobles in the crowd. Most of them hid in the darkened booths in the back, but some of the notorious playboys sat right up front where they could get an unobstructed view.

The more I watched the crowd, the more I felt tension in the air. I couldn't put my finger on it but they seemed a little more keyed up than normal. Then the band hit Ze'eva's entrance cue and the place went silent. Everyone moved forward in their seats as the music rose to a crescendo and then the curtain parted.

For a crowded club, there wasn't a sound as she strolled out to the middle of the stage. She stood there in an off-the-shoulder dress that glittered like it was made of diamonds, her hair draped over one shoulder and long gloves pulled up almost to her elbows. She looked nothing like the person I'd traipsed through the sewers with a few hours ago. I have to admit, my jaw was hanging open too. She stood there, looking down from the stage, and the place was utterly still with every eye on her.

Then the band kicked into the song and the place nearly turned into a riot. I don't know what she sang or how many songs she did sing. It was all I could do to concentrate on watching the crowd through the glass. There was a mesmerizing quality about her voice. Beautiful and haunting pictures seemed to hang in my brain as she sang. I could see why she was drawing in the crowds with a performance like this.

During one of the band interludes, I spotted someone moving along the back wall. He had his hat on and the collar turned up on his coat, making it hard to see his face. He glanced around and then slipped into a booth, sliding all the way to the back. I took a closer look and recognized whose booth it was: Baron Lyndmar's.

The baron had come into his title with the unfortunate—some would say conveniently timed—death of his father a few months ago. Of course, the people who would say that only did so in hushed tones when they were sure no one could overhear them. The baron was known for his temper and his loyal "retainers." He had used his inheritance to pay off a number of gambling debts and was settling in to a life of leisure in his estates to the west of town.

The baron and his visitor seemed to be in a bit of a heated conversation. Unlike my client, I wasn't blessed with extraordinary hearing or vision and was reduced to reading body language. The visitor seemed to be delivering bad news and the baron was not happy. I couldn't watch them too long since I was guarding Ze'eva. Still, something told me this warranted further investigation. I scanned the crowd again and noted they seemed to be hanging on Ze'eva's every note. Not a violent bone in the place while she was singing.

I gave the crowd one last look and noticed a small light above the private booths. I focused the glass on it. I could barely make it out in the dim light but there was a catwalk above the theater leading to what appeared to be a small room with a view of the stage. If I hadn't been in the rafters, I never would have seen it. There was no sign that it was occupied outside of the light, but I suspected who might be there. However, Ze'eva had started her last song of her set, so I knew it was time to head down to the stage. I glanced back at the baron's booth and noted he was alone again. I scanned the room, but there was no sign of his visitor.

She exited the stage—escaped is probably a better term considering the way her fans mobbed the stage—and met me in the wings. I handed her a drink and escorted her to her dressing room. "Nice job, kid. I can't say I've ever heard a better performance."

"Thanks, Theron. I have to get changed for my next set."

"No problem. Let me check the room out first."

She argued and I insisted and she finally acquiesced, which meant that good ol' stupid Theron was the one who stuck his head through the door first. I felt the motion more than I saw it. I had a quick impression of a dark cloak or coat and a hat. I managed to move my head just enough to avoid taking the blow directly. Instead it caromed off the side of my skull. Stars erupted into my vision. For a split second, I had the funniest feeling my legs were made of wet noodles and then I pitched forward into cold, dark nothingness.

"He's waking up. Here give him this."

I didn't recognize the guy's voice, but I recognized the smell of good scotch. I opened my eyes just enough to find the glass dancing before my face. With a little assistance, I directed the glass close enough to my mouth that instinct took over. I sputtered a bit and then tried to sit up.

"Lie still. Don't make any sudden moves now."

"Who . . . Where's Ze'eva?"

"I'm right here, Theron. How is he, Doc?"

"I'd heard Mr. Chase had one of the thicker heads in Calasia. I guess this proves them right. Anyone else would have been killed taking a shot like that. All right, Ze'eva, help me get him upright."

I felt myself raised into a seated position and I chanced opening both eyes at the same time. An older, wizened man stood there, closing a small bag. Doc Griffin. He turned to Ze'eva and patted her on the hand. "I think he'll live. Just try not to jostle him too much. His vision's likely to play tricks on him for a while after a blow like that."

My voice sounded a thousand miles away. "Thanks, Doc. What'd he hit me with?"

"Can't say for sure. Lots of stuff got knocked over in the confusion. Luckily, Ze'eva has some other big friends. When they heard her scream, they came running and the guy who slugged you took off through that open window. Couple of them pulled you out of the doorway while the rest went charging out the back door like a herd of wild beasts. Never did catch the guy, but they're standing guard to make sure he doesn't try to sneak back in. In my professional opinion, I think you'll live. But, you're going to have a heck of a headache in the morning."

"Doc, I got a hell of a headache right now. You mean it's gonna get worse?"

"More than likely. I'd say you should stay in bed for a couple of days. I'd say that, but I know you aren't going to listen to me. I can see that in your eyes."

"I'd love to sleep this one off, Doc, but I think resting will have to wait until I can get this straightened out."

The old man sighed. "I figured you'd say that. You're as hard-headed as Ze'eva. I can see why she likes you so much." I heard an embarrassed gasp and he turned to her. "I may be old, but I'm not blind, young woman. Now, listen closely." He handed Ze'eva some vials with odd-colored liquid in them. "If he's not going to stay in bed—and he won't—then make sure he takes one of these every four hours he's awake. It should stave off the worst of the headaches and the doubled vision."

"I'll make sure he takes them."

"Thanks." The doc turned to look me over once again, staring me in the eyes and making me try to follow his fingers as he moved them back and forth in front of me. "You, I'll expect to see in my office as soon as you decide to quit playing hero and take care of yourself. Here's my card."

I must have been doing better; it only took me three tries to slip it into my pocket. The doc shook his head and grabbed his gear before plunging into the mingling crowd backstage muttering something about hardheaded patients. I, of course, had no clue who he could be talking about. Turning my attention from his disappearing figure, I looked at Ze'eva and noticed she was wearing a jacket, blouse, and a pair of slacks. "How long was I out?"

"Couple of hours. I had to finish the rest of my act, but Stefan and Pietro were good enough to help stand guard for both of us while you were unconscious. Most of the customers have left; just a few are hanging around to see if you'd wake up or not. Money was running three to two against you."

"Why does that not make me feel any better?"

"I said this club drew a higher class of patron. I didn't say they were saints."

I wouldn't say I leapt to my feet, but I did manage to get upright with some help. Ze'eva leaned closer to help balance me, so I took advantage of the opportunity to whisper into her ear. "There's someone in a small room above the booths. I suspect we'll find your missing boss there." I heard a sharp intake of breath, but I leaned heavily on her to draw her attention back to me. "Don't look up there and don't say anything. If he's there, then some of the backstage crew has to know. We do *not* want to make them nervous. If Fitzgerald's there, it's because he's got more than one way in or out. If he takes off running now, we may never catch him."

"But why would he be hiding?"

"You said it yourself, Angel, the constables in this town are basically incompetent. I think we'd both agree the person after you is not. Speaking of which, after we visit with Fitzgerald, we've got another stop to make."

"Who are we going to see this time? Mama Belltre?"

"No, this time we're going need to pull out some big guns. Tell me, have you received anything recently? Maybe from an anonymous fan? A ring, a set of earrings, something you might have on you that you wouldn't normally carry?"

"I do get gifts occasionally. It's one of the perks of the job. However, I've made it clear to a few overenthusiastic customers a gift is a gift, not a payment for services to be rendered later. I return those immediately to avoid misunderstandings. But, now that you mention it, I did get this ring a couple of weeks ago. It was from an anonymous admirer. Louie brought it to me. I believe it arrived sometime after the first attack but before the second. Here."

She handed me an opal ring. Now, I'm no jeweler, but I could tell it was probably worth more than I made in a year. I'm also no wizard, but I'd bet next month's rent there was a spell on it; something that would identify where she was whenever someone wanted to know. If I was right, that meant whoever was after Ze'eva had money to throw around, which made this job that much harder.

We waited until most of the backstage crew had wandered off to start cleaning up the club. I stumbled toward the ladder and unsteadily began to pull myself up. I climbed a couple of rungs just to see if I could. Ze'eva watched with some trepidation, but she didn't say a word. After I made it up a few feet, I could hear her coming behind me. I didn't dare look down; it was hard enough to keep my eyes focused without courting vertigo. After what felt like a small eternity, I crawled up onto the landing and waited for her to catch up and join me.

We gingerly made our way across the catwalk, trying to stay in the shadows. The light was dim but still visible in the darkness. Once we reached the landing on the other side, I saw it seeping out from underneath a closed door. I reached into a coat pocket and cradled my pistol. I'm not sure I could have hit anything if I had to use it, but its weight in my hand was comforting. A wave of nausea swept over me, but I managed to keep my balance and gently rested my head on the door. I couldn't hear anything but the pounding inside my own head. I motioned Ze'eva to move to one side and threw the door open and stumbled inside.

The room looked like a tornado had ripped through it. Lying in the middle of the debris was Tom Fitzgerald. Another man I didn't recognize was pinned to the wall like an oversized butterfly. Someone had driven a huge spike right through him. I rushed over to Fitzgerald. Someone or something had worked him over, but good. He was barely breathing but he was still alive.

He opened his eyes as I propped him up and his voice was barely a whisper. "Chase?"

"Don't talk, Tom. We'll get you to a doctor."

"No time. Listen, you've gotta take care of Ze'eva for me."

"I'll take care of her after I take care of you. Just relax." I started to tell Ze'eva to yell for help when he reached up and grabbed my collar. I don't know where he got the strength, but he clung to me like a drowning man clings to a piece of wood.

"Listen, Chase. I'm done for, but you can get the bastard who did this." Ze'eva came in and knelt down beside me. Fitzgerald turned his face toward her and gave her a smile.

"Sorry about all this trouble, kid. I was hoping it'd turn out different."

Ze'eva held his hand as I spoke to him. "Tom, who did this to you?"

"I don't know his name, Chase. No one does. People call him Mr. X. Yeah, I know, pretty corny, right? He's a shapeshifter. I don't know how he does it. You never see him with the same face twice. Anyway, that bastard broke in here tonight . . . came through the skylight. I don't know how he found me."

"Why was he after you, Tom?"

Fitzgerald coughed, a trickle of blood oozed from the corner of his mouth. "Tabor. He wanted Tabor's identity."

"Did you tell him?"

Fitzgerald's breathing became more labored but he pushed on. "I gave him a name. Not Tabor, though. Tabor is a friend. He's always taken good care of me and Ze'eva. He owns this club. I just run it for him. Everyone thinks it's my place. That's what he wanted."

"Who is Tabor, Tom? We have to warn him."

Fitzgerald coughed again. His voice was getting weaker by the second. He paused and looked at Ze'eva. "Count Aeson. The count goes by Tabor; it's the name he uses when the moon's full. He's a werewolf, same as Ze'eva. He can't let people know or he'd be thrown off the Privy Council and either tossed into jail or killed."

"And someone stands to profit if the count is exposed?"

"Yes. A number of nobles would. There's something else you need to know, Chase."

Fitzgerald coughed again. I felt his body convulse, but he fought to keep his eyes on Ze'eva as he spoke to me. "The count is Ze'eva's father. She's suspected for a while, but she didn't know Tabor was the count. He wanted me to take care of her. Guess I didn't do a good enough job."

"You've always been good to me, Tom."

Fitzgerald's eyes went wide and he turned his head to look at me. "Chase, something just struck me. Mr. X—his face—it was the same as when he attacked earlier. I wonder why?"

And with that, he went limp in my arms. I laid the body back onto the floor, while Ze'eva clung to his hand, crying. Sour racket. I felt like a heel making her leave but we didn't have time to mourn. There was a good chance the assassin would be back to double-check his work and I was no shape for a rematch. We let the guys working backstage know about Tom, told them what we could, and told them to tell Corvinus I'd be in contact with him in a day or so.

Something Fitzgerald had said was pinging around in my brain, but I was still addled from the blow I'd taken and nothing seemed to make sense. I told Ze'eva to leave that ring in a safe place in her dressing room and we slipped out the back. After negotiating some alleys and other unpleasant areas of town, I decided the safest place to sleep was probably the one place no one, to include Corvinus, would look.

"**G**ood evening, Maxie."
"Heya, Chase, what brings you to the morgue?"
"Need a place to hide and rest."

Maxie opened the door and let us in. He had the good manners not to ogle Ze'eva too broadly, but he turned and gave me a sly grin. "Not your typical date spot, is it, Chase?"

"Knock it off, Maxie. She's a client and we're in a jam. You got someplace we can rest?"

Maxie nudged me in the ribs and headed deeper into the basement beneath the constables' Citadel. We followed him down a long dark corridor to a pair of iron doors. He opened one and motioned for us to follow. It grew colder the farther into the morgue we went. After a bit, Maxie stopped at a locker and handed the two of us long fur coats to put on. "So, how long are the two of you gonna hang out around here? Not that the neighbors are going to complain."

"Max, do not start with the morgue jokes. My head hurts badly enough as is."

"All right, Chase, all right. Sheesh. You're in a mood tonight."

"Maxie, I came a couple of inches from being your next client. You'll pardon me if my sense of humor is a tad off kilter."

Maxie paused and gave me an uncharacteristically serious look. "You ain't jokin' with me, are you, Chase?"

"No, Maxie. I am not joking with you."

"Okay, Chase. Come with me, I got a good place to put you up for the night." He pointed to a doorway just beyond the main room. "There's a little spot in the back of the storeroom. We use it for taking catnaps when things is borin' down here. If you open the box on the left, you'll find some more furs you can rest on. I wouldn't sit on this floor too long. It's cold enough you might freeze right to it."

Ze'eva smiled at him. "Thank you, Maxie. We really do appreciate it."

Maxie must have turned six shades of red in about as long as it takes to tell it. "Aww, ain't nothin', Miss. You're in good hands if Chase is workin' for you. He's a good one."

"Yes, I think he is."

While I was enjoying the compliments, it did not change the fact I needed to lie down soon before I fell down. I left Ze'eva and Maxie saying good night to each other while I went into the storeroom and found the furs he'd mentioned. I spread them out and we made ourselves comfortable. I asked Maxie to wake us when he got off shift. The last thing I remembered was laying my head down on a bundle of fur and Ze'eva singing to herself.

I wasn't sure what time it was when I woke up. What I did notice was I was by myself. Without thinking, I jumped to my feet and nearly fell over from the pain. The pounding in my head returned with a vengeance and nausea swept over me in waves. About then, Ze'eva stuck her head through the doorway, alerted to my state of consciousness by the volume of my cursing, no doubt. She rushed over and kept me from toppling forward onto my face and made me sit back down.

"I was just coming to get you, Theron. I've got breakfast out here, if you think you can stomach it."

My head wasn't sure about eating, but my stomach had the deciding vote. I stumbled into the main room and saw Ze'eva laying out quite a spread on one of the tables. Maxie was busy devouring a steaming plate of food over in the corner.

I glanced at the food and then at her. "You shouldn't have gone out, Ze'eva."

"Oh, *I* didn't go. Maxie went. I watched the place for him while he was gone. Now, here, eat something. The doctor said you shouldn't drink these on an empty stomach."

I wasn't in the mood to eat, but the food smelled good and a big steaming cup of coffee sounded great after spending the night in an icebox. I carefully tried a bite, decided it was going to stay where it was supposed to, and then attacked my food with more gusto than I anticipated.

While I was busy stuffing myself, Maxie came over. "You know, Chase, I've been thinkin' about those stiffs that got brought in yesterday."

"The two from the Green Dragon?"

"Well, yeah, them too, but mostly about them first two. The ones Corvinus thinks you killed."

I started to say something, but Ze'eva shoved a glass vial into my hand. "Don't forget to take this."

"Thanks, Angel." I downed the greenish liquid and only

made two weird faces due to the taste. However, it did clear my head some and Maxie's comments started to make sense. I waited a second and then turned to Maxie, who was puttering around the room. "Thanks for the reminder. It seems like only yesterday he was trying to arrest me for that. Well, what about those bodies, Maxie?"

"The big guy, the one that got burned. We was examinin' him and the head spook noticed somethin' peculiar. Seems he was killed with a single blow from a knife. Weird thing was, the knife didn't hit any vital organs."

"That does sound peculiar."

"See, that's what I thought too, Chase. So, the head spook calls in the mage we have on staff upstairs. He verified whatever killed the big guy had somethin' to do with magic because while that blow would have hurt like heck, it wouldn't have killed him. So, we checked out the other guy, the jigsaw puzzle. He was killed the same way. All the other stuff, the dismembering and acid? That happened afterward."

"And wasn't that the body they thought was Tom Fitzgerald?"

Maxie walked over to a couple of bodies covered in sheets. He pointed to the smaller of the pair. Luckily, for Ze'eva's sake, he didn't pull the sheets back like he would have if I had been alone. "Yeah, which is really weird, since we picked up Fitzgerald's body at the theater. That's going to frost ol' Corvinus. He's been looking to pin something on you for a long time, Chase."

"I'm sorry to disappoint him."

"You do have a way with him, Chase. Never seen anyone else get him so riled up. Anyway, these two guys from the Dragon was killed like normal people. Oh, not that normal people usually get pinned to a wall, but I mean, their wounds actually killed them. No magic."

I felt something cold lying against my leg. "So, what kind of knife do you think it was that killed the first two?"

"Oh, I'd say a fairly long blade but not too wide. Definitely not a sword or something like that. Stiletto maybe? I'm just the morgue attendant, Chase, I'm not the examiner."

I pulled out the knife I'd found at Fitzgerald's home. "Maybe something like this?"

Maxie took it and examined it closely with a large magnifying glass and then let out a low whistle. "Yep. Definitely something like this. Where'd you find it, Chase?"

"Someone dropped it at Fitzgerald's place. It might have been kicked under the table during the struggle or while they were mutilating the corpse. Then some goons broke in while we were there poking around. I'll bet this was what they were looking for. And from how thoroughly they tossed the joint, I'd say their boss is awfully desperate to get it back."

"You know, having that knife looks real bad, Chase."

"Yeah, I know, Maxie. It's just the piece of evidence Corvinus could use to pin everything on me. But, I've gotta hang on to it. It might be the only thing that'll lead me to the real killer."

Ze'eva walked up behind me and leaned in to whisper into my ear. "Theron, you said we have to see someone this morning?"

I got Maxie to bring me some cloth and I wrapped the blade carefully before I slipped it back into my coat pocket. "A couple of someones, now that you remind me." I turned back to Maxie and stuck out my hand. "Thanks for letting us hang out here, Maxie. I really owe you one."

He grinned at me before shaking my hand. "Think nothin' of it, Chase. You always have the most interestin' corpses on your cases. Makes working down here much more entertainin' 'cause I never know what's gonna turn up."

And on that morbid note, we slipped out of the police citadel and disappeared into the morning crowds. I knew we needed to meet with Ferendel around noon, but there was another stop I needed to make before we got too far. A short cab ride later, we found ourselves near the North Hills, or as many call it, the Noble Quarter. The nobles had most of their manor houses up here, overlooking North Bay. Lets the well-to-do enjoy the ocean view without having to smell anything or anyone who works down on the docks.

The cab turned onto Batavia Boulevard and stopped in front of Markham's Emporium of the Ancients. I guided Ze'eva past the glowing glass doors and into a carefully laid-out showroom with expensive items displayed behind thick glass. While there seemed to be a hodgepodge of items, they all had one thing in common: very expensive price tags.

A well-dressed man approached us, looking disdainfully at our attire and general disheveled look. "May I help you?" From the tone of his voice, he was hoping I'd say no, but I disappointed him.

"I need to speak to Theodius Markham."

"Oh, I'm so sorry. Mr. Markham is much too busy to deal with clients at this time."

"Look, Jeeves, let Mr. Markham know that Mr. Theron Chase is out in his lobby and needs a moment of his time."

The toady-boy gave me one of those looks and I gleefully returned it. Once he realized I was not going away, he shrugged and disappeared into a back room. Ze'eva and I examined one of the display cases until I heard the sounds of muffled shouting. Seconds later, the young man came flying out of the back looking much less snooty. He apologized profusely and escorted us to his employer.

"Chase, good to see you. And I see your taste in company has improved too." The large man rose from behind his desk, his cutaway coat barely containing his girth, and came around to shake hands with us both. He gave Ze'eva a conspiratorial look, "The last time he was here, he was accompanied by some rather large and disreputable gentlemen. I think he's getting wiser in his old age."

"Those gentlemen, as you called them, belonged to Blackie Carmichael's mob and they're both in Imperial prison as we speak."

He winked at Ze'eva before moving back to his desk, flicking away some imaginary lint from his sleeve. "As I said, young lady, you're definitely an improvement over his usual companions." She giggled at his flirting. I was beginning to feel invisible.

"If you're done harassing my client, I have need of your services."

He shot me a dirty look, but settled into his chair and gave me his attention. "What macabre item have you brought me this time, Chase?"

I carefully pulled out the knife and set it on his desk. "I'm not sure what it is, but I have the feeling it's enchanted. I'd avoid that tip. There's a good possibility there's necromancy involved. It's been used to kill two men that we know of, maybe more. I need to know what it does and if possible who could have made it."

"That's a tall order, Chase. Let me guess, you need this information yesterday?"

"The sooner the better, Theo."

"I'm actually quite busy, but you've done me a favor or two in the past. I'll let you know when I have an answer."

I knew better than to ask how he would do that. Theodius might look like just your average overweight business owner, but he was probably one of the three most powerful wizards in Calasia. The fact I'd solved a small matter of blackmail for him was not well known and he preferred to keep it that way. So, if he told me he would contact me, he would contact me.

Leaving the Emporium, we caught another cab across town to reach Blake Ferendel's. It was a few minutes before noon, so we waited at a nearby restaurant. I flagged down a kid I knew and sent him to my office with a note for Kyra. I didn't know if she'd be there, but I needed information.

After some food and another of Doc Griffin's nasty potions, we crossed the street to see Ferendel. A couple of his boys met us at the door and after a pointed conversation about how they were not going to frisk my client, they led us back to the same den I'd been in only twenty-four hours ago.

"Chase, if I knew you worked with such classy clients, I would invite you over more often."

I turned to Ze'eva. "I always said you were good for business."

"No, I think I told you I'd make a good partner for you."

That caught Ferendel's attention. "You going to work with that bum, Miss . . ."

"Hammacker. We have discussed the possibility once he finishes with the small matter he's looking into for me."

"Miss . . . Hammacker. Gotcha." Ferendel didn't look convinced, but he was willing to let it ride for now. "Anyway, Chase, I've looked into the little matter that you asked me about yesterday. Let me introduce you to my associate, Marcus. Marcus here uses big words on occasion, so feel free to stop him and ask him to speak normally."

With that, he clacked a small hammer against a wooden block on his desk. A small, unimposing man came through a door I hadn't noticed in the dim light and took a position beside the desk. He adjusted his glasses and stared at the two of us. Ferendel pointed to us. "This here is Mr. Chase and Miss Hammacker. They're the ones who wanna know what you've dug up. Chase, Miss Hammacker, this is Marcus. He may not look like much but he is extremely good at getting information from places I might not be welcomed. Please direct any questions you have to him."

Marcus seemed uncomfortable being thrust into the spotlight, but he cleared his throat a few times and pulled several pieces of parchment from inside his vest. He nervously adjusted his glasses and then spoke in a deeper voice than I would have given him credit for.

"It appears Miss Blackthorne, whom you had enquired about earlier, has become the subject of interest to some very influential people. No one is quite sure what she did to draw their attention. However, a significant amount of money has been spent in town to learn what there is to know about her. It appears twenty different people or more are researching her past life as well as her current activities, to include her known associates."

Ze'eva reached out and took a good grip on my hand. I tried very hard not to wince and focused on what Marcus was saying. "Does this exchange of currency have a start and a stopping place?"

"Indeed it does, Mr. Chase. As a matter of fact, Mr. Ferendel himself was approached not twelve hours ago to add his own significant resources to this very matter. However, since he had committed himself to act as your agent, he regretfully was forced to turn down their not-so-insubstantial offer."

I glanced at Ferendel. "I am in your debt yet again."

Ferendel allowed himself the pleasure of a wolfish grin. "Yes, you are. We can discuss that another day. Continue, Marcus."

"Yes, Mr. Ferendel. From what I was able to gather from both the messenger boy and my own investigations, it appears that one Baron Lyndmar is at the apex of the conspiracy against your client."

"Baron Lyndmar? I know him from the club."

"If you're referring to the Green Dragon, then yes, it's possible you have met him, Miss Hammacker. He's become quite the regular since Miss Blackthorne began performing there. However, it appears he believes she knows something of great interest to him. Great enough interest, I might add, that he desires to secure her knowledge before any of his rivals can contact her and make use of her knowledge before he is ready to achieve whatever his ultimate goal is. Whether she actually has this information or not is immaterial—either he will possess it or else he will ensure no one else can access it. Therefore, his own personal feelings toward her—and it appears he does have some interest—must be disregarded and either her capture or her elimination is necessary for his goals."

Ze'eva took in a quick breath before speaking. "That's horrible."

Ferendel broke in. "It is indeed. Now, Chase, of interest to you and your client, it appears whatever the good baron has in mind is aimed at one Count Aeson. I don't have a clue what he's got against the count and in all honesty, I do not care. One noble is the same to me as another. Either they are a direct source of business or they cause others to seek out my resources."

Ferendel poured himself a drink from the crystal decanter on his desk before continuing. He regarded the amber liquid then looked directly at me. "It appears the baron has recruited a big-time hitter from New Beliaria. In other words, he has hired an assassin, one whose personal identity is still a mystery, even to me. He is known in the business as Mr. X, because of his constantly changing appearance—if he is even a he, which I would not lay a single copper penny on. I would not want to cross swords with him, but knowing your overblown sense of right and wrong, I suspect you will do so, if you have not already."

"Is there anything else, Mr. Ferendel?" Marcus asked.

He glanced at us but I shook my head no.

"No, Marcus. You may leave."

With that, the small man disappeared almost as quietly as he had arrived. Ferendel played with a few items on his desk while he waited for the door to shut. I did not take this as a good sign. He waited a few more seconds and then looked up at the two of us. "I'm going to lay it on you straight, Chase. You're in way the hell over your head. This assassin is incredibly good. I've dropped jobs just because there was a rumor he was going to be involved. Take a hint and take a hike, preferably one that would take you away from this city for several months. I would recommend you begin that hike today."

"I'd love to take you up on that, Blake, but it's too late. We've already tangled once. If I blow town, even to keep my client alive, I could never come back here."

"In all honesty, I knew you would say that. However, I felt obligated to make that suggestion. That said, I can now wash my hands of the whole matter. I have fulfilled my part of the bargain and now I am going to ask you to leave before I am associated more tightly with you. I have done work for both the count and the baron, so a neutral position seems to make the most business sense."

"I can't blame you, Blake. It's a tough situation and you have to take care of yourself. Thanks for everything."

As Ze'eva and I reached the door, Ferendel called out. "Hey, Chase."

"Yeah, Blake?"

"Tell you what. You stay alive, I will forget you owe me anything. We will call it even."

"Consider us even then, Blake, because I'm not dying anytime soon."

"Always the optimist. Good luck, gumshoe."

And with that, Ze'eva and I returned to the streets. There was a small flurry in the crowd and the young urchin I had snagged earlier appeared in front of me and handed me a note in exchange for a silver shilling. What I read there was worth the coin and more. I motioned Ze'eva over to the restaurant we'd waited in earlier and we took seats at the back of the place, near the kitchen.

"What's up, Theron?"

"Got a note from Kyra. Pinkie says Louie never arrived at

my place. Says no one's been there all night."

"Has something happened to Louie?"

"Hard to say, Angel. There's a good possibility Maxie's got another customer sometime this morning. If someone was watching my office, they might have seen Louie leaving and followed him, thinking he'd lead them to you. Then again, he could just be hiding somewhere else and be perfectly fine."

She covered her mouth and a few tears welled up, but she held herself together. A few seconds later, she'd recovered enough to talk again. "So, what's next?"

I waited for the waitress to bring our drinks before I responded. "I'm not really sure. We've been on the defensive ever since we went to the club yesterday. We know who's possibly behind this and we know who his ultimate target is, but we don't know why. The worst thing is we can't prove a word of it. If Corvinus gets a hold of me, he's going to throw me into the dungeons beneath Maxie's for so long my nonexistent grandchildren will have gray hair."

"We could go see the count. At least try to warn him what's going on."

"I've considered that. Unfortunately, I'm not exactly on the count's guest list. I don't know how we'd get inside."

Ze'eva grinned at me. "Let me try. After all, he wouldn't refuse to see his own daughter."

"You believe what Tom said?"

"Tom didn't have any reason to lie when he told me the first time, much less when he was dying. It may not be true, but Tom believed it was."

"It's worth a shot."

After we visited one of Ze'eva's friends so she could change into something more suitable for visiting nobility, our cab climbed one of the tallest hills in the city. A couple of guards tried to stop us when we approached the gates. I have to say, Ze'eva put on quite the performance. By the time she was done, they not only apologized for not recognizing her, they provided an escort through the mansion's grounds. From the looks I was getting, it was a good thing Ze'eva vouched for me or I might have been out in the rear alley with the rest of the trash.

A quick word or two with the majordomo and we found ourselves seated in a small library. I examined some of the books on the wall and recognized a few of the titles. There was no question these were original printings, incredibly rare and incredibly valuable. The room seemed old but well used. It had a comfortable feeling, unlike Ferendel's office, or the efficient organization of Markham's. This felt like a place the count used quite often. That he was meeting us here was a good sign. A large smile settled on my face. "That was quite the performance."

"We're lucky those guards never met Lady Siobhan before."

"Have you?"

"Of course not," she said, breaking into giggles. "I made the name and the title up on the spot. From working in the clubs, I know if you act like you know what you're doing, especially if you act imperious enough, people tend to believe you."

The door opened and she drew herself up in a regal pose as the majordomo entered and announced Lord Aeson, Count of Palmora. I bowed out of habit, but Ze'eva maintained her dignified posture. The count swept into the room, moving with a speed and grace that belied his age. His long gray hair framed a noble face and his regal clothing barely hid a body that men many years his junior would have killed for. He waved brusquely at us as he sat behind his desk. He finally glanced up and actually looked at Ze'eva. His mouth fell open and he froze before slowly standing up. A shocked look of recognition crossed his face and he turned to the majordomo and emphatically motioned for him to leave the room.

Once the door was closed, he eased back into the chair. "By the gods, it *is* you. You are the spitting image of your mother."

Ze'eva kept her face impassive. I felt uncomfortable, but it was too late to back out now. Finally, she spoke in a cautious tone. "Hello, Father. It is nice to meet you after all this time."

"I have been many things in my life, child, but until I saw you right now, I had never considered myself a fool. I know now, *that* is my chief accomplishment these past fifty years."

"Provided we both survive the upcoming storm, Father, I hope we'll have the opportunity to get to know each other properly. However, it won't be as easy as just wishing for it."

I wasn't sure if she meant surviving the baron's plot or if she was warning him against a fairy-tale reunion. I don't think either of us had considered what meeting her father for the first time would be like. Still, the tension was rising as they stared at each other, so I took the opportunity to get up and close the drapes to the room. I was uncomfortable with how exposed the room was to the outside world. There'd been enough sniping the past few days to make me leery of open windows.

The count watched with interest as I pulled the last curtain closed before taking a seat. "Are you worried someone may see us together? I fully intend to declare Ze'eva my daughter as soon as it is practical."

"Actually, Your Grace, I'm more worried about keeping the two of you alive. That's what I've been hired to do and I intend to keep doing it."

"Ze'eva what *is* he talking about? I haven't got an enemy in the world. Oh, a few people aren't fond of my positions on the Privy Council and the Hall of Lords can get rather cantankerous at times, but really, my life?"

"That's *exactly* why we've come today, Father. Someone has been trying to kill me and we've just found out they are after you too."

The old man's face went white. "Someone tried to kill you?"

"Several times. Theron saved my life three times in the past two days. I hired him to investigate who's behind this and why. Father, how well do you know Baron Lyndmar?"

"That rapscallion? He sits on the Privy Council with me since his father passed suddenly. He's been hinting he'd like to take my place as King's Exchequer when my term is up. Personally, I don't think he's a good choice—no head for business. Not sure he'd invest the king's money wisely. Is he in danger too?"

"No, Father. We believe he's the one behind the attempts on my life."

When the count rose to his feet, it reminded me of the alley cat I'd surprised behind my office a few nights ago—all bristly and back arched. "Ze'eva, don't be ridiculous. The baron may not be a close friend, but I can't believe he's behind such a plot. I've known him since he was a child. His father was one of my closest friends, both on the council and away. I'm certain you're mistaken. Do you have any evidence to back up this wild story?"

"Evidence? No, Father. No more evidence than I have you're really my father. I only have the words of people I trust."

Ouch.

The count recoiled as if she'd slapped him. When he spoke again, there was almost a pleading sound in his voice. "Now, see here, Ze'eva. There's no reason to speak like that. You have to understand, I have known the baron for years. His father's loss was felt by many of us. The boy, Nathaniel, has gone to great lengths to fulfill his duties. He's served admirably as baron. He's determined to bring his properties into the modern era."

"Isn't it true Baron Lyndmar recently paid off some rather sizeable debts upon the receipt of his inheritance?" The count turned to face me and I continued. "Would it concern you if he was seen talking with a man who attacked me a few moments later in Ze'eva's dressing room at the Green Dragon? The same man we believe is attempting to kill Ze'eva and who's killed four people in the last two days—that we know of."

"It might concern me—if you could prove they were doing

anything more than talking. The baron's choice in company does not conclusively equate him to being involved in a plot against either Ze'eva or me. In fact, you say you saw them speak. Did you hear what they spoke about? Never mind. I can tell from your expression you did not. I'll have you know I am not one who listens to idle gossip. The boy has always conducted himself like a gentleman. I'll hear no more of this."

"Very well, Father. Theron, I think it's time we left."

"Ze'eva?"

She turned toward her father. He saw her resolute expression and his face fell. He reached out a hand and then slowly let it fall onto his desk. She slowly shook her head and took a couple of steps backward. "Father, someone *is* trying to kill me. I cannot simply sit and wait for it. I hired Theron to get to the bottom of this affair and he cannot do it sitting here either. Therefore, we are leaving."

He looked as if she'd just kicked him in the gut. "I can protect you."

"Father, if you refuse to recognize the fact you're in danger, you can't even protect yourself. If we both survive, perhaps we can speak again."

She turned to leave and I rose to follow her. Her father spoke again, anger tingeing his voice. "I could have you stopped."

"You could . . . but, you won't. Good-bye, Father."

I saw the air come out of him as he dropped into his chair. For a second I was afraid the sniper had done his job. However, from the way the count was holding his head in his hands, I knew something else had wounded him, something more devastating than an arrow or a knife. It was the one opponent he couldn't defeat with arms or with a quick turn of words: the loss of Ze'eva's respect.

We left the manor house and I flagged a cab. Ze'eva leaned back in her seat and stared at the roof. "What now, Theron?"

A wild idea buzzed in my head. It was a long shot, but I owed it to my client to run it past her. "That all depends, Lady Siobhan. Do you feel up to a repeat performance?"

Her eyes widened as she grasped my meaning. "The baron?"

"Why not? Maybe confronting him directly will throw him off his game. He's been the one calling all the shots up to now. Maybe if he realizes we're on to him, he'll call off the hounds. Worse comes to worst, maybe he'll make a mistake that we can use against him."

"Or maybe he'll redouble his efforts to prevent us from exposing him."

"That's always a possibility. Still, I doubt he's expecting us to just walk into his place."

"I'm not sure I'm that good an actress, Theron. But, if you think it's worth a try, I'll be right there with you."

Listening to the sounds of the city as we drove through town, I mulled it over in my head. As I had said to Ze'eva earlier, we'd been reacting instead of acting. If we put the baron on the defensive, he might let something slip. I knew we wouldn't scare him off completely. After all, there was no real proof that Mr. X worked for him. There had to be something we could use, some information we were overlooking that would make him believe we were more valuable alive than dead. That would be a start.

The trouble was how to do it? Unlike Count Aeson's, I didn't think we could waltz into the baron's manor quite that easily. Before I could finish that thought, a rather unpleasant buzzing sounded in my ear. I realized Ze'eva couldn't hear it and finally recognized what it had to be and who was causing it. That blow to the head I took last night must have affected me worse than I thought. I leaned forward and gave the driver new directions. A few minutes later, we pulled up in front of Markham's Emporium of the Ancients for the second time that day.

The same young man saw us and immediately took us to a waiting room. We hadn't been there long before Theo came bustling in carrying a box. He appeared dapper as always. However, what he did not appear to be was happy.

"Chase, where did you find this infernal weapon?"

"A crime scene, Theo. Man was apparently stabbed with that and then dismembered. I believe the killer left it behind by mistake."

"I wish you had said so before you left it with me." He put the box on the table as if he was handling a hooded cobra. He glared at me and then his face softened. "No, it's my fault for not asking better questions before I let you leave it. You did warn me it might be necromantic magic, although I tend to discount your ability to recognize magic, much less the school. Nevertheless, I had no idea you were capable of being so precise. I'm giving your secretary credit on training you in the mystic arts. Normally your guesses regarding the realm of magic barely reach layman quality."

"Hey!"

Theo barely registered my protest. He wiped some perspiration from his brow and continued on as if he was afraid that if he got interrupted, he'd never finish. "As I said, my good man, you were more than correct this time. This dagger is not unknown to me, oh dear me, no, although I've never actually seen it before today. It is known as *The Final Kiss* and its owner is an assassin—more than an assassin really—known as Mr. X." Theo chuckled at a private joke before continuing, "Although I'm sure it amuses him to be called that. He's a mage we thought stripped of his powers after he was on the losing side of the Aether Wars ten years ago."

I nodded grimly. "I remember that time. It took years for Calasia to recover. I made good coin dealing with the aftermath. There's a good reason why I try to stay out of wars between wizards. As you've said, I'm not very adept at spell craft."

"Oh, stop pouting, Chase. You have your own unique set of skills. However, magic is not your strong suit. In fact, if you were any less apt, Chase, I'd say you'd almost be invulnerable to the stuff. But, that's neither here nor there." He paused and rang a small bell sitting on the table. The young toady from yesterday appeared and Theo ordered drinks and settled back into the overstuffed chair. I suspected we were in for a bit of a lecture. Once the drinks had appeared and the boy had shut the door behind him, Theo said a few words in a language I did not recognize. The lights dimmed slightly and he turned back toward us with a self-satisfied smile.

"Now, we have good drink and privacy—two things I think we're going to need to continue. As I said, Chase, I know the dagger, because I know the man who owns it—or I *knew* the man. What he has become now, I cannot say. We knew him as Roderick Caupo, but he's much better known in mage circles these days as The Doppelganger. He's not a were-creature or a shapeshifter in the classic sense, Chase. In the Aether War, he was greatly feared as an assassin because he used magic to alter his appearance—forbidden magic and this dagger. When he kills his victim, this dagger drains their soul from their body, allowing him to cast a spell to assume their shape. By storing their soul within the dagger, he is able to access several days' worth of their memories, enabling him to mingle with the victim's associates without being discovered until he reaches his ultimate target."

Finally a light came on for good ol' slow-on-the-draw Theron. I managed to get a word in edgewise to Theo's long-winded explanation. "That would explain how he was able to convince Corvinus that I'd been seen at Tom Fitzgerald's place. Odds are the dismembered body in Fitzgerald's house was the neighbor Caupo was impersonating when he identified me to the constables. So, basically, you're telling me that we can't trust anyone we meet?"

"Yes and no. Anyone you met before you came into possession of that dagger was potentially Roderick Caupo. In fact, it is odd that he did not attempt to attack one of Miss Blackthorne's friends before now. It would have been easier to get to her, if she was really his target. This leads me to believe there's something he wants besides her death."

"Hey, wait a minute. I never told you her name."

The big man chuckled before responding to my challenge. "Chase, my dear boy, do you think you're the only person who knows how to do basic investigation? Besides, I've attended this young lady's performances before. It's good for the soul to take in beauty and the arts. You should try it more often."

Ze'eva laughed and I tried to get his attention again. "Theo, if you're done flirting with my client—again—could we get back to the topic of our opponent? Have your mystical investigations given you any clues to his current employer or what his motives might be?"

"Good gods, Chase, are you actually jealous of the attention I am paying Miss Blackthorne? You really should keep your schoolboy temper in line. The answer to your ill-mannered question is no. I am an accomplished mage but unfortunately, I can only work with what is provided to me, either by you or my own two eyes. The dagger may tell me who its owner was, but it does not give me insight into the owner's thoughts nor whom he meets. I'm afraid you're going to have to rely on old-fashioned detective work for once, Chase."

He rang the bell again and the young man reappeared. They exchanged a few words and the young man took away the drinks. As the lights returned to normal, Theo pointed at the box on the table. "I have taken the liberty to place the dagger in this box. It will only open for either you or Miss Blackthorne. Please, do try not to lose it."

"I'll keep it under close supervision."

"I hope you will. Unless I miss my guess, that box is worth several years of your salary." Theo held up a hand, cutting off my protest, a serious expression settling in over his usually jovial features. "Understand this. Roderick is likely to expend any expense to recover it. You understand that he is trapped either in his own body or that of his last victim. I was unable to ascertain how long the spell lasts; it is not a field of magic I'm comfortable exploring. However, he *is* vulnerable and there are many people who'd relish the chance to take revenge. He will not remain idle long."

Theo's face became almost predatory as an unpleasant smile crossed his face. "If for some reason you render him unable to reclaim his dagger, either through incarceration or more . . . permanent means, I would like to buy this from you."

"I didn't think you dabbled in this type of magic."

"It's not for resale, my good man. I have a rather extensive collection of things that should not be in the wild. It would make an interesting addition. And no, get that idea out of your mind right now. You're not going to get to wander through my collection. With your lack of magical aptitude, you'd probably blow up half the city by accident."

Taking the cue that it was time to leave, we bid Theo good afternoon. One of the clerks caught Theo's attention and said a few words to him. "Ah, Chase, before you go, you might want to know there are several gentlemen who seem to be malingering outside. It might be best to consider alternative means of egress from my business. I do like you, but should your usual bout of fisticuffs bring you back into the showroom . . . well, let's say— it could be disastrous for us all."

"I see your point. Do you have an alternative method for leaving here?"

"You wound me, Chase. Of course I have alternatives. Follow me."

He led us into his basement where we maneuvered past piles of boxes, strange objects covered in white drop cloths and other items I'm not sure I could describe if I saw them in the daylight. He had summoned a small glowing ball to provide illumination, which was useful because I would have killed myself trying to negotiate that maze in the dark. After a hazardous journey, we reached a wall painted as black as anything I'd ever seen. It almost looked oily, it was that black. He motioned for me to touch it. Like the trusting person I am, I reached out and placed my hand on the wall, noting how it gave beneath my fingers at first and then pushed back, like it was covered with some substance.

"Where do you need to go, Chase?"

"I was going to swing by my office and then visit the baron."

"I've never been to your office. Can you please keep your hand on the wall and try to visualize it."

I did as he asked and soon, a lifelike image of the office materialized on the wall. I say lifelike because I could see Kyra moving around the office tidying things up. Theo didn't say a word but motioned for me to step forward. The wall resisted for a second and then dissolved like sea foam. I'd almost caught my balance on the other side before Ze'eva crashed into me from behind. Kyra screamed as we stumbled into her and crashed into the floor. Somehow I wound up at the bottom with two beautiful women attempting to extricate themselves from the pile. I was on the receiving end of numerous elbows, knees, heels and apologies. Eventually, we managed to get untangled and everyone calmed down. I'm certain Theo enjoyed the scene if he was still watching.

"Really, Theron, just appearing in the room like that and then tackling me—you're lucky I didn't turn you into a gnat."

"Can you turn someone into a gnat?" Ze'eva asked.

"Well, no. But, I would have done something if I hadn't recognized him."

"I'm glad you're in such good spirits too, Kyra. Plus, if I have to tackle anyone, I'd much rather it be you. How did things go with Corvinus once he woke up?"

She gave me a quick smile before turning serious again. "I

decided to take your lead and slipped out the back way before that happened. He tore the office up looking for something incriminating and then stormed out. From where I was hiding, I saw he assigned a couple of constables to watch the place. Did you spot them?"

I explained how we had arrived and she vowed to have a word with Theo for scaring her like that. I left her and Ze'eva visiting while I went into my office to prepare for the upcoming confrontation. I was tired of being under-armed. It was time I upped the ante a bit.

Opening the floor safe under my desk, I withdrew two vials of truth serum, a crystal vial filled with a choking gas, and a black blade with silver runes on it. I then went to my closet and pulled out a finely woven chain vest that I slipped on underneath my shirt. It wasn't perfect protection, but it would stop a lot of normal weapons. Along with the magical equipment, I also grabbed my .45 automatic from the desk. I slipped my shoulder holster on and ensured it was reasonably unnoticeable underneath my jacket. I grabbed several magazines and slipped them into a pocket on the inside of my steel-reinforced leather coat. I wasn't sure any of this would do me a bit of good, but it felt better than walking into a manor house filled with armed and armored guards, not to mention one aggravated assassin, with just my bare fists and wits.

When I returned, Ze'eva and Kyra were chatting away like old friends. Ze'eva noted the change in my apparel and nodded. She gave Kyra a hug and headed toward the door. Kyra came over and gave me a hug too. I started toward the door, but stopped when Kyra put a hand on my arm.

"Theron, I know you've been in some tough spots before . . ."

". . . and I always come home, don't I?"

"Yes, you do. Still, I'm worried, Theron. Keep your eyes open. There's more going on here than meets the eye. Call it woman's intuition; call it whatever you want, but I'd feel a lot better coming with you."

"If you want to feel better, get out your earrings, kid. I'll get the ring. That way you can listen in. If things go bad, call Corvinus. Of course, I'd appreciate it if you were to contact Theo. It would be useful to have competent help."

I sat on the edge of her desk and sighed. "I'd like to have a chance to rest and plan, but we just don't have the time. I have two murder charges hanging over my head, maybe four, so I have to get this cleared up before I run out of hiding places. The constables may be idiots, but they *are* going to catch up with me eventually."

Kyra didn't look convinced but I slipped back into my office and pulled a small silver ring out of my wall safe. I didn't like to use the ring too often. It had a limited number of uses, and I wasn't sure if it could be recharged. The guy who made it for me wound up on the wrong end of a wizard's duel. Hell, I didn't know how many charges it even had left, so I only used it for special occasions. Still, I had a feeling Kyra was right—this was the time to use it.

We went to the basement and hiked through the sewers beneath Calasia again. This time, we only went a couple of blocks, just far enough to avoid anyone Corvinus might have watching the office . . . I hoped. We came up in a back room at the Cock and Fox pub, stepped over the sleeping janitor, and left via the alley door.

"You seem awfully familiar with the pubs and taverns in town, Theron," Ze'eva said with a trace of amusement in her voice.

"Between meeting clients and keeping an eye on suspects, I spend a lot of my life in places the nobility would turn their noses up at. That is, when they're not down here slumming."

"I saw that at the Green Dragon too. Those VIP booths exist for a reason. They have to be paid for in advance and there's a waiting list. Don't make a payment and you get bumped back to the end of the line. I noted that only specific staffers served those booths. Tom prided himself in providing 'special services.'"

"How *special* were those services?"

"I don't know. I sang at the Green Dragon, but I wasn't an employee there. I was only there evenings I had a performance scheduled. The employees were nice enough but they always kept me at arm's length. If Tom was doing something illegal, I never saw it."

We turned a corner and went down another alley. I had a feeling staying off the main thoroughfares would help keep both of us out of trouble, given Corvinus's interest in me these days. I thought about what she had hinted at a few moments ago and then began musing out loud. "There's a lot of stuff that's illegal for people like you and me, but the nobles have their own ideas of right and wrong."

"Like I said, Tom liked me, but he kept personal and business matters separate." She paused for a bit before continuing. I could tell she didn't want to talk about something, so I let her take her time getting there. "I liked Tom as a friend, but I had a feeling he was hoping it would develop into more. I didn't like feeling my job was dependent on how well he liked me or how well I treated him versus how well I sang. Once I knew he was thinking of taking our professional relationship in a different direction, I began looking for another place to sing."

She paused for a moment before continuing. "I don't mean to sound unappreciative. I mean, Tom gave me my first break, but there are lines I prefer not to cross. One of the patrons at Mr. Tabor's—my father's—club approached me about singing at his own new club. He didn't know who I was beyond Lyssa, so he figured I was new in town. Said he had connections with other clubs also, if I ever wanted a change of venue."

"If you were uncomfortable at Tom's, why didn't you take him up on it?"

"You're not familiar with the entertainment business, are you, Theron?"

That question caught me off guard. Apparently she saw something obvious that I was missing completely—which would not be the first time either. "Outside of being a paying customer, not really. Several of my former clients have been in the business, both as owners and performers. However, their cases involved customers who get too handy or people trying to use them for blackmail schemes. Occasionally, someone has been known to take losing a part a bit too personally and they've tried to eliminate their competition. But, I've never gotten into the nuts and bolts of it."

"An entertainer relies on two things, Theron: talent and reputation. If a person has no talent, they can't get hired in the first place unless you've got enough money to buy the club. This is a profession where the cream rises to the top. However, that's not enough. If a person develops a bad reputation—too much of a prima donna, doesn't show up for rehearsals on time, or if the manager can't trust them to show up for a performance—they won't get re-hired. I couldn't just walk out on Tom. If I got a reputation of jumping to a new job without giving notice, and by that I mean coordinating it with my manager and helping make sure I had a replacement available . . . well, I'd never get a long-term contract again. No one would hire me for fear of me bailing on them too."

"So, Tom knew you couldn't leave without his permission. Which gave him another thing to hang over your head."

"Yes and that's what bothers me. I liked working for Tom. He was a good boss when he kept his head in the business. If he hadn't started hitting on me, I'd have been willing to sing there for a long time."

"And with Tom's death, you're now free to move to any club you want with no strings attached."

She thought about it for a second. "I guess you're right. I've been so caught up in what's happening around me, I hadn't even considered that."

"You realize, if Corvinus heard this, he'd say you had plenty of motives to entice someone to kill Tom, even if you didn't do it yourself. One way or the other, he's likely to try and tag you as an accessory in Tom's murder."

"Yes, I know. That's why I'm telling you this now in case this comes up later. Tom never told anyone my father was the reason I had a job at the Green Dragon. I thought I got the job on my own when I first started working there. I know some of the people thought I was sleeping with Tom. I wasn't, but that didn't stop the talk backstage."

She stopped and looked me square in the eyes. "I haven't always been proud about what I've had to do to survive, Theron, but I'm not ashamed either. You can't eat pride and it doesn't put a roof over your head. I just didn't want this to become an issue between us later. I'd rather you know the truth, no matter how it makes you feel about me."

"I'm the last person to judge someone else's behavior. You may have thought about holding out on me when we first met, but I think you're being straight with me now, Angel, least as straight as anyone ever is with someone else. I can't ask for more than that."

She leaned over and gave me a kiss on the cheek. "Thanks, Theron. You could have taken advantage of this situation several times and I haven't felt pressured once. I like that a lot."

Well, I liked the fact that she liked that, but it wasn't getting us any closer to an answer. I also asked her more about the patron who approached her at Tabor's. She thought about it for a bit while we continued down another alley before answering. "You know, I didn't remember seeing him there before that night. Now that I think about it, it was right before the first attack."

That stirred some thoughts in my thick head. "So, the initial attacks on you may have been kidnapping attempts. The attack on the doorman may have been an attempt to isolate you. It's possible, since you are a were, they thought anyone providing protection to you might be also."

"So, this may have been a misunderstanding?"

"No. You heard Ferendel. Somehow you've gotten in the middle of a power struggle between Count Aeson and Baron Lyndmar. They may have offered you that job to lure you into a trap. I could make a hundred guesses, but without some type of evidence, that's all they'd be. I'm hoping this visit may change that."

"I'll do my best to get us through the front door."

"I know you will. After that, we'll be playing it by ear. Stay close and keep your eyes and ears open. I have to assume Mr. X will show up eventually. I think he suspects I have his dagger. He cannot afford to be seen too often in the same form. Like Theo said, once people start putting two and two together, he's in danger. He'll have to make a play for it somewhere, either when we're en route to the baron's or perhaps while we're there."

"If he does, what do you want me to do?"

"Stay out of the line of fire, kid. Unless you've figured out a way to take your were shape when there's no full moon?"

"I've heard there are ways, but the further away from the full moon the harder it is to do and tonight is the dark of the moon. I'm not sure any but the ancients could turn tonight. So, that's out."

I nodded. "It makes sense they'd wait to try something as far away from a full moon as possible. If for any reason things go sideways at the baron's and I wind up fighting him, the baron may try something funny. You'll have to cover me. Do you have a weapon?"

"It's not part of the standard stage performer's issue."

I grinned and handed her the sheathed black dagger. "Here. This is an enchanted blade." I whispered something in her ear. "If we get into trouble, use that phrase. The blade will ignore any armor they're wearing."

"Why aren't you using it?"

"You heard Theo. Magic and I don't exactly get along. Things that rely on magic spells or command words tend to backfire on me. You're better off with it. I do pretty well with my own toys."

The look she gave me said she didn't believe a word I was saying, but she took the dagger without a complaint. She stepped behind a couple of boxes stacked in the alley. After a few seconds, she reappeared and I had no clue where she was carrying the dagger. Believe me, it's not like her outfit had a lot of places you could hide it either. I decided it wouldn't be very chivalrous to frisk her, so I let it go and we got out of the alley and flagged down a cab.

I had the driver take a circuitous route through the city to see if anyone was following us. Once I was reasonably sure we were on our own, I directed the cab to cut through the Triangle district and then enter the North Hills along the western edge of the city. The long ride gave me plenty of time to consider all the things that could go wrong. I tried to anticipate every possible outcome. It wasn't the first time I'd walked into a situation not quite knowing what I was going to do, but I always knew something would work out. This time, I had a feeling I was overlooking something.

The rumbling of the cab on the cobblestone streets as we rolled across the North Hills district did nothing to soothe my nerves. Ze'eva, on the other hand, looked like she was getting ready to walk out on stage. If the cabbie had been looking back at her, and I'm sure he was, he'd have thought it was a simple outing. Either she had a lot of faith in my abilities or she was made of stronger stuff than I had ever suspected.

I had the cabdriver stop a couple of blocks from our destination and we walked the rest of the way. I wanted to get a look at the manor house and check for side entrances and such before we waltzed in the front door. However, the few we discovered were either locked or guarded. The idea of an easy escape was rapidly disappearing from my list of possible plans.

After spending some unproductive time outside, Ze'eva and I walked up to the entrance of the manor. Once again, she put on quite the performance and the guards had no clue what hit them. They were naturally more suspicious than the guards at the count's, but after some cajoling and some language I would be loath to repeat, we found ourselves being escorted into a small waiting room.

I found it odd that we had been left alone. I could see that Ze'eva was tempted to check out the desk in front of us, but she slid into the seat in front of it and took up an air of bored expectation. I took note of the two large mirrors on the wall and suspected one or both were being used to observe us. The large tapestries on the other walls worried me. If there was an alcove or a concealed door, we'd never know until it was too late.

We were there for several minutes before a servant appeared. "I apologize, but Lord Lyndmar has been unavoidably detained. Would you like to come back or are you able to wait a bit longer?"

Ze'eva and I exchanged looks. This whole situation felt wrong, but there was no guarantee we'd be able to bluff our way in again. We expressed our desire to wait for the baron and the servant gave us the patented bored look and left. I sat down next to Ze'eva and spoke in a whisper. "This could get ugly, Angel. They're stalling. It sounds like they're waiting for someone to arrive. I don't know if that's the constables or if they're lining up the firing squad. You have that knife where you can get to it quick?"

"I've got your back, Theron."

"Thanks, kid. You've been a real trouper so far. Hopefully we can pull this off with a minimum of fuss."

I casually turned to face her so I could watch the tapestry out of the corner of my eye. It might have been my imagination, but I swore there was the slightest rustle behind one section. I stretched and shifted to get more comfortable in my seat, using the opportunity to slip the strap off my automatic. I wanted it ready to go if something happened. Once I was sure it was ready, I leaned back in my chair and tried to look as calm as I could for the people watching through those mirrors.

After what seemed like hours, the door finally opened and the baron came in. He was a young man, probably in his early twenties, dressed in the latest fashions from the Imperial capital. He was escorted by an older man who carried a large piece of parchment and some writing equipment. The baron motioned for him to sit in the corner and then took a seat behind his desk. He played around with some of the items on it, seemingly oblivious to our presence. It was an old stunt and I'd used it on a few occasions myself. I glanced at Ze'eva and she remained as imperious as ever. Only when he had completed what he was doing and poured himself a glass of sherry from a crystal decanter did he finally acknowledge our presence.

"Ah, Mr. Chase and Miss Blackthorne, I'm glad we've finally had this opportunity to meet. You do know that charade you used to get past my guards was completely unnecessary. I told them to be looking for you. You actually made it harder to get in trying to be clever. But, that's what you do, isn't it, Mr. Chase? Try to be clever?"

He was too self-assured. I was immediately on edge but decided to try and seize the initiative. "Well, I admit I'm a bit surprised at the warmth of your welcome, Baron Lyndmar. Then again, many of the things you've been involved in recently have surprised me. I'll just chalk it up to not running in your circles very often."

He looked down his thin nose at me. "No, I suppose we don't have the same social schedule."

I noted the older man was copying down everything being said. It was another tactic to try and intimidate us, and generally it was a good ploy. What the baron didn't know was my own secretary was copying everything down back in my office. There would be no doctoring of the record this time. I *hoped* Kyra was getting everything. If the baron had any magical shielding on this room, we might be in trouble.

"Ah, but you're wrong, Your Lordship. After all, we both share an interest in local music. Why, you and I were at the Green Dragon last night right before all those unfortunate incidents. It was really too bad that Tom Fitzgerald was still alive when I reached him. Your man didn't do a very good job—on Tom or on me."

The baron's expression flickered ever so slightly and I could tell he was getting annoyed. He wasn't used to people treating him like an equal and he didn't like it. "My man? Good gracious, Mr. Chase, to hear you talk, you'd think I was this master criminal, manipulating things from behind the scenes like a puppeteer. But, is it not true that *you're* actually the wanted criminal? I believe there are two murder warrants out for your arrest."

This sounded nothing so much as a rehearsed script for an unseen audience, but two could play at that game. "It *is* true that the local constabulary gets confused from time to time, especially Captain Corvinus, although he means well. I chalk it up to professional jealousy. Still, there is a small issue that needs to be resolved. I'm hoping we're going to be able to come to an understanding today."

"Indeed? What issue could that be?"

Ze'eva leaned forward in her chair slightly, drawing the attention of the baron to her. "There's a small issue of murder. Well, let me rephrase that. There's a small issue of intent to commit murder."

"Murder? I thought that was Mr. Chase's purview."

"No, I'm speaking of your intent to murder Count Aeson and myself."

I shifted in my chair apparently to look at her and saw the tapestry flutter again. I didn't see any fans in the room, so I had a good idea what was back there and who.

"Murder the count and you? My dear Miss Blackthorne, that's a heady charge to toss at one of the nobility. I appreciate the fact you're upset over your misadventures, but how could you possibly blame me? I assume you have some proof of this."

"I have some proof. I have additional proof being collected as we speak and soon enough we will capture Roderick Caupo, and when given the choice of spending the rest of his life in the penal colony on Death's Head Island or turning his employer over to the constables, I'm quite certain the trail will lead directly to your door."

The baron's eyes narrowed and for the first time, I saw a small crack in his confidence. "You might have some noble blood running through your veins, but do not believe that will protect you against charges of slandering a member of the Privy Council."

Ze'eva continued on as if she had not heard the threat in the baron's last statement. "I am puzzled by one thing, though, Baron. Why my father? You've recently been elevated and he speaks quite highly of you. Why would you want to hurt him?"

The baron brought his hands together to form an inverted V in front of his face as he watched us through half-closed eyes. A cruel smile edged onto his lips and then he leaned forward to rest his chin on the backs of his hands. "You know Ze'eva, I've taken an interest in your career. I was going to talk to Tom about buying your contract. Along with inheriting my father's position, I also inherited a number of businesses he owned or had a controlling interest in. Among these were several clubs both here and in the Imperial capital. I was considering you for my headliner. I even had a few venues set up especially for you . . . Lyssa." He let out a dramatic sigh before continuing. "Now, I see you're nothing but a cheap tramp with no vision at all. You're someone who will spend the rest of her life singing in two-bit taverns and dumps before winding up in an alley somewhere. Pity that."

I was about to reach across the desk and wipe that smirk off of his face with my fist, but Ze'eva placed a hand on my arm to calm me. I could tell she was in her element now, so I sat back to watch.

"It's true I didn't get everything in life handed to me because of the accident of my birth. It's also true I may never live in a house this fancy with my own personal retinue of thugs and assassins. However, whatever I have, I have earned. I didn't get it by simply outliving someone—or should I say, ensuring I outlived someone."

The baron's face turned red. It seemed his attempt to intimidate and belittle Ze'eva had backfired on him. "You little gutter tramp. You know how I knew you'd be here? Your dear father thought enough of *me* to let me know what you had been saying. You see, I know your father better than you do. You're nothing more than a momentary mistake. I have nobility going back generations on both sides of my family and I was acknowledged by my father from the day of my birth. Do not presume to tell me what I have or haven't earned."

"If in the grand scheme of things I mean so little to you, then why are you trying to have me killed? Why are you trying to have my father killed?"

The baron leaned back in his chair and took a sip of sherry

to calm down. When he spoke again, there was still a fire in his eyes, but it was smoldering embers now. "Let me try to put this in simple words for a peasant girl like you, Ze'eva dear. Hypothetically speaking, why would I want to kill you beyond the fact that you're an impudent wench who is way out of her element?"

She gave him a wolfish grin. "Hypothetically speaking."

He moved ever so slightly and I saw him push something on his desk. I tensed, assuming he was signaling for someone, and then he motioned for the scribe to leave. After a few moments, the baron visibly relaxed, but his voice grew icy. "Have you ever held power, my dear? Not just the power of your raw strength when you're in your were form, but *actual* power? It's probably the most intoxicating drug in the world. Once you get a taste of it, it's something you never want to lose. Like a drug, though, after a while the highs are not so high and the lows seem deeper, so you need to get more power to stay on top of your game."

Ze'eva stretched in front of him, giving me a chance to glance at the tapestry, which was now standing out slightly away from the wall. "This is all very fascinating. I'm assuming this is the reason why your father had his unfortunate accident."

"My father died peacefully in his sleep, thank you very much. Although since we're dealing in hypotheticals, his death did occur at a most opportune time."

Ze'eva started to say something, but I broke in, wanting to see if we could push him into losing his temper again. "I hear your father's unfortunate death was mourned by many in town but not all. However, I understand the bookies were rather pleased by the turn of events. Word on the street is several large debts disappeared in the days immediately following his death. I find that very convenient. According to a few people I've spoken to, they were getting ready to speak to your father over your inability or unwillingness to pay."

I was bluffing there, but the sudden stiffening in his shoulders and back told me I'd hit pretty close to the truth. He tried to play it off by waving a hand at me, keeping his attention on Ze'eva. "There are always some who profit from death and some who lose, Mr. Chase—you should know that better than most. After all, not only have you lost two partners, but 'word on the street' says your first partner's wife was seen leaving your apartment the evening he was killed. I would think you would know better than to mix business and pleasure. And then to lose a second one two years later in that messy blackmail case with the Lord Mayor's wife. Really, I'm surprised you still have a license in this town."

I bristled at his comments, but they weren't unexpected. Ze'eva wasn't the only person in this room with a reputation. "It's touching you've taken an interest in my career, Lord Lyndmar. However, it appears your sources have only been talking to the local constables. I've learned over time they're usually pretty good at arresting jaywalkers and people the nobles take a dislike to, but I wouldn't rely heavily on their detective skills. My first partner was killed by a maniac who was gunning not only for him but his family. His wife and two kids were hiding at my apartment while I was dealing with that maniac's mob down on the south docks. My second partner walked into an ambush the blackmailer had set up for the Lord Mayor's wife. Yes, I've lost partners and I may lose more in the future, but I've always ensured there was justice for their deaths. Their killers are either dead or at Death's Head Island."

The baron softly clapped his hands together when I finished. "How noble of you, Mr. Chase. Unfortunately, when one deals in finance and politics there are usually debts of a more monetary nature to be considered. You certainly wouldn't expect me to take the law into my hands and kill someone, do you?"

"Hypothetically?"

"Of course, Mr. Chase."

"No, I suspect you'd simply hire a really good assassin. People with money tend to do that."

"Yes I suppose they do. Then again, most people, if they want something bad enough and have money enough, they tend to get what they want. After all, our history books are filled with ruthless people who rose to seize kingdoms and empires by not waiting or relying on being born to the purple. No, some people reach out and seize what is rightfully theirs."

"And spend the rest of their lives trying to hang on to what they've seized."

"True. And that is the drawback to the direct approach. If a person is too obvious about their desire for power, they tend to give away their plans before they're ready to act. Their target has a chance to secure their own borders or their bedroom windows. But, we're getting off the subject now. Getting back to your ridiculous question, Ze'eva, let me ask you. Why I would want to kill your father?"

"I'm certain *I* have no idea or I wouldn't have come to speak to you."

He chuckled before continuing. "Since you brought up this ridiculous scenario, I'll try to answer you. Now, for the record, I have nothing but the highest admiration for him. However, hypothetically speaking, why would I want to kill him? What possible motives could I have to commit murder? Let's see. Could it be he holds a higher position on the Privy Council than I do? No, that's such a petty thing. Then again, there is also the small matter he's blocked my attempts to become Lord of the Exchequer, which would give me direct access to the Empire's treasures. But again, it's only a matter of time before I influence enough of the council to vote for me. Ah, but there is *one* reason he might be a viable target. He has no living heirs—recognized heirs that is—and well, I'm about as close to a son as he has."

He stared at Ze'eva, a look of pure loathing on his face. "In fact, it was thought I was to be named his heir *until* he heard rumors he had a bastard daughter running around town."

The baron's eyes narrowed dangerously and his voice became softer. It was obvious this message was not for his hidden audience any longer, which worried me more. "It's well known your father's county holds some of the richest farmland in the kingdom. Considering the majority of his lands abut mine, it would be a perfect merging of lands and powers if something unfortunate were to happen to him and a will should turn up naming me heir. So, you see, dear Ze'eva, you are more than just an annoying entertainer who doesn't know her place, you're actually a threat to my plans."

Ze'eva began to laugh. It was a soft, almost sympathetic laugh at first but it soon shook her body. It took her a few seconds to calm down and she had to wave an apologetic hand at the baron. "Oh, my. You've been wasting your time sitting in your booth at the Green Dragon. You should have been up on stage with me. You have a way of spinning a story that almost makes me believe you. Theron, I think it's time to leave."

I looked at her and she gave me a quick wink. "Leave? But we haven't asked the baron the questions we were going to."

"We don't have to, Theron. I can tell from that little mono-logue that Nathaniel here . . ."

The baron slapped his hand down on the desk, "Baron Lyndmar to you."

She turned her head slightly and stared right at him. ". . . Nathaniel here cannot be the person we suspected. He's too immature and too much of a dreamer to actually be the master-mind behind any plot against my father."

She gave the baron a pitying look before continuing. "I mean, he speaks poorly of my birth, but the only difference between he and I is his mother was married to his father and mine was not. Regardless of the circumstances of my birth, I love my father for who he is and if he never acknowledges me, I will still love him because he's my father. This child could only see his father as an obstacle and a source of money for his gambling and whoring. He's no threat to my father because he doesn't have the balls to actually do anything about it." She gave him another sad smile. "I do apologize. It appears our information was incorrect. So sorry to bother you."

I stood up and extended a hand to her. "I think you're right, Ze'eva. Don't worry, Nathaniel, we'll show ourselves out. I'm sure your nurse will be here in a bit anyway. Must be nap time."

I guess that last shot did it. His eyes bulged out and his face went three shades of ever deepening red. "And to think that once I learned of your existence, I nearly went to your father to ask for your hand in marriage. I figured if I couldn't inherit his lands outright, then I would gain them legally through you. Besides, you'd make quite the trophy wife to parade around town. Then I learned you were a half-breed bitch, for real. Can you imagine polluting the Lyndmar line with a contemptible creature like you?"

His veins stood out as he continued his rant. "You think you're so high and mighty because you've got adoring fans who'll come running to do whatever you ask if you snap your fingers because you're Ze'eva Blackthorne. Well, let's see how long that lasts once word hits the street you're a werewolf and your father is a werewolf. How long do you think your father will hold his position on the Privy Council once his secret comes out? You'll be Exhibit A at his trial before the Star Chamber standing there in your leash and muzzle. I suspect the inquisitors will make his death last a while to see what other vermin he'll expose. I was going to just kill you both, but now I think I'll watch you suffer before you die."

I felt her tense up but she stepped out of my grasp and slapped him right across the jaw before I could stop her. He reeled back into his chair, nearly knocking it over. He brought his hand up to his face in shock and went pale. His voice climbed into a higher octave as he screamed at her. "You'll pay for that! I'll see you pay for that! Kill them! Kill them now!"

I felt the approaching figure more than I heard him coming. I spun around, my automatic barking as he rushed at me. He slammed into me and I went tumbling over backward, my pistol going one direction and the vicious dagger he'd been carrying the other. I climbed back to my feet and noticed he was bleeding from his left shoulder. I knew I hadn't hurt him very much, just thrown him off balance. I motioned for Ze'eva to move out of the way and prepared for the fight of my life. My opponent, still dressed in a long coat with the collar turned up and a wide-brimmed hat, turned to face me. He gave me a slight nod as if to congratulate me for surviving the first rush and then he eased into an unfamiliar fighting stance

He was several inches shorter than me and I had twenty pounds on him, but if there was a fighting style Roderick Caupo didn't know, I hadn't seen it. There was no quarter asked or given in this fight, and to be honest, I don't think I've ever enjoyed a fight more. I knew after the first couple of exchanges why Blake and Theo said he was known as the best in the business. I must have hit him square on a dozen times and he just shrugged off the blows and focused on hurting me. Wherever he'd picked up his reputation for toughness, he'd earned it legitimately.

We used every dirty trick in the book and I think we invented a few new ones that afternoon. I managed to nail him with a shot as he rushed me, rocking him back on his heels. I tried to follow up with a rush of my own, but all I got was kicked in the private parts for my efforts. My knees went wobbly for a moment and it was only by pure instinct that I managed to grab him by the coat as he came in for the kill, spinning him around and tossing him into the baron's desk. He tried to bounce back up, but I kicked out and caught him on the side of the knee. The sickening *crack* told me I had either broken it or dislocated his kneecap. Before he could finish screaming, I followed up with a shot to his temple, which buckled him and he dropped down onto his good knee, his other leg behind him at an odd angle. The fight seemed to go out of him and I moved in to ensure the fight was over.

I heard a scuffling behind me and turned my head to see Ze'eva and the baron tangled up in front of his desk. Suddenly, I felt a stinging sensation in my leg. I looked down to see a small stiletto sticking out of my thigh, an ominous green oil still running down the blade mixed with my blood.

Caupo—Mr. X—looked up at me from the floor. He spoke for the first time, a dry, whispery voice that seemed to reach from beyond the grave. "Just a matter of time, now, Chase. Just a matter of time."

I didn't waste time talking. I could already feel my leg going numb. I brought my fist down on his face as hard as I could, over and over again to wipe that grin away. He dropped limply to the floor. I turned to help Ze'eva, but by now my legs were turning into jelly and everything seemed to be moving in and out of my vision. I crashed to the floor on top of Caupo, staring up at the plastered ceiling.

It was as if time was stopping and starting as I lay there. I had a vision of Ze'eva rushing toward me. I heard a crash and so help me, Corvinus appeared at the edge of my vision. I saw Ze'eva saying something but no sounds came out of her mouth and then I knew nothing.

———

Over and over, I had a nightmare where I was trapped in a well and every time I got near the surface, Caupo would appear at the edge and pour more water on me. My eyes suddenly snapped open and I saw a stone ceiling above me. My mouth and tongue felt thick and dry. I tried to raise my hand, but I couldn't seem to move it more than an inch or so. Through some trial and effort, I found I couldn't move my hands or my feet and something was strapped across my chest and legs. Taking a deep breath, I managed to croak out something vaguely like words and a young redhead appeared in front of me, wearing what seemed to be a nurse's outfit. If this was the afterlife, it was starting out pretty well—except for all the restraints. That worried me.

"Welcome back to the land of the living, Mr. Chase. Here, drink this."

I'm not normally a big water person, but that drink tasted like it had come down from the gods themselves. After a few sips, she moved out of my line of vision and I felt the upper half of the bed begin to rise. She ratcheted me into a seated position and then let me drink a bit more.

Once she was sure I wasn't going to fall back asleep, she summoned the doctor. There was a flurry of movement by the door and then Doc Griffin appeared. That's when I knew I had not moved to the life beyond.

"Ah, Mr. Chase. I warned you to take it easy. What part of getting into a fight with a trained assassin falls under taking it easy?"

"Not letting him win?"

"Good point. Anyway, he used some nasty stuff on you. Between the poison and sustaining another concussion when you hit your head on the floor, it's been touch and go the past few days. Luckily, it appears you're going to recover. That is," he added with a laugh, "until you see my bill. Might cause a relapse."

I would have laughed too, but it hurt too much to consider it. "This is one bill I won't mind paying. What's with the restraints, Doc?"

"Well, as I said, he hit you with some nasty stuff. If it didn't kill you outright, it was designed to cause seizures. Your body was literally trying to shake itself apart and your heart was racing. Not only did I have to apply an antidote for the poison, we had to restrain you to keep you from hurting yourself—or one of us. You nearly knocked one of my poor nurses unconscious before we realized what was happening."

A wave of drowsiness swept over me. When I could see straight again, the doc was checking my pulse. "How much longer am I going to have to stay here?"

"Oh, I wouldn't say too much longer. No more than a couple of days. Poison's just about out of your system. However, that head injury worries me. I'd say you're going to have to take it easy, and I mean *easy* this time. You should do nothing too strenuous for a minimum of a month to be sure."

"A month! But, Doc, you don't understand. I've got mouths to feed—my landlord, my bartender, my bookie, they're all counting on me."

"And I'm telling you, Mr. 'I know more than the doctor' Chase, that if you take another blow to your head before this heals, feeding them will be the least of your worries. It'll be more about who's stuck feeding *you*—permanently, Mr. Chase. I'm giving it to you straight. Your health is precarious. You screw this up and there's nothing anyone's going to be able to do for you."

"Yes, Doctor."

"That's better. Oh, and you have two visitors. Against my better judgment, I'm going to let them in. They're under strict orders not to get you excited, although, good luck with that. Ten minutes and then I'm throwing them both out."

He checked my eyes and my pulse one more time before leaving the room. I could hear him talking to someone and then the door opened. Kyra came in first, holding a handkerchief up to her eyes. She rushed across the room and grabbed my left hand as Ze'eva entered. She made her way over to the bed and took my right hand. If the gods had taken me to my rest right then, I could have died happily.

"Theron, are you all right? Doc Griffin said you could have died. You promised me you'd come back all right."

"Kyra, I *am* all right. And I *will* come back. I just have to stay here a bit longer and then you'll have me in your hair just like always."

"Oh, Theron." She buried her head against my hand and I could feel the tears rolling out. Poor kid.

I looked over at Ze'eva. "How are you, Angel? Last I saw, you and the baron were scuffling behind me. Sorry I couldn't help."

"I'm sorry too, Theron. When he saw you were going to beat Caupo, he pulled a dagger out of his desk drawer. He was going to stab you in the back. I screamed and the next thing I knew, he was laying backward on his desk with your black dagger sticking out of his chest."

I felt her hand tighten on mine as she relived the moment. Then there was a change in her voice. "However, my father is safe and that's the important thing. Him—and you, that is."

"Was it my imagination or did Corvinus show up, late again as usual? Kyra, you did great getting them there."

"It wasn't me, Theron. I didn't have anything to do with it. I tried to summon him, but he was out of his office when I called."

"Wait, if you didn't call him, then who did?"

Ze'eva spoke up. "He was there all along, Theron. Once Lyndmar knew we were there, he summoned the constables. That's why we were waiting around for so long. The constables were in a room behind one of the two-way mirrors, hoping you'd do something stupid like take a punch at him. Lyndmar suspected you had Caupo's special dagger on you. When he signaled for the constables, they could burst in and arrest you with the murder weapon on you. With you out of the way, he thought Caupo would have no issues dealing with my father and me."

"Well, that son of a gun. He was smarter than I gave him credit for."

"He was smarter than a lot of people gave him credit for. He was playing up the irresponsible image to keep people from looking into his business too closely."

"But wait, while this isn't exactly my vision of paradise, what happened with Corvinus? I'm surprised I'm not talking to you from the hospital wing of the Citadel. Knowing our dear captain, I would've expected him to be measuring my noose as we speak."

Kyra and Ze'eva exchanged glances and Ze'eva went first. "Well, it was looking pretty bad, Theron. You were unconscious with the murder weapon on you and the baron was lying there with your dagger stuck through his chest. Apparently when he lost his temper, the baron blacked out the mirror with a switch on his desk and locked the doors. It took them a while to break out and then break into the room where we were. They missed the entire fight."

"Glad to hear Corvinus is as efficient as always. So, I'm guessing a couple of constables are posted outside this room?"

Kyra piped up then. "Oh, no, Theron. Right after the fight was over, Count Aeson and I arrived with his personal guard. When I couldn't get ahold of Corvinus, I flew over to the count's place. Luckily his guards don't look up much. Or, they didn't. He was awfully mad that I just flew past them."

"The count, Kyra?"

"Well, once I told the count what was going on, he grabbed his personal guard and we rushed over to the baron's estate. The baron's guards didn't want to let us in, but when Count Aeson picked one up and tossed him over the outer wall into the courtyard, the others quickly moved to the side. We arrived as Corvinus was putting the manacles on Ze'eva. Oh, Theron, I wish you could have seen it. The count chewed Corvinus out in front of his men and everything. By the time he was done, Corvinus was ready to do anything he could to get out of there. The count swore this was a Privy Council matter; that the constables had no rights to be on this property. With the baron dead, Corvinus had no way to prove he'd had been invited there by the baron. The count threatened to take this to the king and the lord mayor before his men escorted the constables off of the property. That's when Ze'eva insisted bringing you to this doctor. And, here you are."

"And here I am, but for how long? I'm sure the count can work out something for the fiasco in the baron's chambers, but what about those four murders Corvinus is trying to pin on me? It's not like there's a statute of limitations on murder."

Ze'eva took over the narrative. "Not a worry, Theron. Seems your friends Mr. Ferendel and Mr. Markham have provided the constable general enough evidence against Roderick Caupo to send him either to the gallows or to the prison colony for life. And from what I hear, people are lining up to testify against Caupo in other cities around the kingdom. Ferendel also provided enough information to round up the rest of Caupo's gang. Seems they were living on a country estate owned by the baron. I hear they're busy blaming every crime in the past three years on Caupo to save their own hides."

"Well, that was . . . Wait. Did you say Blake Ferendel actually provided evidence to the constables? I didn't think he would go within a mile of the Citadel."

"You're right, Theron, he didn't," Kyra said. "An older gentleman—Marcus, I believe his name was—appeared with an affidavit signed by Mr. Ferendel. The gentleman also stopped by our office and delivered a payment of two hundred gold crowns and a note for you. All it said was, 'We're even.' What did he mean by that?"

"It means I'm still alive and knowing Blake Ferendel, if he

gave us a payment of two hundred gold crowns, he made a lot more betting on me to still be breathing after my fight with Caupo."

'He was betting on you? I'll send that money back right away."

"You'll do nothing of the sort. We're going to need that to pay this doctor bill. You heard Doc Griffin. I'm not going to be able to work for a month. Between Ze'eva's payment and the money from Ferendel, are we gonna be able to cover this bill?"

Kyra's eyes filled with tears again. "Not even close."

Damn.

Kyra smiled then. "Luckily, your new partner has already brought us business. Not only are we caught up on the bills, we've rented that empty office next door and are remodeling it. We're going to be okay, Theron."

Now I *knew* I'd taken a blow to the head. "New partner? I haven't taken on a new partner and I certainly didn't authorize renting new space. We're broke as is."

Ze'eva exchanged a smile with Kyra before looking at me. "Sure you have, Theron. Besides, your old office was too small for me to get a desk in there and as much as I like you, I'm not sharing a chair with you."

"Ze'eva?"

"That's right, Theron. And our first client is my father. He's put us on retainer. He owns several businesses in town and the nearby countryside and he's having a devil of a time keeping all his employees honest. He'd like us to drop by every so often, check the books, get a feel for what the workers are thinking about management, and try to cut down on the pilfering. It's not a full-time job, just something to do between cases."

I frowned and that simple motion brought back my headache with a vengeance. "I'm not sure I like it. I've gone to great lengths to stay out of politics. I don't want my regular clients thinking I'm a toady for the guys on the hill."

"Theron, it's a retainer. You're independent and he wants it that way. He needs someone who'll tell him the truth. Most people tell him what they think he wants to hear. He likes you."

"I'm guessing you and he had a few heart-to-hearts while I was sleeping?"

Ze'eva smiled at Kyra. "You told me he was one of the best."

Kyra patted my hand. "He's not one of the best, he *is* the best."

"Anyway, we have to go now, Theron. The doc will be back in a minute and we've got to meet the contractor. He's measuring for the new offices and we've got new furniture to buy and paint and office supplies. We'll be seeing you."

I shuddered to think what I was going to find when I got back to the office. The nurse came back in with some pills and a potion for me to take after they left. I forced myself to swallow it all and leaned back. My eyelids grew heavy as I heard the door open again.

The voice sounded miles away, but I swear I heard Ze'eva in the distance. "Oh, since you can't work for a month, Father lent his yacht. We're going on a cruise and we'll be stopping on a private island to ensure you don't overdo things. Doc Griffin put me in charge of your therapy, so rest up as much as you can. You'll want to be in good shape." She giggled and shut the door as my eyes closed.

I remember dreaming of yachts, sandy beaches and were-wolves in bathing suits.

Case 2:
The
Pearls of
Darkness
Affair

THE PEARLS OF DARKNESS AFFAIR

I t had been a slow week for the detective business. Even the flies circling the dusty overhead light in my office looked bored. I heard my secretary, Kyra, typing up the files for the last case in the outer office, while my partner, Ze'eva, flipped through a magazine. There hadn't been a hint of business for the past couple of weeks. If it wasn't for the retainer Ze'eva's father, Count Aeson, paid us to keep an eye on certain properties of his, the landlord would have been scraping Ze'eva's and my names off the smoked glass door and measuring the room for new tenants.

I tossed my pencil into the air one last time and glanced at the clock. My stomach already knew the answer, but the clock confirmed it was nearly noon. "What do you say we go get lunch?"

Ze'eva slapped the magazine she'd been reading closed. "Might as well. Doesn't look like anyone is coming by today. What are you in the mood for?"

I ran down an all-too-familiar list in my head. "I think we owe Pete the least on our tab. Might as well see what he's got on special today. I could go for a Reuben and a side of fries."

Ze'eva nodded in agreement and we rose from our respective desks. Just four months ago, Ze'eva had been a client of mine; a singer here in Calasia, mainly working at a high-class caberet called the Green Dragon, but also on certain nights of the month at a club catering to were-creatures. Yes, Ze'eva herself is a werewolf, which doesn't bother me, but not everyone in Calasia is as open minded about nonhumans as I am. She still performs on occasion, just to keep her agent happy. I think there are times like today when she misses it, but she never mentions it.

The fact we were also dating was a nice side benefit of the job, though. However, there were a couple of drawbacks. You see, I don't normally date women who could tear my arms off and I couldn't seem to get Kyra to quit leaving wedding magazines around the office.

We had just reached the office door when I heard the outer door open and Kyra's pleasant voice call out. "May I help you?"

An older woman's voice respoded, "Is Mr. Chase in?"

I smiled. There was a distinct advantage to hiring a Sylph as my secretary. Most people aren't used to dealing with the fae, so Kyra's diminutive size, gossamer wings and incredible good looks tend to throw them off for a bit, which gives her a chance to size them up for us.

"I think you're in luck," Kyra replied, a signal I should go back to my desk.

We crept back and picked up a stock conversation. "So Ze'eva, do you think we can fit in Colonel Morton's missing stocks into our schedule?"

"I think we might be able to, since we've almost wrapped up Mrs. Anderson's."

Kyra paused in the doorway, her wings fluttering softly. "Excuse me, Mr. Chase, there's a Mrs. Sherwood out here to see you."

I looked up with a harried look on my face. "Miss Sylvari,

does she have an appointment? We *are* rather busy at the moment."

Krya had played this game before and only the small quiver in her wings gave away her amusement. She turned so the older woman could see her concerned expression. "Mr. Chase, I really think you should talk to her."

I thought for a moment and then nodded. "I've always trusted your judgment. Send her in."

Ze'eva and I pivoted in our chairs and watched Kyra escort our new client into the office. She appeared to be in her sixties, her white hair was done up in a flattering style, and her clothes were conservative but I could tell they were expensive. I had a feeling this could be a profitable case.

I motioned to a leather chair in front of my desk. Ze'eva pulled her chair over so she could see us easily. "Please have a seat, Mrs. Sherwood."

"Thank you for seeing me on such short notice, Mr. Chase."

I nodded and motioned for Kyra to grab her notebook and join us. "Please make yourself comfortable and tell us what seems to be the problem."

"Well, I'm a little embarrassed to admit this, Mr. Chase, but I'm afraid I've been foolish. There was a young woman in my employ, Penny Fairbanks. She's missing—and so is a rather unique pearl necklace of mine."

There was an awkward silence before Ze'eva asked the question on everyone's mind. "Do you believe Miss Fairbanks is behind the necklace's disappearance?"

Mrs. Sherwood started as if noticing Ze'eva for the first time. I thought I saw a look of irritation cross her face, but it was gone so fast, it was hard to say for sure. "Oh dear, that's so hard to say, Miss . . ."

"Blackthorne, Ze'eva Blackthorne. I'm Mr. Chase's partner."

She gave Ze'eva a warm smile before answering. "Miss Blackthorne, Penny's been in my employ for a number of years.

Her mother and I were friends years ago. I took Penny in after my friend passed away. She's been the daughter I never had, so I really hope that's not so. Penny's been gone nearly three days. At first, I thought maybe there was a boy involved, but I've checked with everyone who knew her. No one seems to know anything about it."

I broke in. "Was Miss Fairbanks in the habit of just disappearing?"

"Good gracious, no. If she was, I wouldn't be here. I'm afraid she may have interrupted whoever stole the pearls and something may have happened. Perhaps she was kidnapped?"

I nodded, but kept my face impassive. "That is one possibility. However, I'd rather not guess before we know the facts—we might send ourselves chasing after phantoms. Now do you have a description of the necklace, a picture, anything? An idea of how much it's worth? That might help us track it down and get a lead on who may have taken it."

The old lady pulled out a small mirror and set it down on my desk. She said a few words over the mirror and an image began to form above it. Shortly, a strand of perfect black pearls appeared. It rotated slowly, letting us see it from all angles. I'm no expert in jewelry or magic, but I've handled enough cases to admire the workmanship of both the necklace and the spell. It looked like the pearls were suspended in midair above my desk—real enough to reach out and touch them.

"These are exquisite! What would pearls like that run?"

I recognized the tone in Ze'eva's voice. And who could blame her? I could feel the attraction and I'm the last person in the world to ask about things like that. I'm lucky if I can make sure my socks match. We were both so absorbed in looking at the necklace, it sounded like a small explosion went off in the room when Mrs. Sherwood spoke.

"I don't know how much my necklace is worth, dear. It's been passed down for generations. I suspect it might be worth forty to fifty thousand crowns, if you could find a buyer for it." She leaned forward conspiratorially. "After all, there is the matter of the curse."

I felt the hair rise on the back of my neck at those words. "The curse? How interesting . . . " I surreptitiously scooted my chair backward, which seemed to amuse Mrs. Sherwood.

She smiled sweetly before continuing in a voice that sounded like she was giving me a recipe for chocolate cake. "There's nothing to worry about, Mr. Chase. This is only an image; there's no threat to you. As long as you don't put the real necklace around your throat, there's no way to transfer the curse. It's there to prevent anyone other than the rightful owner from profiting from the necklace."

"So, what happens if someone who's not supposed to own it gets their hands on it?"

Mrs. Sherwood gave me a benevolent smile before responding. "It's simple. If someone handles the necklace with the intention of returning it, then the curse has no effect. But, if someone handles the necklace intending to keep it for himself? Then the pearls will vanish, leaving nothing behind but a corpse."

After some more questions regarding Penny—who she knew, who she might hang out with, where she might go and so on—we thanked Mrs. Sherwood and Kyra escorted her out. Ze'eva looked closely at me and smiled. "Those were gorgeous pearls, weren't they, Theron?"

I saw the way her eyes were sparkling and tried to rein her in. "Yeah, those were gorgeous *cursed* pearls." I leaned back in my chair, listening to the familiar squeak, and stared up at the ceiling. There was something about those pearls gnawing at the back of my mind. I swear I'd seen something like them before, but I couldn't put my finger on it..

Ze'eva stretched and looked at me, her dark hair falling down into her face. "I seem to recall someone offering me lunch a bit ago. Since we now have Mrs. Sherwood's retainer, we can even go somewhere we don't have a tab."

My stomach rumbled at the mention of food and we both laughed. I stood up and offered her a hand out of her chair. "That sounds like an idea. While we're there, we can figure out our next step. We've got two goals—finding the missing girl and finding the missing necklace."

The puzzled look on Ze'eva's face prompted me to continue. "I'm not convinced they're necessarily connected. For all we know, Penny met some guy and took off for a vacation. She's over twenty-one according to Mrs. Sherwood, so she's legally able to go wherever she wants with whomever she wants. She simply might have forgotten to leave a note. It'll be more effective to look for them at the same time. Would you rather look for the girl or the pearls?"

A breeze rustled the papers on my desk. I glanced up and saw her give me a knowing look; I knew what she was thinking before she spoke. "While the pearls are tempting, I'm not sure I should trust you searching for the missing girl. After all, I was your client once; now I'm your partner. I'm not sure we've got enough room in this office for another desk." She paused for effect. "Nor do you need another girlfriend."

I nodded sagely before speaking, "So, as I said, you should look for the girl while I look for the pearls."

Ze'eva looked out the door and grinned at Kyra. "See? He can be taught."

I spoke over their laughter. "Har-dee-har-har. If we're done being clever, perhaps we could get started on that lunch date?"

Kyra spoke up. "Could you bring me back something? I'll keep an eye on the place while you're out."

Ze'eva nodded as Kyra settled into the chair behind her desk. We moved through the outer office toward the door, only to stop when there was a knock at the door. Well, not really a knock, more like a loud heavy *thump* from someone who demanded entry. We retreated into our inner office and then motioned for Kyra to let our visitor in.

A deep male voice responded to Kyra's initial greeting. I didn't catch the person's name at first, since I was busy slipping my pistol out of its hiding place in my desk . . . just in case.

Kyra stepped into the doorway. "Captain Horace Grantland to see you."

"Show him in," I said with more enthusiasm than I felt.

Kyra stepped to the side and a mountain of a man walked in. He was dressed in a white fisherman's cap and a dark blue overcoat and his sweater strained at holding in his mass. Seven foot tall and probably 400 pounds of pure muscle stood framed in the doorway. Between his size, the grizzled tufts of gray hair, and scraggly features, I suspected there was ogre or troll in his bloodline somewhere.

He spoke with a huge gravelly voice. Somehow it seemed appropriate. "You Chase?"

I sat up and leaned forward, reaching under my desk for my head knocker. It's been my experience that conversations that start out like this tend to wind up causing damage to my office. "I'm Theron Chase, yes."

The ogre grinned. "Good, then you're the man I'm lookin' for. Some of my mates down on the docks say you're pretty good at finding stuff, especially things others don't want found."

I relaxed slightly, but kept my fingers on my head knocker. He wasn't showing any signs of hostility, but I've been fooled before by much smaller men. No sense in taking chances now. I motioned him toward the sturdiest chair in the room. "I get lucky now and then. What's missing and why do you think others don't want it found?"

A huge smile split his face, showing off a mouthful of jagged teeth. The chair groaned under him as he shifted his mammoth frame to include Ze'eva in his gaze. "Pearls. Twelve of the most beautiful black pearls you've ever laid your eyes on. Some people seem to think they don't belong to me no more. That's 'cause some people think I'm dead. However, those people are about to get the surprise of their lives—their short lives."

I didn't care for the direction this conversation was going. I don't enjoy some of the jobs I do to make ends meet, but something about this case was starting to smell rotten. I decided to pass on whatever Captain Grantland had in mind. "Well, it sounds like you've got everything under control, so I'm not sure why you need my services. Plus, I try never to get in the middle of a vendetta."

He leaned back in his chair and smiled again. "Vendetta? Nah, I ain't mad at anyone. But I got more claim to those pearls than most. I figure the curse will get the rest of them." He paused for a second and then laughed before speaking again. "I get it! The old-lady act fooled you too, eh?"

That caught my attention. "Old-lady act?"

The ogre shoved his thumb over his shoulder at the door. "Yeah, I seen her coming out of here. She ain't changed that look in ten years. It's real useful to get people to do your dirty work when they think you're a little ol' lady who might be a little dingy. She's about as addled as I'm handsome and buddy, I ain't about to win no beauty contest."

Something in Captain Grantland's voice made me believe he was telling the truth—as far as he understood the truth. However, this was turning out to be a personal matter, and those get messy. I saw Ze'eva's signal there was something she wanted to say, bit we needed to finish this interview first.

"Captain Grantland, you claim these pearls are yours, and I believe you're telling the truth." The ogre started to say something, but I held up one hand to stop him. "I also believe the 'old' lady believes *she's* the owner of those pearls too. However, neither of you know where they are. Why should I believe you have any more claim on the pearls than she does? Where's your proof?"

The ogre threw his head hack and laughed. "Chase, you *are* as good as they say. Tell you what. Come by my room in the Black Prince Hotel later this evening. I can introduce you to the guy I got them from then."

"Seven o'clock?"

Grantland nodded before rising from his seat. If an inanimate object could sigh in relief, I knew the chair would have done so right then. He looked from me to Ze'eva and then back to me. "Seven, it is. I look forward to hiring you after the meet-up. You both coming or is it just you, Chase?"

"That'll depend on what I find out between now and seven."

"I knew you were the man for the job. See ya later, Chase."

He wandered out and Kyra shut the door behind him. When she returned, there was a peculiar look on her face. "Doesn't that beat all, Theron? Two people show up, both claiming to own the same item. What do you think is going on?"

"I'm not sure, sweetheart. Right now, I think I'm going to take Ze'eva to lunch. After that, we're going to do some research on our two visitors. The pearls and the missing girl will keep a bit longer."

After dining at a more upscale restaurant than usual, we split up to take care of our assignments—Ze'eva set out to find out what she could on Mrs. Sherwood while I went to the docks to see if anyone was familiar with Captain Grantland. It was a pleasant day, so I decided to walk. On the way there, I bumped into Officer Mortiva coming up the hill from the direction of the waterfront.

"Good afternoon, Chase. Out chasing bad guys—or did you have something a bit more shapely in mind?"

I laughed and waved my hands to caution him. "Not so loud, Mortiva. You'll have Ze'eva leaving pieces of me all over town."

He laughed and gave me a slap on the shoulder. "She's got you on the run, does she? Well, don't worry none, Chase. I'll keep it to myself. So, what does bring you down to my beat?"

Mortiva had been working the docks for nearly twenty years. He'd been a fisherman before he took the job with the city. I figured if there was anything going on, he'd be the one to know. Some dock people don't like talking to policemen but most of the workers still see Mortiva as one of them.

"I'm headed toward the port, but maybe you can help me before I get there—point me in the right direction, so to speak. Ever hear of a Captain Grantland?"

That stopped him for a moment. From the look on his face, I thought he was getting ready to tell me something funny. It *was* funny, but somehow the punch line left me cold,

"Captain Grantland? Captain Horace Grantland? He's been dead for ten years."

I did a double take before I could respond. "Are you certain we're talking about the same Captain Grantland?"

"Ain't likely to be forgetting a mug like that. Big guy, must have had some ogre or troll in his family and probably not too far back, if you catch my drift. Never was big on saying where he was going or where he'd been. Liked to play it close to the chest. Anyway, ol' Cap Grantland had been gone overseas maybe three years. When he came back, I had to break up three parties in three different bars that night. Seems he'd hit it big down south in the islands. Next day, we pulled his body out of South Bay. Weirdest thing too."

I felt a shiver run down my back. Must have been a breeze kicking up off the bay. "Sounds like he got drunk and fell in the water. Nothing strange about that."

Mortiva paused and squinted as if he was looking at some-thing off in the distance. "That's just it. He didn't drown—he'd been strangled. There weren't any finger or rope marks—just strange round marks evenly spaced around his neck. Honestly, big as he was, I can't believe anyone was strong enough to strangle him."

I stood there with a dumbfounded look on my face, trying to process what Mortiva was saying. "And this happened ten years ago?"

He looked at me intently. "Yeah, as far as I can remember. Why are you so interested in him anyway?"

I tried to keep my voice even as I answered him. "Because Captain Grantland was in my office less than an hour ago, trying to hire me to find something. Said people thought he was dead, but he had a surprise for them."

Mortiva gave me a strange look and then burst out laughing. "That'd be one heck of a surprise. I'm the guy who pulled him out of the water and identified his corpse. If he wasn't dead, he's one hell of a magician." Mortiva paused to laugh some more. "That's a good one, Chase. You had me going for a moment. I know you have some weird clients, but I didn't know you we're working for a ghost."

"I'm not kidding. Someone calling himself Captain Grantland tried to hired Ze'eva and me to find something for him. To be honest, you mentioning the southern islands makes me think *whoever* was in my office knew what they were talking about."

He looked like he was sizing me up for a straitjacket and then rubbed his chin with one hand before speaking. I noticed it wasn't the hand closest to his billy club. "Chase, someone's playing a joke on you. Grantland's been dead for a decade and he didn't have no brothers I ever heard of. Nope, sounds like someone's setting you up for a gag. But, if you want to prove it to yourself, he's buried up on Sailor's Peak, that graveyard on the islands just beyond Pelican Cove to the north. Weren't that many mourners for him, as I recall."

I decided not to spend more time trying to convince Mortiva the guy he fished out of the bay was still walking around. I wasn't sure how he'd done it either. Still, ghost, ghoul, or escape artist, Grantland had gotten me interested in his story. I figured it wouldn't hurt to see what I could find out about him. I bid Officer Mortiva a good afternoon and continued down to the docks—but with a new set of questions.

I got pretty much the same story everywhere I went. Captain Horace Grantland had lived in a series of flophouses along the bay when he wasn't at sea. He was well-regarded as a ship's captain and a navigator, and no one worked harder on a ship under sail than him. He was also considered irresponsible, known to disappear at the drop of a hat to chase a tale about lost treasures, and he could consume more alcohol in one sitting than any five sailors in Calasia or any other port around the world.

He was also, most assuredly, dead.

A fter a few more fruitless stops I left the waterfront and made my way back downtown. When I called the office Kyra told me Ze'eva hadn't checked in yet. It was starting to get late, so I instructed Kyra to go ahead and lock up. There was no sense in her waiting around. I hadn't found out anything that wouldn't keep until the morning.

I stopped at a local diner about a block from the office— Ze'eva and I frequented it probably more than my wallet and waistline needed—and grabbed a quick dinner. One of the waitresses came over when the crowd thinned out a bit.

"Hey, your girl was in here earlier."

I looked up and recognized her. Gina hadn't been working there long, but Ze'eva and I tried to sit in her section whenever possible. She was a good kid and a hard worker and we tried to make sure she got tipped whenever we were there. Most of the counter help couldn't be bothered if you didn't look or smell like money, but she seemed to actually enjoy working here.

"Oh, when was Ze'eva here?"

Gina shifted to let some customers pass her before answering. "About an hour ago. She seemed kinda distracted. Only ate half her sandwich before she took off. Seemed really interested in some other woman who was in here most of the afternoon. She'd taken a seat near the window and stayed there while it was quiet. The lady she was watching seemed to spend a lot of time looking out the window, like she was looking for someone or something."

I thought about it for a second and then turned to the waitress. "Where was she sitting?"

She pointed toward a booth near the window. "Right over there."

Another waitress was cleaning the booth. I grabbed my cup of coffee and slid into it before another couple could sit down. "Sorry, folks. I need to get some sunlight. Doctor's orders."

The lady raised her eyebrows and sniffed disdainfully in my general direction, but Gina stepped in and directed them to another booth and poured them each a cup of coffee on the house. While she grabbed my food and moved it to the new booth, I glanced out the window to see what this mystery lady could have been so fascinated with.

It didn't take long. From where I was sitting, you could stare right into the windows of my office. I was going to have to tell Kyra to start keeping the shades drawn at night. With a small telescope or a magically enhanced device, you'd be able to see almost everything going on in the office from here. That's bad for client confidentiality.

I thought about it for a bit, but none of it made sense. We hadn't had any business in weeks and except for our two surprise visitors today, I couldn't imagine why anyone would be interested in what's going on at our place. Secondly, why was Ze'eva keeping an eye on the woman watching our office, if that *is* what she was doing? After all, there were other things you *could* see from the diner. Still, if Ze' was interested, then I should be too.

I handed Gina a few crowns and said if the woman returned and took that seat again to call Kyra and let her know. She gave me an odd look, but she wasn't going to turn down the money either. Honestly, if she had asked me what was going on, I couldn't have answered her. There was something odd with the whole situation.

I checked my watch and saw it was nearly six o'clock. I was going to have to hustle to meet the "late" Captain Grantland. I really wanted to ask him what his secret for coming back from the dead was. Seemed like it would be a useful thing to have in my line of work.

The Black Prince Hotel was over in the North Point area, which wasn't that far if you have a car. Since I don't drive, I had to flag down a cab and of course, they all decided to take their coffee breaks right then. Finally, I managed to get one and we worked our way into the heavy traffic going over the bridge separating downtown from the north side of the city. I fumed at how slow we were going, but there was no way I would have made it there on time if I walked.

I climbed out of the cab at nearly 7:10. It had taken longer to get to the hotel than I had counted on and I hoped the good captain hadn't gotten bored and wandered off. I hurried through the lobby and had the clerk get me Captain Grantland's room number. The clerk must have been working off the effects of a big dinner, because he moved like he was half asleep, but eventually he came back with the information. The person calling himself Captain Grantland was in room 630. Not wanting to climb six flights of stairs, I decided to take the elevator.

After a short wait, the door opened and a large man pushed past me as I tried to enter. He was in a hurry and had his collar turned up and his hat pulled low, so I couldn't get a good look at his face. Still, there was something unusual about him. He wasn't quite as large as Grantland, so I filed him under "big and rude" before riding the elevator up to my floor.

The floor was dimly lit and quiet as I made my way down the hall to room 630. A few doors from my destination, I paused. Even in the poor lighting, I could see the door to 630 was slightly ajar. I loosened the .45 in my shoulder holster and eased my way up.

One glance inside and I realized I could have been leading a marching band and the occupant wouldn't have noticed. I could see the row of dark bruises spaced out circling his throat. But that wasn't the strangest thing I noted in the room.

It wasn't my client.

I took out a handkerchief and opened the door wide enough to slip in. The dark-skinned man was dressed in the latest fashions, but it was obvious he was from the southern islands. I checked his pockets and found a wallet and passport. Glancing through them, I learned three things: his name was Torombo Inohuaye, he was from Walikamba Island, and robbery had nothing to do with his death—not with a blank check for eight thousand crowns still in his wallet.

I walked over to the phone in the room and carefully dialed the front desk. A few minutes later, Smokey Davis, the hotel detective, was standing next to me, staring down at the stiff. We stood there for a few moments and then he turned to me.

"You know the guy, Chase?"

I turned and spread my hands out flat in a negative motion. "Never saw him before, Smokey. I was supposed to meet one of your guests here—a man name of Horace Grantland."

Smokey turned and an odd look crossed his face. "You sure you never met this guy before, Chase?"

That was an odd question. However, Smokey is a straight guy, so I wondered where he was going with this. "Yeah, I'm sure. Why?"

"'Cause that's Horace Grantland. Or that's the name he registered under, anyway."

"Smokey, I think we've both been sold a bill of goods. Better call Homicide. There's nothing more we can do for him. Besides, I think I saw the guy who did this."

That caught Smokey's attention. "Thought you said this guy was dead when you got here, Chase."

"I did, but a big guy shoved his way out of the elevator when I was trying to board. There was something about him that sticks in my head. I'll figure it out soon enough."

Smokey drummed his fingers against his leg, staring down at the body again. "I don't know, Chase. It's a bit of a jump to go from getting run over by a guy in a hurry to accusing him of murder. He could have been late for an appointment or just rude. You'd need more than that to go to the constables. Corvinus ain't exactly your biggest fan. He'd think you're trying to blame someone else to try and get yourself out of trouble."

I had to grin sheepishly. "Okay, maybe I am jumping the gun a bit. Still there's something about it that makes me think something more was going on. You don't normally pull your collar up and pull your hat down when you're going out for an appointment." I was moving toward the door when Smokey spoke up.

"Ain't you gonna hang around, Chase? You know Corvinus is gonna have some questions for you."

That brought me up short. I was so busy trying to figure out how Inohuaye fit into this whole mess, I hadn't even considered what would happen when the constables made their usual mess of the entire thing. "Do you need me to?"

Smokey grinned and waved a hand toward the door. "Nah, I'll deal with the constables. They know where to find you if they need more information."

T his case was getting more complicated by the moment. My client was or wasn't who she was supposed to be. The other guy who wanted to hire us to recover the same items may or may not be a dead guy—except when I went to meet him, there was another guy registered in his name who was definitely dead. I was beginning to think I should check my own license to be sure I was who I thought *I* was.

So far, the only thing I was getting out of this whole situation was a headache. If there had been any money in the bank account I would have told both Mrs. Sherwood and Captain Grantland—or whoever they really were—to both take a hike and tried to get a more normal case involving a serial killer or a blackmailer or something I could understand.

But, since I've seen cobwebs with more things in them than my bank account, there wasn't much of an option. I had to attempt to earn the money Mrs. Sherwood had paid us. I had a feeling I wasn't going to get anything else done this evening, so I decided to swing by the office and leave a note for Ze'eva in case I was late getting to the office the next day. I've never been much of a morning person anyway, but given all the screwballs I was being thrown on this case, I wanted someone to know where to start looking if I didn't make it in.

I was about to put the key in the door when I noticed a light on in the inner office. I eased my pistol out of my pocket and checked the door. As I suspected, it was unlocked.

I opened the door quietly and let myself in. Inching my way toward the light, I smelled something familiar—not perfume or cologne, this was more like faintly burning wood. I peered into the office and saw four small sticks had been placed into one of my empty bottles and small tendrils of smoke rose from them, sending a faint but unmistakable scent through the room. However, that wasn't what surprised me. It was who was sitting at my desk . . .

Major Sebastian Fielder.

Major Fielder of His Majesty's Royal Dragoons and fortune hunter extraordinaire. We'd crossed paths a few times in my career and neither of us had ever been able to claim a clear victory. I was still alive, which was more than many of his opponents could say. To see him sitting in my office, drinking my booze, and, in general, making himself right at home was not what I had expected.

"Ah, Chase, there you are. Do come in and sit down."

I walked over and took the bottle away from him and poured myself a drink. I found a spot to sit where I could watch both the door and the window. If Major Fielder was here, you could bet Victor would be nearby. Victor was a small mountain of a man who served as both his valet and bodyguard. We'd had a few dustups and it was usually me who finished facedown in the dust after them. I don't think I've ever hit anyone so hard and had them laugh and ask for another.

After fortifying myself with a drink, I stared at him over the edge of the glass. "You look pretty comfortable in my chair, Major. Things getting too hot for you in Granville?"

His lips pursed together as if he'd bitten into something sour. "Dash it all, Chase, why must you always think the worst of me?"

I leaned back in my chair, feigning a nonchalance I certainly did not feel, and prepared for our usual banter. It's become almost second nature between the two of us. "It's not that I think badly of you. It's that people have this bad habit of dying when you're around."

He sipped his drink and stared back at me, his bland expression as hard to read as ever. "I'm certain I have no clue what you're talking about, Chase. Anyway, I'm not here to debate rumors and bygones. Instead, I understand that you have been hired to acquire some missing pearls. I would like to make you a counteroffer."

"For someone who's *persona non grata* in Calasia, Major, you have some interesting contacts. How is it you happen to know about an assignment I only received today?"

"Simple. You've been asking around town about Captain Grantland. Your charming associate has been making inquiries about Mrs. Sherwood. I happen to know both of them are in pursuit of the aforementioned necklace—one, I should make note here and now, that is actually mine by right. Since you are making inquiries both about them and for them, I have no choice but to assume you are employed by one or the other if not both."

I tipped my glass in his general direction. "You do get around, Major."

He lifted his in my direction in return. "I make it a point to keep track of you, Chase. While we may not have the same goals, we do seem to keep crossing paths. It's only good military tactics to know one's . . . competitors, especially one who seems entirely too adept at thwarting my own schemes."

I made a production out of putting my glass down so I could slip my pistol out of its holster, just in case. Once I had regained my chair, I chose my words carefully. "You have a counteroffer for me? With all due respect, Major, we haven't been on the same side of anything in the past. I'm not sure why you're being so generous now."

He straightened up and placed both of his hands palm down on my desk. "Look, Chase, I am willing to place my cards on the table—"

"Facedown."

He allowed a look of frustration to glide across his face, but he soldiered on. "—if only to right them at the proper time. Regardless of what you may have heard, those pearls are mine. I paid a small fortune for them twelve years ago. However, the pearl merchant was found dead the morning he was to have delivered them into my hands. Neither the pearls nor my money were ever recovered."

"I'm certain you had a good alibi for that morning."

"Quite, not that one was needed. I soon learned a young man had been found strangled down by the docks in Caprisia. It seems the young man was a servant in the merchant's house and he was either the murderer or he aided the murderer, and subsequently, was betrayed by him. Further inquiries showed a ship had sailed about an hour before his body was found. I suspect whoever stole the pearls was aboard."

I paused and let my amazement show on my face. "I'm not sure what surprises me more, Major—the fact you let someone slip in and snatch the treasure right out from underneath your nose, or your willingness to admit it to me this openly."

"It was not one of my finer moments, I must admit, but I'm a humbler man than I was those many years ago. Anyway, Victor and I caught the next ship out and began our pursuit. We followed innumerable clues to the same number of dead ends. To tell you the truth, I was beginning to despair of ever finding those pearls again."

I managed to suppress a yawn. "I'm assuming there's a point to this sea tale of yours?"

He paused to top off his glass and take a healthy swig before continuing. "What I'm saying, Chase, is those pearls have claimed eight lives I know of so far. If someone approaches you regarding them, do keep that in mind." He lifted the glass and let the light filter through the amber liquid. "The natives call them the Pearls of Darkness. There is an eerie beauty to those pearls and to have seen them is to be inexorably drawn to them, Chase. They're a prize beyond measure. I have tracked the pearls to this city and I will have them."

"So, you're hiring me?"

It was the first honest laugh I'd ever heard come from him when I said that. "I love your conceit, Chase, but, no. I've tracked those pearls for this long; I think I'll finish the hunt. However, if you do find them, do contact me first. I'm certain I can make you an equitable offer for them—and this time, you'll be on the side of the angels."

And with that, he stood up and walked out of my office without a backward glance. I heard movement outside and knew Victor had joined him in the hall. He must have been lurking on the landing while the major was visiting. I waited for a few minutes to be certain they actually left; the major had a bad habit of doubling back on his trail. The last thing my office needed was a new set of bullet holes in it.

I finished my note to Ze'eva and slipped out a different door into the night. Not that I specifically distrusted the major, but there was no reason to make it easy for him either.

I swear I hadn't been asleep for more than a few minutes before I heard the pounding on my door. I managed to lift my head and saw the sunlight streaming through my window and the clock near my bed read 10:00 a.m. I heard the pounding again and realized it hadn't been a dream. I tossed on a robe and stumbled to the door.

"Chase, open this damn door. I know you're in there."

I would have recognized Captain Corvinus's dulcet tones anywhere. I opened the door and motioned for him to come in. I also noted the two constables at either end of my hall and knew this was no social call. He stomped in and made himself at home in my overstuffed chair. Between the major and him, I was beginning to wonder who was paying the rent around here.

"Please make yourself at home, Captain. I was about to put on the coffeepot. Should I make some for you too?"

I knew he wanted to rip into me for something, but my manners caught him off guard. His expression softened for a second and he tapped himself on the stomach with a fist. "Nah, the doc says I have to cut back on my coffee. Says I'm working hard on an ulcer and the last thing I need is more acid in my stomach. Go ahead, though. I can wait long enough for you to perk some for yourself. Coffee's one of the first things you learn to miss when you're sitting in a cell down at the Citadel."

I scooped coffee into the urn and ran water into the pot. Once I had it going on the stove, I grabbed one of the chairs from the dining room table and dragged it over to where the captain was sitting. "The Citadel? The goons in the hall told me you're not here to check on my health, Captain. Still, isn't the Citadel a bit extreme?"

"Cut the crap, Chase. You were at the Black Prince Hotel last night. You discovered a body in room 630 and contacted the house dick about it. Then you left before we could ask you any questions. Why?"

"Well, first off, the person in that room wasn't the person I went to meet. The man I *was* supposed to meet stopped by my office earlier that afternoon wanting to hire me. Said if I met him at the hotel, he'd give me good reasons to take him on as a client and drop the one who'd hired me just before that. However when I showed up, the stiff was already lying on the floor and it was *not* the man I'd met earlier. So, seeing how it probably didn't concern me, I turned it over to Smokey and had him contact you. I figured if you really wanted to talk to me, you'd find me soon enough, and here you are."

Corvinus paused from taking notes and used the pencil stub to push his hat farther back on his head. "Okay, Chase, what's going on? I can count on the fingers of one hand the times you've volunteered anything. What's different this time?"

I went over and saw the coffee was done and poured myself a cup before I answered the captain. Hey, he had come to my place uninvited; I wasn't under any obligation to be hospitable. Once it was ready, I returned to my chair and took a sip before finishing. "It's real simple. The guy who tried to hire me—one Captain Horace Grantland—isn't a client yet. He hasn't paid me a cent and he led me straight to a stiff in his room. To my surprise, said stiff was registered in Grantland's name. I don't owe him a thing. Besides, according to your own department's records, my prospective client died ten years ago. Last time I checked, a dead man can't sign a contract, verbal or otherwise."

He leaned back in the chair, surprised by my vehemence. "Hey, Chase, I can't blame you for being sore about the bum deal. Still, you usually like to solve these things yourself. It's not like you to give me information without a fight."

"Look, Corvinus, I'm sorry if it felt like I was jumping down your collar. I'm tired and I don't like being set up. If you can catch up to this joker, he's all yours. What I'm still trying to figure out is how he managed to look so much like what everyone says the late Captain Grantland did. From what I was able to find out, he didn't have any brothers or close relatives."

"That is a puzzler, Chase. Still, there was a report on the stiff when I came in this morning. When I saw it, I thought you might be interested."

"Captain, you have my attention."

"Now, I'm not privy to your cases, but I've heard you're looking for a strand of pearls, twelve in number, black in color. Said pearls are supposed to be cursed, depending on who you talk to. Sound familiar?"

"You know I can't divulge what a client may or may not have said to me regarding an investigation I'm working on."

Corvinus let out a hearty laugh. "That's the Chase I've come to know. Anyway, did you know those pearls were harvested from a sacred lagoon—a lagoon in Walikamba Island?"

"Walikamba Island, eh?"

"Yeah, pretty odd considering that's where the stiff is from. Oh yeah, did I also mention this Torombo Inohuaye's father was killed twelve years ago and the pearls were stolen from his home safe? Apparently, he'd received threats from one of the local priests for possessing those pearls. The priest insisted Inohuaye return them to the tribe to be replaced in the lagoon, but Inohuaye assumed the priest was running a scam to gain possession of them. He sold the pearls to an anonymous buyer the night before he was killed. However, the pearls and the money disappeared before the local constables discovered the crime."

"Did anyone check the priest's story?"

Corvinus shook his head and leaned back in the chair. "You've obviously never spent any time in the southern islands. Everyone lives in fear of those priests. Some claim they have dark magic at their command. Of course, it could be nothing but superstition. Either way, the locals believe and they believe hard. Hell, sometimes I think they 'make' things happen because they believe so strongly. No, the constables took the priest at his word and did not investigate further. They were afraid of being cursed."

I'd like to say I scoffed at their superstition, but I knew better. One of my best friends is a court mage and I've encountered enough things that can't be explained logically. Some call it miracles from a god; others call it magic. Others still call it advanced science. Me, I avoid it as much as possible.

I got up and poured myself another cup. When I returned, I had decided what I was going to do, provided he would cooperate. "Look, Captain, I've got some ideas on how to help track down your killer. You've got Smokey's story and you've got the information from the stiff. If you can give me a day or so, I think I can get enough evidence to hand you a murderer. But, I can't do it if I'm stuck in the Citadel answering a bunch of questions and I sure can't do it if you hang a tail on me. What do you say?"

"I say I'm probably going to take a butt chewing from the Chief Constable for letting you do this. However, something tells me I'm giving you enough rope to hang yourself along with this mystery person, so it would be a win/win in my book. You've got seventy-two hours, Chase. If you don't have proof for me—proof I can take in front of the magistrates—then I'll be booking you for Inohuaye's murder."

———

I wandered into the office an hour later to see Ze'eva and Kyra huddled together over at Ze'eva's desk. Clearing my throat to get their attention, I waited until they looked up before I sauntered in. I set my hat in its usual spot on top of my file cabinet and then looked over at the two women.

"How did things go with your investigations yesterday, Ze'?"

"Apparently not as well as yours. You really need to work on your poker face, Theron. I can tell when you think you're ahead of me on a case."

I plopped down into my chair and spun it around to face the two of them. "Why, Ze'eva, such a suspicious mind you have."

She turned to Kyra and sighed dramatically. "What did I tell you, Kyra? As soon as he didn't show up on time, I knew he'd come in here crowing about something."

"Argh, you wound me, Ze'eva."

"Not yet, I haven't. Don't push it, Chase."

When Ze'eva broke out my last name, I knew I was close to the edge and it was time to back off. I grinned sheepishly before continuing. "Yes, I have been busy since last evening. But, tell me what you found yesterday and I'll see if any of the information I picked up fills in the gaps."

Ze'eva pulled out her notebook and flipped a few pages in to find her place. "I found a jeweler who'd been approached about buying the pearls, but the seller never showed up after their initial conversation. I also learned from a friend of my father's the pearls have quite a history. He says there are six murders and nine mysterious disappearances associated with them."

"That ties in with what I've learned. Although I think we can add two more murders to that total. Oh, Kyra, do you remember Major Fielder?"

She didn't even try to disguise the look of frustration when she heard that name. "Theron, is he involved in this? You remember what happened last time?"

Ze'eva's ears perked up. "Major Fielder? I don't believe you've ever mentioned him before."

"That's because I was hoping I'd seen the last of him. He's always been good at staying just this side of the law, at least on the surface. No, he showed up here last night claiming he was the rightful owner of the pearls and he's been trying to recover them for years. It seems there are more players in this game than we thought."

I related the details of yesterday's events and between Ze'e-va's notes and mine we were able to put most of the pieces together regarding the pearls. However, trying to figure out who was the actual owner, who was really our client, or who any of our clients really were was anyone's guess. From what we could gather, none of the people who wanted to hire us were the legitimate owners and the one person most likely to be their legal owner was the person I wanted to have them least of all.

Ze'eva leaned back in her chair, twirling a strand of hair in her fingers as she thought. Finally she stood up and began pacing around the office. "What do you think we should do, Theron? I mean, we can't work for three different clients who all want the same thing."

"Before we go much further, I think we should talk to someone who knows a lot more about magic and curses than I do. Let's try and determine how likely there is to be a curse on those pearls and whether or not it could do what Mrs. Sher-wood hinted at."

"Who do you have in mind?"

I stood up and grabbed my hat. "I think we need to drop in on Theo again."

Kyra frowned at me. "If you visit him again, remember to leave by the front door. Pop through the wall again and I am not responsible for my actions."

I laughed as I held the door open for Ze'eva. "I'll keep that in mind."

A short cab ride across town and we were standing in the entrance of Markhams's Emporium of the Ancients. A well-dressed young man in a gray cutaway coat walked toward us as soon as we entered and stopped. It was obvious he recognized us and motioned for us to wait as he disappeared into the back of the store. A few moments later, he stiffly escorted us past the gleaming glass cases, pausing only to wipe a stray fingerprint off with his silk handkerchief, and led us to a short hallway with offices. He knocked on the one at the end of the hall and then opened the door for us to enter.

A familiar voice boomed out. "Theron, please come in. This is an unexpected surprise." Theodius Markham spotted Ze'eva and jumped to his feet to greet her. After giving her a kiss on the back of her hand, he straightened up and positioned himself between the two of us. "Ah, Ze'eva, you're still wasting your time with this reprobate? Knowing Chase as I do, I'm surprised one of the unpleasant gentlemen he normally hangs around with hadn't parted his hair down to his shoulders by now. I guess you're good luck for him. However, should you ever decide to leave this disreputable field, I'm certain we can find a position for you here."

I tapped him on the shoulder. "Uh, Theo, I'm still right here."

He looked at me as if he hadn't seen me before and then turned to wink at Ze'eva before responding. "Oh, Chase, sorry, I guess I got carried away. Anyway, what brings the two of you here?"

"Have you ever heard of the Pearls of Darkness, Theo?"

I've seen a lot of expressions on Theo's face in the six years I've known him, but I'd never seen him grow pale before. He swallowed hard, walked over to his desk, and lowered himself gingerly into his chair. I grabbed a glass off the rack on the wall and poured him a glass of water. He felt well enough to glare at me, so I poured out the water and sloshed a dollop of scotch into it. He tossed that back with one motion and, after wheezing a bit, looked up at me and shook his head sadly.

"Why can you never come to visit me about something small and innocuous? No, first you bring me one of the deadliest knives in the world and now you come inquiring about the cursed pearls of Walikamba Island. What next? Will you bring me an invitation to meet the Witch-King of Blackhaus?"

"That bad, huh?"

Theo favored me with a look usually reserved for explaining things to small children. He stood up and walked over to a small library he had behind his desk. Running his finger along the spines of the books, he found the one he was looking for, a dark leather book, and brought it back to the desk. He flipped through it and stopped at a passage. "According to this, the original Pearls of Darkness were stolen from a sacred lagoon on Walikamba Island one hundred and fifty years ago. Traders found the Walikamba oyster beds and harvested the original black pearls. It took mystic investigators forty years to track down the pearls that had been woven into a triple-strand necklace. In that time, two hundred and sixteen people were killed by the curse. In every case, the cause of death was the same—a mysterious pattern of black spots around the neck of the victim."

I slowly raised my hand to halt Theo. "Torombo Inohuaye and Captain Horace Grantland were killed by person or persons unknown. The only sign of injury was a single row of black spots around their necks."

"So, the rumor I'd once heard that a second necklace had been created is true?"

"Looks that way, Theo. Apparently a merchant tried to sell twelve of them in the form of a necklace. So far, there are twelve deaths associated with these pearls. Inohuaye was killed last night."

"So, you're saying the pearls are here in Calasia?"

"I thought I'd made that perfectly clear, Theo."

He paled further and motioned for me to bring him the scotch. After slamming down another shot, he continued. "The priests of Walikamba refused to remove the curse when the original necklace was finally secured and contained. They claimed that since the pearls had been handled by nonnatives, they had been tainted. Whoever found them afterward deserved whatever happened. After every attempt to remove the curse failed, it took seven of the greatest mages on this continent to finally destroy the pearls. The feedback killed three of them and two never were able to cast a spell ever again."

Ze'eva's voice broke in. "That's horrible."

Theo glanced over at her. "There was talk about interdicting the Walikamba Islands for fear of this ever happening again. It was about as close as we'd ever come to getting all the kingdoms and realms of this world to agree to anything. However, after a few years, we learned all the interdiction was doing was making the regular pearls from there so valuable smugglers would risk anything to reach the islands. Soon, the only pearls outlawed were the black pearls. Those are still illegal to own in every civilized country in this world. For some of the less-civilized places . . . well, let's say, money speaks louder than laws there."

"And if the major is involved, let's say, even civilized countries aren't safe."

"Major Fielder has been around, Chase? Oh, that's not good. Even though I attempt to avoid the circle of friends you seem to collect, even I am familiar with that name. Last I heard he was trying to bilk a young lady out of a mountain of gold."

I nodded and then turned to Ze'eva who was gazing at me with a quizzical expression. "He was trying to scare her into marrying a confederate. I suspect she would've shortly thereafter had an unfortunate accident at which point her widower would've sold the mountain to Major Fielder for a pittance, or else suffered their own unfortunate accident. You know, accidents seem to follow that man. I swear he's part poltergeist."

"It sounds like this major should be worried. After all, accidents can happen to anyone," she said, with a rather unpleasant look on her face.

While I might have agreed with her, I thought it might be prudent to get back to the original subject. I turned to Theo. "After some rather delicate maneuvering on my part, I encouraged Fielder to seek shelter in another part of the world after that incident. However, believe it or not, he claims to be the rightful owner of these pearls. I'll admit, I didn't ask him for the bill of sale, but his story has the strongest air of truth to it. And if Fielder's telling the truth, then you know something strange is happening."

Theo nodded and then stood up. "Oh, quite. Chase, I can't help you locate them, but I do have something that might come in handy. You'll have to follow me, though. There are parts of this store I cannot send the staff into for their own safety. I'm afraid I'll have to escort you myself."

"So, it's too dangerous for your staff to go into, but it's all right if we follow you?"

"Certainly. After all, *I'll* be with you."

I swept my hand magnanimously in front of me. "After you."

Theo gave me a dirty look but then walked to the door and motioned for us to follow him. We went into the hall leading to his office, but instead of heading into his showroom, he walked directly across the hall and pushed up on a lamp sconce, causing a door to slide back and then to the side. I could see a narrow passage leading down. He flipped a light switch and we descended. The light broke the darkness, but the dimly lit passage felt oppressive. I was glad to reach the bottom landing.

At the bottom of the stairs, Theo paused to work the tumblers on a vault-like door and carefully pulled it open to reveal a large dark opening. He stepped in and muttered something under his breath. Suddenly, the room filled with light and he motioned for us to continue following. Ze'eva and I crowded in behind him and I saw we were on a balcony overlooking a large room that sank into the ground ahead of us. Apparently Theo had spared no expenses on the room because I know it was below the water table and yet it was perfectly dry. Not even a hint of moisture in the air.

He said something else I couldn't quite make out and a small platform rose in the air to hover at the end of the balcony. Theo moved a rail to the side and stepped onto it. I figured if it could hold his weight, it could certainly hold Ze'eva and me. We stood close to the center as the platform descended and came to a gentle stop on the floor of the room. Theo took a couple of steps and then turned to face us.

"Please stay close to me"—he paused and gave me a knowing look—"and don't touch anything. Most of the stuff in here is incredibly powerful and incredibly deadly. Given your lack of aptitude with magical devices, well, you know the rest."

"Theo, if you make that 'blow up half the city joke' again, I'm going to feed you your tie."

"Perish the thought, Theron. Given what's in this room, you'd probably take out everything in a hundred-mile radius or more. Now, if you'll follow me, I think you'll find this helpful."

If I didn't know he was right, I might have put up more of a squawk. I do all right with magically enchanted weapons, but most magic items and I don't get along—which is strange since items are supposed to be inanimate. On the other hand, I hear the fae have issues with modern technology. Anyway, I'm not a magic-phobe like some people but I prefer things that make sense like a good head knocker or a .45 automatic.

We followed Theo down the rows until he came to a shelf along one of the walls. He pulled a small wooden box from the top shelf and pointedly handed it to Ze'eva. We looked it over together—some kind of dark red wood with some silver inlay, a silver clasp holding the box shut. When we opened it, it was lined with some type of white silk padding. All in all, it seemed quite normal, but from the way Theo was looking at us, I knew it had to be more than that.

"All right, Theo, you're acting like the cat that ate the canary and all its relatives. What gives with the box? It's magical or it wouldn't be down here. What is it? One of those boxes you can shove a whole lot of stuff in and it never weighs like it should?"

"Oh no, but score one for Chase; I do have one of those. Not for sale, though. No, this is a replica of the box the original set of pearls was contained in when they were finally tracked down. Once they're inside, the curse, while not lifted, is neutralized. When you find the pearls, carefully place them in here and lock the lid. In fact, it might be wise to not actually touch the pearls." He handed me a set of long-handled forceps from another shelf. "You might want to use these to handle them."

I took the box from Ze'eva and began examining it from all different angles before Theo took it away from me and handed it to Ze'.

"I'd prefer you held this, my dear. I don't want Theron's bad luck rubbing off on the box."

Ze'eva grinned and carefully tucked the box into her purse. "We can't thank you enough for this. When we do recover the pearls, what do you suggest we do? Bring them to you?"

Theo actually blanched at that thought. "Good gods, no. After all, you said you have three clients who claim to be the rightful owners. Give them the pearls inside the box and let them know what I told you about the curse. If they're wise, they'll take the pearls back to Walikamba Island and give them to the priests. If they're not, I highly recommend an armored neckpiece."

"Thanks, Theo," I said, as we followed him back to the floating platform. "What do we owe you?"

"Find those pearls and secure them. If you can do that without getting killed yourselves, I'll consider it payment in full."

Z e'eva and I spent the rest of the day trying to track down any new leads on our clients or the pearls, but it was like trying to find the proverbial needle in a haystack. There was no reason to even believe the pearls were still in the city. If this Penny Fairbanks had lifted the pearls from Mrs. Sherwood, the smart thing would have been for her to hightail it out of town and find another city to pawn them. Then again, that was assuming she hadn't already fallen victim to the curse.

Ze'eva called it a night, but I wanted to run down a few more ideas. I went back to the office to find it empty—for real this time. I put in a call to the Citadel to catch up with Captain Corvinus. He really didn't want to give me any information, but after a while, he did let me know no other corpses had shown up with weird black marks around their necks. I'm not sure it told me anything, but thankfully, the body count wasn't rising.

I was about to put in a call to Maxie down in the morgue when I felt a nearby presence. I couldn't see anyone, but the feeling was unmistakable. I hung up the phone and pulled out a pad of paper as if I were going to write a note, keeping one eye on the door.

Unfortunately, that's not how she arrived.

If not for the lingering scent of the incense the major burned last night, I might've noticed her perfume. As it was, my first clue she was there was the soft, dusky voice from behind me.

"Good evening, Mr. Chase."

I spun around in my chair to see her leaning against the wall next to the window leading to the fire escape. Her red hair highlighted the deep tan of her skin. Her dark green dress left little to the imagination from the way it clung to her curves, and there were plenty of those. From the way she stared at me with those blue eyes, it was obvious she enjoyed the effect she had on me.

"And good evening to you too, Miss . . .?"

"Penny Fairbanks. I heard you might be looking for me?"

"As a matter of fact, I am . . . I mean, I was. Your former employer seems to believe you might be in possession of some of her property—a strand of black pearls, to be precise. You wouldn't happen to know anything about that?"

"It's possible. Buy me a drink and we can discuss it."

I waved my hand at my desk. "I've got a bottle right here if you're thirsty."

"Uh-uh," she said with a quick shake of her head. "If we drink up here, there won't be any talking. That wouldn't do at all. See, I hear your partner and you have more than a business relationship. You're cute, but it's never a good idea to make a pass at someone's boyfriend if you need to ask her a favor. I don't mind flirting, but I think it's safer keeping this a *very* professional relationship."

She walked past and I grabbed my hat. We went across the street to a small bar called Joey's. They knew me there and they've got some out-of-the-way booths they let me do business in. The waitresses know to keep the busybodies away.

We found a quiet booth in the back and ordered our drinks. Penny didn't say much until after the drinks arrived and the waitress got busy with her other customers. Once she was sure we weren't going to be bothered, she started her story.

"All right, Mr. Chase, I know something about the pearls, but I didn't steal them—well, not from their original owner anyway. I suspect my 'former employer'—and I use that term loosely— has dirtier fingers than I do, especially given how she wanted to use me. I was to set up the pigeon, wine and dine him, and get him in the proper mood for our business in return for ten percent of the profits. Yet, when the theft was noticed, it was me they came after, not her. No, she'd set it up so I was the one everyone remembered, not that 'dear sweet old lady' who's not as daft as everyone thinks she is."

"You're not the first person to cast aspersions on Mrs. Sherwood."

Penny laughed. "Mrs. Sherwood? Really? It was Mrs. Northrup when I 'worked' for her. She changes aliases the way I change dresses—and get that look off your face, Chase."

"My thoughts were nothing but the purest."

"Pure malarkey is more likely. Still it doesn't surprise me the old bat put the finger on me. She's obsessed with the pearls. If that means leaving a few bodies in her wake, I'm sure she wouldn't lose a second of sleep over it. This is the reason I don't have the pearls at the moment. I figure it's safer that way."

"So, you're implying there are other people involved in this pearl hunt? People who might be interested in eliminating the competition?"

"Implying nothing, I'm flat-out stating it. However, don't worry about the guy I helped liberate the pearls from. Apparently he developed a breathing difficulty not too long ago. You might have heard about the condition—tends to leave black marks around the neck. Almost always fatal."

"Yeah, I've run into a couple of them lately."

"Besides, she doesn't have to worry about me; if I never saw her again, it'd be too soon. I hear she's got her own fan club who'd love to see she doesn't get any older." She paused for a moment and then asked, "Who else spoke to you?"

I took a drink before replying. "Captain Horace Grantland stopped by after she hired me. Claims he's the rightful owner of the pearls."

She didn't bat an eye. "I've heard of him. Part ogre or troll, but he's got no more right to the pearls than me or half a dozen other claimants. Ever since the pearls left Walikamba Island, there have been a number of people who've had a chance at them. Those who aren't dead aren't likely to give up the hunt either. I'm not sure the hunt will ever end. I just want to find a buyer, get rid of them and get on with my life."

She let her guard down for a moment and I took a chance. "So, if you sell them, what're you going to do with the money?"

A real smile appeared and her face almost lit up. It was a nice change from the ice queen act she'd been handing me all along. "Head back west . . . maybe open up a nice club—a classy joint with music and entertainers. You know, I caught your girl's act a few times. She's got talent. I mean, she had the audience eating out of her hand."

"Yeah, you'd probably do well."

And just like that, the ice armor reformed around her. "But first, I need a buyer."

"Which I'm assuming you've done."

She looked at me with a triumphant smile. "Indeed I have, Chase—a merchant down in South Point. He'll buy the pearls—no questions asked—for a collector in Pyang-yan. If I bring him the pearls, they'll be on a boat within an hour and out of reach forever."

"Pyang-yan? So, this collector isn't afraid of the curse? I mean, I'm no believer, but I'm not sure I'd want to chance it."

She picked up her drink and gave me a mock toast. "I heard you have a good head on your shoulders, Chase. The curse is real, but I paid a lot for protection. It'll take more than some island witch-doctor's hoodoo to keep me from turning a profit on this venture. And don't worry about the collector, either. He specializes in collecting cursed items. It's win/win, as far as I'm concerned. However, if you could distract everyone for, say, three days, I'd be happy to cut you in on a share of the profits. I'm certain it'll more than make up for having to return the retainer when you . . ." She paused to chuckle. ". . . fail to find me."

"But you said you don't have the pearls."

Her eyes narrowed and I knew I wasn't going to like what she'd say. "I said I don't have them *on* me. I never said I couldn't get to them."

T he next morning, I made my way into the office and poured myself a cup of coffee. I could tell Ze'eva was upset about something and I knew why. Before she could say anything, I held up a hand, took my usual seat behind my desk and tried not to scald myself with the coffee. Once fortified, I began.

"Yes, you're smelling perfume and if it's the perfume I think it is, it runs about fifty crowns an ounce. The owner of said perfume was one Penny Fairbanks who made an impromptu visit to the office via the fire escape. We spoke here and at Joey's across the street. She's an attractive woman and about as dangerous as a lion shark."

"I'm assuming discussing the case was *all* you did."

"You can get that suspicious look off your face, Ze'. She's heard about you and she figured staying on both of our good sides was safest. We discussed how she came into possession of the pearls, she warned me about Mrs. Sherwood, and to alert us there are more players in this game than even we suspected. Also, she's located someone interested in buying the pearls and wants us to *not* find her for three days. In return for our ineptitude, she'll cut us in handsomely for the profits of selling the pearls."

"And you believe her?"

I tried another sip and found the coffee had cooled to the temperature of molten lava. A few sips later, I responded to Ze'eva's question. "Yes and no. I believe there's no love lost between her and Mrs. Sherwood. I believe she may have worked for the woman at one time and was used as the foil when the old lady acquired the pearls. I even believe that the guy she helped steal the pearls from is dead. What I don't believe is her sharing a single copper from the sale of the pearls. I suspect there's a ship captain standing by for her probably two days from now."

"So, now we have to figure out where she's hidden the pearls."

"Or figure out who the buyer is and get there before she does."

Ze'eva looked past me at the map of the city I had pinned to one of the walls. "Have you actually looked at Calasia lately? Do you realize how many stores handle jewelry in this town?"

"Two hundred and sixteen according to the phone book. Yes, I looked them up when I got home last night. However, ninety percent of those we can eliminate immediately. It takes a special kind of person to handle *magical* jewelry. If we narrow that down to someone who's willing to handle *hot* magical jewelry that leaves four jewelry stores."

"Assuming the buyer is actually a jeweler and not just a magical fence."

"Assuming she uses a storefront jeweler. There aren't that many fences who'll handle magical jewelry; they're not exactly the bravest guys. If they were, they'd be doing the heists themselves and not paying someone to do it for them. I only know of two guys who'd handle something like the pearls. Of course, there could be new guys in town, but we don't have time to find out. No, we've got six places to investigate regarding jewelry.

On top of that, we need to check both Northport and Southport to see if anyone's got a special cargo going out day after tomorrow."

"Which you believe would be Penny."

"I can't imagine why she specifically asked me to wait three days unless she was leaving in two."

"You're a suspicious man, Theron."

"I'm still alive, so I see no reason to change at this point in my life."

Ze'eva favored me with a smile that I hoped meant she was getting over being upset with me. "Good point. So, what do we do if we recover the pearls? I mean, if they're stolen, shouldn't we turn them over to the constables and let them dispose of them."

"I wouldn't trust those guys with disposing of a lollipop, much less a cursed piece of jewelry." I paused for a moment and then an idea crossed my mind. "Then again, it's really not our problem what happens after we recover the pearls. After all, all of our clients—to include the major, even if he isn't one officially—claim ownership of the pearls. What if we get them first and deliver them to the trio? It might be fun to sit back and watch the fireworks."

"I think that's cynical, even for you. Besides, you don't even know where the pearls are. You said Penny had them."

"No, I said she knows where they are and *I* know what room she's in at the Hotel Garfield. I have a plan on getting her to lead us right to the pearls and then it'll be a matter of getting all the actors together in one place."

Kyra came in as I was explaining my plan to Ze'eva. After laying out my surefire plan to the two of them, Ze'eva was convinced I had taken leave of my senses and Kyra was certain we didn't have enough in the account for bail money. Still, Silver-Tongued Chase continued elaborating on the plan until they both agreed to aid me in this noble quest. Personally, I think they went along with it so they could laugh when it blew up in my face, but regardless of their motivation, they agreed to meet me at the Hotel Garfield at nine that evening.

Before that, we had jewelers to investigate and ship captains to question in case there was a flaw in my plan I hadn't anticipated. Ze'eva took the jewelers while I headed back to the docks. I stopped in at a dive called the Grinning Shark and took a seat at the end of the bar. There were only a few down-on-their-luck sailors sipping ale this early in the morning. After a few minutes the bartender made his way over to me.

"Whatcha want, mate?"

I took a special coin out of my pocket and slid it across to him. He took one look at it and pushed it back. "Sharkey's down in his quarters."

"Give him a call and let him know I'm on the way. I know he hates surprises."

"I'll do that. You gonna go around or should I open the trapdoor?"

I stood up and motioned toward the door. "I'll go around. I could use the fresh air."

The bartender laughed. "There ain't no fresh air on land, mate, but if you can find your way without help, then Sharkey does know you. Good luck. If I hear a splash, I'll fetch out a net for you."

I smiled back and left the bar, walking around the corner to make my way down a narrow shelf toward the water. Once I reached the back of the bar, I spotted the row of pylons rising out of the water. If you looked closely and knew what you were looking for, you could see the path up the pylons toward a carefully hidden door in the floor of the bar jutting out over the water.

Taking a deep breath, I hopped onto the first one and then took my time jumping from one to the other, gaining altitude with each one I precariously perched on. *This was a lot easier ten years ago. Maybe I really should think about that diet Ze'eva's been suggesting.*

Reaching the last pylon, I spotted the hidden landing and stepped onto it. I knocked on the door above my head. A gravelly voice called out, "You sure you weren't followed, Chase?"

"Sharkey, if you know it's me, that means you've been watching me hop around here like an idiot. You also know I haven't had time to look over my shoulder. It was all I could do not to take a nosedive off these damn slippery poles. Now, open the door, if you don't mind. I'd like to talk to *you*, not a moss-covered door."

"All right, Chase. Can't blame me for being careful. I don't know why you don't go through the trapdoor like everyone else."

The door opened and a large arm reached down and grabbed my upstretched hand. With a sudden tug, I was propelled through the air by a grayish-green man who deposited me on the floor of his office. He didn't say anything, just padded back over to his desk with his bowed legs and sat down, waiting for me to explain why I was there.

Sharkey Pavanovish was an old customer of mine. I'd gotten him out of a bad situation when everyone assumed he was the Northshore Mangler because he was a sea troll. I was the only one who actually looked at the clues and figured out the son of the former lord mayor of Calasia was behind the gruesome crimes. That had cost me my job on the Calasia police force fifteen years ago, but it had won me Sharkey's friendship and the friendship of most of the nonhumans who worked the docks.

"You ain't been around for a while, Chase. 'Course, if the rumors are true and you're hanging out with Miss Blackthorne, I can understand why. I guarantee I never missed a night when she was performing—at either club. What a woman. Why she's hanging out with a loser like you, I'll never understand."

"I think she appreciates my sparkling wit and my boyish charms."

"The only thing buoyish about you would be if I tossed you in the water to see if you float."

"Why, Sharkey, and here I thought we were friends."

"All right, Chase, cut the small talk. You wouldn't climb up here for no reason. What's on your mind?"

I picked up a piece of kelp and tossed it out of the only guest chair before I sat down. "I need to know if someone might have booked passage out tomorrow. It would've been on the sly—too many people looking for her to go out on a regular passenger ship. Redhead, about twenty-five, carpenters would kill to use her as a model for a ship's figurehead. Might be known as Penny Fairbanks, but that's probably an alias. She'll be paying for passage with cash and probably paying extra to keep her presence off the manifest."

Sharkey leaned forward and put his elbows on the desk. "Hmm, sounds like I'd enjoy meeting her."

"You would as long as you kept her at arm's length and even then I wouldn't turn my back on her."

"Oooh, beautiful and treacherous. I might have to get involved personally, Chase. When do you need the information by?"

"I needed it yesterday, Sharkey, but if it's out there to be found, I know you'll find it."

Sharkey smiled, and even though I'd been his friend for years, the three rows of teeth still disquieted me. "For the usual fee."

I nodded. "If you can find out by tonight, I think it's safe to say there would be a bonus."

He leaned back in his chair and tucked his arms behind his head. "You must want this one really bad, Chase. Who'd she kill?"

"No one yet, Sharkey"—that I knew of anyway—"and I'd like

to ensure it stays that way. You might even be saving her life too."

"Now, that's a new one, Chase. Ain't never been no knight in shining armor before. I'll see what I can do. And, Chase . . . ?"

"Yeah?"

"Next time, use the trapdoor. I had them install spikes below the waterline around those pylons. I'd hate to have to explain to Kyra what happened if you slipped. She ain't the forgiving type."

I thought about the times I'd nearly taken a header on my climb up and swallowed hard. "Trapdoor, got it."

Sharkey's laughter followed me up the ladder.

K yra and Ze'eva showed up at the Garfield a little before nine. I knew it was a bit of a long shot, but I figured if I could get Penny to listen to me for a few moments, I could spin this tale right. Then it would just be a matter of waiting for her greed to take over.

It couldn't lose.

Luckily, I knew the house detective there, so Sweets Baker ran interference with the hotel staff for me. So, at ten o'clock exactly, I knocked on Penny Fairbanks's door. I waited a few minutes and then knocked again.

"Hey, Penny, it's me, Theron."

There was no answer. Sweets had assured me she'd gone in and no one else was in the room. Ze'eva and I had been watching things from our positions at either end of the hall while Kyra was outside, keeping an eye on the fire escape. There are advantages to being able to fly, after all.

Something felt wrong so I tried the door. It was unlocked. Now I really had a bad feeling. I pulled out my .45 and pushed the door open with the muzzle. I slipped in, moving to the side out of the doorway to give my eyes a chance to adjust to the low lighting.

Penny Fairbanks lay sprawled on the bed, eyes gazing life-lessly up at the slowly moving ceiling fan spinning overhead. I moved closer to examine her body without touching anything. There was no sign of a struggle, but it was obvious someone had been there before me because the room had been tossed. Her clothes were strewn around and her bags had been dumped out on the bed beside her.

I looked closer and noted there were no wounds—just a series of small round bruises circling her neck.

I was staring down at her when Lieutenant Jameson of the homicide detail came in. He gave the scene the once-over and then reached down and closed her eyes.

"Did you know her, Chase?"

"Met her last night; wanted to hire me for something. I was supposed to meet her here. Seems someone got here first."

"I spotted your partner lurking around. You two expecting trouble?"

"From the looks of this room, I'd say we should have been if we weren't."

Jameson ran a big meaty hand over his face and wiped the sweat off his forehead. It wasn't particularly hot in the room, but he wasn't used to exerting himself this late in the day either. He walked around the room carefully, noting the condition of Penny's luggage—how the linings had been ripped out, how her clothing showed signs of being turned inside out—and came back to stand in front of me.

"Chase, you didn't happen to pick up something before I came in, did you?"

"Like what, Lieutenant?"

"Dammit, Chase, don't go down that path already. You recognize a toss job as well as I do. Someone wanted something your 'client' had and either they got it or they didn't. Either way, they left you to get blamed for this. If I didn't know you so well, you'd be at the station right now booked on suspicion of murder."

"Which would be stupid. What's my motive for killing my own client?"

"Calm down, Chase. I said I'm pretty sure you didn't do this. However, if you know someone else who might have a motive or maybe an idea what this person could have been looking for, I'd appreciate you sharing."

"Jameson, I can tell you she either had or knew of the location of a strand of pearls a whole lot of people want. I also know she's the latest person who's died because of that knowledge. Captain Corvinus has already met one of the victims. What I can't tell you is who is doing the killings because I don't know yet. Nor do I have a clue how it's being done. As soon as I know something, I'll let you know."

"You can't tell me who else might be involved?"

"Look, Jameson, my clients are confidential until they're no longer my clients or they turn up like her. I don't want to name people who might not be involved without more clues than you or I have to go on here. I can't even blame the ones I think might. You're going to have to trust me on this one."

"You're really trying to get me hauled in front of the chief, aren't you?"

I patted him on the shoulder. "Thanks, Lieutenant, you're a pip. Hey, wait a moment. Why are you here anyway? I found her a few minutes before you walked in. I hadn't had a chance to report this yet."

"We got a tip about a body in this room. Kind of a weird accent, but nothing you could pin down. Didn't stay on the line long enough for us to put a trace on it."

Somehow, that didn't surprise me. However, it made me begin to wonder about the whole curse thing. Evil spirits normally didn't report their kills to the local constabulary. I spent some time visiting with Jameson and then left the room while he sealed it for the lab boys. I knew I could check in with Maxie down at the city morgue if I wanted to see the body later. He owes me a few favors and he's got a big crush on Ze'eva.

Still the more I thought about it, things seemed too pat. I gathered up Ze'eva and Kyra and we sat down in the hotel bar talking about what had happened. The waitress brought a round of drinks for everyone and Sweets Baker came over to join us a short time later.

"Say, Chase, that's a strange set of events that went on upstairs. But, I'm telling you, no one went in or out of that room before you all got here. I tried to listen in while Jameson was talking to the lab team, but he chased me off before I could hear anything interesting."

"Thanks, Sweets. I appreciate everything you did for us. This one's going to take a bit to figure out."

"Well, if anyone can figure it out, Chase, it'd be you. Well, I'm going to go make my rounds. If you're still here when I get back, I'll buy the next round."

We waited until he'd left before turning our attention back to the case. "Ze'eva, either tonight or first thing tomorrow, try to talk with Sweets and find out everything he knew about Penny—who she saw, when she came in and out, anyone who might have left her a message, any phone calls she placed through the switchboard. We lost our only real lead to the pearls, so we're going to have to do this the old-fashioned way."

Ze'eva looked up from her pad of paper and stared out over the bar patrons. It was a light crowd, but this wasn't one of your ritzy hotels either. "Theron, do you think someone already has the pearls?"

"If they do, they got them from someone else. Penny may have been many things, but stupid wasn't one of them. She must have known she was being watched. I'm convinced she believed as long as she didn't actually possess the pearls, no one would kill her."

"Unfortunately, that didn't work too well," Krya said, leaning forward over the small table we were sitting at. "What are you going to do now, boss man?"

"I'm not sure. Penny's death could mean a couple of things: either whoever killed her already has the pearls, in which case we'll probably never see them again; or, they think they know who has them, which meant Penny became expendable."

Ze'eva noted the change in my voice. "So, you don't think this has anything to do with the curse?"

"Not on your life. I'm not a big believer in curses to begin with, but this one's a bit too pat. No, I think when all is said and done, Penny's murder has a very mortal agent involved. Last time I checked, cursed pearls don't rip open suitcases or rifle drawers. I'm pretty sure Jameson's boys will come to the same conclusion too. Which is why I need to get on the street before they grab me for a bunch of useless questioning."

We finished our drinks and I excused myself. I told Kyra I might not be by the office tomorrow. There was no mistaking the questions on Kyra's face and the concern on Ze'eva's, but I smiled and disappeared into the night as quickly as possible.

See, I didn't want to mention there was another option that would have made Penny expendable. If someone saw us together last night, there was a good possibility they might think I had the pearls. That would mean someone likely was watching us, trying to figure out who might have the pearls now. The only way to take the heat off of Ze'eva and Kyra would be to make myself the clay pigeon and see who showed up to take a shot.

I spent the next few hours dropping in at several watering holes where I have a friend or two. Some were uptown, some were downtown, and a few were even below downtown. I made sure to position myself where I could watch the doors and windows, but no one seemed to be tailing me. So, either that meant I was being paranoid and no one was actually interested in me, or whoever was following me was a real pro, which made me even more paranoid.

Three in the morning found me down near the docks, so I decided it was time to go visit the one place I was reasonably sure I'd be safe. Soon enough, I was sitting down in Sharkey's room under the Grinning Shark, lifting a glass of blood ale with my host.

"Really, Chase. I know it had been a while since we last hung out, but two visits in one day? It must be my birthday or you're really in trouble."

"A bit of both, Sharkey. Let's say your place here is probably the safest spot in Calasia right now."

"Wow, you must be really worried about whoever's after you. It ain't like you to take it on the lam, Chase."

"I'm hoping it's only for the night. However, when someone I'm supposed to meet gets strangled in their room but no one is seen going in or out, well, let's say I don't think my old apartment is that secure."

"And since you know this room is lined with a magic-resistant wood, it's not likely someone's going to apparate through the walls and attack you in your sleep."

"Well, you gotta admit, it helps."

"Fine, Chase, you can spend the night. The john's through that door over there. My room is through the other door. You can sleep out here. But, if you're a snorer, you're likely to get tossed out the window if I can't get any sleep."

With that cheery thought, Sharkey let himself out and I stretched out on his couch. Just before I passed out, he stuck his big head into the room. "Oh, I got something you might find interesting. If you're still alive in the morning, it's in the manila envelope on my desk marked Chase. Sweet dreams."

S harkey had been right; what he had found out was interesting. So, the morning light found me standing at the base of a gangplank leading up to a tramp freighter. I looked it over from dockside and marveled that water would support that much rust. It looked like if you even waved a paintbrush at the tub, it would fall apart from the breeze. Still, since it was there and obviously not sinking before my eyes, I decided to wait until someone on the deck noticed me.

After about fifteen minutes, one of the crew came out on the deck to relieve himself over the side. I politely waited until he was finished before requesting permission to come aboard. I wasn't sure what shocked him the most: the fact I was there or the fact I said something before walking up the gangplank. There was a small rustling as people relayed my request and then a deep voice told me to come aboard.

Reaching the main deck, I came to one conclusion: if I were going to cast a pirate movie, I would have hired every one of these guys and still been accused of being stereotypical. About all they lacked were a few peg legs and hooks for hands, otherwise, they would have been dead ringers for the latest Redbeard the Pirate movie. Most stood by watching and I was beginning to wonder if I was being sized up for the latest crew member when the first mate appeared and led me below to the captain's quarters.

The captain was a huge man with dark eyes and beard and hair to match. He gave me a once-over and pointed toward a chair in front of his desk. I sat down. For a big man, he moved quickly and noiselessly as he sat down behind the large wooden desk. He reached into a drawer and pulled out a bottle of alcohol. I didn't ask what it was and he didn't volunteer any information either, but if I ever need paint remover, I'm getting myself a bottle. I wheezed a few times and when the world stopped spinning, he grinned and spoke up.

"So, what can I do for you . . . ?"

"Chase. Theron Chase. I'm a private detective here in town and I've got a few questions about some supercargo you're supposed to be carrying today."

He leaned back in his chair and casually put his hands behind his head. I pretended not to notice the small knife handle sticking up out of a neck sheath back there. "Do you now? And how do you know about my supercargo?"

"Mutual friends of mutual friends. However, I do hope she paid you up front."

"Only way I work. Why?"

I leaned back in my chair and politely declined a top-off of that engine acid. "She isn't going to be leaving town anytime soon."

"Pity. She in jail?"

"She's dead. Murdered last night."

The only emotion the captain showed was to shake his head. "Now, that's a real pity. She was a fine-looking woman."

I lifted my glass to salute that comment. I took another sip, immediately regretted it, and pushed on. "However, there are a couple of questions I'd love to get an answer to before you set sail. Let's say it might help me catch whoever did it to her."

"And why would I care?"

It was my turn to shake my head. "I doubt you would, especially if she already paid you. However, you can tell me and I can conveniently forget I stopped by until you're under sail and gone. That's one option."

For a moment, the only sound in the cabin was the muffled sound from the docks coming through the small porthole nearby. The captain's face took on a nasty expression and it was obvious he didn't like being backed into a corner. "You act like there's another one. The only other one I can think of is you simply not getting off this ship until we're well past the breakwater."

I sat my glass back down on his desk as if I hadn't a care in the world. "You know, Captain, I suspected you might take that attitude. If you would, have one of your people take a look at the warehouse down the pier from where you're moored. I think he'll see someone wearing a peacoat and a white hat."

I let that sink in for a moment and then continued as if we were talking in my office rather than his. "If I don't leave this freighter in thirty minutes, he'll contact the Coast Guard and hand them the same information that led me to you. Now, you and I both know the Calasian constables aren't real efficient nor are they inclined to hurry, but the Coast Guard is. They'd probably have your ship impounded before you could even build up steam. Why, it might be months before you sail again. I suspect your cargo is due wherever it's going long before then."

The captain sent for one of his sailors and whispered in his ear. The guy shot out of the room like his tail was on fire. A few minutes later, he was back and his nod told the captain I hadn't been kidding. His face turned red and I knew he was imagining stretching my guts all over his engine room. After a few moments, he calmed down and fixed a phony smile back on his face. "All right, smart guy. What are your questions?"

"Where were you taking her?"

"Bear Island, just off of the coast of Pyang-yan."

"Bear Island? I've heard about it, but why would she want to go there?"

He leaned forward and placed his elbows on the desk. "The island used to belong to the Empire of Xianton but it was conquered about a hundred years ago by the Kingdom of Albion. Now it's a trading colony. If an item can be bought anywhere in this world, it can be bought in the markets of Bear Island. That's about all I know about that. She didn't volunteer why she was going there and I didn't ask. You said you had questions, so what else is on your mind?"

"Did she have any cargo of her own here? After all, if she's dead, there's no sense in shipping it now. I mean, you've already gotten paid. You can fill the spot with more cargo and double dip."

The captain let out the first honest chuckle since we'd started talking. "You're part pirate yourself, ain't you, Detective? All right, come on. She left two boxes here. You're welcome to them, but if you want help getting them off of my ship, that'll cost you. Dockworker's Union rules, don'cha know."

Two hours later, I was back at my office with the two boxes belonging to the late Penny Fairbanks. I asked Kyra to give me a hand going through the possessions. Not that I was uncomfortable about going through a dead girl's belongings, but being a Sylph, Kyra has the ability to spot magic auras. I didn't want to set off any traps, intentionally placed or otherwise. There was already a set of cursed pearls floating around. The gods knew what else might be lurking around the corner in this case.

The larger of the two boxes contained what must have been her worldly possessions—clothes, unmentionables, shoes, fake jewelry, two wigs, and a book about the Walikamba Islands. Kyra informed me the majority of the stuff was fashionable, but most of it was knockoffs of more expensive brands; based on the tags, it had been bought on Bear Island earlier this year. Neither of the wigs really seemed to be the kind of things Penny might have worn, but by the time we got to the bottom of the box, we were encountering more mundane articles and even some men's clothing.

"I think she was worried about something," Kyra said, holding up the short black wig.

"I think she was right to be worried."

"No, Theron. Look at this wig. Imagine her with no makeup on, this wig, and those men's clothes. With the right chest wrap, she could probably pass for a young man, especially at night or at a distance. This wasn't just a disguise, this was an escape plan."

"But, escaping from whom?"

Kyra gave me an exasperated look. "If we knew that, we'd be collecting the reward for solving this case, now wouldn't we?"

"Yes, Mother. Should we open the other one?"

Kyra picked it up—a box no bigger than her palm—with her fingertips and examined it carefully. After a few moments, she sat it down on my desk, but she was frowning.

"There's nothing magical about the box or its contents, Theron, but I didn't like holding it at all. There's something odd about the contents."

"You don't think the pearls are there?"

"No. No, that's not it." She paced around the office for a bit and I let her work out whatever was nagging at her. I learned a long time ago not to ignore Kyra's hunches. They're another reason she's worth a lot more to me as my secretary than I can afford to pay her. She's steered more than her fair share of crazies and people with mayhem on their mind out of the office before they could reach the inner rooms.

Finally she stopped and put her finger on the box. "Be careful."

I approached the box lying on my desk as if I was getting ready to do battle with a cobra. I stared at it and then slipped a long-bladed letter opener out of my desk drawer and plucked away at the strings holding the box closed. Once I had loosened them all, I eased the tip of the letter opener under the lip of the lid and lifted it gently. The box lid refused to budge for a bit, but after some coaxing I was able to exert enough pressure on it to get it moving. A few seconds later, I saw daylight under the edge of the lid and then eased it over to the side. The lid slipped off of the tip of the letter opener and clattered to the top of the desk, sending Kyra and me skittering away. When nothing blew up, no evil beings appeared, and my landlord failed to materialize with my eviction notice, I decided it was safe enough to take a look inside.

The box contained a small velvet bag held closed by a leather drawstring. It was surprisingly heavy when I lifted it out of the box. I eased it onto my desk and used the letter opener to pluck at the leather cord until it came loose and then worked the bag open. When nothing crawled out, I picked it up by one corner and, using the letter opener yet again, pushed the object out onto my desk without touching it.

An iron key fell out of the bag and lay there on my ink blotter. I started to pick it up but stopped before my fingers touched it. Even my all-too-mortal senses could feel something was wrong about this key.

Kyra motioned for me to back away and then held her hand over the key, her eyes closed in concentration. After a few moments she turned to face me. "No, there's no magic on the key or the bag. Still, something's wrong. I can't tell you what, but there is something odd about it."

"That's not very specific, Kyra."

She narrowed her eyes at me. I've seen that look before and knew she was as frustrated about not being able to identify the source of her concern as I was. "If I knew more, Theron, I'd tell you. I get a bad feeling. It's like something's telling me you don't want to find whatever this key opens."

I was about to ask her more, but as I opened my mouth to speak, a loud pounding came from the other room. It sounded like the outer door was trying to come off its hinges. Krya went to see who was there and to stall them while I slipped the key back into its pouch and box and then tossed them both into the wall safe. There was no mistaking the booming voice echoing through the room once Kyra opened the door.

"Where's Chase? I need to talk to him right now."

I spun the dial on my safe and put the picture back over it before I stepped toward the connecting door. "Let him in, Kyra. I need to speak to the good captain too." I motioned for the huge man to follow me into my inner office. Kyra followed him to the door and I could see the concern on her face as he pushed past me and walked directly to my desk. I signaled to her to try and contact Ze'eva and then shut the door behind me.

Captain Horace Grantland smacked a fist down on the desk and bellowed. "Dammit, Chase, what the hell have you been doing on this case? I told you I'd meet you at the hotel and you never showed. Then the hotel is swarmed with cops and I have to move somewhere else. Then I don't hear from you for a couple of days. I tell you, I'm beginning to think you're not taking this case seriously. Do you want my money or not?"

I pulled a bottle of my better scotch from my desk drawer and poured him a drink. Capping the bottle, I sat it down between us. I made sure my drawer was left open and my spare pistol could be reached with a minimum of movement before I responded.

"It seems we had a bit of a miscommunication, Captain. You see, I went to the address you provided me at the appointed time. I didn't find *you* in the room, Captain, but I *did* find a fresh corpse. Even more mysterious was the fact the corpse was a Walikamba Islander with the prettiest set of black dots around his neck. The police can't say he was strangled, but they can't say he wasn't either. They're quite confused, but what they're not confused about is the fact I was the first person spotted with the corpse. They'd like some answers and soon. So, you see, I'm *very* interested in this case."

Grantland looked confused at first and then a look of realization swept over his face. "Torombo Inohuaye's dead? But he was alive when I stepped out to get us some food. When you didn't show, I thought you'd stiffed us. I knew he was missing but I didn't know he was dead."

"That's what the unfortunate gentleman's identification read. Judging from how he died, I'd say he had gotten his hands on those cursed pearls while you were out. But don't worry, he's probably not going to be the last person to end up like that—unless I get my hands on those pearls and soon."

Grantland slumped forward and lifted a hand to his forehead. "Torombo was my contact. He'd located someone willing to buy the pearls, no questions asked. He was prepared to handle the entire transaction for a percentage of the take."

"Well, it's possible he may have been working a little action on the side. He may have tracked them down himself. It almost sounds like he was trying to cut a deal with someone without cutting you in."

"That bloody heathen. I should have known better than to trust one of those island devils. They're all too afraid of those damn witch doctors to keep a promise to an outsider."

"Speaking of not trusting people, I've met two other individuals who've pressed a claim for those pearls. Everyone is convincing they were the actual owners too. So, refresh my memory, Captain. Why should I believe you're the rightful owner in the face of all the competing claims?"

The huge ogre of a man leaned back in his chair and laughed. "Ah, I knew I made a good choice when I sought you out. You know I don't have any proof. None of us do, because there ain't no rightful owner, lessen you want to talk to the oyster where those pearls were born. Everyone wants them, but even the person who harvested them from the deep was doing so illegally. Ain't no one supposed to have Walikamba black pearls, not even people from Walikamba. They're supposed to be turned over to be destroyed as soon as they're found. So, ownership tends to belong to whoever is the last one standing."

"I suspected as much as soon as Major Fielder made an appearance."

Grantland's face paled for a second and then he tried to bluster past his momentary slip. "That sea dog is involved in this too? I should have known. If there's money to be made and you don't mind getting your hands a little dirty, then Fielder is your man. Him and that man-mountain he calls a servant."

"By the way, there's something I probably need to settle before we go too much further, Captain. If you recall, I never officially took you on as a client."

"By the gods, you're right, Chase. I plumb forgot after we didn't meet that night. Let's see, how much do I owe you up front?"

"Well, that depends. I don't normally take on people who don't tell me the truth. And, if you are telling me the truth, I can't sign a contract with you. Because, you see, the courts are as open-minded as the next person, but I've got it on good authority you can't enforce a contract on a ghost."

"Now, wait a minute, Chase, what the hell are you talking about?"

"Why, my good Captain Horace Grantland, you died about ten years ago. I've talked to the cop who fished you out of North Bay and I've been to your gravesite. I'm no expert on graves, but I doubt it's been disturbed since that day. So either you're a ghost or you're not Captain Grantland. Either way, I can't see how I could ever work for you."

The man seemed to deflate a bit and then a low chuckle erupted from his weathered face. He glanced over at me and then probably the first honest smile I saw from him split his face. "All right, Chase, you got me. I ain't Horace. I'm Tobias Grantland. Horace and me were twins but we were separated a long time ago. He learned sailing from our dad. I lived with

Mom down near Iron Mountain most of my life. I didn't even know I had a brother until Mom died and left me a way to find him. I only met him a month before he died."

Grantland looked out the window and then back at me before he continued. "So, when I heard about his accident, I decided to take his place and see if I could find his murderer. His first mate covered for me until I learned how to be a ship's captain and we've been working together this past decade to try and learn the truth about how he died. It's taken quite a while to get this close, which is why I needed your help."

"You could have told me this up front. It doesn't matter to me if you're Horace, Tobias, or really named Jenny. I just hate feeling like a patsy."

"Can't say I blame you, Chase, but I had to be sure about you. Too many people'd like to see me dead—mostly for stuff Horace done. He was a mean son of a bitch, ain't no denying it, but when I took his place, I took his troubles too. No, I need to find who killed him first. If I find the pearls and if I survive long enough to sell them, that's gravy on my biscuits."

I topped off his glass again. "So, I can believe this story . . .?"

"Hell, no, Chase. I ain't asking you to believe nothin'. I mean, it's the truth, but I got no proof. I destroyed any papers tying me to Tobias Grantland. For all purposes, I *am* Horace Grantland."

"In that case, I think you need to leave your retainer with Miss Sylvari on your way out. I've got work to do."

The big man paused and took another shot of scotch before continuing. "To be honest, I never thought you'd figure it out this quickly."

"Call it blind luck, if you want. If I hadn't bumped into a friend of mine on the force who's been covering the docks for most of his career, I might never have tumbled to the truth. I'll take you on as a client, but if I discover you haven't been straight with me, I'll drop you like a hot potato and ensure the maritime authorities know who you really are. I suspect you enjoy being a captain, so let's ensure nothing happens to your license."

"You play hardball, Chase, but I can respect that. Your neck's on the line too."

That caught me off guard. "And what does that mean?"

The ogre leaned back and lifted his glass of scotch to me. "Why, rumors are going around the dock that you've taken quite an interest in the affairs of Penny Fairbanks. Said you were the last one seen with her before she met an unfortunate accident. Why, it's even been hinted at you might be in possession of her personal effects. You know she was rumored to be the last person who had those pearls. Some might begin to think you're holding them for yourself. Now, I know you're too honest for that, but some might not trust you like I do. I'd be sure to sleep with your doors locked, if I were you."

With that, he got up from the chair and, still chuckling to himself, made his way to the door. He left, but a second later, he stuck his head back through the door. "I'm staying at the Black Castle Hotel in the Downtown area. Just ask for me at the desk. They'll know who I am. Hope to hear from you soon, Chase. I certainly do."

Z e'eva showed up about an hour after Captain Grantland had departed. I gave her a thumbnail recap and watched her reaction. "How long had you known Captain Grantland wasn't who he said he was?"

"I suspected it as soon as Mortiva said something, but I wasn't sure until he was sitting in front of me today. I made up the whole thing about going to the grave site, but he didn't even try to argue. So, I decided to bluff and managed to draw to my inside straight."

"And what if he had decided to protect his secret? You took a big chance without me there."

"Darling, that's one of the reasons I love you. You're the only person who'd worry about me doing something like that. I've been playing poker with clients for years before we met. That's also why I have several weapons secreted around this office— just in case a client decides to get frisky."

"Most of your former clients couldn't rip your arm off and beat you with it."

"I seem to remember a certain young female client who needed a detective to take a chance on her too. I came out of that one in fairly good shape."

"After several weeks in the hospital and several months of R&R afterward."

"Details, details. However, I'm still not certain about something. The desk clerk identified Inohuaye as Captain Grantland. So, did he check in *for* Grantland or *as* him, and why? Did Grantland think someone might be gunning for him? Considering how we found Inohuaye, I think he was right to do so, but still, why send me there without telling me who I'd find?"

"So, you don't trust him yet?"

I laughed before responding. "I don't trust *any* of the people involved with this case. I barely trust Sharkey and he's not even involved other than tracking down information for me. None of our clients are who they appear to be and that includes the major."

A soft, almost polite knock on the outer office door stopped our conversation. I heard Kyra's heels clicking across the floor and then a murmur of conversation. I heard the door shut and then Kyra approaching the connecting door.

"Theron, a Xian Daisong here to see you."

"Did he have an appointment?"

"No, but I think you probably should talk to him. Apparently he represents a client from Bear Island."

I gave Ze'eva a signal and then made certain my voice was all sweetness and light. "Then please show Mr. Daisong in."

Kyra escorted an elderly gentleman into the room. His hair, mustache, and beard were white, but he moved with the grace of a much younger man. From the way he placed his weight on his feet as he walked, I had a strong feeling Mr. Daisong had been a practitioner of martial arts for a long time. I tapped my fingers in a prearranged code to let Ze'eva know not to take our newest customer lightly. Her return tap let me know she had figured it out on her own, but thanks.

"Welcome to our office, Mr. Daisong. How may we be of assistance today?"

The gentleman declined my offer to sit down and merely bowed his head slightly to Ze'eva first and then to me. "I understand you have acquired the estate of the late Miss Fairbanks."

"Well, I've removed possessions of hers from a tramp steamer. Whether or not they belong to her estate is another question altogether."

"Be that as it may, the items from the steamer are of interest to my client and me. You see, Miss Fairbanks was operating as my agent. While her death is most regrettable, her obligation was not discharged by her passing. As our agent, her goods rightfully belong to us. We would like to acquire them with a minimum amount of fuss."

I leaned forward, putting my fingers in front of my face in an inverted V to hide my expression from our guest. I was hoping Ze' would be able to see me clearly. "I sympathize with your position, Mr. Daisong. If you have the proper papers to claim these items, I'll turn them over to you. However, the Calasian constables have an interest in them also since Miss Fairbanks was a murder victim. I'm sure you understand I cannot turn them over to you based on nothing more than your say-so."

While his features remained placid, there was no mistaking the threat in his voice. "You are refusing my request?"

"I am refusing to hand over possible evidence of a crime to someone who appears at my office without something to validate their right to the items. After all, I'm in no hurry to go to jail for tampering with evidence."

"Yet, you have not turned the items over to the local constabulary either. Therefore, are you not also tampering with evidence?"

I sighed dramatically before responding. "Such is the life of a private investigator, Mr. Daisong. However, I've compiled a complete inventory in front of witnesses and can produce the list should I have to appear in court. The constables are en route to retrieve these items as we speak. Therefore, again I must ask to see your written authorization to remove these items. I'm sure that if Miss Fairbanks was in your employ, you have some documentation."

The old man looked at me, then at Ze'eva, and then back at me with an incredulous look on his face. "Mr. Chase, may I ask you bluntly—did you ever actually meet Miss Fairbanks?"

"Yes. She came to this office one evening and then my partner, Miss Blackthorne, and I arrived at her apartment right after her death. It was a short acquaintance, but I have a feel for her personality."

"Then you should know she was not the type of person to sign anything. She worked in a shadowy world, Mr. Chase—one where a person collects powerful enemies, whether one wants to or not." He drew himself up erect and I could feel his dark eyes boring into mine. "In fact, Mr. Chase, it is considered quite unwise to make enemies when one does not have to. It is for that reason I have approached you directly rather than sending people to relieve you of those items. So, for the last time, will you give me her possessions?"

I saw Ze'eva tense up, but I smiled and motioned for her to

remain still. "Mr. Daisong, I'm afraid you've given me no reason to believe you're here acting as the executor of her estate. I agree Miss Fairbanks was unlikely to have signed anything with her real name. I also know the laws of Calasia are pretty clear. You're asking me to go to jail and possibly lose my license simply on your say-so. In fact, outside of the card you gave my secretary, I can't prove who you are or whether you had any relationship with Miss Fairbanks at all."

I stood up and walked over to the window, resting my hands on the windowsill. As I had suspected, a long, dark limousine sat at the curb with two men leaning against it. Along the street outside, four other men lounged about in strategic positions. I turned back to him and put on my most disarming smile.

"However, I'm not an unreasonable man. If you'll provide me with a way to reach you, and after I verify your connection with her—and if the police don't object—I'll be happy to bring Miss Fairbanks's possessions to you."

Mr. Daisong bowed his head toward me. "You play a dangerous game, Mr. Chase, but you play it well. I am staying at the Royal Lion in North Point. I will remain in this town for one week. Even allowing for the notorious inefficiency of the Calasian constables, it should give you plenty of time to clear her items and also investigate me. You will find I am involved in the import/export business and I truly am from Bear Island. Please do not mistake my politeness for weakness, Mr. Chase. Others have done so to their regret."

"Mr. Daisong, underestimating you is the last thing I intend to do."

He walked toward the door, pausing only to bow to Ze'eva and then me. "Then we understand each other perfectly, because I do not underestimate you either. Good day."

We both waited until he had exited the outer office and his footsteps had disappeared down the stairs before either of us relaxed. I returned to the window, but this time, I positioned myself where I couldn't be seen from the street. He emerged from the building and, without a backward glance, got into that impressive limousine which merged into the afternoon traffic. The goons were gone, but I didn't believe they'd gone far. I pulled down the blinds in my office and stepped over to the safe. I withdrew the small sack from inside and tucked it into my jacket's inside pocket.

"Ze'eva, remember the exit down in the basement?"

She scrunched up her nose. "It's not something I'm likely to forget. We haven't had a good rainstorm in quite a while, Theron. It's likely to be a bit ripe down there."

I grabbed my coat and hat and grabbed a spare pistol and ammunition. "Get whatever you need and meet me down there." I went out into the main office and pulled down the shades there too. "Kyra, we're taking off. Give us a half hour, gather up anything irreplaceable and then take off yourself. Go to Theo's, tell him the situation and then ask him to find you a safe spot. I'll have him let you know where we wind up."

"Theron, you've never let someone chase you out of your office before."

I stopped directly in front of her to be certain she understood the gravity of the situation. "Kyra, I suspect Mr. Daisong was the polite face of a much uglier organization. If everything goes the way I think it will, this office will be tossed tonight. They're not going to care who or what gets mangled when they don't find what they're looking for. So, while our insurance agent won't like replacing furniture and such, better that than them finding us here."

From the look on her face, I decided I never wanted to get on her bad side. "Don't worry, Theron. I've got a few favors owed me. I'll make sure no one messes with the office."

I wasn't happy and I'm sure it showed on my face, because she put a hand on my arm. "Listen, boss, my friends won't do anything if they come in and search. They'll only intervene if they try to do permanent damage. You've met some of my cousins before and they have friends who're even bigger. Not all of the fey are petite like me, after all. They'll keep an eye on the place."

"All right, but don't take chances. I don't want anyone getting hurt on my account—fey *or* human."

Kyra pulled on my tie to make me bend over and kissed me on the cheek. "See, that's why I love working for you, boss. Now, get Ze'eva and get out of here. I'll make it look like you're still around as long as I can."

Ze'eva came out of the main office. "I stuck a bunch of stuff in the hidden bedroom and locked it. It may not be perfect, but it'll take them a while to find anything back there. So, what's the plan?"

"I'm thinking we visit Mama Belltre and then we set up shop at a spare office I had down near Southport. I haven't used it in quite a while, but Joe owes me a big favor, so he keeps it available for times like this."

"Joe?"

"Yeah, just Joe. Don't worry, you'll like him."

Ze'eva went to the front door and glanced out through the window to the stairwells. Over her shoulder I heard her mutter, "I've heard that before, Chase."

I checked my pistols one more time and then joined her. "All right, let's go."

―――――――――

No one seemed to be hidden in the building and a few minutes later, outside of an amazing smell, we were alone in the sewer system running beneath Calasia. Following the maze of connecting tunnels and walkways, we made much better time crossing the city than we would have above ground. No one seemed to notice us except for a small colony of man-sized rats. However, instead of threatening us, they bowed respectfully to Ze'eva and withdrew farther back into the darkness. I got along with most of the ratmen, but there's nothing like having a werewolf accompany you to ensure you're left alone.

After about an hour's walk, we emerged in Mama Belltre's back room. Apparently a large shipment had recently arrived since the back room was filled with boxes and unpacked crates. I moved some stuff around to make enough room for Ze'eva and me to rest and then I let Ze'eva go get Mama's attention. I heard some talking going on up front and then Mama called out a name I didn't recognize, telling her to watch the shop while she did something in the back. Mama pushed her bulk into the back room and made a beeline for me, her dark eyes boring straight into me.

"All right, Chase, what's going on? You've never come to the shop this way before. You're in serious trouble this time, aren't you?"

"And it's good to see you too, Mama. Ze'eva and I are doing fine, no we're not married yet, and business has been keeping us busy. How're things here?"

"Don't pull that crap on me, Theron. You're in over your head again and this time you're dragging this beautiful woman into it." She turned to Ze'eva with an evil smile. "Honey, you say the word and I'll turn him into a frog or a newt for you. I think it would improve his looks, honestly."

"Hey!"

Ze'eva suppressed a giggle before answering Mama. "No, he's been treating me well. We're in the middle of a tough case and a new player showed up—one apparently backed with a lot of muscle. Theron and I are merely relocating until we can get momentum back on our side."

"Humph. He's probably hiding from a bill collector. I would

have said a jealous girlfriend, but even he's not stupid enough to cheat on you, honey. Still, what do you need?"

"We could have simply come by to say, 'Hi', Mama. After all, it's been a while," I said, setting down on a box and stretching out my legs.

"Hey, get off that! That's expensive stuff. Here, let me get you a couple of chairs." She bellowed at me before stomping off up the stairs leading to her apartment on the next floor. A few minutes later, she came chugging through the back room with a couple of chairs—only one had a cushion I noted—and she set them down for us.

"Look, Theron, I love you like a son, but don't try to pull the wool over my eyes. I can count the number of times you've come by to visit on one hand. You come here because you're in trouble. Thankfully, your lovely secretary makes sure I get paid reasonably on time or I'd toss you right back down that trap-door into the sewers."

"All right, Mama, you're right. We need your help."

Mama Belltre's face hardened. "You're really in trouble if you don't want to banter, Theron. What's the matter?"

I laid out the events of the past few days, right up to our visit from Mr. Daisong. She nodded at the mention of his name and sat down on a box. "So, you had a visit from one of the Four Winds. Yes, you are in a bit of a pickle, Theron. It's going to take some doing to extract yourself, especially since I know you have no intention of giving them what they want."

"The Four Winds?" Ze'eva asked, glancing from Mama Belltre to me and back.

"The Four Winds of the Storm, the guild leaders of the largest group of criminals associated with Bear Island and Pyang-yan. Xian Daisong is the West Wind and his particular section of the Storm focuses on acquiring items and selling them. Their interests run from weapon smuggling to industrial espionage to petty theft. If there's a crown to be made, they're involved. I don't know if they're representing someone or involved for their own interests, but if Xian Daisong made a personal appearance, it's not something they're taking lightly."

Ze'eva glanced nervously over Mama Belltre's shoulder. "There was no doubt in my mind he was not a man to be ignored. Unfortunately, the next full moon isn't for six days. Every instinct in my body told me not to let him leave that office alive."

I smiled at her. "Lucky then for both of us you're still not able to change. If he put in a personal appearance you can be certain he had both physical and magical protection. He was too confident. He never would've walked into our office if he wasn't absolutely certain he could walk out, also."

Mama Belltre nodded slowly. "You can count on that, Ze'eva. He did not rise to the head of a crime family by taking unnecessary chances. He is a schemer of the highest degree. Theron here might give him a run for his money, except for one thing."

"What's that?" Ze'eva asked.

"Theron's got a conscience; Daisong doesn't. If he thought it would improve his odds, he'd have simply burned down the entire office building and killed everyone in it to be certain he got you two. Theron's a good man. He'll do everything he can to accomplish his task without hurting people. That means he'll hesitate; Daisong won't. Keep that in mind if you face him again."

Ze'eva looked even more worried, but she kept her voice steady when she spoke. "So, Theron, what's the plan?"

I patted her on the hand to try and reassure her before I answered. "We have three things we need to do. We need to locate the pearls, preferably first. Then we need to figure out who's leaving the trail of bodies around Calasia—the gods know we've got plenty of suspects for that. And third, we need to decide what to do with the pearls. We're going to have to turn them over to someone, but whether we turn them over to an individual, the Calasian constables, Theo, Xian Daisong, or whomever Penny Fairbanks was working with to sell the pearls in Bear Island."

"Is that the order?"

"Not necessarily, Ze'. I think if we can discover who Penny was going to turn the pearls over to, it may answer quite a few questions. Daisong may have been the ultimate buyer or he might be trying to intercept the pearls, but only the middleman would know for certain. Besides, we can see if one of our other candidates for the murderer has been in contact with this person."

Mama Belltre leaned back against a crate and looked at us like we'd both lost our minds. "Do you have a clue who this middleman might be?"

I took a deep breath and let it out slowly. "Not at the moment. I'll bet Sharkey can find out for me though. I have a feeling this person is down at the docks, although whether the north, east, or south ones, I'm not sure. Everything that's happened up to this point has led to the docks or the sea. Between finding the body of the first Captain Grantland, to Penny's ship, to the islander in the captain's room, to the pearls themselves, this affair will be solved the closer we get to water."

There was a moment of silence and then Mama slowly climbed to her feet. "If you're going to continue on this foolhardy adventure, Theron, you'll need a little help. Wait a moment." With that, she glided through the cluttered room like it was an open field and then disappeared through a door I could barely make out behind a pile of boxes.

Ze'eva's eyes followed Mama's disappearing form and then turned back to meet mine. "So, should we split up to cover more ground?"

"I think we're better off sticking together. Do you have any weapons on you?"

She reached into her purse and came out with a small automatic and a sheathed dagger. She sat the pistol on a crate and then pulled the dagger partway out. I could see blue light and smelled ozone coming from the blade. She smiled at my confusion. "Theo gave it to me the last time we were there. He thought it might come in handy one of these days."

"I've known Theo for twelve years. He's never offered me a lightning blade before."

"He didn't think you'd need it. Besides, you've said yourself magic and you don't exactly get along. Theo figured you'd wind up shocking yourself at an inopportune time."

I glanced at the dagger nervously and brought my hands together, hinting for her to close it. "He's probably right. I hope we're not going to need them, but it's better to have and not need . . ."

". . . than need and not have. Yes, I've heard that song before too. I think I've performed it on stage."

"You did. I was lying in the rafters above you that show."

"Do you have any idea how creepy that sounds, Theron?" Mama Belltre's voice rang out as she re-entered the back room. "I'm telling you, Ze'eva, that boy just ain't right. Musta been dropped on his head a lot as a child."

Ze'eva giggled and I did my best to look offended, but Mama didn't even look at me as she pushed her way in-between us and set a small tray on the nearest box. She put a meaty hand down on the tray and pushed one small pile toward me and the rest toward Ze'eva. While we examined the items, she stepped back and I swear I saw the slightest blush on her cheeks.

"Ain't much, but you both know I'm no wizard. I know a few tricks and some spells, but I think this here might be useful. Those amulets there should protect you against most tracking spells for twenty-four hours. Those vials can be used to hide your scent if they hire some rat people to track you down." She turned toward Ze'eva. "Ratfolk got the sharpest noses in the business. Put a canine to shame."

"No offense taken, Mama."

Mama pointed to the small caltrops on the tray. "If you think you're being followed, prick your finger with one of those and then throw it. It'll not only carry your scent, but they'll animate and keep moving for an hour. At the end of an hour, or if they're picked up, they'll burst and send a shower of caltrops all around whoever picks them up. Won't kill them, but it'll make it damn difficult to leave the area."

"These are fantastic, Mama. But, aren't you worried Theron's jinx won't do something to them?"

"Don't you worry your pretty head none, Ze'eva. Theron's jinx, as you like to put it, only seems to work around big magic. Me? I'm a hedge witch. Most of my magic is small and benign, so his jinx doesn't seem to even notice."

Ze'eva gave Mama a big hug. "Well, I think your magic is wonderful."

I spoke up once more. "Mama, I need you to take a message to Theo."

She gave me a dirty look. "What? Am I running a messenger service, too?"

I leaned over and whispered in her ear. She pulled back and a huge grin grew on her face. "Theron, you surprise me. You actually do have a brain in that thick skull of yours. I'll get word to him as soon as you're gone."

"Thanks, Mama. I knew we could count on you."

Mama Belltre waved her hands at us, shooing us back toward the trapdoor. "All right, that's enough of that. Go on; get out of here so I can get back to tending to my paying customers." She turned to leave but then gave us one last look over her shoulder. "You be careful, you hear. And don't worry, Theron. I'll send Kyra a bill for those things."

"Now that's the Mama Belltre I've come to know and love. See you later, Mama."

The sun was sitting out over the bay when a teenage boy found the two of us sitting on a park bench near South Point. He looked at us, down at a piece of paper he had, and then back at us. Finally, he walked over. "You Theron Chase?"

"Who wants to know?"

He pushed his cap back on his head and gave Ze'eva an appreciative look. "Never mind, you gotta be him because the Shark told me you'd be with a beautiful dame and I haven't seen anyone in this town who'd meet that description better than her. You must be that singer, Ze'eva Blackthorne."

Ze'eva blushed in spite of herself and I coughed to get the young Lothario's attention. "And I believe you have something there for me?" I asked, standing up and moving slightly between Ze'eva and him. He frowned at me for interrupting his view, but he pulled his cap off and reached inside it. He handed me a small piece of paper and then held his hand out. I tossed him half a crown and he stepped around me to bow to Ze'eva.

"If there's anything you need down on the docks, ma'am, just ask for Louie. I'll get the word soon enough and there ain't nothing going down on the docks I can't find out."

"Thank you, Louie. I'll keep you in mind."

"You won't be sorry, Miss Blackthorne. I'll even cut you a break on my usual fees. All right, I gotta get back and let Sharkey know I found you. See ya later."

He disappeared into the milling crowd and I could see Ze'eva was amused at the way I was acting. I offered her my hand and as she rose from the bench, I leaned forward to speak softly. "Let's take a walk into the crowd. These amulets might protect us against magic detection, but not much protects against good ol' eyes."

"Now, Theron, you're jealous! I never would have believed that of you," she said for the benefit of anyone walking past us.

Then speaking almost without moving her lips, she continued. "Do you think someone followed him?"

"I'm telling you, Ze'eva, if that kid doesn't have wolf blood in him, I'll buy you a new outfit." I took her arm in my hand and we moved quickly toward the lookout point at the edge of park overlooking South Bay. "I don't *know* if he was followed or not, but there's no point in taking chances."

She leaned her head against my shoulder as we walked, acting like she didn't have a care in the world. "So, is going toward the point a good idea? Seems like we're trapping ourselves there if we're being pursued."

"One would think so, yes. However, this isn't the first time I've had to disappear quickly."

We walked through the crowd and I scanned the crowd surreptitiously, pointing out this and that to Ze'eva. I saw two worrisome things as we moved closer to the observation point. One was one of Corvinus's men following us at a discreet distance, which of course meant there were more lurking around. Apparently he was starting to run out of patience with my habit of turning up around dead bodies. The other was the large dark-skinned man who was moving through the crowd without attempting to disguise his intent; he worried me more. He resembled a Walikamba islander, but more importantly, I recognized him. He didn't have his coat or hat, but he was the guy I'd seen coming out of the Black Prince. I decided not to tangle with him, though. Unlike the guy we found in Grant-land's room, this one looked like could have made a living lifting boats out of the water without using a crane.

I nudged Ze'eva and pointed out the dreadnought heading straight for us. She nodded and patted her purse. I knew she had several weapons in there, but I shook my head. I picked up my pace and headed toward the farthest telescope out on Observation Point. Ze'eva's look made it clear she was begin-ning to doubt my sanity, but she followed me anyway.

I could tell by the commotion Corvinus's men had noted the large man tailing us and were trying to fight their way through the crowd. We reached my target and I put a silver penny into the slot to activate the telescope. I pointed toward it and said to Ze'eva. "Go ahead and take a look, the islands to the southeast are known for the sea lions and seals."

The look on her face was priceless, but she sighed and bent over to look. While she did that, I used her body to momentarily hide me from the approaching islander. I slipped my belt out of my trousers and eased it over the brown cable leading from the bottom of the telescope out over the small cliff on the point.

"Ze'eva, when I say 'now,' grab hold of my waist and hang on for dear life."

"What are you . . . ?"

"Now!"

The big islander had shoved the last person between him and us out of the way when I stepped back with a death grip on both ends of my belt. There was the momentary shock of free fall when my body sailed through space before my belt caught on the thin, but sturdy, cable. The added weight of Ze'eva nearly pulled my arms out of their sockets as we rocketed down the cable. I could hear the incoherent cries of the islander and the sound of police whistles in the distance behind us.

A few seconds later, I warned Ze'eva to get ready to drop. There was a small wooden wall on the top of a warehouse and I let go of my belt the second our feet were over it. I hadn't realized how much speed we'd gained coming down as a tandem and we nearly missed the pads I'd arranged here months ago. We hit the roof hard and I had the wind knocked out of me. I crawled to my hands and knees and glanced up the rope, but there were no obvious signs of pursuit. Ze'eva was sitting up, trying to pull herself together from the wild ride and the sudden stop and I managed to stumble to my feet and go retrieve my belt from the cable.

"Theron Chase, if you ever pull a stunt like that again, I'm going to do serious bodily harm to you when it's over."

"You have to admit, it was fun."

Ze'eva tried but she couldn't quite hide the excitement in her voice. "I do not have to admit anything. Besides, you could have warned me before I went flying over half of Southport in a skirt."

"I'll keep that in mind. But, since we needed to come to Southport anyway, we might as well catch up with Bobby Seward."

"Who is that?"

I waved the piece of paper I'd gotten from Louie. "The gentleman Penny Fairbanks was using as a middleman. He's supposed to sell the pearls to a collector on Bear Island. I'm hoping he can shed some light on the situation."

Once we were presentable again, I showed her the hidden door from the roof to the warehouse interior and in less time that it takes to tell, we were out on the streets of the docks and heading for a small curio shop down near the waterfront. Now, Southport area is an industrial area and mostly freighters and ore ships dock here, but if you go to Seal Row, they do a thriving business taking tourists out to the rocky islands nearby where we have a huge population of seals, sea lions, sea otters, and other assorted critters. Bobby Seward ran a curio shop that catered to the tourists, specializing in product from Bear Island.

Normally, the streets aren't crowded in this section of Southport. The warehouse workers are inside loading and unloading containers, trying to get ready for the next set of ships coming in on the dawn tide. Most tourists are out on the boats and won't be coming back until before sunset. So, it was concerning when I turned onto Seal Row and saw a number of vehicles outside a store and a number of people milling about on the street.

"You don't think someone's beaten us here, do you?" Ze'eva asked.

"Only one way to find out."

We wormed our way through the crowd. I saw a constable I knew and angled over to him.

"Hey, Jack."

"Oh, hey, Chase. What brings you down here?"

"Checking out a few things. What's the commotion?"

"Strangest damn thing, Chase. Some tourist walked in and found a guy dead in one of the aisles. There was no sign of a struggle, in fact, he looks perfectly normal except—"

"—for a row of black dots around his throat?"

Jack eyes scrunched together and he stared at me with that look cops get when you know more about something than they do. "Hey, now how did you know, Chase?"

"Because Bobby Seward is the third guy to die lately with the same marks on his neck. It's becoming an epidemic."

"Hah, gotcha, Chase. So, you don't know everything."

It was my turn to look at him with a dumbstruck look on my face. "What don't I know, Jack?"

"That ain't Bobby Seward in there."

"What?"

"Yeah, it was some guy named Xian Daisong. I never heard of him, but I know Captain Corvinus showed up here in a hurry once we identified the body. Apparently he's some big shot, that's all I know."

"Thanks, Jack. Well, we'll be going now."

Jack reached up and scratched his head with his night stick. "Huh. That ain't like you, Chase. Normally you'd be the first guy going in to see what's going on."

I waved a hand at him and called back over my shoulder as Ze'eva and I left. "Just trying to turn over a new leaf. You know how Corvinus gets whenever he sees me."

"Madder than a wet hen. The way he's acting, I wish I wasn't here either. See you later, Chase, Miss Blackthorne."

We hurried down the street and I caught the first cab I could find. With Daisong murdered, there was no point in setting up a new office. I called Kyra and asked her to bring our stuff back and to warn Theo about the turn of events. I doubted it would directly affect Theo, but it never hurts to have a mage of his caliber on call, just in case. Things were going to start moving and poor stupid Theron was going to be at the center of the maelstrom. If I wanted to head off a possible gang war in Calasia, we were going to have to find the pearls and the murderer fast.

K yra and Ze'eva kept Captain Corvinus and everyone else off my trail for the next couple of days while I searched around in places I'd rather not have visited and cut deals with people I didn't enjoy hanging out with. Many crowns lighter and a few bruises both taken and given out, I discovered where the lock was that fit Penny's key. Now, it was only a matter of getting to it first.

I hired one of the city's ratmen, Black Sid, to take me through the sewers to the basement of an old dilapidated hotel down in the Commons. It had been a respectable hotel once upon a time, but now it was a flop house for people who couldn't afford anything better. Black Sid opened a sliding door from the sewer into the basement. It was obvious this is where they stored the stuff even the winos and derelicts didn't want and it smelled like it too.

Black Sid pointed toward an opening in the far wall. "If you go through there, you will find what you are looking for. However, if I were you, which thankfully I am not, I would not go through that door."

"Why wouldn't you go there, Sid?"

"Death waits beyond the door. I can smell it from here. But, if you want an answer to your question, you will have to find out for yourself."

"Thanks for the encouraging words, Sid."

Sid glanced at me and with the typical bluntness of his race, replied, "I am not encouraging you. I am trying to discourage you. But, I know you, Chase. You are stubborn, even for a human. Still, I hope you survive. You have always treated us well. Please, try not to die." With that, he spun around and padded into the darkness of the sewers.

Cheery thought.

I pushed on into the basement and made my way past the junk and detritus that had accumulated over the years. Approaching the open door, I realized what Black Sid had been talking about—the stench of decaying flesh was more and more overpowering with every step. I lifted the glowing gem that was my light source even higher and scanned ahead. From this angle I couldn't see much, but there was no mistaking what appeared to be a pair of legs in the pool of light.

I slipped my .45 out of its holster and stepped into the room. If someone was there, they were there in spirit only. I counted six bodies in the room in varying degrees of decomposition. Now, given the hotel and its less than respectable inhabitants, I can't say I was surprised to find bodies in the basement. The fact I hadn't seen more was more of a surprise. I couldn't tell what had killed these people, but given the gold watch on one corpse, I was sure these weren't hotel residents. Add in the various burglar tools and crowbars lying around the room and I decided Penny Fairbanks's hiding spot wasn't as well hidden as she'd hoped.

Once I was certain the bodies were non-ambulatory, I moved through the room, paying particular attention to where, and into what, I was stepping. It took several minutes, but I finally spotted the metal door in the wall. I double checked and ensured I had the box with the key in one pocket and the small thin box Theo had given me in the other.

I approached the safe but stopped dead in my tracks. I heard soft footsteps crossing the basement toward this opening. I set my gem down and moved to the side, avoiding stepping on the bodies. I had secured a place in the shadows when a skinny dark-skinned figure appeared in the doorway. I didn't recognize him at first, but then I realized it was Bobby Seward.

"That's far enough, Seward. No, keep those hands where I can see them."

"Who's there?"

"The name's Chase. Now, with just two fingers, open up your jacket buttons and then pull your jacket open."

"I am carrying a gun, Mr. Chase."

"Yes, you are. And you're going to show me it's the only one you've got before I have you toss it away."

Seward was angry, but he did as he was told. I had him lift his jacket up and turn around so I could be sure he didn't have a spare tucked into his belt before I had him withdraw his automatic with two fingers and toss it behind him into the room. Once I was certain he was alone down here, I stepped into the light to face him.

"Come to observe your handiwork?"

"I admit nothing, but if these people died trying to get the pearls, then they brought their deaths upon themselves. The pearls are cursed and only the rightful owner can handle them safely."

"The rightful owner being you?"

"Why not? They were stolen from me twelve years ago."

"Oh, not you too."

"Are you so surprised, Mr. Chase? After all, I believe you have spoken to a certain Major Fielder? Did he not mention the pearls were first stolen by a houseboy who turned up dead? Did you never wonder if the person the houseboy stole the gems from might not be searching for them too?"

Actually, I hadn't considered that, considering I'd been told the owner was also dead. Given the way bodies were piling up around here, it made sense. I could see why the first person attacked might want people to think he was dead. Meant nobody was trying to kill you while you worked in the shadows. "So, the curse killed these people?"

"No, Mr. Chase, the only curse that killed these people is the curse of greed. I suspect the traps installed to protect that safe worked as they were intended. I have no intention of following their example and blindly attacking a well-protected target."

Something about the way he spoke worried me. He was a little too assured for someone who'd been caught so easily. Still, he was disarmed so I decided to press my advantage until a better idea came to mind. "So, why are you here? Were you stopping by to see if your traps had caught someone else, or did you have something more immediate in mind? After all, with your seller, Penny Fairbanks, dead and the Four Winds breathing down your neck, you needed to collect the pearls in a hurry."

"You're partially right, Mr. Chase. While these are not my traps, Miss Fairbanks's death did complicate things. Mr. Daisong was unhappy when I told him the pearls remained out of reach. After his talk with you, he was convinced I had double-crossed him. However, the cursed pearls claimed another victim."

I motioned Seward into the room. "That's interesting. So, if you didn't set these traps, then I suspect the bodies belong to people you sent to recover the pearls so you wouldn't have to pay Penny."

"You are as good as your reputation says, Chase."

I guess word gets around. And yet . . . "No, I'm still slow on the uptake. I'd considered everyone who was after the pearls except you. Why would you be after them since Penny was going to hand them to you for what I'm sure was a fraction of the price you could get for them? But, see, that's where I made my mistake. I hadn't considered you'd get greedy and try to cut out the middle girl. Why pay Penny when you could just take them?"

I paused and watched his face closely. When he didn't flinch, I pushed on. "So, when your thieves here couldn't break into the wall safe, you decided to scare Penny out of the only thing that would work; a key she possessed that would open the safe. You and your accomplice killed Torombo Inohuaye for two reasons: he could identify you as the owner of the pearls—a man who was supposedly dead—and his death might frighten Penny into surrendering the key to you. When that didn't work, you made your big mistake. You went after her yourself. The pearls might be cursed, but I've never seen a string of pearls, cursed or not, search through someone's baggage."

He slowly raised his hands in front of him and gave me mock applause. "You weave a skillful story, Mr. Chase. If I didn't know better, I'd almost believe you. Still, your story is just that—a story. You have no evidence and you certainly can't prove I killed anyone."

I nodded slowly. "You're absolutely right. Then again, I'm not a constable. While I'd love to haul you in on a murder rap, I'm not getting paid to prove who killed whom. But, I do have a client who's willing to pay me for the recovery of the pearls and I do have a reputation to consider. So, it's up to you, Seward—either you're going to let me take the pearls or you're going to stop me. There are no other choices."

"But, Mr. Chase, how could I possibly stop you?"

"Maybe you can't. But, where's your accomplice?"

Seward smiled, but there was nothing friendly about it. "May I show you something, Mr. Chase? I promise it will not endanger you, but it might prove most illuminating."

I gave him the briefest of nods and I took up a bit of slack on the trigger of my .45. He slipped off his jacket and tie and carefully sat them to the side. He mumbled a few words and the air shimmered around him. It couldn't be true, but the little man known as Bobby Seward disappeared and the large Walikamba islander I'd seen at the Black Prince stood before me.

"As you may have guessed, Bobby Seward was merely an alias. A skin to be put on and taken off as necessary. I was Palimiba Tuhaika, a priest of Walikamba, but for now, I am content to live among you until I recover what was mine and will be again." He waved his hands and the large man disappeared, returning to the shape of Bobby Seward.

I waited while he slipped his jacket back on. "Besides, Mr. Chase, I am unarmed. What possible threat can I pose you?"

"The same threat you posed to your houseboy, Captain Grantland, Penny, Inohuaye, Daisong and the gods know how many others over the years. I don't know how you do it, but it's effective. So, the question is, can you stop me from pulling this trigger before you can strangle me?"

His eyes narrowed. "I guess there's only one way to find out."

Before I could fire, there was a roar and two large hands reached into the room, grabbing Seward and jerking him out of the room. I could hear roaring and screaming coming from the other room. I paused only long enough to grab the glowing gem so I could see and headed for the doorway. Captain Grantland had Seward in a bear hug, trying to squeeze the life out of him. A black nimbus had settled around the huge man's neck and I watched as Seward tried to ignore the pain he was in to concentrate on maintaining it.

There was a sick snapping sound and Seward let out a bloodcurdling scream. At the same time, the captain dropped the broken man to the ground, grabbing at his neck. A black ring had manifested around his neck and was tightening.

Seward's eyes never left his target and the ogre tumbled backwards clawing away at the phantom necklace.

Grantland let out one more rattle of breath and fell still on the ground. I looked back at Seward and knew he'd never be able to do that to anyone again.

I stood there for a moment, staring at the two combatants, which to my everlasting shame, allowed the third person to slip into the basement behind me.

"Please lift your hands, Mr. Chase. I assure you, I cannot miss from this range."

I turned around to see Mrs. Sherwood standing there. She held a small automatic pointed at my midsection and extended a hand in my direction. "Please toss your gun over there. Now, the pearls, if you please."

"I'm afraid you're a bit early. The gentleman there stopped me before I could get to them. I'm surprised to see you here. This isn't an easy part of town to get to, much less navigating those stairs. You're quite spry for someone your age."

There was a shimmer and Mrs. Sherwood was now a middle-aged islander dressed in western clothes. "Appearances can be deceiving, Mr. Chase. But then again, I've spent years searching for these pearls. I've used a number of disguises over the last twelve years to seek them out." She glanced over at Seward's broken body and then at Grantland's corpse. "It's a pity, Mr. Chase, but I did warn you these pearls were cursed. All who sought the pearls who were not the rightful owner would die."

"And *you* are the rightful owner?"

"Did I not tell you so? I am Palimiba's sister." She pointed toward Seward. "What he said was true, in a way—he *was* one of the priests of Walikamba, but turned away from our faith when he decided to sell the sacred pearls. He knew the legends, he knew our gods would never allow him to get away with something so foolish, but he persisted and now he has paid the price."

"Why do I have the feeling you led Captain Grantland here?"

She bowed her head, but never took her eyes off me. Her automatic didn't waver either. "You don't miss much, do you? Yes, I decided to let the good captain be the instrument of my revenge. I knew the chance to get back at the killer of his brother would be bait too enticing to ignore. However, I didn't anticipate them killing each other. That is simply a bonus."

"And now, you're going to finish me off and get away scott free."

"Mr. Chase, you misunderstand me. Why would I kill you? I haven't killed anyone involved with this. You have your murderer, one Bobby Seward. He was killed by Captain Grantland. You have led me to the pearls and as the high priestess of Walikamba Island, who can possibly have a greater claim to them than I? Your secretary received a payment by messenger for your services with a large bonus for your good work earlier today."

I smiled humorlessly. "I see what you mean. After all, you *are* the rightful owner."

"Thank you. Now, if you'll give me the key to the safe and then move over by the entrance to the sewers, I'll recover my property and leave on the next boat."

I fished out the box holding the key and set it down on the floor. Once I was safely away, she picked up the box and went into the death room. I debated on leaving, but decided to wait until she left first. No sense in blundering into an ambush she might have set for me.

A scream came from the room and I rushed to the door. I glanced in and saw her holding her hand, froth forming around her mouth. She looked at me with a pleading look and slowly collapsed on the ground in front of the now-open safe. I moved forward, glancing at every inch of the floor with the gem to ensure I didn't set off any new traps. Reaching the safe, I realized two things. One, Kyra had been right to think there was something wrong with the key—it was booby-trapped. Once turned to the side, a needlelike projection had come out, sticking Mrs. Sherwood in the palm.

The other thing was Mrs. Sherwood would never be returning to the islands.

I opened up Theo's box and, using the forceps he'd provided, I hooked the pearl necklace and slipped it into the box. Then, I trudged up the stairs and placed a call to Captain Corvinus.

"Theron, you could have been killed."

I looked over at Ze'eva and nodded in agreement. "And I undoubtedly would have been if Mrs. Sherwood hadn't taken the key from me. It's ironic the pearls' curse caught up with her too."

Kyra brought me a fresh cup of coffee and took a seat on the corner of my desk. "So, what now?"

"Did that messenger really show up?"

"Oh yes, Theron. She actually paid us double what we were originally supposed to get."

"Then I say we pay off all our outstanding bills, put some aside for operating capital and spend the rest on a celebration."

There was a harrumph at the door and Major Fielder marched into the office. He motioned toward the coffee urn and settled into one of the office chairs. "Not so fast, Chase. After all, I think we have some unfinished business."

"Now, Major, surely you don't think I'm going to just hand you the pearls?"

The major accepted the cup of coffee from Kyra and then turned to face me. "Blast it, Chase, those pearls belong to me. I purchased them ten years ago and I mean to have them. Victor and I have a buyer lined up for them and it would be poor form to not deliver the same to him."

"And you are getting what contraband from him in return?"

"Contraband?" The major let out a nervous laugh and then carried on. "Really now, Chase, enough stalling. Where are the pearls?"

I glanced at Ze'eva and she nodded slightly. That told me Victor was lurking in the outer office. "Major, if you read the morning paper, you know the pearls are in the possession of the Constabulary of Calasia. Are you hiring me to steal them back for you?"

"By the gods, man, why must you always assume there are nefarious ends in all of my activities? No, I am not going to hire you. First of all, it would be most unseemly for a Royal Dragoon to resort to hiring a private detective in the first place. Secondly, you had an obligation to return those pearls to me. I *am* the rightful owner and as such I demand my property be returned."

"Major, let me make this as clear as I can with you. One, those pearls were taken in as material evidence in a series of murders. Now, the fact the murderer was killed by one of his victims in return does simplify the matter somewhat. Two, those pearls are under damn near universal interdict. It's illegal in almost every country in the world to own Walikamban black pearls."

I leaned back and tried on my most disarming smile. "The only possible resolution I can see is either you confess those pearls are fakes, in which case I'm certain the police will return them to you after they're done investigating things. You do have your bill of sale, I hope. The only other resolution would be for you and Victor to try storming the Citadel to break into the vault where they're holding the pearls. Because, I suspect there's no way the Imperial Wizards College is going to let you take them if they're real."

"I will not allow you to do this to me, Chase. I really do not care what your opinion is of me, but I am the rightful owner and I will be satisfied."

"Look, Major Fielder, I sympathize; seriously, I do. For once, you're on the side of the angels. That still won't make the pearls magically appear here. Take it up with Captain Corvinus—he's the officer in charge of the investigation. That is, unless there's a reason why you can't?"

The major gave me a dirty look but finally resignation set in. "Very well. Let it never be said a Royal Dragoon doesn't know when to sound retreat." He stood up and bowed to both of the ladies before turning back to me. "You've won this round, Chase, but there are many moves still ahead in this game."

He walked to the outer office and I heard him call out, "Come along, Victor. We're off to Sinegar. There is a jeweled bird there waiting for the proper person to claim it. Why not us?"

A loud childish voice echoed from the outer room. "Oh, very delight, Master. A jeweled bird just for us."

"Yes, Victor, now come along."

I heard the outer door shut and after a few minutes, Kyra got up and checked. I heard locks being thrown and then she came back in. "He's gone. Now, what was that all about? You didn't give Captain Corvinus those pearls."

I glanced down at the middle drawer of my desk where I knew a black wooden box lay with twelve of the deadliest pearls I'd ever encountered inside. "No, I didn't. But I knew there was no chance the major would walk into the Citadel to check. I'm glad to see Theo got the message from Mama Belltre. I'm delivering them to Theo in the morning." I caught a look from my partner. "Yes, Ze'eva, he didn't and still doesn't want anything to do with them, but the finder's fee he negotiated for us with the Imperial College is going to be a nice bonus for this caper—minus his personal cut, that is."

Ze'eva stretched at her desk and looked at the empty calendar on the wall. "So, what's next? We're out of clients again."

I stood up, reached behind a bookshelf and came out with my best bottle of scotch before walking around the room, pouring Ze'eva and Kyra each a drink. Returning to my desk, I put my feet up and leaned back in my chair, admiring one of the nicest sunsets I'd seen through my office window. "Let's worry about that tomorrow. Tonight, let's enjoy the fact this case is over and the guilty were brought to justice. Who knows? Maybe a vacation is in order?"

Kyra spoke up, "A vacation? Where?"

I felt myself relax for the first time in days. "I don't know—maybe a dude ranch or a mountain retreat. Anything as far away from oceans, islands and cursed pearls as we can get. Now, who's up for dinner?"

Case 3:
The
Unquiet
Corpse
Affair

THE UNQUIET CORPSE AFFAIR

The fog was rolling in off of the Palymir Sea, coating the city in a damp blanket. From my window, I watched as section by section the gray clouds swallowed the surrounding districts and began to slink around my building. In a few minutes, there was only the fitful glow of the streetlamps against the encroaching mist and small, blurry shapes moving along on the street or making their way from the neighboring buildings to flag down the few taxis.

The painted letters on my window, advertising CHASE AND BLACKTHORNE, PRIVATE INVESTIGATIONS, blocked some of my view, but then again, what was there to see? I'd finished dictating the report of my latest case to my secretary, Kyra Sylvari, and now, with nothing pressing, I wondered what new mysteries this city held. That was one thing about my profession: someone was always doing something they shouldn't, which meant the slow times never lasted long. I'd learned to enjoy them while I could.

I heard the sound of heels clicking across the floor and knew Kyra was ready for me to review the report for the Calasian constables and our client. However, I wasn't prepared for her reaction when she came into the room. She took two steps in and froze, her translucent wings fluttering, as she stared at something behind me. Being a naturally curious man, I slowly turned to see what had caught her attention.

There was a swirling black circle on the back wall of my office. I moved backward away from the wall and drew my pistol from my shoulder holster as I saw a shape moving in the darkness toward me. To be honest, it wasn't the first time something weird has happened in my office, but it usually came through the front door or the windows.

I nearly dropped my pistol though once I recognized who came through the darkness. It was Theo Markham, a good friend and proprietor of Markham's Emporium of the Ancients. He was immaculately dressed as usual, but he was carrying a large ebony-colored box in his arms. Before I could say anything, I knew something was wrong—Theo moved like he was sleepwalking. He looked around the room and walked to my desk.

I put away my .45 and looked at Kyra but she just shook her head. "He's under a spell, Theron. Let him do whatever he's doing. I've got a few counter-spells prepared, but I'm no match for Theo in a one-on-one battle."

"Let's hope it doesn't come to that."

Theo set the box on my desk and eased the catches on it open. After removing the lid, he lifted out a square bronze mirror and propped it up against the box before stepping away. Two steps later, he started and shook his head. "What am I doing and where the hell am I?"

"You know, Theo, I was about to ask you the same thing."

"Chase! I should have known you were behind this. What has your infernal poking and prodding of the city's underside gotten me into this time?"

"I'm glad to see you too, Theo. I have no idea why you're here, but we'll worry about that in a moment. Don't blame me if your magic went astray. Remember I'm the one who says a good wooden club is more reliable than a spell."

"Only because you'd probably turn yourself into a toad if you tried."

Kyra, who was neither familiar with nor fond of our bickering, stepped between us and got to the point. "Theo, why *are* you here?"

For once, Theo was at a loss for words. He settled himself into the leather chair we usually reserve for paying clients, while Kyra poured him a shot of scotch. I took the opportunity to examine the bronze mirror. It was ancient and bore marks on the frame in no language I'd ever seen before. However, the mirror itself showed no sign of its age. I couldn't find a blemish on the surface anywhere.

My hand inched toward the mirror, but Theo bellowed at me: "Oh no you don't, Theron! Do *not* touch that. I've seen you destroy more magical items simply by touching them to last a lifetime. We don't need yet another example."

"Well then, Theo, can you please explain this thing's presence on my desk? I mean, it makes a great paperweight, but beyond that, I think it's a bit ostentatious for my current décor."

"Theron . . ."

"All right, Kyra. Theo, you seemed not quite yourself when you arrived. Can you tell us what happened?"

Theo sipped at his scotch, took a deep breath, and settled back in the chair. "That's the damnedest thing, Chase, I was cataloging some new items the Wizards Council had dropped off for safekeeping in my vault, when I was summoned by a messenger. He had a large package that was to be delivered to me and no one else. Not an uncommon occurrence, but something in the messenger's demeanor told me I'd want to check it out immediately. I carried the package into my office and discovered this box."

Kyra frowned, looking up from the notepad that had

appeared in her lap as soon as Theo had started talking. "You didn't just open it, did you?"

"Miss Sylvari, one does not get to be a wizard of my advanced age by not taking proper precautions. No, I set the usual wards and protective spells in place. However, what we're dealing with here is obviously not 'the usual'. I remember opening the box and then the next thing I knew, I found myself in this . . . " Theo paused and glanced around my office. "No offense, Theron, but when was the last time you dusted this room?"

"It's the maid's week off, Theo. Focus."

"All I can say is, this must be a most powerful magic device; I'm not one easily caught by such traps. That's why I don't want you touching it until we get the chance to examine it."

Kyra spoke up, her voice guarded. "You may want to examine it right now, because it just turned on."

White light emanated from the mirror, growing brighter by the second before erupting in a brilliant flash. I tried to close my eyes in time, but I was too late. I dropped to my knees and tried to draw my pistol, although between the spots and my eyes watering, I'm not sure what I could have hit. I didn't hear a commotion so I decided to just wait it out; after a few seconds, my vision began clearing and I saw I was surrounded by two balls of mystical energy. It seemed Kyra and Theo had had the same idea. Luckily for me, their spells hadn't canceled each other's out, which would be more appropriate for my luck.

Once I could see normally, I realized a young woman was standing in front of my desk. No, not standing—she was floating a few inches off the floor. She appeared to be around five foot four, with a figure that demanded your attention, and hair the color of a roaring fire. There was a certain insubstantiality about her body that did nothing to detract from her beauty. Her blue eyes gazed steadily at me as I stood up and the two mages in the room removed the protective shield.

"You are Theron Chase?"

"The one and only. Now, who are you and why are you here?"

"My name is Naomi Talgoti. I want you to find my killer."

Her response caught me off guard, but once again, Kyra came through like the champion she was. "Would you take a seat, Miss Talgoti?"

The specter smiled and took a spot on a nearby chair. I stood there like a poleaxed steer for a moment until Kyra pointed toward my desk. I scrambled over and took my usual seat, while Theo moved the mirror off to the side. He returned to his seat and crossed his arms across his ample frame.

"Now, Miss Talgoti . . ."

"Call me Naomi."

Her voice turned my insides into melted marshmallows but I took a deep breath and continued on. "Naomi, obviously the first question is, do you know who killed you? The second one, before you answer the first is, why me? Why not the constables?"

"That was three questions, but I'll let it slide. First, no, it happened too fast. Secondly, you're known around Calasia for not being afraid or too snooty to deal with supernatural beings. And lastly, I didn't go to the constables because I'd like my killer to be caught before he dies of old age."

Theo snorted and then looked insufferably pleased with himself. Being the consummate professional I am, I ignored the interloper and concentrated on my new client. Not that it was a chore, mind you, but there was something familiar about her. It felt like the buzzing you get in the back of your mind when you know you should remember something "Since your opinion of the constables coincides with mine, I'm inclined to take you on as a client."

"I know you don't work for free. Do not worry. I may not be able to access it, but I guarantee I'll direct you to a healthy cache of funds when you catch my killer. You can even have Mr. Markham there place a geis on me to ensure I don't refuse, if you desire."

I glanced over at Theo and he shrugged as if to say, "Don't ask me." Deciding there'd be no help in that direction, I refocused on my client. "These are questions I'd normally ask the coroner, but since you're here I'll go ahead and get some of the preliminaries out of the way. When were you killed, where were you killed, and how were you killed?"

"I was on my way home from a pickup mission two nights ago. I was carrying my cargo in a special briefcase. No one had paid attention to me, which is normal since most people can't see me unless I choose. I had reached the docks and spotted my ship when there was a flash of light, a sharp searing pain in my back, and then I was falling. Next thing I knew, I was wandering around the city. Took me quite a while to pull myself together"—she ran her hands down her sides—"so to speak. As you may have noticed, my cargo is missing."

"Pardon me for being dense, but I'm not sure what a pickup mission is."

"You should. You've seen me on one of my missions before."

I laughed, finally starting to relax. "Naomi, no offense, but you're not the type of woman a man would forget meeting."

"Don't let it worry you. You were a bit too busy trying not to die yourself to pay much attention to me. I seem to recall you warning me to keep my head down . . . as if a normal bullet could have ever harmed me."

Theo chuckled. "Ah, my dear, I'm afraid our poor detective is unlikely to recognize you in your current form. You're much too civilized at the moment."

"All right, Theo. What are you not saying?"

"Naomi, would you please show him your true form?"

"As you wish, Mage. After all, without your aid, this meeting would have been impossible."

Before I could say anything, the mirror glowed with a red light. There was a burst of light and hot winds swept through the room. When I uncovered my eyes, Naomi's fashionable dress had been replaced by an old-style suit of armor and her hand bag was now a nasty-looking spear. She also now sported a pair of white feathered wings.

Moving quicker than I thought possible, she stepped around the corner of my desk and touched my shoulder.

"Sergeant Chase, think we're going to see some action tonight?"

I looked over and saw my partner, Corporal Timmons, walking a few feet away. I knew the rest of the patrol was strung out a few dozen feet behind us. "Nah. We spent three weeks taking this hill. I don't think the Parijans will regroup for a couple of days. About all we have to worry about are stragglers."

"I don't know. I've got that creepy feeling. Something doesn't feel right."

I raised one hand to alert the patrol. Timmons's hunches were right more often than not, but before I could say a word, machine gun fire ripped into us from the right flank. Three of the men went down before we realized what was happening. I dove behind a tree and came up firing, just trying to get the enemy to duck while the others could move.

"Sergeant, I'm hit!"

I saw Timmons lying there, an ugly dark splot growing bigger on his tunic as he tried to stanch the flow of blood. There was another burst from the hidden machine gun and Timmons's body bounced off the ground from the heavy-caliber slugs ripping through him.

I fired into the darkness again, trying to spot the gun flashes. A sudden movement behind me caught my attention and I saw someone squatting next to Timmons's body. "Get to cover! You're a sitting duck there!"

The figure started and for a split second I stared into the eyes of someone who had no business being in my unit. Before I could ask why one of the nurses was this far out of camp, the enemy opened up again.

I spotted their weapon and lobbed a couple of grenades at it. I was luckier than I deserved because as soon as the pineapple went off, there was a secondary explosion and the hidden enemy bunker went up. I turned around but there was no sign of the nurse anywhere near Timmons.

I caught myself on the edge of my desk as I nearly fell out of my chair. "You. You were the nurse that night."

"I was never a nurse, Theron. Your mind saw me and thought I was a nurse because you couldn't accept what you were seeing. Then again, you weren't supposed to see me at all. It was not your time. You saw through my mystic veil while I was collecting Jeff Timmons's soul. That is why I came to you tonight. I figured you'd be the easiest person in Calasia to convince to help me since you already knew of my existence."

"Your existence? Look, Naomi, I still don't quite know what to make of you."

Kyra tapped her pencil on the arm of the chair a couple of times and then a smile crossed her face. "You're a psychopomp!" she crowed triumphantly.

Poor dumb Theron stared at her blankly. "She's a whatsit?"

Theo grabbed the lapels on his waistcoat and fluffed them at me, grinning from ear to ear. "She's a psychopomp, Theron. She guides souls to the afterlife. Although, given her wings and weaponry, you'd probably know her from legends as a Valkyrie."

"Oh, come on, Theo. Those are stories we learned as kids—barbarian warriors being taken to a mystical land after dying valiantly by beautiful women on winged horses who would swoop down on the battlefield to select the bravest to go to an eternal land of feasting and fighting? There's no such thing as the Shadowed Lands."

Naomi coughed just loud enough to get my attention. "Theron, have you ever died?"

"No. But not for a lack of people trying."

"Then you have to admit, you're really in no position to say whether the Shadowed Lands exist or not. Let me tell you, they do. Mine lay several weeks journey from here, but there are shadowed isles all around the world, catering to fallen heroes. I don't blame you for being skeptical though. Again, you're among the living, so they should only be a myth."

Sure, I deal with trolls, ogres, witches, magicians, merfolk, sprites, fairies—hell, I even have a werewolf for a partner—but to have a servant for one of the gods standing in my office? *That* was a little bit much for even me.

I walked over to my chair and plopped down behind my desk. I glanced over at Naomi and she had resumed a more *modern* form and was sitting down next to Kyra. "All right, say I take you on as a client. You say you didn't see your killer, that's going to make it a bit tougher. Can you guide me to the place you were killed? Wait . . . I know you said you were murdered, but how can you be killed?"

She moved her hands down her translucent body. "My corporeal body is much easier to kill, but even this form can be destroyed with the right magic. As long as this form exists, I can be restored once I return to the Shadowed Lands, but it's going to take some time and it's not without pain. However, retrieving my cargo must take precedence over anything else we do with this case, including capturing my killer."

I didn't like the sound of that. "What aren't you telling me, Naomi?"

"We are on a strict deadline. If I do not arrive with my cargo within the next four days, the ship sails without me. I cannot board the ship without my cargo. If I do not arrive, my sisters will assume something has interfered with my mission."

"Which it has."

"Which it has, yes. Therefore, they will attempt to recover my cargo and take vengeance on the person who interfered. The problem is, since I don't know and can't tell them, they'll do the next best thing and wipe Calasia off the face of the earth."

"What?"

"My sisters tend to be rather straightforward in their thinking . . . very cause and effect-oriented. So, if they can't find the individual, they'll assume the entire town was in on it." She put a finger beside her face and glanced at the ceiling before continuing. "You know, that probably was more effective against a village or seaport in the old days."

"Well sure, why kill a couple hundred thousand when you can just terrorize twenty or so people."

"Exactly, Theron. Oh, you do understand. That's so refreshing."

Apparently Naomi wasn't good at reading expressions, so I spelled it out for her. "No. No, I don't understand. I don't understand any of this, but if solving your murder prevents the wholesale slaughter of this city, then that's what I'm going to have to do." I glanced at my liquor cabinet but decided it could wait until I had all the bad news. "By the way, what's the cargo?"

"The soul of a firefighter who died saving three children. That's also part of the deadline. If I don't get him there in time, the seal holding his soul inside my case will fail and his soul will be lost somewhere in this land, free for any soul eater to seek out."

Valkyries. Soul eaters. Next thing you know, an actual goddess will arrive in my office to explain everything. Why not? You've had worse cases, Chase, even if you can't remember when.

I turned to Theo. "All right, you brought her here, can you put her up somewhere?"

Naomi tilted her head slightly and pointed toward herself again. "I don't need to be 'put' anywhere, Theron. After all, in this state, I don't notice the passage of time or feel weather."

"No, but I need to know where to find you when we go search the spot you were killed. I also need to be certain whoever killed you doesn't get another shot to complete the job. We need you alive and intact . . . well, mostly intact, when we find your cargo. Go with Theo. I have research ahead of me before I start this case."

Naomi looked over at Theo and he shrugged in mock defeat. "No sense arguing with him, Naomi, you did hire him. You should let him get to work."

I waited until everyone was gone before I picked up the phone. My first call was to my friend, Maxie, who worked at the coroner's office beneath the Citadel.

"Maxie, this is Theron. Did you get a new customer tonight? About five foot four, red hair, blue eyes, nice figure, probably found down near the docks with something stuck in her back?"

"Nah, Theron, nothing tonight. But if you'd asked any other night, we might've had something for you. 'Course, I ain't seen the red-hair, blue-eyes one, but I've got about every other combination here."

"Maxie, once again, you're getting ahead of me. What're you talking about?"

"Well, I ain't supposed to talk about it, 'cause the High Constable doesn't want to start no panic, but apparently someone's going around town killing pretty girls. We've had six in the past three weeks. Each of them stabbed in the back, but no trace of the weapon and no one ever sees nothin'. Just they're there, and then they go down a street and *poof*! Next time anyone sees 'em, they're dead."

"Do they all go down the same street, Maxie?"

"Figure of speech, Theron, but you know, most of them *have* been found in the same area. Down by the docks, just like you said. Should I send a wagon out to pick up the body you're talking about?"

I paused and realized I had no idea where Naomi had died. Technically there were three sets of docks in Calasia, but I was pretty certain she wasn't killed near the Northport marina. That place has way too many watchmen to ensure the hoi-polloi don't pollute the air of their masters. The docks down on Southport deal mostly with freighters and other large ships. She didn't seem like the kind who'd be taking one of those to get to this "Shadowed Lands" she was talking about. No, it had to be the East Docks, where those who couldn't afford the docking fees for the North Shore tied up their boats and several excursion boats sailed from.

"Hey, Chase, you still there?"

"Oh, sorry, Maxie. I was just thinking. I had a tip about something happening tonight but the person just said 'docks.' I guess I should have gotten a better location out of them. I'm guessing they were talking about the East Docks."

There was a pause as Maxie's voice came garbled over the phone. Sounded like he had covered up the mouthpiece to talk to someone at the morgue. When he got back on the line, he sounded more nervous than usual. "Yeah, Mom, I'm going to be a little late getting home tonight. The captain wants to meet with me. Now, remember what I told you earlier, Mom. No, don't worry. I'm not in trouble, just going to be busy for a bit. Talk to you later."

As he hung up, I knew he was warning me Captain Corvinus was in the area. However, from what I gathered, they'd just brought a body in. Whether it was Naomi's or not was still to be seen, but I decided to drop in on Maxie and see what I could find out about all the other corpses who were appearing on his tables. If I could get a hint about our killer, I might be able to track him down and recover Naomi's cargo before it was too late.

A short cab ride later, I pulled up a couple blocks away from the Citadel. I casually strolled through some of the better-smelling alleys in Calasia until I spotted the back entrance to the building leading down into the morgue. I found a comfortable spot to rest and waited to see if Corvinus would emerge. After about fifteen minutes, I decided he'd already left and walked across the street. Letting myself in, I strolled down the stairs and opened the door to the morgue. I heard an explosion of words on the other side as the door stopped partway from hitting something hard and spotted Captain Corvinus waving his hand around in obvious pain.

"Chase, I should have known. I ought to run you in for assaulting a peace officer in the commission of his duties."

"Now, Captain, how was I to know you were trying to leave just as I was coming in?"

"I don't know. I do know you're walking right out with me. This is a police morgue here, Chase, not a public park. You have no business here."

Maxie gave me the high sign, so I decided discretion was the better part of solving this case. "Actually, Captain, I was coming to see you. They told me you'd be here and here you are."

"Well, *they* ought to mind their own business. I have too much going on to play twenty questions with you, Chase." He swallowed hard, but when I held the door for him, he harrumphed and went up the stairs. I signaled Maxie I'd be back and trotted up the stairs behind Corvinus.

We stepped out into the night air and I followed him around to the front of the building. To my surprise, he made no motion to go inside. "What's on your mind, Chase? I'm a busy man."

"I think we're working on the same case, Captain. I figured we could compare notes and see if we could help each other out."

Corvinus started to say something but his eyes narrowed and he shifted from friendly to suspicious. "The same case. So, what case are you walking on?"

"I'm trying to solve the murder of a beautiful woman who was stabbed down at the East Docks this evening. About five foot four, red hair, blue eyes, very attractive, and apparently very dead. I understand through my sources she's not the only one and you're keeping a lid on it to not panic the city. I know you don't approve of me, Corvinus, but we need to put our past aside and let's bring in this maniac before something worse happens."

"What woman killed down at the East Docks? If there's a body down there, why didn't you call it in right away? Who knows how much evidence has been tainted because you've been doing whatever the hell you've been doing? Chase, you know better."

I held up a hand to cut off his diatribe. "I don't know for certain where the body is, if there even is a body. My client just said she was killed down at the docks. I'm assuming the East Docks because she was supposed to meet a chartered boat tonight. However, it sounds like she was killed by the same person who's been picking off the others around there."

"Oh, your client told you this. Did you ever think your client might be the killer?"

I shook my head. "No, this time I can say with complete assurance they didn't do it."

"Oh you can. And just how can you make that guarantee, Mr. Smart Detective?"

"Because *she* was the victim. Now are you coming or not?"

Corivinus just stood there, his face looking like a fish out of water, his mouth opening but nothing coming out for several seconds. I flagged down a passing constable and asked him to have the captain's car brought around for him before Corvinus came out of his mild shock. I expected him to explode in some tirade, but he simply started laughing.

"Okay, Chase, you got me. I didn't see that one coming. No, seriously, who's your client?"

"Her name is Naomi and she was carrying a special package for delivery when she was killed down by the docks. If you don't believe me, go check with Theo Markham. He's watching her for me while I'm trying to figure this out."

Corvinus's reply was drowned out by the motor of his car pulling up, but I'm certain he might have been making some comment about how smart I was coming to get him. I mean, what else could he have been saying? I piled into his passenger seat as he climbed behind the wheel and we headed toward the East Docks.

"I don't have any clue why I'm agreeing to this, Chase. This story is preposterous and the docks cover about fifteen blocks. If there even *is* a body—which I doubt—it could have been moved a dozen times from where the 'murder' happened. We could be there all night."

"I know it's a long shot, but she was supposed to be on a chartered boat. I suspect she came in on the train. She was just passing through Calasia, so she wouldn't have driven. Air travel might have been too slow since she was on a deadline. She also doesn't seem to be the type to sightsee, so if we search on a direct line between the railroad station and the charter docks, we should find her body."

"Seems like your client could have been a bit more specific about where she got killed."

"She's a stranger to Calasia, Captain. She couldn't probably name a street to save her life. . . so to speak." He gave me a dirty look. "Well, anyway, she didn't know more than 'the docks,' so that tells me we can skip downtown and the theater district."

Corvinus didn't say anything else, but he stepped a little harder on the gas and we shot across town. We parked right at the edge of the docks closest toward the direction we guessed Naomi would have come and started walking. Between people who knew me or recognized Corvinus's badge, we must have spoken to fifteen or twenty people who might have been around when Naomi was killed, but no one saw, heard, or suspected a thing.

I was considering going to get Naomi to walk us through her route when I heard a voice out of the shadows. "Hey, Chase, I understand you're looking for something."

I held up a hand to signal Corvinus, who was across the street at a drugstore. "I'm always looking for something, friend. Can you think of something I might be interested in specifically?"

I heard the footsteps drawing closer, stepping carefully as if they weren't sure of their footing, and then I heard the soft tapping of a cane. The figure stepped out of the alley's shadows and a rumpled man walked toward me. His clothes and hat showed signs of better days and the cane he loosely held in one hand was white.

"You'd be surprised what a blind man sees, Mr. Chase. People get awfully careless around blind people assuming that because we can't see, we don't know what's going on. Especially people who're doing things they ought not."

"Provided they're blind to begin with. I know enough people who claim to be blind but they can tell the difference between a five-crown coin and a five-pence coin without too much trouble."

"That would be the weight, Mr. Chase. The crown, being made of gold, is slightly heavier than the pence, which is a bronze/silver compound. But let me put your mind at rest." He lifted the dark glasses covering his eyes and there was no mistaking the milky fluid covering his pupils. In a world of charlatans, he was the real thing.

He settled his glasses back down and leaned lightly on his cane. "I believe you are here searching for any more unfortunate victims of the 'Night Stalker.' Not very imaginative, I admit, but that's what people down here have named him or her. No one's quite sure because as far as I know, no one's seen him. I know I haven't." He let out a wry laugh, more biting than happy, before continuing. "I know where most of them happened. Again, no one *pays* me much attention."

I fished several crowns out of my pocket and let them drop, one atop another in my palm. He smiled. "And that is why you have your reputation, Mr. Chase, you don't miss many clues."

I guess word does get around. "That's my earnest money. More where that came from based on how good your information is."

"Understood. I wouldn't buy . . . sight unseen either." He chuckled at his own joke before continuing. "You're wondering about someone who's been killed recently. Tonight, perhaps?"

I paused as a cab stopped and dropped off a couple who hurried past the bind man and me into a nearby apartment building. After convincing the cabbie I really didn't need a ride, I turned back to my companion. "Since I have Captain Corvinus with me, he would know where the others are, so yes, if something happened tonight, I'd like to know about it."

"Don't assume the captain knows everything that happens at the docks, Chase. The constables see what they're paid to see. While the captain is a good man, some of his underlings are less than honorable. It's a pity, but what are you going to do?"

"Just how many women has the Night Stalker killed . . . ?" I let the sentence trail off as I fished for his name.

"You can call me Blind Bob; that's the handle I have down here. Now, mind you, I can't say for certain, but I'd say there've been nearly twenty. Oh, he or she's gotten a lot bolder lately, but like any good hunter, it was one at first. When no one raised much of an alarm, then it was a couple more and so on. Now, I suspect the Stalker is convinced they can't be caught and they'll continue to hunt at will. It's unfortunate it had to happen around here. Once word gets out, there won't be a lady within blocks of here. They're usually much more generous with old Blind Bob than the gentlemen."

"But the one tonight. That's the one I'm most interested in right now."

"Of course. Gather up your captain and follow me. I can show you where it happened."

I waved for Corvinus and he hurried across the street to join me. We fell into step behind Blind Bob and he led us in the direction I suspected Naomi had gone. About halfway through the dock area, he paused at the entrance of an alley that looked no different from the dozen or so I'd already passed that evening.

He pointed toward it with his cane. "This should be the place. I'll just wait here." Before I could say anything, he'd walked over to a nearby stoop and taken a seat.

Corvinus had fished a flashlight out of his coat pocket and motioned for me to follow him. There were the usual smells in the alley—half-rotted food, trash several days old, animal musk, all competing with each other—but this alley had a new scent— the unmistakable coppery scent of blood. It didn't take Corvinus long to spot the blood spatters everywhere. Incredibly, whoever or whatever was killed here had died within six steps of the mouth of the alley and no one had apparently noticed a thing. It wasn't even hidden from view. The nearest dumpster was another twenty feet down the alley, so this had to happen where anyone could have glanced in and seen it or heard the attack happening.

We followed the blood trail down the alley until we came to that same dumpster. I glanced inside and as I suspected, Naomi's body—or what was left of it—was lying there. The name 'Night Stalker' didn't do justice to the carnage I saw. She might have been stabbed in the back, but whoever had killed her had disassembled her body like he'd been preparing it for market.

I let Corvinus get a look and he shook his head. "No, he's never done that before. The first bodies just had a single stab wound. Lately, there had been signs he was spending more time with the bodies, but nothing ever like this before."

I took his flashlight and carefully lifted the lid of the dumpster again. I didn't want to disturb the scene any worse than it was, but I had to prove to myself the case was not here, and, of course, it wasn't. I followed Corvinus out of the alley where Bob was waiting.

"Bit of a mess, isn't it?"

"And how would you know that, Bob?"

"Remember, when you lose one sense, the others tend to sharpen to compensate. I can smell with the best of them, Chase. I'd never smelled so much blood before at one of his attacks. Something about this one really set him off."

"We'll want you to come down to headquarters to give us a statement, Bob," Corvinus said. "Chase, secure this area for me while I go phone this one in. I'll be back in a few minutes."

One Corvinus was out of earshot, Bob rose from the stoop, stretched, and started walking down the street in the opposite direction. "You have a good what's left of your evening, Chase. I think I'm going to go mind my own business. I'm good at that."

I caught up with him and pressed the rest of the crowns in to his hand. "You know the captain will put out a call on you as a material witness."

"Oh, I'm certain he will. But what kind of a witness does a blind man make? I don't think the judge is likely to look favorably on his warrant request."

"Bob, you're a scoundrel from a long way back, I wager. So, tell me, when you discovered this, you didn't happen to stumble across a case of some kind, did you? Not certain what it looked like—"

"Not that I'd be able to tell," Bob said dryly.

"—but it was average sized and locked. Now, I'm not saying you took it, but as you said, you're a person who hears things.

There is a significant reward for its return, but it has to be returned soon."

There was just a small tremble on Bob's face when I mentioned the case, but his voice betrayed nothing. "A case?"

"Yes, a case. Probably like a briefcase, but nothing too big. Definitely smaller than a suitcase. My client is offering good money for its return, no questions asked."

There it was, that small twitch again.

"Don't know how much help I'll be, but I'll get the word out. Now, if you don't mind, I'd like to get a bit of a head start before the captain gets back here. I'm not much of one for hide-and-seek at my age."

"Don't kid a kidder, Bob. You probably know these streets better than anyone. I suspect you've outrun your share of people in your day. But, go on, I'll tell Corvinus you sneaked off while I was busy."

He started shuffling off, getting more stooped and feeble-looking with each step. "That's a good lad, Chase. I'll not be forgetting your generosity, either." By the time he disappeared into the darkness, you'd have never known it was the same person from the body language. Still, I knew Blind Bob, whoever he really was, knew a lot more about this Night Stalker business than he was volunteering. However, who was I to judge? I've been known to play my cards close when it suited my needs too.

His reaction to the mention of the case surprised me. If he wasn't the one who had it, I'd bet next month's wages he knew who did. There was no point in trying to tail him, though. If his hearing was as good as I suspected, he'd lead me anywhere *but* where the case was. I had to hope the offer of a reward would make him bring it to me, either in-person or through an inter-mediary.

I waited near the mouth of the alley. I was surprised Corvinus hadn't returned yet, but maybe he was still hung up on the phone. I kept glancing at the dumpster where my client's body lay and shuddered. I'd seen a lot of dead bodies in my career, but I'd never seen anyone dismembered like that before.

The hair on the back of my neck rose and I knew I wasn't by myself any longer. Before I could move, something hit me in the back of the neck hard and I went down like someone had cut the strings suspending me. I was awake, but my body refused to work. I saw a flash of light and realized it was reflecting off a large blade a few inches from my face.

Whoever had attacked me bent over and a voice sounding like it came from the grave whispered in my ear. "So, Mr. Chase decides to get involved in something that should not concern him. This is a poor career choice for Mr. Chase. As a matter of fact, Mr. Chase is likely to live much longer if he wisely quits now while he's mostly ahead. If he doesn't, then Mr. Chase is likely to be missing his head if we meet each other again. Does Mr. Chase understand?"

I managed to make some kind of noise and I felt the flat of the blade rub against my cheek. There was something about the voice, a mixture of creepy and deranged that frightened me in that moment like I'd never been afraid before. The voice told me its owner was capable of anything and I was lying there helpless to defend myself. "Mr. Chase should keep this in mind the next time he comes down to the docks, because it's likely to be the last time he does."

I waited for the blade strike, but nothing happened. After a few moments, I realized I was alone in the alley. It was a bit longer before feeling started coming back to my limbs. I managed to climb to my feet and brush myself off before the first squad cars arrived. There was no sign of my assailant. Whoever it had been had come and gone without leaving a trace, but I had no doubt I'd encountered the Night Stalker in person and lived to tell about it.

Once Corvinus had secured the scene, I talked one of the

officers into giving me a ride back to my apartment. After a few drinks and writing down notes about all the things that happened that evening, I decided I wasn't getting anywhere so I decided to call it a night. I double-checked the locks on my doors and windows, put my .45 under my pillow, and lay there for quite a while staring at the ceiling before I fell asleep.

I opened the door to Chase and Blackthorne just as my partner, Ze'eva Blackthorne was about to enter the inner office. "There you are, Theron. I was wondering if you were going to make it in today or not."

I rubbed the back of my neck before responding. "It was a rough night last night. We have a new client and I met her killer."

Ze' stopped in midstride and carefully pivoted on one spiked heel to face me. "Wait. Would you like to repeat that entire sentence again . . . only with a hundred percent more explanation?"

I motioned for Kyra to follow and I led the two women into the office. Kyra handed me a package and then eased into her favorite chair, steno book at the ready, while Ze'eva took her spot at her desk. I poured a glass of scotch, but just sat there letting the light reflect through it before setting it on the desk. "I take it Kyra hadn't mentioned our visitor last night?"

"Was just about to do that when you walked in, boss. Oh, by the way, that arrived this morning from Captain Corvinus. It's a list of all known locations of the bodies and another list of missing women who might be earlier victims before they knew what to look for. The constable who delivered it said he'd never seen the captain look so nervous before."

I toyed with the glass some more, wondering what Corvinus had seen to make him so cooperative, before sliding the glass a few inches away and resting my elbows on the desk. Taking a deep breath, I started explaining all of the events last night, including my encounter with the gentleman in the alley. "The fact he knew my name and why I was there is a tad concerning. Usually, I have to work at it to annoy people, but he got on me entirely too easy. This is not going to be a walk in the park."

Ze'eva let out a most un-ladylike snort before responding. "A serial killer at the docks, a horde of Valkyrie preparing to descend on Calasia, and a mysterious carrying case containing one soul . . . What part of any of this made you think this would be an easy case?"

"So I'm overly optimistic."

Kyra tapped her pencil on the edge of her pad. "If you want, boss, I can call in some of my cousins to help. Braggo has been hoping to help you out again if you can use him."

I considered it for a moment. Kyra might be a Sylph, but most of her relatives tended to be a bit more on the large side for the fae—Braggo , an eight-foot-two spriggan, was among the larger of them. "Tempting, Kyra, but I'm not sure how much stealthy snooping I could do with him along. He does tend to draw a crowd even in a town as used to unusual sights as Calasia."

"Good point, Theron. He also tends to be the hit first and ask questions after they wake up type. Probably not a good interrogation technique."

"However, it might be a good idea to put Braggo and a few of your other cousins on standby. If things get tight, I'm not against pulling out all the stops. Ze'eva, you up for a little snooping?"

"I thought you'd never ask."

I gave Kyra a list of some other contacts of mine and told her to round up as many as she could, just in case, along with her relatives. After that, Ze'eva and I caught a cab across town back down to the docks. Even in the daylight, I couldn't seem to shake the feeling I was being watched and laughed at from somewhere in the shadows. It had been a long time since someone had gotten the drop on me that completely, and I don't mind saying I didn't care for it one bit. Still, Naomi's deadline was hanging above our heads and time wasn't going to slow down just because I had the shakes.

It became clear after a few blocks Ze'eva could tell something was bothering me. Outside of a few questioning glances though, she didn't say anything. She seemed content to let me work it out on my own, but I knew we'd need to talk back at the office this evening. That was one thing I loved about her; she knew I was a private person, even around those I cared the most about, so she was willing to wait for me to bring it up. However, she'd made it clear enough she wasn't going to put up with being kept at arm's length permanently—and that applied to both work and our relationship.

Having Ze'eva along helped out quite a bit. The girls down on the docks "knew" me, which was good and bad. They knew I was a straight guy and they could trust me, but they also knew which side of the fence I stood on and were cagey with their answers—especially if they thought it could get them in trouble. However, Ze' was able to get them to lower their guards a bit and we made some headway.

Most didn't know much more than rumors, but after a while, even the rumors started to paint a picture. The Night Stalker had first struck about eight weeks ago. At first, everyone thought it was just some random thing because there were no signs of struggle and mostly just the one or two stab wounds. But, over time, the killings got more and more graphic. It was like whoever the Night Stalker was, he wanted them to admire his work. It felt like he was showing off, trying to generate as much fear as he was death. Most of the girls said they'd have left the area long ago if they could.

Somehow, the fact they couldn't leave didn't surprise me.

Unless the Stalker started targeting some of the major pimps down here, it was unlikely a few deaths would really cut into their bottom line. They would just recruit new women to replace their losses.

As we walked away from our latest interview, Ze' turned to me with a cold fire in her eyes. "I've dealt with some slimy operators on the club circuit, Theron, but this is beyond wrong. There are nights, when the moon is right, I wouldn't mind coming down here and realigning a few necks."

"I understand your feelings, but that's not going to solve much. Like any cockroach, you kill one and six dozen try to replace them. Let's settle for taking a serial killer down and then we can work on this problem."

She didn't stop muttering to herself for another block, but finally she pointed to a diner. "Let's grab a bite and go over our notes. Maybe getting something to eat will put me in a better mood."

"Perhaps, but don't get your hopes up. I've eaten at Louie's before. He's not known as the bicarbonate king for nothing."

Two servings of what passed for a pork chop, corn-on-the-cob, a salad, and a big helping of apple pie later, Ze'eva and I both felt a bit more like ourselves. I had just pulled out a map of Calasia to start plotting all the points our interviews had mentioned when a shadow fell over the table.

"Hello, Chase, long time no see."

I glanced up and saw Rocko Avilon smiling at me. Rocko had been big in the gambling rackets years ago before the authorities shut him down. I'd been one of the main witnesses at his trial so if he was back in town and looking for me, I could guarantee it wasn't because he wanted to wish me well. I frowned and nodded my head toward the door. "Not long enough, Rocko. Last time I saw you, you were being loaded into the wagon headed toward the work farm."

Rocko smile grew bigger. "You know what, Chase? I never

would have believed it, but it was a nice three-year vacation—fresh air, clean sheets, raising fruits and vegetables. Makes a man appreciate things in life. All that exercise is good for you, too. Never felt better than the day I walked out. You know, I bet ol' Fish Clayborne wishes he'd come out to the farm with me. I heard things didn't go so well for him after I left. Funny, if you think about it. Who knew a guy named Fish couldn't drown?"

Against my better judgement, I introduced Ze'eva to Rocko. I also explained to Ze'eva that Fish Clayborne had been Rocko's right-hand man and had been running Rocko's "businesses" after his boss's forced vacation. That was until he had his "unfortunate accident," as the coroner called it. "Well, I'm certain you've got a lot of catching up to do now that you're out, Rocko. I don't want to keep you."

His smile stayed plastered on his face. "Mind if I join you?"

I moved over next to Ze'eva and motioned for him to take my spot. "I'd say yes, but it's obvious you're not going to leave until we talk, so let's get this over with as quickly as possible."

Rocko gave Ze'eva a glance . . . just long enough to be annoying but not quite long enough for me to object without seeming insecure. Rocko liked to push until he had your measure. He wasn't reckless like most gangsters here in town, but he also wasn't someone you'd take lightly—not more than once.

Ze'eva gathered up the papers we'd been going over and slipped them inside her shoulder bag. I coughed to get his attention. "What's on your mind, Rocko?"

"Chase, I want to hire you."

I tried really hard, but I'm certain the fact my lower jaw nearly hit the table might have given away my surprise. "You . . . want to hire . . . *me?*"

"Well, it ain't so much want to as I need someone I can trust and I can't imagine going to no one else in this town than you."

"I'm flattered, Rocko, but I can't imagine this will end well."

He put both of his hands down on the table and for a split second, the expression on his face made me think he might be about to tell me the truth. "Look, Chase, this is real simple. I need you to do something and in return, I'll give you the name of Fish Clayborne's killer. That sound like a fair trade?"

I shifted uncomfortably in my seat before responding. "First off, I'm not a constable, so why tell me? Secondly, I'm the guy responsible for sending you to prison, so again, why tell me? You're up to something, so lay all your cards on the table faceup or take a hike. I don't have time to waste on a bunch of doubletalk."

Rocko waved his hands as if pushing me back down into my seat. "Relax, Chase. I told you, I enjoyed my time out on the farm and that's the truth. I suspect if I hadn't been there, ol' Fish might have had some company. I'm not above taking a hint. After we finish our business, I'm going to retire to a place south of town. Bought me a vineyard and I'm concentrating on getting into the winemaking business. Not quite as cutthroat as my old job, but there's still plenty of competition."

His grin grew even bigger. "Besides, you don't think you found all my dough, do you? I don't need to spend the rest of my life wondering who's walking behind me. I think retirement sounds rather nice. You oughtta consider it sometime."

I picked up my glass and lifted it to him in a mock toast. "Here's to your retirement. So, again, why me?"

"You're the only guy in this town I trust. I couldn't scare you and I couldn't buy you, so if you're involved, everyone will know it's on the up and up. You handle this one transaction for me and I hand you Fish's killer. Can't ask for a better deal than that."

"Let me be the judge of that. What, pray tell, is this simple transaction?"

He pulled an envelope from inside his jacket and handed it to me. "You take this. You put it in your office safe. Tonight at ten p.m., Black Tom and Drago are going to come by. You remember them, don't you? You open your safe. You hand this to them. They leave."

I remembered them, all right. The constables had been trying to pin enough murders on them to fill the diner we were currently sitting in. I waved a hand at him, trying to act nonchalant about the whole situation. "That's it?"

"That's it. Tomorrow, a messenger will deliver a package to your secretary. The package will lead you to Fish's killer as well as some very interesting evidence that can be used to pin the killing on them. Some former business associates of mine looked it up before I was released from the farm. Is that straightforward enough for you?"

"As straight as anything coming from you has ever sounded." I handed the envelope over to Ze'eva and she slipped it into her purse.

Rocko stood up and smoothed out his jacket. He started toward the door, but paused and doubled back to lean over the table again. "Oh, and Chase, I know you're a detective and all, but this is one time where you probably should keep your curiosity to yourself. I won't say Tom and Drago might be a bit upset if the envelope is tampered with in any way, but I won't say they won't be . . . if you follow my drift. Well, here's seeing you in the funny papers, Chase."

He left the diner without a second glance at us. I watched through the window long enough to see him get into a low-slung gray coupe driven by a young blonde woman wearing enough fur to make a grizzly jealous and drive off. I didn't recognize her, but then again, Rocko and I never hung out in the same social circle before he went away.

However, it didn't surprise me when Ze'eva muttered, "Phyllis Androfos. I wonder if her dad knows who she's hanging out with these days?"

I sipped my coffee a bit longer and then turned to Ze'eva. "Professional or social?"

"Definitely professional. She's a singer, but she works some of the classier clubs in North Point. Her dad is a big promoter. He's been working on getting her out of the Calasia circuit and up to the capital. Hanging out with Rocko isn't going to go over well with him or their publicity guy if the press gets ahold of that."

"Curiouser and curiouser. So, what do you make of this?"

Ze' stared out the window and I knew she was checking the alleys and streets to see who might have observed the transaction. "I've never met Mr. Avilon before, but I have a feeling you two were not best friends before you sent him to prison."

I laughed and felt some of the tension in my stomach wash away. "Ze', he's the one person who's come closest to making me the ex-Theron Chase of anyone I've ever known. Don't let his demeanor or his 'aw shucks' talk fool you. That man's memory would put most mentalists to shame and he's as cold blooded as a shark. We've traded shots, blows, and I've replaced more office furniture because of his bombs thanks to his ideas of 'fun.' If he came to me for anything, I guarantee you, it's good for him and bad for me."

"So, do we just dump this envelope and forget about it?"

I took another sip of my coffee to give me a moment to think and then shook my head. "If there is the slightest chance he will come through with the goods to get Fish Claybourne's killer, I've got to take the chance. However, I also know we won't be keeping it in the office safe."

"No?"

"No. Because there's a greater chance whatever is in this envelope is something Captain Corvinus would love to get his hands on and if I'm found with it, it's probably a one-way trip to that same farm he just left. After all, besides you, do you see anyone else who would testify they saw Rocko give it to me?"

Ze'eva glanced around and noticed both the cook and the waitress had conveniently disappeared. "I see they both decided to take a smoke break at the same time."

"Healthier than getting involved in Rocko's business. However, fear not, young lady. Thanks to certain remodels of our office space, we've got more nooks and crannies that don't show on any designer's plans—including a few that are bomb-proof. I suggest we retire to the office and resume reviewing the map there."

Ze'eva grinned. "I also seem to remember you brought in a new brand of scotch you wanted to sample the other day too."

"Well, what's the point in being a boss if you can't enjoy your office from time to time?"

To my surprise, the rest of the evening passed uneventfully. No mysterious visitors appearing on the fire escape, no surprise visits from Captain Corvinus, not even the cleaning lady made an appearance. It was a most congenial evening spent with a beautiful woman.

I'd never been so nervous in my life.

Ze'eva patted the seat on the sofa beside her. "For the gods' sake, Theron, sit down and relax. You're worse than a sheep at a werewolf convention. We've taken all the precautions we can. It's just a matter of getting rid of the envelope now."

I glanced out the window. The lights of Calasia shone all around peacefully, mocking my feelings. "I can't help it, Ze'eva. Things normally don't go this smooth. I must be overlooking something."

Sighing in resignation, Ze'eva stretched her legs and then stood up to join me at the window. "Is it possible Rocko was telling you the truth? Maybe he's squaring the books before he goes into retirement?"

"Rocko's ideas of squaring the books usually results in someone making gravesite visitations. It's against his nature to do something this simple. That was how I was able to catch him in the first place. If he'd just done the job and caught a freighter that evening, he'd have been out of reach before we even knew a crime had happened. No, he had to taunt the constables and leave clues, most of which were red herrings, and then try to catch the freighter just ahead of the dragnet. When we caught up with him on the gangplank, he was angry. Not because we'd caught him, but we were not following his script."

"Wow, that's some serious ego."

I cocked my head in the direction of the window to draw Ze's attention. "And speaking of scripts, there's one of Drago's boys over on the corner across the street. What time is it?"

"Nine forty-five."

"Right on time. If you glance out Kyra's window, I'll bet you see another guy on that corner, too. That would be one of Black Tom's men. If things go according to plan, they'll take every other corner."

"Oh, Black Tom and Drago aren't partners."

"Partners of convenience. They have had designs on Rocko's business ever since he went to the farm. I suspect they're none too happy ol' Rocko got an early release and I wouldn't be surprised if his sudden interest in retirement might not have been strongly suggested by the two gentlemen we're going to meet in a bit. I suspect both of them are looking for opportunities to consolidate the partnership into a sole proprietorship. As long as they don't involve bystanders, I really don't care who comes out on top."

Ze'eva tensed up and put her hand on the pistol in her purse. "I hear steps outside."

"The hallway or the fire escape?"

"Both."

I turned on the lights in Kyra's office and dimmed the lights in ours. I motioned Ze'eva to a spot where she could keep an eye on the windows as well as the outer office and I walked over to Kyra's desk and sat down on one corner. I spotted several shadowy shapes through the frosted glass, but they didn't move toward the door. A bell tolled the hour from down the street just as someone started knocking on the door.

"Come in, gentlemen. I've been expecting you."

The two men who entered couldn't have been more different. Black Tom was a short, compact man who moved with the grace of a dancer or a professional athlete. His black hair was slicked back in the latest style and his clothes were elegant without being flashy.

Drago was tall and thin, almost skeletal in his appearance. His bald head shone in the light from the bulb and I swear the quick grin he gave me as he entered showed sharpened teeth. His clothes were so rumpled, I wouldn't have been surprised if he slept in them; they were years out of fashion.

But the two of them did share one thing in common: There wasn't a trace of humanity in either of their dark eyes. I knew both of them would kill me as quickly as they'd talk to me and neither would lose a second of sleep over it.

Tom broke the silence. "You have something for us, Chase?"

I stood up, keeping my hands in clear view. I had no doubt both men had snipers on the rooftops—trained on both of them and me. "I do, but not on me. If you'll accompany me to the inner office. My partner is waiting inside there."

"We know. Come on, Drago. Let's get this over with."

Now, that's comforting.

I motioned to the chairs near my desk, but both Black Tom and Drago stopped just inside the door and waited. Ze'eva gave me a signal telling me the fire escape landing outside our window was clear—for now—so I went over to my desk and gently opened a drawer. I felt more than three pairs of eyes on me as I slid the envelope out and then carried it over to Tom.

"Here you go. Please examine it. You'll find nothing has been tampered with. It's as pristine as it was when Rocko handed it to us."

Black Tom examined it and then handed it to Drago. He balanced the envelope in his hand and then sniffed it. "You done good, shamus. There's a scented capsule in here. If you'd opened this, the smell would have dissipated in seconds. You gotta have a nose like mine to spot it, though."

"Rocko asked that it be delivered intact and so I have. I hope you'll report I kept my side of the bargain."

"You have indeed, Chase. We will be happy to inform our former boss and current benefactor you proved yourself quite the trustworthy gentleman. While we will not divulge the contents of this package for your own health's sake, let us say it will prove highly profitable to us and will ensure Rocko enjoys his upcoming retirement."

"What my overeducated partner is sayin' to you, shamus, is if you don't wake up tomorrow, it's not our fault. Good to know there's one honest Joe out there."

"I don't think I could have said it better myself, Drago. Now, if we have no other business to transact, gentlemen, it's been a long day and the lady and I would like to retire for the night."

Drago gave Ze'eva an appreciative look. "I have to say, Chase, I didn't know being a detective had such *fringe* benefits."

"Gentlemen, my partner, Ze'eva Blackthorne."

Black Tom bowed to her. "An absolute pleasure, my lady. I've caught a few of your shows at the Black Dragon and I must admit I'm quite taken with your talent and beauty. It is an honor to finally get to meet you in person, even if under such unusual circumstances."

Drago let out a dramatic sigh. "Damn it, Tom. Always using forty words when ten would work. He's a fan of yours, Toots. Come on, Tom, we're done here."

"Indeed we are, my impetuous friend. If you'll pardon us,

Chase, Miss Blackthorne, we have yet another appointment this evening."

I escorted the two men out of the office and locked the door behind them. I turned out the light in the outer office and rejoined Ze'. I pushed a buzzer on my desk and watched as the windows darkened and the noises of the city became muffled. A few minutes later, one of the hidden panels in my bookshelf slid backward revealing Theo and Naomi in the spare office. Naomi floated over to the darkened windows and concentrated for a bit before rejoining us.

"There is consternation because of the screen Theo has erected, but more because they cannot observe us. I did not detect any intention of attacking, but there are some out there who have orders to watch us."

Theo chuckled and then sat down in my chair at my desk. "Let them wonder. Unless they have an imperial-grade wizard with them, they're not getting through that barrier until I drop it."

I gave Theo a dirty look for sitting in my chair, which he pointedly ignored, so I took a seat on the sofa. "One package delivered. Now, what was so important about that package and how is it going to backfire on me for delivering it?"

Theo smiled broadly and leaned back in my chair. "Ze'eva, spotting that capsule was brilliant." He turned to Ze' and smiled, "I still don't see what you see in that lump on the couch, but it can't be for his deductive abilities. It appears the mystic jar I opened the letter in prevented the capsule from activating. It was only a minor bit of prestidigitation to get the envelope resealed."

"Actually, Theo, it was his idea for me to check for something like that."

Theo had the decency to blush before he leaned forward and blustered on. "Be that as it may, the envelope contained three things: a set of keys, a piece of paper covered in mathematical symbols, and a compass. I was able to make a copy of the keys and reproduce the script on the paper. However, the compass was a bit of a challenge."

"Wait. Are you saying there are things an imperial-grade wizard can't do? Ze'eva, mark this on the calendar. I want to remember this."

Theo slowly turned in the chair to face me. "I said, 'a bit of a challenge,' not an insurmountable task." His face fell, though. "It will take me a bit to decipher and reproduce the compass though. Its magic is unfamiliar. It appears to be divinatory in nature, but is not." The smile returned to his face. "A worthy challenge indeed."

"That's all well and good, Theo. However, considering the fact we're facing annihilation in a few days, I think that's a project for another day."

"Nonsense, Theron. After all, Naomi hired you because you're a detective. I was merely the means for transporting her to meet you. If it was something I was good at, I certainly wouldn't have bothered you with this."

Naomi suddenly stiffened and turned toward the darkened window. "I hate to break up your mutual admiration society, but something is happening across the street. I felt three lives disappear and there is a great hunger out there looking for more."

"The Night Stalker?"

"I'm not certain. Remember, I was in my human form when I was assaulted. Even though I'm stronger and quicker than the average human when manifested, my senses are no sharper than yours. This form, while inconvenient, does have its advantages. The question is, since whatever is out there is killing potential enemies, should we let it continue without interference?"

I shook my head as I grabbed my pistol out of my desk and headed toward the door. "Not the way I work, Naomi. Ze', stay here and guard these two—I don't want the trinkets Theo has disappearing."

I headed up the stairs, taking two at a time. Simply knowing they were on nearby rooftops wasn't enough of a clue, I needed to see what was happening before I blindly rushed over to another building. After the third set of stairs, I resolved to either get a new office closer to the top floor or to move into a shorter building. I paused for a second at the door to the roof and eased it open. I gave my eyes a moment to get used to the darkness and then slipped out and pressed my body up against one of the pipes running across the top of the building. After ensuring I was alone on my own rooftop, I began scanning the others. There was no sign of movement, so I worked my way over toward my office's side of the building.

The dim moonlight didn't reveal much at first, but after a while I noticed several dark shapes that did not belong where they were. Seconds went by and there was no sign of move-ment, so I assumed they were either unconscious or dead, if Naomi's senses were correct. There was no sign of anyone on the other roofs or down in the street, so I headed back to let everyone know what the situation was.

Stepping out of the stairwell on my floor, I came up short. There was a piece of paper stuck to the door with a knife. I took a deep breath and eased my way over, feeling like I was being watched by someone or something I couldn't quite spot. I unlocked and opened the office door, carefully stepping inside. I pulled out a handkerchief and worked the knife out of the door and then shut and locked the door behind me.

I recognized the click of Ze'eva's heels coming up behind me as I flipped Kyra's desk lamp. "What do you have there, Theron?"

"Not sure, Ze'. This was left in our door. I spotted several bodies on the roof across the street, but whether they're alive or dead I couldn't tell. You might want to give Corvinus a call and let him know he's got some pickups."

She moved over to the phone while I set the knife aside and opened up the folded piece of paper. The note inside was written in a crude hand.

"I took care of a small matter for you. Don't worry, I'll be around to collect."

I felt Ze'eva come up behind me and read over my shoulder. "No, that's not creepy at all."

"Ze'eva, there hasn't been a single thing about this case that hasn't been creepy. However, what is the Stalker's tie-in with Rocko, Black Tom, and Drago? It's not normal for serial killers to hunt gang members. Most gang deaths are retaliation for something."

I folded up the paper and stuck it in my jacket pocket. "Another question we can ask when we catch him. What did Corvinus say?"

"'Tell Chase not to leave before I get there. I want to know what he knows about this and I don't mean tomorrow.'"

The clock showed 11:30, so I sent Theo and Naomi home to get some rest. Ze' and I settled in to wait for Corvinus . . . well, Ze' settled in and I paced the floor. I was fuming over losing time in trying to find Naomi's briefcase and the Night Stalker, and meeting with Corvinus was not high on my list of things to do. After a bit, I decided if he was en route to my office, he wasn't at the morgue, so I might as well follow up with Maxie.

"Chase, glad you got back with me. I was surprised when you didn't stop by later."

"Sorry about that, Maxie. Things came up. Just how many women have come in from around the East Docks?"

"Total of nine so far. Don't hold me to that, 'cause some of the most recent are cut up so bad, we're not a hundred percent sure we've matched all the pieces to the last few bodies. Officer

Jabrok tells me he's had reports of at least another five or six missing from that area."

"Any signs of women attacked like that in any other area of Calasia?"

"Nothing so far, Chase. If I were more than just a morgue tech, I'd say the guy has his hunting ground staked out. From what the M.E. says, serial killers tend to stay around areas they're comfortable with and won't move until something makes them uncomfortable."

"Well, Maxie, you're likely to have some more bodies coming in tonight. Not women, but I think the same guy killed them. In fact, you're going to be getting a knife probably used in tonight's killings. See if it compares to the wounds on the female victims. I need to know if this is the same guy or a copycat. Can you get me a copy of the coroner's notes when he's done?"

"I don't know, Chase. I could get in big trouble . . . ah, what the heck, if they haven't fired me now for helping you, what's one more infraction?"

"That's the spirit, Maxie. I think I hear Corvinus coming up the stairs, so I'll see you tomorrow for that report."

"Be careful, Chase. You're working with a real wacko out there."

I had no sooner hung up the phone when Ze' let the captain into the room. He was his usual charming bull-in-a-porcelain-shop self. "All right, Chase, what's going on? My boys found six guys cut to ribbons on two separate building within a block of your place. How did you know and what's your connection?"

"Honestly, Captain, I was hoping you could tell me. Ze'eva and I were reviewing some cases when we noticed the commotion. I spotted the bodies and thought we should call you immediately. Just being good citizens."

"I can see why you teamed up with Miss Blackthorne—probably the only one who can read between the two of you. And don't think I'm buying this cock-and-bull story of yours for a moment, Chase, but it's not important now. The few who had enough left to identify were members of Black Tom's and Drago's gangs. They were also packing enough artillery to start a war. From what we can tell, most died without even getting a shot off."

"Were they knife wounds?"

"Yeah, and a big one . . . Hey, how did you know that?"

I pointed at the desk. "Apparently someone left me a present in my door while I was trying to get a good look at the carnage from my own roof. You'll find a nice notch in my door outside where it was left."

Corvinus gave me the side-eye. "All right, Chase, what's the gag? Normally, you don't hand stuff over to me without some kind of angle."

"The only thing I want from you is for you to check this knife against the wounds from the Night Stalker killings. I want to know if he might have done it or if someone's trying to throw the blame on him."

"Whether it does or not is no concern of yours, Chase. That is a police matter and will be handled within police channels." He glared at me, but then said *sotto vocce*, "If we find a match, I'll let you know."

"Thanks, Captain, I knew I could count on you."

Corvinus blustered some more about staying where they could find me and then headed out the door, the knife secured in an envelope. Personally, I was glad to see that thing leave. Whether or not it actually belonged to the Night Stalker, it gave me the willies just looking at it.

"So, Ze'eva, have you had enough excitement for one day or should we head down to the docks and see what we can stir up there?"

"Let's call it a night. I want to try and follow up on something that's been bugging me. I'll tell you more once I have an answer."

"And you fuss at me for keeping secrets. All right, I'll meet you at Josie's Drugstore at seven p.m. tomorrow. We'll grab a bite and head out from there."

"It's a date," she said, grabbing her coat. She blew me a kiss as she let herself out of the office. A few minutes later, I grabbed my own coat and made my way over to my apartment building, but it took a while for sleep to come. I kept wondering how everything tied together. Somewhere around Theory Number 40, I nodded off.

T he fog was as thick as it had been two days ago and it wasn't making me feel any less edgy as I made my way down to the East Docks. It wasn't so thick I couldn't make my way around, but everything had taken on that out-of-focus look. The few people I could see on the streets were keeping their distance from one another. Even on streets where no one was visible, there was no mistaking the fear seeping out of the darkened apartments and businesses.

Just the perfect situation for looking for clues to a serial killer or a missing briefcase. With any luck, I might be Maxie's next customer.

I shook off those dark thoughts and worked my way deeper into the warehouse district of the docks. We hadn't had time to get this far the other night when Corvinus and I conducted our initial search. I had a map of the area I'd borrowed from a friend in the City Planning Board's office, but I also knew these maps were out-of-date the moment they were created. People set up buildings, tore down buildings, and turned parking lots into storage areas at the drop of a hat.

After an hour of searching, I had found four unmarked alleys, two illegal storage sheds, and an illegal bar serving smuggled rum to the longshoremen, and had worn a year's worth of leather off my shoes. I was thinking about trying to contact

Shady Quickbite, a ratman who knew the sewers beneath this area like I knew my apartment, when I heard a familiar clicking sound heading my way. I took a seat on a nearby trashcan and waited.

The old blind beggar came even with me and stopped. "Ah, you had lunch at Simon's today. It's hard to disguise that onion-and-garlic sauce he puts on his sandwiches."

"And good day to you, Bob. How's life treating you?"

Blind Bob smiled in my general direction. "It's been a good day so far. The fog is keeping most people off the streets, so no one is around to bump into me or get annoyed because I'm not walking fast enough for them. I actually love the fog."

I fished a five-crown coin out of my pocket and handed it to him. "So, Bob, have you heard anything new since the last time I saw you? I believe I mentioned something to you about a case. Maybe someone found a briefcase they can't open and wants to sell it as quickly as possible?"

Blind Bob froze for just a split second before he ran a hand over his chin. "I do recall you mentioning that the other night. You see, I have heard something since then. Someone found one in an alley not too far from where we met. The first person to find it didn't do too well. Seems there was a booby-trap on the case and all Sheila found was a set of empty clothes and the vague sooty outline of a man against the wall of the alley."

"Sheila?"

Bob rubbed his hands in a peculiar manner before responding. "Oh, yes, Sheila. One of the young ladies who earns her living down here on the docks after sunset. She's always been nice to me, but that's not what you want to hear about. You want to know about what happened to the briefcase next."

"That is the general idea yes, Bob."

"Well, you see, that's the problem. Apparently Mouse didn't approve of Sheila finding something and not turning it over to him immediately. There was an argument in one of the apartment buildings a few blocks from here and somehow Mouse wound up going right out the window. No one's sure if he was trying to push Sheila out and missed or if she did it on purpose. Either way, Mouse's associates are now looking for the young woman and I'm afraid they're not in the mood to listen to explanations."

"Bob, you're well on your way to earning another five crowns if you can point me toward Sheila. Have you heard if she still has the briefcase?"

Bob cocked his head from one side to the other and then shook his head. "I'd love to help you, Mr. Chase, but in case you hadn't noticed, our conversation seems to have drawn the attention of a number of people. I'm going to take my leave of you here, but please do come to Madame Illysa's house tonight, say around midnight. I'll do what I can to procure the young lady and the case."

I could feel the eyes on the back of my neck, but I kept my face focused on Bob. He wasn't worried yet, so I decided I had time for one more pitch. "Bob, I'll remind you, there is a significant reward for the return of the case intact, but we have to find it soon."

"Again, I do remember something about that. That certainly piques my interest. Ah, company approaches. I think you might want to turn around now and duck."

I heard the scrape of a shoe behind me and I ducked and spun around. I felt the wind from a blackjack split the air just inches above my head and I buried my fist into my assailant's midsection, driving the air out of his lungs. Two other men, slightly smaller than your average ogre, were rushing at me from the right, so I did the intelligent thing and ran as hard as I could to my left. I didn't know why they were after me, but neither of them seemed to be in a talkative mood—if you ignore the various invectives they hurled my way as we ran.

I don't know how many blocks they chased me, but after a

while I spotted a familiar waterfront bar and dove through the door. Sharkey rushed out of his office to see what the hell was going on, but he stepped to the side and let me pile into his office as the two ogres came charging in behind me. Sharkey bellowed something in a language I didn't know and a few seconds later, a door at the far end of the bar popped open and several sea trolls came bounding up the stairs. The ogres took one look at the odds and decided one private detective wasn't worth the beating they were about to get. They barely got out the door one step ahead of the trolls, who invited the retreating ogres to come back anytime with as many friends as they wanted to bring.

Sharkey walked back into his office and shut the door behind him. He took a seat at his desk and let out a belly laugh. "Oh, Chasie, you do liven up the place when you stop by. Wish your friends hadn't been in such a hurry to leave. We haven't had a decent donnybrook in here for a least a month. The boys are worried they're losing their edge."

"I'll try to see if I can't find a better quality of leg-breakers the next time."

Sharkey slapped a palm on the table and laughed again. "You do that, Chase. You do that. Well, since you're here, what can I do for you?"

I decided to play a long shot. "Sharkey, apparently my newest client had a run-in with the Night Stalker. In the middle of that, she lost something very valuable and *very* dangerous. Now, I've a rather unimpeachable source who swears he knows where it might be, but the young lady in possession of it is in a bad situation herself. Following so far?"

"I swear, Chase, one of these days you're going to get a normal case and die of boredom. So, I'm going to make a couple of guesses and if it doesn't break your client-detective confidentiality thing, you let me know if I'm right or close. Okay?"

"Sure, Sharkey, I just didn't want to get you involved more

than you already are. After all, someone apparently doesn't want me to make that meeting tonight. I don't think they're going to appreciate your interference."

"Chase, I wouldn't have lasted as long as I have down here on the docks if I couldn't deal with stepping on a few toes. Now, you say your client had a run in with the Night Stalker. I'm assuming she's an ex-client, then?"

"Yes and no. She is ex- but not an ex-client. After all, she hired me afterward."

I saw Sharkey's forehead wrinkle as he pondered what I'd said before a smile spread across his ugly mug, showing way more teeth than a normal human would have. "Oooooh. Now, this case has gotten even more interesting. So, she wants you to find the Night Stalker?"

"No, although I've already had one meeting with him. She's more interested in recovering the briefcase lost during the incident. She was bound for a private boat at the East Docks when she was waylaid. To be quite honest, Sharkey, it's beyond vital that we recover the case. Almost end-of-the-world vital, if you follow me?"

Sharkey held up a big paw. "Whoa, wait up, back up. You met *the* Night Stalker . . . in person . . . and you're here talking to me?" He rose from his chair and walked up to me, poking me in the chest and shoulder areas. "Nope, you're not a ghost . . . anyway, not yet. How do you account for that?"

"Maybe he'd met his quota for the night? How the hell do I know? All I know is I'm not in a big hurry to meet him again. While I'd love to catch him, it's vital that I recover the case. If my client can't deliver it by a specific date and time, her employers are going to hold the entire city responsible for what happened to her, and that's not going to be pretty."

Sharkey poked me one more time on the shoulder just to be sure and I slapped his hand away. He rubbed the back of his hand and grinned. "Okay, you ain't no ghost if you can hit that hard. So, tell me, Chase, what do you need me to do?"

"First off, what can you tell me about a guy named Mouse?"

"You mean the pimp who fell to his death two nights ago? Not much. Wasn't a very pleasant fellow from what I heard, but most of Drago's boys aren't. I think he tries to find the most obnoxious men around. I hear his associates took a dim view of his death, which is sorta weird 'cause I figured they'd be too busy splitting up his operations. Go figure."

"Wait, one of Drago's boys?"

"Yeah. Drago took over the flesh trade down on the docks when Rocko went to prison. Thought you knew?"

"Vice isn't something I usually stay on top of. You know a girl who used to work for Mouse, named Sheila?"

"I hear she's the one who helped him take a dive into a concrete pool."

"There are differing versions of the story. However, she may have a line on this briefcase I really, really need to get my hands on. If you could have a couple of your boys find her and make sure nothing happens to her before my meeting with her at midnight, I'd be happy to return the favor to you in the future."

"Aw hell, Chase. No worries. Besides, I seem to remember you saved my life once or twice when I was getting established here. We've been friends too long to keep track of who owes who."

"And that's why we get along so well, Sharkey. Mind if I use your back door?"

"Sure, Chase. We'll be talking soon."

I slipped into the alley behind his bar after ensuring none of my earlier playmates were hanging around. Then I counted my fingers, toes, checked my back for knives and made sure all of my teeth were still in place. Sharkey had agreed to this deal just a little too easy—he was up to something and I could only hope

Mrs. Chase's favorite son would wind up on the right side of the deal when it was all said and done.

"Kyra, this is Theron."

"Hey, boss. The package you were expecting arrived this morning. You coming into the office this afternoon?" I could hear her keeping her voice light, which told me someone was in the office with her.

"I can be there in about a half hour. Anything going on I should know about?"

"If you could stop by the deli, it'd be great. I really could go for a Reuben."

I felt my stomach tighten. We had a few phases we'd use on the phone when we didn't want people to know what we were actually talking about. In this case, the deli meant there was trouble and a Reuben meant I was about to walk into an ambush.

"No worries, Kyra. I'll have them make it just the way you like. Anything else you want?"

"Some coleslaw, pickles, and a soft drink."

"You got it. See you in a bit."

Kyra's list told me there were three people waiting for me. I didn't know if it was the same three who'd tried to waylay me while I was talking to Blind Bob or if this was a different pack, but either way, I'd have a surprise for them. I hung up the phone and flagged down a taxi. I gave him the address for Markham's Emporium of the Ancients. While the cabbie maneuvered his way through traffic across town, I went over a few of my options before a nasty grin spread across my face as I decided on just how I wanted to handle this.

I walked into the Emporium and the head clerk motioned for

me to follow him. A quick walk down a dark mahogany hallway through the thickest carpet I'd ever stepped on and we were in front of a door marked PRIVATE. A quick knock and a muffled reply led to me being let into Theo's sanctum sanctorum.

Filling in Theo as quickly as possible about everything that had happened today, I told him what I had in mind to get Kyra and myself out of our predicament. He smiled evilly and motioned for me to follow him. Several hidden doors and disguised stairwells later, we arrived in his laboratory. Naomi was sitting on one of the benches, idly toying with some chemicals.

"Now, my dear, what did I tell you about that?"

"Honestly, Theo, you're worse than my mom. I'm already dead. What can I do that's worse than that?"

"If you have to ask, you really have no business doing what you're doing," he said as he slipped the vials from her hands and put them back on their shelves. "However, if you don't mind, I could use an assistant for this project."

Naomi joined him at a table and Theo pointed me toward a small room next door. As I watched through a glass window, he slipped behind a screen and emerged a bit later wearing a lab coat, pristine white apron, and heavy rubber gloves. He set up some retorts and other lab equipment and ignited several burners. Naomi grabbed several vials and potions off the walls as he pointed them out and he measured out varying amounts before she returned them to their spots. I'd always known Theo was an imperial-grade wizard, but I hadn't realized just how into alchemy he was.

After twenty minutes, he carefully poured the contents into a container and motioned for me to return. "Here you go, Chase. I think this will do fine."

"What exactly have you done, Theo?"

He patted me on the shoulder. "I think I'll leave it as a

surprise. However, as soon as Kyra opens her coleslaw hit the floor and take her with you."

He noticed me giving him a dirty look as he stripped his gloves off of his hands, and continued. "Don't look at me like that. I will tell you it's not fatal nor is it long-lasting, but you *really* do not want to breathe this in."

"All right, Theo. Think you can get me to the hallway outside my office quickly?"

"If you're asking if I'll make a portal for you, yes, but not right this moment."

"Why not?"

Theo looked at me as if preparing a lecture for a rather slow student. "Because, Theron, before you just go blundering into a trap, wouldn't it be easier if you could survey the situation first?"

"Theo, do you have my office bugged?"

"Theron, I am a wizard. If I can't cast a simple scrying spell into an office I have been in numerous times, either someone's specifically blocking me or I should turn in my wands. I did need help that first time, remember? However, your charming partner has invited me over several times. Seems she has much nicer manners than some I could mention. Which reminds me—Ze'eva had me put a block around your hidden rooms. I need to send you my bill."

"A little less bragging and a little more casting, Theo?"

He made a harrumphing noise, but I could see he was pleased he'd gotten under my skin again. He pulled a mirror down from one of his lab shelves and set it on the bench. A few words later, the mirror's surface swirled and the interior of my office appeared in the glass. To my surprise, it wasn't my playmates from earlier. These appeared to be three normal, well-dressed men. If not for the revolvers in their hands, I'd have thought they were businessmen or lawyers. Kyra seemed to be unharmed but from the way her hands were flat on her desk, they weren't taking any chances on her doing something.

"So, you sure you want to go in the front door?"

"Yes, actually. Look at how they're arranged. They're expecting me to come in through the fire escape or from my interior office. I think coming in the front door will give me time to try and pull off my plan."

Theo glanced at the glass. "I believe you're right, for once. Do you want either Naomi or me to come with you?"

"For three guys in my own office? I'd never live it down. No, but keep an eye on us just in case they've got backup."

Theo muttered something about overconfidence, but began chanting. A black swirling circle appeared on one wall of the lab and after he nodded, I picked up the "deli order" and stepped through. For once I managed not to stumble as I appeared on the other side and made sure to check Theo's surprise was in place before I entered my office.

"Here you go, Kyra. One Reuben with the works, just like you requested. Good afternoon, gentlemen, what I can I do for you?"

I could tell my sudden appearance had startled them, but they recovered quickly. Two of them adjusted their guns to cover me while the third kept his trained on Kyra. I sat the sack on her desk, pointedly ignoring the gunmen. I pulled out the prepared container and slid it across the desk to her. "Sid said he did the coleslaw extra spicy just like you like."

"Hold it just a minute, shamus. You might notice we've got the guns here."

"And so you do. I'll be right with you after I finish delivering my secretary's lunch. I mean, after all this, you object to her eating? I admit I'm curious why you're here."

"Stinks to be you then, 'cause I don't think you're gonna like the answer. Hey, give me that container."

"You like coleslaw, too?"

He snatched the sealed cup out of my hand. "No, you jerk, I want to be sure what's actually in there. Pass the rest of the sack over here, too."

"As you wish."

I moved closer to Kyra as he began fumbling with the lid. The second he broke the seal, I grabbed Kyra and hit the floor. I heard some shouts, curses, and then nothing. I looked up and saw a cloud of black smoke hanging about a foot above the floor filling the rest of the room. Kyra was muttering something next to me and I realized she had formed a wall of hard air around us, keeping the smoke away. After a few minutes, the smoke began to lighten and then slowly faded away, revealing the three gunmen frozen in place. Kyra kept the spell up for a few more minutes until she was comfortable the gas had dissipated.

"As much as I'm enjoying snuggling with you, boss, you can let go now."

I quickly unwrapped my arms from around her and stood up. Not knowing how long Theo's concoction would keep them paralyzed, I confiscated their guns and frisked them. The other weapons they'd been carrying were piled into one of Kyra's desk drawers. I took a seat on the edge of her desk while we waited for the effects to wear off. About five minutes later, they slowly began moving and as they became more mobile, I waved them over to the couch. They grumbled but decided they didn't want to argue with my .45, much less the very angry Sylph standing beside me.

"Boys, we're going to make this short and sweet. Who do you work for? Why are you here? Why should I let you leave?"

They stared at one another before the one in the middle edged forward on the couch cushion to speak. "We work for Black Tom. Not full time, but he hires us from time to time for special jobs."

"And what's special about this job?"

They shared glances again and the two on either side of the

spokesman shrugged. He turned his attention back to me. "We were paid to find out what's inside that package."

"That's it?"

"That's it. Once we knew, we were supposed to report back to him, get paid, and get out of town."

"So, you're not from here?"

"Like I said, we're contracted help. We come in, do a job, and leave."

I tapped my fingers against my knee. "Well, Kyra, you had the most time with them. Should we let them report back empty-handed or do you want to dump them off the fire escape one at a time?"

One of them started to say something but the guy in the middle cut him off. They sat stock-still, but three sets of eyes watched Kyra closely as she moved toward the door. With a sudden swing of her arms, the door flew open and a gust of wind tossed the three men into the hallway. They rolled across the landing with a satisfying thud before Kyra slammed the door behind them.

"That work for you, boss?"

"Yeah, that should do. Now, where's the package you mentioned?"

"Stuck it in your office safe as soon as it arrived. The messenger said you'd be the only one who could open it, so I didn't bother checking."

I filled her in on today's events as we walked into my office. She took her usual seat next to my desk as I walked over to the safe. I reached up but paused just inches away from the safe dial. "Do you find it curious how both Drago's and Black Tom's men are so interested in this package? You'd think they'd know since they both used to work for Rocko—unless they think it contains information that pins Fish's death on one or the other of them. I wonder if they think it would allow either of them to take over the other's territory without a war?"

"Well, there's only one way to know, boss. You're going to have to open it."

I reached up again and then paused. "Then again, it also could be a little going-away present from Rocko. After all, I am the one who sent him to prison. He might not be as ready for retirement as he was letting on."

A knock on the doorframe nearly made me jump out of my skin, but before either Kyra or I could react, Theo's voice stopped me. "I was wondering if you were going to be stupid enough to just open that package without some kind of protective spell. Really, Chase, what if it is a bomb or say, poisonous gas as opposed to my mere paralytic one? I know you're cavalier with your own life, but *do* think of your poor secretary there."

"Ah, Theo, somehow I knew you were due to put in an appearance. Is Naomi with you?"

Theo motioned for me to open the safe before answering. "Unfortunately, no. That delightful creature had another appointment, or so she claimed. I felt it was best not to inquire too closely into her personal business. When one gets to be my age, it pays to stay on the good side of any avatar of Death. She will be here this evening, though."

I gingerly took the package out and handed it to Theo. He carried it over to my desk and began examining it. I couldn't tell if he was muttering to himself or casting a spell, but after a few minutes, his shoulders relaxed and he plopped down into my chair. "Well, it's not going to explode, fill the room with a toxic fume, or ignite on contact with air. What happens after you open it, well, even I can't see that far into the future."

"Wait, did I just hear Theo Markham, the pride of the Calasian wizardry community, just admit he might have limitations?"

"Remember, Theron, I'm not the magical enigma. Neither magical artifacts nor divination seem to work well around you.

If I didn't know better, I'd say there are some skeletons in your ancestry."

"We'll take up my genealogy another time. Let's see what's in here."

I opened the package carefully and glanced at the small stack of paper inside. I tipped it up to slide them out and a rather familiar-looking key and compass dropped out and bounced on my desk. "Theo, what do you make of this?"

With a flourish, a matching key appeared in Theo's hand and he set it on the desk next to the new one. "Apparently, Rocko wants you to have a shot at whatever Drago and Black Tom are after. These keys are identical."

Kyra picked up a magnifying glass from my desk and examined the two keys. "Which we'd have never known if we hadn't checked the contents of the first envelope."

"But what does it mean?"

Theo looked up from the papers he was thumbing through. "You'll know that answer as soon as I finish translating the documents I already have. This is the same cipher. Someone wants you to go somewhere, but he doesn't want to make it too easy."

"Then perhaps you should get back to that?"

"Then perhaps I should. Do try to stay alive, Theron. My life would be so much more boring without you in it. See you at midnight."

Kyra closed her notebook after I finished dictating a report on my encounter with Drago's men. Before she could get up though, Ze'eva came in, smiling enigmatically, and made a motion toward doors. I secured the office and took a seat on the corner of my desk as she took off her coat and brushed her dark hair out of her face. Kyra walked over and tapped the bottom of my jaw with her pencil.

"You're drooling again, boss," she whispered before taking her usual seat.

I had the decency to look sheepish before turning back to Ze'eva. I caught the momentary smirk before she took center stage in our little play.

"I know we weren't supposed to meet before dinner, but I didn't want to wait. It's not often I get one step ahead of you, Theron." She pulled her notebook from her purse. "While I may not know Calasia as well as you do, I do know the theater district. I discovered some interesting information on Phyllis Androfos."

I thought for a second and then snapped my fingers. "Ah, the young blonde lady we saw with Rocko last evening. The one with the gorgeous sports car."

Ze' gave me a glance. "I'm glad to hear you were more interested in her car than her."

"I only saw the back of her head and her shoulders, remember? Should I take a closer look?"

She gave me a dirty look and then flipped her notebook open. "Needless to say, she is well known in the theater district. Her father's position as a promoter helped her get into some of the better theaters at the start of her career. That didn't win her many friends in the business."

Nope. No professional jealousy at all.

"However, she does have talent—no amount of money can keep you on stage if you don't have *some* talent. However, this isn't a review of her career. She's been building up an interesting résumé the past few years off-stage."

"Yeah, you mentioned something when we recognized her last night. However, you also said her father wouldn't be happy with her hanging around our Mr. Avilon."

"I did say that. Apparently I was wrong. They've been together a lot longer than I realized."

Ze' found the page she was looking or and continued. "She met Rocko five years ago and from all reports, it was a whirl-wind romance. However, it appears Phyllis was the one doing the pursuing. Shortly after they met, Rocko's mistress, Tiana Hooper, had a fatal car accident. Apparently, her brakes failed on the Coast Highway twenty miles south of Calasia. The car failed to negotiate a curve and plunged a hundred feet into the sea. No trace of the car was ever found, so there was only a cursory investigation and it was chalked up as an unfortunate accident."

"But you don't think so."

"The constables did find Tiana's body at the bottom of the cliff. Her injuries were consistent with falling from a great height. However, Maxie looked up the autopsy report and said it was impossible to swear if she'd been ejected from the car when it hit or if she'd been thrown off the cliff. He said no one had ever asked that question before."

I nodded, listening to Kyra's pencil scraping as she furiously took notes. "Interesting. So, she set her eyes on Rocko and possibly eliminated the competition. But, for what purpose?"

Ze'eva flashed that infuriating smile she gets when she knows something I don't. "Not only did she move in with Rocko shortly after Tiana's death, but—five months later, Rocko's personal accountant was arrested for tax fraud. On Phyllis's recommendation, Rocko hired Phyllis's agent's partner to take over the books. Over the years, she's wormed her way into his organization, but always in the background. When you sent Rocko up a few years ago, even though Fish was left in charge, Phyllis was running things. When Fish met his unfortunate demise, she stepped in to lead the gangs until Rocko was released."

"And she was still performing on stage during all this? Impressive."

Ze' poured herself a small drink and flipped to a new page in her notebook. "Never let it be said Phyllis isn't ambitious. She used Rocko's money and power to get herself better gigs as well as investing in new forms of entertainment while he was away. She's working through dummy companies and shills, but from what I've found out, she's part owner of three nightclubs and two of the new motion-picture theaters. She fronted the money for the new radio station, and she has a partial interest in a floating casino off the coast of Calasia. All very legitimate businesses and *all* very profitable. She'd been a very busy person . . . until Rocko was sprung."

"Oh? I suspect things get even more interesting here?"

"Depends on your definition of interesting. When Rocko said he was retiring, he wasn't kidding, Theron. From what I've found out so far, he's sold his properties around Calasia and divided his criminal holdings between Black Tom and Drago. He's in the middle of selling his legitimate businesses to an unknown consortium. It also appears his vineyard is legitimate."

I sat forward and picked up the key Rocko had left for me. "I doubt Black Tom or Drago care that Phyllis has been dipping into the till. It sounds like something they'd have done in her place, except they would've spent the money on themselves. However, this business group is likely to go over the books with a fine tooth comb, which could be a problem if she was using legitimate funds for her purchases too."

I paused and looked over at Kyra. "Don't you have a cousin who works down at City Hall?"

"Jasypth. Why?"

"Could he try and track down this unknown consortium? After all, no one can legitimately buy a business, much less get licenses, if there isn't someone's name on some piece of paper. Even if they're staying back in the shadows, there must be a lawyer or broker fronting for them. Have Jasypth talk to the various licensing boards, secretaries, go through the property register, contact the utility companies, whatever it takes. Someone had to sign for something and I need that information. Something doesn't set right here."

"What about Naomi and the deadline?"

"That's why I want your cousin to look into it. We've got a good lead on Naomi's situation. It appears someone might have Naomi's briefcase, or know where it is. Ze' and I will be running that down tonight. We'll focus on catching her killer once we've averted the whole 'burn Calasia down with holy fire or whatever it is Valkyrie do' thing. I don't know why Rocko decided to involve me in this little game he's running, but it's against my personal ethics to play the patsy for anyone, much less Rocko."

I turned back to Ze'eva. "Is there any reason to suspect Phyllis was playing fast and loose with Rocko's investments? You said the investments she's made are turning a nice profit. I can't imagine him resenting that. But Phyllis seems like a city girl. I also can't imagine *her* being happy about retiring to quiet country living."

Ze'eva flipped through her notebook and then shook her head. "Nothing came up to make me think she's actively working against Rocko. She likes his money and power and he seems genuinely interested in her and her career." She paused and looked over at Kyra. "Sounds like a certain detective I know, minus the money and power."

I squawked before replying. "Ah, but how can you overlook the perks of late-night stakeouts, cold food, and warm beer? What's not to love?"

Kyra laid a hand on my shoulder. "Boss, you really don't want her to answer that."

Maxie's report came in while we were waiting. Unfortunately, it wasn't as helpful as I had hoped. The knife found in my door matched the wounds on the gunsels found on the roofs across the street from my office, but while it was close, it wasn't a match for the wounds on any of the female victims. However, his report did show something interesting: the M.E. had picked up faint magical traces on the wounds. Naomi's body had the strongest residue being the newest and the one most dismembered, but even the earliest known victims showed hints of necromantic magic.

"So, what exactly is Maxie saying here, Theron?" Kyra asked, as she filed the report with Naomi's case file.

"Not exactly sure. Without seeing the knife, I don't know if it's just an enchanted blade, which would make it do more damage, or if it's a knife where death is ensured from just a simple hit. Think of it as being magically poisoned."

Ze'eva pulled the file back out of the drawer and flipped through it. "No, I don't think that's it, Theron. Magic that potent would leave a bigger imprint. I know the Citadel can't afford to hire the most compentent examiners, but even a low-grade wizard would notice magic that potent. Could it be a summoning spell?"

"Ze', honestly it could be anything. You know me. Magic and I do not get along and personally, I'm pleased with that. I wouldn't know the difference between a wand of fire or a wand of ice until it was used on me. Even I could figure it out then."

Ze'eva afforded me one of those looks you bestow on a rather slow child. "No, Theron, what I mean is, what if the Night Stalker is able to summon his weapons and then unsummon them? He would be able to walk past anyone at any time without drawing attention. He'd even be able to be at the scene and be frisked by the constables and have no trace of his weapons on him. Kyra, can you have Maxie get with the examiner and see if they can determine the nature of the magic they've discovered. It could make things much easier if we knew what we were up against."

Kyra nodded and went out to her office to place the call.

"You think it's that important, Ze'eva?"

"A good detective once told me you can't overlook any possibility. We know so little about the Stalker, anything we can learn is better than nothing."

I glanced at my watch. "As long as we can learn about it in less than fifty-four hours."

After treating Ze'eva to dinner at Josie's, we headed toward the East Docks. It was several hours before we were supposed to arrive at Madam Brigitte's, but there was nothing to be gained by sitting around the office, either.

The fog swirled over the city as the sun set, and the street-lamps gave off a sickly illumination. The shadows were even darker than usual, making it perfect for dealing with a serial killer. Ze'eva slipped her arm through mine and even though she kept up a tough front, I could feel a slight trembling in her arm.

She glanced over at me and I noticed a faint change in her face. Most people wouldn't have noticed, but I'd stared at that face often enough to notice the difference. She smiled and the slight elongation of her canine teeth was visible.

"The full moon will be out soon, Theron. The wolf is rising. My eyes, ears, and nose are more sensitive." She pulled out a handkerchief and held it up to her nose. "And given what's in that alley, I wish it wasn't."

A few more steps and even I noticed the sickly sweet smell in the air. There's something about the scent of a dead body you never forget. I slipped my .45 out of its holster and Ze'eva's .38

appeared as if by magic. We approached the mouth of the alley and glanced in but between the darkness and the fog, it was impossible to see more than a few feet into the narrow passageway. I glanced overhead, but the fire escape stair must have been down around the middle of the apartment buildings lining the street.

Once I was certain no one was around, I stepped into the alley and struck a match. In the fitful glow, I spotted what was left of a young woman. She'd been pretty once, but someone hadn't liked her. Her face was a mass of bruises and her throat had been sliced so deep the blade had nearly severed her spine. However, that was apparently the only wound on her.

Ze'eva joined me and we searched the body for any clues. She found a purse a few feet away, but shook her head. "Nothing in it. No identification, no coin purse, no nothing, but then again, I doubt it's her purse."

That brought my head up. "Why do you think that?"

"It's the wrong shape and color. Look at her clothes. She's not rich, but she's well put together. She'd never go out of her place with a purse that didn't match her outfit, much less without a hat. Did you see her hat anywhere?"

Muttering to myself about fashion and vanity, I scoured the immediate vicinity, but turned up nothing unusual. After my negative report, she left me to guard the body while she went across the street to phone for the constables. I glanced down at the young woman once again, wondering who she was and how she'd wound up here. Did she tie into all the other mysteries swirling around me right now, or was she simply a woman in the wrong place at the wrong time?

After Ze'eva rejoined me, I had a hunch and walked down the alley until I found a pile of refuse cans. Using one of my few remaining matches I rummaged through four of them until I found what I thought might be there. I called for Ze' to hurry over while I still had a light and she carefully removed a purse and examined it. "This is probably hers—it matches her outfit. No money, but her identification's in here. Says she's Ruby Kilgore, twenty-two, One-oh-five Greenleaf Way, apartment eight."

"Greenleaf Way? That's all the way over on the west side of the city." I glanced over at the corpse lying in the dirt, tossed aside like yesterday's newspaper. "Kid, you came an awfully long way to die. What brought you to the East Docks?"

A soft voice spoke up from behind me. "That's a very good question, Theron."

I yelped and spun around, bringing up my .45 before my brain registered it was my client's voice. "Naomi, do *not* do that. Are you trying to get yourself ki— " I grimaced. "Sorry. Anyway, *what* are you doing here?"

"Theo did not need me this evening, so I decided to join Ze'eva and you. He will meet us at the appointed hour."

"Well, that's all well and good, but I seem to remember asking you to stay with him. If someone was able to kill you once, he might want to finish the job if he discovers you're still mostly around."

Naomi drifted over to the body, pointedly ignoring me and knelt down next to the woman. She placed her hand on the corpse's forehead and her body stiffened. There was a flash of . . . something . . . and Naomi's head gradually turned until she was looking right at me.

A voice, low and melodious but definitely not Naomi's, came from her lips. "Good evening, Mr. Chase. I understand you're concerned about what happened to me here."

Nope, not creepy at all.

"Yes, Ruby, we are," Ze'eva said, stepping into Naomi's sight. "We wondered who you were, why you were here, and who did this to you."

"I'm a clerk at Marcus Wells—we deal in curios, both magical and mundane. When I was leaving work this evening, a customer asked if I could deliver his package to an address in the building next to us. I told him our usual courier had left for the day, but I could have it there in the morning. He was quite insistent it must be delivered this evening and offered me fifty crowns plus cab fare for my troubles. Fifty crowns is more than I make in a week, so I decided to take him up on it."

"Go on, Ruby. What happened after you arrived?"

"There was a terrible row going on inside the apartment. Two men were arguing about something . . . one of the voices was very deep and the other was sort of normal. They stopped when I knocked on the door and the customer came to the door. While I was handing him the package, the other man came pushing out past me. He seemed very upset I was there and he hid his face with his coat collar, but he was very distinctive. He was very skinny and bald. I thought he was sick or something at first, but when he pushed me, he nearly knocked me across the hallway."

Drago.

"My customer helped me up and paid me extra for my troubles. However, he asked that I not mention tonight to anyone. For fifty crowns, I'd forget my own name, if you know what I mean. I came back downstairs, but before I could get to the cab stand, someone grabbed me and dragged me back into the alley. His face was covered with a scarf, but his hat came off and I saw he was bald. He beat me, trying to find out what was in the package. I managed to break away and ran for the mouth of the alley, but he caught me again and then I felt pressure against my throat and then I went to sleep. I'm still quite sleepy, so if you'll excuse me . . ."

With that, Naomi's eyes returned to normal and her shoulders slumped in exhaustion. "I didn't realize making contact without having my own body would be so tiring." She began leaning to the side and I jumped over to catch her, but she passed right through my arms and wound up half sunk into the ground.

"Naomi, are you all right?"

She glanced up at me with some of the feistiness she'd exhibited when we'd first met. "No, I always phase into dirty alleys to get a better look at city sanitation efforts. Idiot." She rose gently into the air and stood up. "I hadn't realized how much energy I was expending to maintain this form. If we do not recover my case and return both it and myself to the Shadowed Lands in time, I may suffer the same fate as our missing firefighter."

"So we know who did it, but not why. Naomi, do you remember which apartment Ruby went to?"

"Two-D."

I was about to say something when the first squad car came rolling up. I glanced back into the alley but Naomi had disappeared just as quickly as she'd appeared. It took us the better part of two hours before Corvinus and his boys were finished processing the crime scene, which included interviewing the firm of Chase & Blackthorne. We told him everything we had done and knew, which wasn't a whole lot if you didn't include what we'd learned from Ruby. And really, with no witnesses, no murder weapon, and no fingerprints, there was nothing for Corvinus to bring Drago in on and any lawyer worth the ink on his degree would get him sprung in twenty minutes.

We still had some time before we had to be at Madame Brigitte's, so we went into the building Naomi/Ruby had pointed out to us and headed for apartment 2D. Three knocks later, I slipped my picks into the lock and, with a couple of deft twists, we were inside the room. Ze'eva and I spotted the alchemical set-up in the dining room and realized someone had been doing some experimenting and not that long ago. The retorts and tubes were still bubbling and the alcohol lamp was still warm. The open window showed where the former occupant of the room had gone and by the time I got to the window,

I spotted a dark figure drop from the second-floor landing to the ground and take off toward the far end of the alley.

I watched the shadowy figure turn the corner and glanced back into the room where Ze'eva was examining the contraptions on the table. "Wonder why he ran off so fast? Worried Drago was coming back?"

"Or we were the cops. These are not necessarily legal ingredients he was working with here. But you might find this interesting."

I moved over to the table and saw what Ze'eva was pointing at. In the middle of the table was a set of papers covered in unusual symbols—symbols I'd seen just the other day and again this morning. However, above each symbol was now a letter or a number, spelling out words. It seems the concoction had revealed hidden writing on the paper.

"From what Ruby's customer's notes say, the symbols aren't a cipher, they're an alchemical formula to reveal this hidden writing. You said Rocko never did anything straightforward. The answer was right in front of us, but we were trying to force an answer in where it didn't belong."

"Which is what I told Theo this afternoon after I returned to his lab," Naomi said, rematerializing by the window.

"You really have to stop doing that. So you recognized this as a formula before Theo did?"

"I did, but then again, these formulas were lost over three thousand years ago. The fact the person who fled this room was able to decipher them is an impressive feat. What I cannot understand is why he didn't take these pages with him when he fled."

I spotted a pad of paper on the table next to the original notes. Following a hunch, I picked up the pad and tilted it toward the light. There were faint impressions on the paper and I pulled a pencil out of my pocket and lightly rubbed the edge of the lead against the paper. The impressions from the page above formed faint letters against the graphite background. "He didn't, but why make a copy instead of taking the originals?"

Ze'eva backed toward the door. "Because the originals are a trap."

Naomi floated across the room to join Ze'eva. "The chemicals required to reveal this writing are rather unstable when mixed together. As long as they're fresh, you're able to handle the paper, but the more it dries, the more dangerous it becomes."

I gave the table another glance. The fan above the table barely ruffled the damp pages and I noted a faint wet stain slowly disappearing around the pages. "I suggest we clear the building quickly and alert the fire brigade. If this goes off, it could wind up setting the whole block on fire."

While Ze'eva went to find the building manager to start evacuating the tennants, I turned off the overhead fan and dumped out a wastepaper basket and eased it atop the paper. It wasn't a perfect solution, but it might slow down the evaporation rate for a minute or two.

Naomi was still floating near the door with her eyes closed. "Theron, there's no time. There are sixty-four people in this building. Given the rate of growth of the impending fire, thirty or more will die before they can get out of the building. You must do something with those pages."

Now was not the time to ask how she knew. Glancing around, I spotted a frying pan and spatula on the stove. "Naomi, can you interact with solid things?"

"Briefly, if they're not too heavy."

"Okay, I need you to lift the edge of the basket when I signal. I'm going to try to move the papers in one movement into the pan and then dump them into the alley. Get ready to move fast."

I opened the window to the fire escape as wide as it would go and made sure nothing could trip me. Then I gave Naomi a nod and she inched the basket up just high enough for me to get the spatula underneath the papers. I slid them to the edge of the table into the waiting pan. Then with one sudden move, I rushed toward the window and leaned through as far as I could, tossing the frying pan over the fire escape railing.

Before I could pull back, the frying pan erupted into a ball of flame and a shock wave shook the building. The next thing I knew, the wall I was resting on gave way and I collapsed on the iron grating of the fire escape. With a sickly creak, I heard the weakened escape start to pull away from the wall. I fought down the instinct to scramble to my feet and inched my way toward the opening back into apartment 2D.

Just as I reached the opening, I heard metal scream and the fire escape pulled away from the wall and collapsed on itself. I grabbed onto the window ledge, but the bricks give way as soon as I put my weight on them. I found myself in midair, but before I could add to the wreckage in the alley, something grabbed me by the shoulders. I floated down to the ground.

"Thanks, Naomi. But I thought you said you couldn't hold heavy things?"

When she didn't respond, I turned around—and found myself face to face with a horse. The first thing I noted was the very sharp teeth and then the red eyes. As I stepped back, I noted the coal black coat, the dark wings, and the smoke rising from the creature's hooves. Naomi was perched atop the beast, petting its neck and talking to it.

"Naomi, I don't mean to seem ungrateful, but who or what is that thing?"

The creature's eyes narrowed as it bared its fangs at me, but Naomi stroked its neck again and it settled down. "This is Ebonfire, my assistant. He's been hanging around the city watching over me ever since my murder. He normally doesn't like, much less help, the living, but since we have a contract he decided to help you *this* time. To be honest, I am as surprised as you are."

Ze'eva came tearing around the corner, but pulled up short at the sight. "Theron, you're all right?"

"Thanks to Ebonfire, yes. It was a close thing. Naomi realized it was going to go critical too soon, so I tried to minimize the damage. Just didn't expect to follow it out of the building."

Ze'eva walked up closer and gently patted Ebonfire on the nose. "Thank you for saving him."

I swear the horse winked at her before it spread its wings and took off into the night sky. Before I could say anything though, I heard a familiar voice behind me. "All right, Chase, what in the hell were you thinking trying to drop the building on my men?"

"It's a little more complicated than that, Captain."

Corvinus grunted. "With you, it always is. Well, like the saying goes, wiseguy, you can tell me all about it downtown . . ."

Two hours later, we managed to extract ourselves from Corvinus's grasp and Ze'eva and I caught a cab over to Madame Brigitte's. It might have been a manor back around the turn of the century, but the years and the changing neighborhood had done it no favors. Still, the wrought-iron fence surrounding the property was rust free and freshly painted and the house itself seemed immaculate from the street.

Ze' and I walked into the lobby where a half-clad young woman handed us both champagne flutes. "Evening, Ashley. I need to speak to Madame Brigitte."

"Hey, Theron. Didn't recognize you. Give me a moment. She's in her office."

As the young woman glided across the carpeted floor, Ze' gave me a curious look. "You seem awfully familiar with this place, Theron."

I sipped my champagne and smiled at her. "I've done several jobs for Madame Brigitte over the years. We did a stakeout up on the third floor to take down Mad Dog Mullins. Seems he was head-over-heels in love with one of the ladies here and loved to brag about his latest jobs with her. We finally got enough evidence to put him and his gang on ice for quite a while. He never did figure out how we did it. Ashley was just getting started back then, so she was my runner with my partner on the outside. Wound up sitting in one bedroom for nearly three weeks because we were afraid he might spot me by accident."

"I see."

"What can I say? Not everything about detective work is glamorous."

"And sometimes it even has its perks, right, Chase?"

I recognized that husky voice right off the bat. Madame Brigitte was maneuvering through the lobby like a battleship surrounded by PT boats. She had been a model and actress in her younger days, but that was about thirty years and a hundred pounds ago. I didn't know how much money she spent a year on rejuvenation spells and clothes, but she managed to still look elegant in the latest outfits.

Brigitte walked right over to Ze'eva and patted her on the arm. "Ah, so you are the dark-haired beauty who stole Theron away from me. It's all right, dear. After meeting you, I forgive you. After all, how could he resist those . . . eyes of yours."

Ze blushed and then smiled at both of us. "I'm honored you consider me competition."

Madame Brigitte laughed. "Honey, you and I are gonna get along all right. Tell you what, when you and the handsome guy there aren't busy with a case, you come back here. Oh, I've got a few stories I can tell you about Theron. After all, you can't spend almost a month here without getting to know someone."

She grabbed both of us under her arms and half-pulled/half-guided us to her office. "But you didn't come here tonight to discuss old times, Chase. What can this old woman do for you?"

"We're supposed to meet some people here at midnight, Brigitte; Blind Bob and Sheila are either here or should be shortly. Figured your place was the safest place for her given the circumstances."

"That poor dove. She has the worst luck. Used to work for me before that jerk, Mouse, talked her into going 'independent.' Tell you the truth, not many tears were shed when he took that nosedive. Still, you don't have to wait until midnight—Sheila and Bob are upstairs. They got here an hour ago. Third floor, second door on the right."

"Thanks, Brigitte."

We climbed the stairs to the third floor. Just as we arrived, I heard the sound of smashing glass and Bob's shout. Without waiting, I pulled my pistol and kicked the door open. Bob lay sprawled in one corner, a large bruise on his forehead. Sheila lay on the bed with a large knife buried up to its handle in her chest. I rushed to the broken window, but saw no movement on the grounds behind the building. I glanced up and spotted a rope hanging from the roof just beside the window. I motioned for Ze' to secure the room and rushed to the roof-access ladder.

I inched the trapdoor open and eased out onto the roof. There were only a few places someone could hide behind, so I cleared them and made my way over to the rope. Something about it seemed odd and I realized it was tied with a slipknot. If anyone had tried climbing it, the knot would have immediately released, sending the climber crashing to the ground.

Realizing this was nothing more than a red herring, I rushed back to the room. Ze'eva had finished going over the scene and was helping Blind Bob to his feet. I found a broken vase near where I'd seen him when I first arrived. He held his hand up to his head but he let me examine the bruise running from his temple toward his widow's peak. The window was smashed and small shards of glass lay on the sill. Turning to the victim, I noted there were no defensive wounds. Someone had stuck her so quickly; she hadn't even had time to raise her hands before she was dead.

I glanced over at Ze' and she shook her head. The briefcase was still in the wind and we were back to square one with two more days to solve this case. We told the girls gathered at the doorway to stay out of the room, help Bob to another room to rest and call the constables. I left my card and told them I'd be in to see Corvinus in the morning about this.

We caught a cab back to the nearest bar where we could keep an eye on Madame Brigitte's. I ordered Ze'eva and myself a drink and I sat there watching the light twinkle against the liquid as I swirled it in the glass.

"You know, Theron, it was a setup. That scene was staged for our benefit."

"You mean besides there being no glass on the carpet? Yeah, the window was broken out, not in. The only way that makes sense is if the killer was already in the room and jumped through the window to escape. No one climbed that rope. I'd bet my license on it."

"Then why the phony rope trick?"

"Delay and confuse. The knot gave the trick away, though. Whoever set it up isn't an experienced climber or a sailor. That's one of the first things they teach you not to do when tying knots. But there was one even more damning piece of evidence there if you think about it."

Ze'eva's brows furrowed as she thought, reconstructing the scene in her mind. "I guess I must have missed it, Theron. What did you see?"

"Bob's bruise. He hit himself."

"What?"

I picked up a glass and held it in my hand. "Imagine this is the vase. Lay this against my head as if you were trying to hit me."

I felt the cool glass touching my skin and I stopped her. "Look, with me facing you, the bruise you'd give me would run from my temple backward on the side of my head. Even if you backhanded me with that, the bruise would be centered on my forehead but it wouldn't produce the marks we saw on Bob. But"—I said, taking the glass from her—"if I were to hit myself and not really want to concuss myself, I'd take it in my left hand and smash it against my head like this . . ."

"Producing the temple-to-forehead bruise."

"Exactly. It looks horrible and bleeds a lot, but it's thick bone there."

"So you're saying Bob knocked himself out. But why?"

"That, my dear, is why we're here. I'm waiting for Corvinus to release Bob and we're going to try and follow him. I think he has or knows where the case is. I made it very clear we were offering a big reward for it and, for some reason, that old blind man has inserted himself into our business. I remember he said something about how he 'sees' more than most people know. Makes me wonder just how much he does see."

"Surely you're not thinking that blind guy is the Night Stalker?"

"I'm not thinking anything, I'm looking for clues to the truth. Is the idea of a blind man being a serial killer any more bizarre than an assassin who can change shapes . . . or a beautiful singer who just happens to be a werewolf? Hell, I'm working for a dead woman this case. This is Calasia. The whole city was built on weird."

We watched the prowl cars pull up and the constables spread out to cover the grounds. We were on our fourth cocktail when the ambulance took the body away and the constables began filtering out. A half hour later, only Corvinus's car stood outside the gate and there'd been no sign of Bob emerging from the house. A bad feeling came over me and I slapped some money on the table and motioned for Ze'eva to follow. We met Corvinus as he made his way down the walk.

"Thought you wanted to talk in the morning, Chase. What're you doing back?"

"Just figured I'd give your boys time to process the scene without our help. After all, they need the practice."

"Har-de-har-har, Chase. What can you tell me about this?"

"Not a lot more than you should already know. I'm trying to find something for my client."

"Your dead-but-not-dead client."

"You remember! Corvinus, there's hope for you yet. Anyway, the deceased—"

He jerked a thumb at the ambulance as it pulled away. "You mean, *that* deceased."

"Right. That deceased. Sheila, either had my client's missing briefcase or knew where it was. Blind Bob meet with us here at midnight so we could arrange to recover the item. However, they arrived early and by the time we learned they were there, the girl had been stabbed to death and Bob was unconscious from a beaning with a vase."

"I see. And did you notice anything odd about the room?"

"Besides everything?"

"Ze'eva must be rubbing off on you, Chase. You're making sense these days. Yeah, everything about that room was staged. According to the M.E.'s initial examination, the girl was already dead before she was posed on the bed. Nowhere near enough blood on the bedclothes for a recent stab wound. In fact, we're not even sure the knife in her is the murder weapon. Oh, she'd been stabbed, but several times in the back. Someone went to a lot of trouble to confuse things."

"What did Blind Bob have to say?"

"Who knows? The madame says she was in her office when he arrived and told her Sheila was already in the room and to direct you up there. She never actually saw Sheila arrive and apparently none of the other girls did, either. I have a witness who saw him slip out the back door right after you left. He's been gone about two hours now."

I slammed my hand down on the hood of his car. "Dammit. I

didn't think of that. I figured he'd walk out the front. After all, who'd suspect a blind man of killing a girl?"

"So, what now, Chase?"

"I don't know about you, Corvinus, but I'm going to take this beautiful woman home and go back to my apartment and get some shuteye. We've got two more days to save Calasia and I'm out of ideas at the moment."

M y alarm went off way too early for my taste, but three cups of coffee and a bagel later, I was en route to Theo's store. Hopefully he'd teased the answers out of the papers and had some good news for me.

"Hey, mister!"

I looked down and saw a kid wearing three weeks of dirt tugging on my coat. "What can I do for you, kid?"

"You Theron Chase?"

I moved away from the curb and pulled the kid along with me. No sense in making myself an easier target than I was there. In the entrance to a store, I turned to face the kid. "And, if I am, what is it to you?"

"It's worth a crown to me. I was told to wait here until I saw a guy that looks like you. If you're Theron Chase, you should have your detective's license on you."

"Suspicious fellow, aren't you?"

"Just careful. I want that crown. So, you got a license or don't you?"

I didn't see anyone else paying too close of attention to our exchange, so I decided to take the kid's word. I fished my wallet out of my pocket and showed him my license. He looked it over like a jeweler checking a diamond, but once he was satisfied, he pulled the cap off his head and handed me an envelope. Before I could say anything, he bolted into the swirling crowd on the street. I took two steps toward him, but he was swallowed up by the Calasians moving up and down the sidewalk and had vanished.

I tucked the envelope into my jacket pocket and continued up the street to Theo's. I was escorted to Theo's office and he hurried me down to his lab. "By the gods, Theron, your discovery last night was more than fortuitous. I think I've got the whole thing figured out now."

"Whoa, whoa. Slow down there, Theo. I just walked in and the coffee is still percolating in my system. Which discovery are you discussing? And why didn't you show up at Madame Brigitte's?"

"Oh, Naomi and I arrived right at midnight just as the first patrol car came screeching up. I deduced something had gone wrong and decided introducing our lovely guest and myself to Captain Corvinus at that particular place and time was a bad idea." He grabbed me by the elbow and dragged me over to a table. "But that's neither here nor there, my boy. Thanks to your discovery, we have a solution to the mysterious papers and the compass."

I saw a set of alchemical equipment strewn about and a set of papers floating inside a glowing green box. Theo picked up a pad of paper and shoved it at me. The more I read, the wider the frown grew on my face.

"You see the implications of this missive?" Theo said, taking a seat at the table.

"I would say our friend Rocko is up to his old tricks. This doesn't tell me who killed Fish Clayborne. These are directions to where he's supposedly stored most of the funds he's acquired over his career—his personal vault, so to speak."

Theo nodded. "Not quite what we were expecting, but then again, from what you've told me about Rocko, that's not surprising. I've checked out the directions and the coordinates. They lead to a series of caves just south of Calasia. They're underwater during high tide, but at low tide, they are accessible. You won't have a lot of time to go in and out without getting trapped. The compass is enchanted to direct the holder to the location once you get there, but according to this, both Drago and Black Tom have to turn the key simultaneously or it won't open. I checked and the key we have has no such enchantment on it. Perhaps, if Drago and Black Tom could not be persuaded to work together, then you were to claim the contents of said vault."

I leaned on the table, staring at the floating pages. "But Rocko also knows I'd never take the money, so either they cooperate or no one gets the treasure. Ah, so that's why they were after my envelope—with my key, they wouldn't need each other."

"That does sound like the ruthless Mr. Avilon. The question is, what are you going to do?"

"Rocko said he'd give me Fish's killer. I suspect that's why he gave us the same clues as the others. The killer will be present when the vault is opened. It's up to me to figure out who it is."

Theo pushed a buzzer on the wall and then plopped down in a chair near the alchemical equipment. "And that is why you earn the big bucks, or so they say."

I laughed and grabbed a chair near him. "If that's what *they* say, I'd hate to see their bank accounts."

One of Theo's assistants brought in a silver pot and some cups and poured coffee for the two of us before exiting as quietly as he'd entered. Theo stared at his cup for a bit and I decided to focus on the coffee and let him think. As I leaned forward to set the cup down, I felt a crinkling in my pocket. I extracted the envelope and noticed it had no return address or postmark, so it had been hand-delivered all the way.

Inside was a short note written in a crude hand:

Chase,

Sorry to skip out on you last night, but some things just can't be helped. I have the case. You find Fish's killer and I'll give it to you. No other reward needed.

Bob

"Something upsetting?"

I crumpled the note into a ball and shoved it and the envelope into my pocket. "I hate to admit I've been taken by someone I thought I could trust. Apparently, Blind Bob has been playing both sides against each other. How else could he have known I was looking for Fish's killer? I never mentioned it to him. Hell, I don't even know how he could have killed that girl. I've seen his eyes. He's not faking being blind. Who is he working with or for?"

Theo looked at me over the edge of his coffee cup. "Now, that's an interesting development. So, do you go looking for a treasure vault or Blind Bob?"

I thought about it for a few moments and then finished my cup before responding. "I suspect he'll find me before this is all over, so let's go get us a treasure."

"You mean, Ze'eva and you should go get a treasure. I don't go spelunking anymore. I hire people to go searching for magical treasures these days. My job is marking them up enough to ensure I turn a profit."

"I happen to know you're nowhere near as sedentary as you claim to be, Theo, but you're right—this is Ze's and my case. Besides, if I need rescue, better if you're not trapped down there with us."

"By the gods, Theron, you need to marry this woman soon. She's damn near civilized you."

I made a few friendly suggestions to Theo about what he could do while I was gone and headed out to gather up a few supplies and one particularly attractive partner. One way or the other, this was going to get settled today.

The sun was sinking over the coastal mountains as we arrived at the cave complex. The cabbie swore we were crazy wanting to get out twenty miles from the nearest town, but finally sped off, leaving us on a desolate overlook with a rough set of stairs descending toward the ocean.

We inched our way down the narrow passage until we got to the small white beach at the bottom. From the marks on the wall beside us, we were easily five or six feet below the high-tide mark. I noticed Ze'eva was getting more and more irritable and nervous as the sky darkened.

"You feeling all right, Ze'?"

"Tonight is the first night of the full moon, Theron. I don't know if being underground will slow down the change, but you're going to get to meet Lyssa Darkmane for the first time."

"Isn't that your stage name?"

"It is and it isn't. Yes, I've performed under that name, but my personality changes drastically under the influence of the wolf. It's almost as if another person occupies my body during the night. Just prepare yourself."

I clicked on my flashlight and motioned her forward. *And just when I thought things couldn't get much stranger.* We moved into the cave system and followed the main passage until we came to a split. I pulled out the compass and found it glowing and pointing toward the right passage.

"Guess that's a hint," Ze'eva said, pointing her flashlight down the narrow passage. "Let's hurry. I thought I heard something back by the mouth of the cave."

I focused on the compass and it guided us through a series of twisting passages until we reached a central passage. From what I could tell, the water only reached halfway up the walls here, but even so, being stuck in a dark cave and standing in cold water wasn't my idea of fun, so the quicker we could wrap this up, the happier I would be.

It wasn't hard to miss the vault door against the far wall. I gave it a cursory examination. It looked like a bank vault door, but instead of a combination lock, it had a simple keyhole. I toyed with the idea of opening it, but Ze'eva pointed to a side passage and motioned for me to follow.

We had just found a good hiding place and doused our lights when other flashlights lit up the room. There were more people in the room than there were lights, but it was impossible to tell how many because they kept shuffling around. They seemed to be looking for something other than the vault door, though.

"If our information was correct, my esteemed friend, the switch should be to the left of the vault door."

"Yeah, yeah, keep your shirt on. These stone thingies all look alike."

"I believe the word you're searching for is 'stalagmite.' They're the ones that grow up from the ground."

"I don't care if they grow out of unicorn crap as long as we can find it. Ah, here we go."

I heard a click and then I heard a low hum as a generator started and then the room began to brighten. There were light bulbs hidden up among the stalactites. Apparently, Rocko hadn't been satisfied to work by flashlight when he visited his vault.

As my eyes adjusted to the light, I counted twelve men in the chamber. Black Tom and Drago stood on opposite sides of the room and each had five heavily armed men with them. I heard some heavy breathing behind me and turned to see what was going on with Ze'eva—and swallowed a yelp.

A dark-furred humanoid wolf stood behind me, her fangs visible in the dim light. She was staring at the gang of men in front of her and it was clear she was trying to fight down the urge to jump into the middle of them and rip them to shreds.

"Ze'eva?" I whispered as she put her hands up to the side of her head and shook it hard.

"Theron, Lyssa is fighting me. I'll be back in a bit," she said softly as she retreated farther into the passage.

Even through it killed me to do so, I let her go and settled in to watch what was going on in the chamber. Besides, as Ze' had pointed out on numerous occasions, a were was just as likely to rip my arm off for interfering as it was to thank me for helping. She was going to have to work it out for herself.

"Okay, Drago. We've managed to maintain a suitable truce amongst us for now, but I can tell some of our companions would rather fight than cooperate. Perhaps we should see about opening the treasure vault and returning before we have to spend the night when the tide shifts."

"One of these days, Tom, I'm going to gut you just to see where you keep that damn dictionary inside you, but I agree. The last thing I want is to spend the whole night listening to you use big words. Let's get this over with."

The two gangsters stared at each other with mutual loathing but then they moved to the vault as one. Drago put the compass down and Black Tom produced the key from his pocket and inserted it into the lock with a flourish. There was no questioning the greed on either man's face as they both took hold of the key and turned it.

There was a high whine from the generator as the lock engaged and then their bodies arched and screams rang out through the chamber. The smell of cooked flesh and burning clothing was overwhelming After a few seconds, the generator returned to normal and the blackened bodies of Tom and Drago collapsed to the floor.

Before either set of gunsels could move, two submachine guns opened up from a different passage and cut them down. The gunfire continued to rip into the bodies as they lay there until whomever was hiding was certain everyone was dead.

I pressed myself against the wall, pulled out my .45, and waited. I knew it was no match for what lay across the chamber from me, but I wasn't going to go down without a fight. I still had no idea where Ze' was, but unless they were pumping silver bullets into their magazines, I knew she was safe enough.

"Yo, Chase. You all right over there?"

Rocko.

"I thought you were retiring, Rocko."

"I am, Chase, just clearing up a few loose ends. Last thing I wanted to do was turn all my hard work over to those two louses—they'd have screwed up everything before I had my first crop in. Besides, they knew too much about me. Sooner or later, they'd have tried to cut themselves into my legitimate businesses. You know there's only one sure way to stop a blackmailer."

"Especially if you can stop them before they start, Rocko?"

I heard the mirthless chuckle before he responded. "You're a smart guy, Chase. Too bad it had to end up this way. I figured this trap would either get Black Tom and Drago or it'd get you and I could blame your death on them. Now I'll have to leave your body here and make sure one of them is holding the 'murder weapon.' See, I can't leave you behind to testify against me. After all, they don't send you to the farm for Murder One."

"There never was a vault, was there?"

Rocko laughed. "Oh, there's a vault, but do you think I'd put it in some place where I couldn't access it on a moment's notice? I mean, I like my privacy, but this is a tad too remote for my tastes. Nope, I had this built while I was at the farm by a couple of guys I know who love traps. I made sure the key would only work with both of them holding it to ensure I got those rats at the same time."

I shifted positions so he couldn't focus on my voice for a free shot. "So you never did know who killed Fish Clayborne?"

"Of course I did—he was killed on my orders. I mean I was at the farm the night he was killed, playing cards with the warden, so obviously I couldn't have done it personally." There was a small pause, and then Rocko continued. "Poor ol' Fish thought I wouldn't notice him skimming. I mean, I appreciate a little bit of larceny in any man, but he was being stupid about it. I couldn't let it go or I'd never be able to control the rest of the gang. So, I trusted my finest operative to handle it. When I got out, I knew if I dangled that as bait, you wouldn't be able to resist it and we could settle a few old scores. So, why don't you come on out and we can get this over with?"

"Let's not and say we did. In fact, why don't you come get me?"

There was that infuriating laugh again. "Chasie, you're in a bad situation. Unless you're a mer-man, just how good are you at holding your breath when the tide starts rolling in here? Oh and do you have any idea how much your heat signature stands out against the cold wall you're kneeling next to?"

I immediately scrambled back a few feet down the passage as a round cracked off the wall where I'd just been. There was a momentary silence and then that laughter started up again. I inched forward again until I could make out the chamber again, but I knew Rocko could have slipped out of the passage across from me and taken up a firing position somewhere just out of sight.

"So, where's that pretty little partner of yours? I don't see her anywhere, but the passage you're in is a dead end, so you have to get past this chamber to escape. Face it, shamus, you're in over your head here. You know Rocko always has an ace hidden somewhere."

Even though the cave was cool, I felt the sweat rolling down my back. Ze'eva and I were in a bad spot here. I knew regular bullets couldn't kill her, but they would still hurt like hell when they hit. If she went into full feral mode, there was no guarantee Mrs. Chase's boy wouldn't wind up as a detective fillet by the time she calmed down.

While I was trying to figure out my next move, another shot

rang out. I tried to bury through the limestone floor of the cave with my fingers before I realized the round had come nowhere near me. After the echoes of the shot had finally settled down, the only sound was the whirring of the hidden generator and I realized there was someone lying on the ground right behind me.

A dusky voice came from the darkness. It was Ze'eva's voice but lower and huskier than usual. "I smell blood, Theron. It doesn't smell like you, though."

"I'm pretty sure I wasn't hit. How about you, Ze'eva?"

There was a momentary hesitation. "I am uninjured. Should we investigate?"

"He has an infrared scope over there. Odds are, he'll drop us before we get anywhere near him."

I heard a scrabbling noise and recognized claws on the stone. "Wait here. I'll be right back." Before I could say anything else, there was a black blur shooting across the chamber, bounding between stalagmites at inhuman speed. I'd always heard weres were fast, but I'd never seen one in action before. All I can say is I'm glad Ze's on my side. A few seconds later, she waved a paw at me, beckoning me forward.

I rushed over to her to find Rocko's body. He was slumped over a rifle with a bullet hole in the side of his head. A still-warm submachine gun lay on the ground next to him.

"Wait, there were two people over here. I saw flashes from two separate guns when they mowed down the gunsels over there. Where's his partner?"

Ze'eva sniffed the air. "There's a faint scent going down the passage toward the outside. I suspect whoever shot Rocko wasted no time escaping. We need to do the same if we want to avoid the oncoming tide."

I glanced over the scene and decided this was a mess for one of Corvinus's buddies in the Sheriff's Department. We rushed down the passages, Ze'eva having to pause and wait for me—to her obvious displeasure. The closer we got to the entrance, the more splashing I heard and I realized the tide was coming in faster than I'd anticipated.

By the time we got outside, the full moon lit up the beach like a spotlight and we were wading in calf-deep water. We spotted someone coming down the stairs. Ze'eva wrapped a scarf around her head and ducked off to the side as the flashlight caught me.

"Did you just come from the cave?" the newcomer asked.

"That's Phyllis," Ze'eva said from the shadows.

I shaded my eyes from the glare of the flashlight, my .45 still in my hand. "Yes. Don't come down much farther. The tides coming in. Why are you here?"

"I was waiting for Rocko in the car. Someone came rushing past me a few moments ago and tore off toward town. I got scared something had happened to Rocko and decided to come down here."

I moved up closer to her and grabbed her by the elbow. "We have to get to dry ground while we can." I pointed out the rising waves. "This is going to be a bad tide with the full moon."

She tried pulling away from me. "No, I need to find out what happened to Rocko."

I tightened my grip on her arm. "Rocko's dead. They're all dead in there. If we don't move, we're going to join them. Now, come on."

Protesting all the way to the top, Phyllis finally reached the top of the narrow staircase with me right behind her. A silent black form came up behind us, pausing a few feet below the edge of the overlook. There were five cars that hadn't been there when Ze' and I arrived earlier. Night birds flew overhead, screaming their call and there was the faintest scent of sulfur in the air almost hidden by the scent of the ocean.

Phyllis broke away from me and rushed over to the sleek coupe I'd seen her driving the other night. "Look, you can't just shove me around. How do I know Rocko is dead? How do I know you didn't kill Rocko yourself?"

"Name's Chase. I'm a private detective and you're Phyllis Androfos, Rocko's girlfriend and business partner. Rocko's dead because that's what a high-caliber bullet does when it hits you in the side of the head. I didn't kill Rocko, but it's not because he wasn't shooting at me first."

Her hand went to her mouth. "So, that's why Joe sped off so fast. He must have done it."

"Joe?"

"Joe Brisco, Rocko's right-hand man."

A soft voice came from the steps below. "She's lying, Theron. There was only the scent of her perfume in the passage."

I guess my poker face needed some work, because before I could move, there was a flash in the moonlight and a nickel-plated automatic appeared in her hand almost by magic. "Drop your weapon, Chase. As you noticed below, I am an expert shot. I mean, Rocko spared no expense on my theatric career, which included learning shooting from some former Imperial marine snipers."

I eased my pistol to the ground and stood back up, trying to shield the top of the stairs from her sight. I knew Ze'eva would spring out at any moment and I didn't want to give Phyllis any warning. She motioned for me to go to my knees and I decided to humor her.

"That's a good look for you, Chase—you and all the jerks like you. Everyone has always looked down at me because I'm a woman, because I'm a singer, because I'm just Rocko's girl. No one ever gave me credit for keeping Rocko's business afloat when you sent him to jail. No, everyone just assumed I'd be an easy mark because I'm just an ornament for Rocko. Well, now look at them. They're all dead—*dead*—just like Fish Clayborne. He was stupid and let me put three bullets in his chest while he was walking on the pier. He was dead before he hit the water.

He was too stupid to cover up his tracks. I learned from his mistakes. I made sure Rocko knew what I was doing, but never the full extent of it. Like the big dummy he was, he just thought I was some cute bunny and never saw the claws I was hiding. So, now he's dead and I'm in charge. I guarantee, no one is going to look down at Phyllis Androfo again."

I heard Ze'eva shift on the stairs but there was a sudden movement behind Phyllis. Before I could say anything, a hand went across her throat and her body arched as something hit her over and over in the back. The look of surprise on her face would have been classic if not for the bloodstains sprouting through the front of her blouse. There was one last jerk in her body and then she collapsed like a puppet whose strings had been snapped, revealing Blind Bob standing behind her with a glowing knife.

"Bob!"

The blind man turned toward me, a demonic snarl on his face. "There never was a Blind Bob, you idiot. The name is Fish—Fish Clayborne. Thanks for flushing out my killer for me. All I knew was she was a beautiful woman. Mentezis made that clear. But Mentezis couldn't tell me which one, so I decided to kill them all until I got the right one. Mentezis is my guide. He led me to you and told me to stay close. He told me you'd find the right one, so not to kill you until afterward."

There was no missing the crazy in his voice. I put my hands out flat to try and calm hi down. "Mentezis? Who's he?" I asked as I inched my hand toward my pistol. There was a flash and a knife hit the ground right next to my .45, sending it skittering away.

There was another flash and the knife disappeared from the ground and reappeared in his hand. "Please don't be stupid, Chase. I can't see like a normal man, but then again, I'm not exactly normal anymore." Fish began walking in front of me, almost as if he was on a stage. "I'm not much of one for melodramatics or making speeches, Chase, but since you asked, you deserve a short answer. Who is he? He's my partner, the Shining Knife. You might know him as the Night Stalker."

"How is this possible? Phyllis must not be quite as good a shot as she thought."

"Oh no, Chase, she's probably better than she bragged. I was quite dead, but Mentezis woke me up in the morgue. For a price, he helped guide me on my hunt, but he's greedy. I have my revenge—so now it's my turn to help him out. You see, he's not easily satiated. He likes the blood of beautiful women. We've been careful up to now. We didn't want to scare my killer away. Now, though, there's nothing to hold us back. We will turn Calasia into our personal hunting ground. It will be glorious."

"Fish, listen to me. You really don't want to do this. You've had your revenge. Why take it out on the rest of the city?"

The blind man pulled off his glasses and I could see the glowing red eyes staring back at me. There was no sanity left in that face. Whoever or whatever Mentezis was, it had full control of Fish's body.

"Why, Chase? Does the hunter need a reason to kill beyond the thrill of the hunt? Do not appeal to Fish Clayborne's honor or decency. Fish has been dead for quite a while. I have sustained his body because it suited my purpose. I promised to aid him in his hunt in return for his body when it was done. You will fall. Your beautiful partner hiding on the steps there will go next, and then the city."

"Do you have the case? You promised you'd deliver it."

"Why do you care? You're a walking dead man."

"Because I held up my part of the bargain. You owe me that."

Mentezis paused and a grim smile spread across his face. "Ah, you're a quick learner. Yes, it's in the front seat of Phyllis's car. Perhaps I should take your body instead of killing you. You're in much better shape than Fish and I wouldn't have to spend so much of my energy maintaining a corpse."

"Thanks, that's all I wanted to know."

A puzzled expression crossed Mentezis's face. Then he glanced down to see a ghostly lance sticking through his chest. He threw his head back in a voiceless scream and an explosion of energy ripped out of Fish's body. With a quick twist, the spear was withdrawn and Fish's corpse slumped to the ground for a final time.

I picked up my pistol and stood up. "You took your time, Naomi."

The ghostly Valkyrie stepped from the shadows between the cars. Her wings folded behind her and with a shimmer she returned to her more modern appearance. "I couldn't move before now. I had to be absolutely sure the case was here. Otherwise I would have had to continue following him. You distracted him enough to let me get into position and I appreciate that. Speaking of which, you seemed sure I was nearby."

"Your horse has a distinctive odor."

She laughed. "Indeed."

Ze'eva joined us—Naomi didn't even bat an eye at here were form—and we went over to Phyllis's car. True to his word, the case was lying undisturbed in the front seat. Naomi inspected it and, with a nod, verified everything was as it was supposed to be. With a whistle, she summoned Ebonfire and strapped the case to his saddle.

"So, what happened to Mentezis?"

"I severed the link between him and Fish Clayborne's soul. He was sent back to the Abyss. I suspect it will take several centuries for him to regenerate down there. He's not gone, but considering how long your lifespan is, you won't have to worry about him again."

"Thanks, I think."

"This will do well. Tell Theo Markham he may keep the mirror, but to be careful with it. Opening a passage to the Shadowed Lands is dangerous even for those who know what they're doing. I think it would be a good idea if he kept it in his vault with his other curiosities."

She climbed into the saddle with one swift move and took the reins in her hand. I patted Ebonflame on the neck and he gave me a look that said if I did that again I would be missing a hand. I cautiously withdrew my hand and apologized.

"Will you be able to catch the boat back to the Shadowed Lands in time?" Ze'eva asked as they started to take off.

"With Ebonflame, I won't need the boat, so yes we should arrive well before the deadline."

I held out a hand. "Wait, I have two questions before you take off."

"Please be quick, Theron. We have some margin for error but very little."

"One, why didn't you just fly the soul back on Ebonflame to begin with?"

Naomi laughed. "Because I can't summon Ebonflame in my corporeal body. Novice Valkyrie must spend most of their time corporeal until we finish training. Only when I complete my training will I be allowed unfettered flight both on my own and with our steeds. Now, hurry, what's the last question? I must be airborne soon."

"Where's my payment?"

The next day I reached the office to find Ze'eva on the couch with an ice bag on her head. "Oh my goddess, I'd trade half a dozen other ailments than the pain of transforming back into a human in the morning."

"The wolf won't go away quietly?"

"Not even." She peeked at me from beneath the ice bag. "You're in early—and chipper too. What's going on?"

I took a seat at my desk and propped my feet up. "Just

waiting for the courier to arrive. Naomi said our payment would be here this morning, remember? Oh, and Jasypth found out that the 'unnamed group' buying up all of Rocko's businesses was a front for Phyllis. She'd set up two dummy corporations to hide her activities. It's obvious that Rocko's retirement wasn't quite the future she had planned for herself."

Ze' stretched out, wincing as she forced her arms and legs into different positions. "I can't believe you let her go with that promise. How would you track her down if she welshed?"

"Ze', part of being a good detective is being able to read a client. If Naomi says she's good for it, then she's good for it.

There was a knock on the door and Kyra stuck her head into our office. "Hey, guys, a messenger just dropped off a package addressed to the two of you."

I gave Ze' my best "I-told-you-so" smile and bounded into the other room. It was a narrow envelope and very light. I held it up to the light and saw only a couple of sheets of paper inside.

"Odd."

Ze'eva snickered. "Or not. Go ahead and open it, o master of reading people."

The first page was a list of locations. The second page was a note in beautiful cursive script.

Theron,

Valkyrie don't have a lot of worldly wealth, but hopefully this will help. These are the locations of all of Rocko's vaults. I know you won't keep the money because it's stolen or gained through nefarious means, but I suspect there should be quite the finder's fee for returning the items. Use the money to set up a foundation for the needy of Calasia—you could call it the Valkyrie Foundation if you like irony. Either way, it won't make you rich, but you should at least catch up on all your bills.

Until we cross paths again.

Naomi

We stared at the note until Kyra broke in. "Does this mean you're going to make up my back salary, boss?"

I stared out the window at the sunlight washing over Calasia, knowing just how close to death the city had come. Finally, I turned around and swept up Kyra and Ze'eva in my arms, spinning them around the room. "I should certainly say so, and bonuses all around. In fact, let's go find these treasures and secure them."

Kyra gasped. "Quick, Ze'eva—you call the asylum, I'll knock him out. All this wealth he's imagining has made him nuts."

"Nonsense, my faithful fae. In fact, as soon as this is over, I'm authorizing vacations with pay for all of us."

Ze'eva slipped out of my arms and grabbed the phone. "Forget the asylum, I'm calling Theo. He's obviously possessed."

"Maybe," I said with a grin. "But in a good way."

Case 4:
The
Sparkly
Reaper
Affair

THE SPARKLY REAPER AFFAIR

I stood at the window, staring at my little slice of Calasia. The evening breeze caught the sounds of the city starting to wind down and swirled them through the concrete canyons of Downtown. The half-moon was rising higher in the sky, but there was enough light for some of the local kids to be playing stickball in the nearby alley. I glanced over at the empty desk across from mine. Ze'eva Blackthorne, my partner, was off visiting relatives in the Imperial capital with her father, leaving me to my own devices.

It had been another "exciting" day at the office, which translated into the phone ringing once and that was the local rag trying to convince my secretary, Kyra, to take out a subscription. If business didn't pick up soon, I might need to do that—mainly for the want ads. The shadows creeping across the floor of my office told me it was time to go home. I grabbed my coat and hat, shooed Kyra out the door, and locked up behind her.

Kyra's wings fluttered, indicating she was upset, even though her voice betrayed nothing. "Bills are due next week, Theron."

It was an old story she was tired of repeating, about the financially challenged gumshoe and the surly debt collectors, co-starring the harried secretary who had to keep them at bay while her boss was out hustling the next assignment. I hated leaving her in that situation, but unfortunately that's one of the complications of being a detective's secretary. Still, I don't know what I'd do without her.

I patted her on the shoulder. "Kyra, this is Calasia. We both know it's just a matter of time before someone does something they're not supposed to do. Eventually, they're going to need a detective and I still have a pretty good reputation in town."

"If you say so, Theron. The landlord stopped by yesterday with a rent reminder. I don't think he'll accept your reputation as payment."

I clamped my mouth hard to keep a few choice words I'd learned in the Imperial military police from curling Kyra's hair even more. Only when we reached the outside door did I feel I could speak civilly again. I flashed the smile that always worried her. "I may have to schedule a little talk with our esteemed landlord."

She grabbed my arm and shook her head vigorously, her curls swirling around her face. "I wouldn't do that, Theron. Face it, someone shot up our office a few months ago—and not for the first time either. He took it better than I expected, but some of the other tenants wouldn't mind seeing us kicked out. He appreciates you helping him out of that jam with the protection mugs, but he's a businessman first. If we cost him tenants, we become a liability."

I hated it when she made sense.

"All right, Kyra, I'll try to line something up before the end of next week. Now, you'd better run home before your mom gets worried and sends one of your cousins out looking for me . . . again."

"Now, Theron, you know Mom likes you."

"Sure, she does. But your cousins . . . ?" I pantomimed stretching my neck. How a young lady who's barely over four foot tall can have two cousins who tower over seven, I'll never understand, fae or not.

Kyra punched me on the arm before hurrying across the sidewalk and flagging down a cab. Once I saw she was safely en route, I decided to walk the twelve blocks to my apartment building. The sun had almost set and the streetlamps were fighting against the remaining glow in the sky, creating deep shadows. I took comfort in the familiar weight just beneath my left armpit and set off.

I'd like to blame concentrating on where I might score a new case for distracting me—but I simply didn't hear the guy behind me. However, when he put his hand on my shoulder, I didn't spin around or try anything stupid. The feeling of naked bones and the cold radiating from that hand brought me up short.

Turning around, I tried to put a nonchalant smile on my face. The figure towered over me, his black hooded robe hiding his features. I took a quick glance and, yes, his legendary scythe rested comfortably in his left hand. However, as imposing as he was, I had the strangest feeling he felt as awkward as I did.

"Wow, I-I didn't think it was quite my time," I stammered, staring up at him.

A deep voice rumbled from the open hood and damned if he didn't sound embarrassed. "No, Mr. Chase, it is not your time. Sorry, I didn't mean to startle you. People have a hard time seeing me if I don't make physical contact. Goes with the job."

My knees nearly buckled with relief. "I never thought about the Reaper being a job."

"It's a hereditary position. My family has served the Imperium for eight generations. But that's not why I sought you out."

I pulled out a handkerchief and wiped it across my brow. "Believe me, that's the best news I've heard in weeks. So, why *are* you looking for me?"

I heard scuffling behind him and before he could say

anything a small, sparkling, hooded figure stepped out from behind him. It took my hand in its bony fingers and spoke in a young girl's voice. "Please, Mr. Chase, my bin chicken is missing and I need help finding it."

Now, I never thought I'd ever consider a reaper being cute, but something about her melted my heart. Maybe it was the glitter. Her scythe, while very effective looking, was as sparkly as her robes. I glanced at the dark figure and he rested a hand on her shoulder.

"What my daughter has said is essentially correct. Her bin chicken *is* missing. We discovered the empty coop when I got home from my afternoon rounds. However, it is not merely a missing pet. The lock was picked and discarded. It is *imperative* that we recover the creature as soon as possible."

I held up a hand to give myself a chance to sort everything out. "Let me take this in. Someone has birdnapped the Reaper's daughter's pet—knowing what you could do if you caught them? We're obviously not dealing with run-of-the-mill crooks here."

"Obviously. I'm familiar with your work, Mr. Chase. You show a distinct lack of prejudice toward nonhumans . . . a rather rare trait. This is why I wish to hire you. Most people would not aid me due to my profession. Of course, you will be paid for your services."

However much he paid me, I had no doubt I'd earn every crown. No one *just* takes on the Reaper.

"Tell you what. Don't touch anything and I'll swing by in the morning to look over the scene. Maybe I can pick up some clues or perhaps the birdnappers will contact you between now and then."

"I'm afraid that won't work, Mr. Chase. You'll need to get started immediately."

The small numbers in my checkbook fought with my desire for a meal and bed. "No offense, Reaper. I realize this is your daughter's pet, but why won't this wait until morning? And what is a bin chicken anyway?"

The two reapers glanced at each other and it was obvious there was a conversation going on I was not privy to. I hate it when my clients decide how much to tell me, because they invariably don't tell me enough. I find the truth eventually, but much later than I should have. However, their scythes convinced me to keep my opinions to myself.

After a few seconds, the father looked down at me and spoke in resigned tones. "A bin chicken is another name for a white ibis, a bird associated with wetlands and marshes."

"An unusual choice for a pet, I agree, but why is this one so special?"

"The creature is demonic, Mr. Chase. It is quite carnivorous and when outside of the special coop we designed for it, it has an insatiable taste for human flesh. As you can see, it's quite imperative we recover this bird."

For once in my life, I had no comeback.

F ollowing my new client, I soon discovered a maze of alleys I didn't even know existed in Calasia until we reached the Reaper's home. It looked like your typical brownstone, except it wasn't attached to any other buildings. Stepping onto the property, I swear I felt the air temperature drop a few degrees, but I'm certain that was my imagination.

I turned to my host as he led me to the back of the house. "Excuse me, but since 'Reaper' is more of a job title than a name, what should I call you?"

"Oh, sorry. I don't usually have enough time to introduce myself. I'm Mort. This is my daughter, Winks."

Of course.

The backyard was hidden in shadows, so I started to pull out my flashlight, but Mort stopped me and held his scythe aloft. After a few seconds of it glowing, the area was lit up like it was noon. I noted the light didn't seem to spill beyond the edges of the property. I chalked that up to magical weirdness and began my investigation.

Mort was right about one thing: the lock had been picked and the lack of scratches suggested it had been done by a pro. I checked the ground next to the coop and found two sets of footprints. One looked like it had belonged to a boot; given the depth of the impressions, I figured the owner was about my weight. The other set appeared to be made by feet with scales and long toes ending in talons.

"So, does your bin chicken have a name, Winks?"

"His name is Stymph."

I made a big deal of writing that down in my notebook. "And what does Stymph look like? How big is he?"

"He's very handsome and has a lot of *really* sharp teeth. I feed him a lot of my extra bunnies. He's about three foot tall and doesn't weigh a whole lot. His feathers are white except for his head and the ends of his wings, which are black."

"Are his feet this big?" I asked, pointing to the claw tracks I was examining—and sincerely hoping they weren't.

She giggled. "No, silly, his feet are only this big." She held her hands much closer together.

"Winks is technically correct. The magic of the coop keeps Stymph at a normal size for an ibis. However, once the magic wears off, he's going to grow a lot bigger."

That didn't sound promising. "How much bigger?"

"Well, he's not going to be stomping buildings like some of the sea creatures I've heard about." Mort raised his hand and continued. "Imagine a nine-foot-tall bird, with razor-sharp talons, three-inch teeth, and an insatiable appetite."

No, nothing to worry about, Chase. Only the end of Calasia if you don't find it in time.

I reviewed what I had learned in my visit. Given the footprints, I had an avian and something wearing boots for initial suspects. In a city the size of Calasia, that narrowed the field down to about 450,000 humanoids. Given the size of the tracks, I could eliminate the troll and ogre populations, but that only removed 3,000 suspects, give or take. No, to get anywhere, I had to hope the avian tracks led me to someone who could give me some answers before I was introduced to a very large, very hungry man-eating bird.

I looked around Mort's place a bit longer, but that was the sum total of what I had to go on. Mort told me the bird had been fed about an hour before it was spotted missing, so we probably had until dawn before it would expect to be fed again. All I could do was hope whoever was stupid enough to swipe something from the Reaper had the sense to keep it caged. A long shot, yes, but I've dealt with worse odds.

"Okay, Mort, I've done all I can here. What's your number, so I can call you if I find the bird?"

"I don't have a phone. It's not exactly required for my business."

Of course. "Well, how do I get a hold of you?"

He thought for a second and then handed me a copper coin. "Touch this to your tongue when you need to reach me."

I thought about bringing up the fact that magic tends to not work—or works oddly—when I'm around, but hey, he was a reaper. I figured he knew what he's doing, so I pocketed the coin and said good-bye. Just in case the coin trick didn't work, I tried to memorize the route back out to the main streets. If I couldn't reach him, I wanted to be sure to deliver Stymph well before feeding time.

The sound of traffic as I retraced my path was just starting to relax me when I heard soft footsteps from behind. Before I could turn, I felt something cold and hard connect with the top of my head.

And then I didn't feel anything at all.

"Hey, mister."

The voice sounded a million miles away, but like a drowning man I grabbed hold and let it drag me out of the swirling darkness that filled my head. When I could force my eyes open, I saw two guys standing over me. "What happened?"

"I guess you had too much to drink, mister. We found you passed out in the alley over there."

I reached up and felt my head; beneath the dried blood was an egg-sized lump. "There was a shot involved, but no alcohol."

"Got mugged, did you? Sorry to hear that. Do you need an ambulance?"

They helped me back to my feet. I wobbled a bit, but after a few seconds, I found my balance. "No, but thanks anyway."

The one guy shrugged. "Okay, mister, but do us a favor, will you?"

"What's that?"

"Wait until we're out of sight before you fall down again? We done picked you up four times already."

Ah, Calasia, you're all heart.

I waited for the cobwebs to clear, checked my pockets to make sure the "good citizens" hadn't charged for their services, and started off again. I made my way to a drugstore for some aspirin and a diner for some food and coffee. Once the pounding in my head settled, I caught a passing streetcar and headed toward the South Hills. If an avian was involved, odds were it was a harpy. There were a few other winged folk around town, but only a couple of races had avian feet. Of those, most of them were native to the Southern Islands, hundreds of miles from here. If something was going on, someone in Aerie should know about it.

Of course, the trick was going to be finding someone who'd talk. Humans weren't popular among harpies and I rated a bit lower than most since I'd broken up two of their burglary rings last year. I decided to call in a favor from Kova Illisi, one of the few harpies I knew personally. He'd been set up to take the fall for a robbery, and his family had approached me for help. Like me, they had little faith in the Calasian constables' ability to find their noses with both hands, much less uncover evidence needed to clear him. With luck, and some help from Kyra's family contacts, I was able to spot some overlooked evidence and put the finger on the right person. Hopefully Kova could point me in the right direction if nothing else.

Fifteen minutes later, I hopped off the trolley and began walking into the South Hills district. Like the street in front of me, the buildings of the South Hills have all seen better days. It's one of the older districts in town and it shows its age. Even a fresh coat of paint wouldn't hide the run-down feeling that oozed out of the area.

Don't let the tourist guides fool you; Calasia has some nice places, especially the theater district or the fancy spreads up in the North Hills, but the South Hills they tend to ignore. The place is bad enough in broad daylight, but now, with the dark sky and absence of streetlights, the area seemed to grow grimier and more run-down with every block.

I paused in front of a diner to take advantage of the dim light spilling out the windows and check my watch. It was ten o'clock, which meant I had *some* time before the oncoming disaster, but not as much as I'd like. When I resumed my hike, I felt someone watching from the shadows. I hadn't expected to be invisible, but I didn't think I looked *that* out-of-place. I guess other than the locals people don't hang around the hills after nightfall.

My eyes adjusted to the dimly lit streets the farther I moved into the district. The sidewalks were buckled and crooked, which forced me to spend more time watching my feet than the surrounding area. That could be a recipe for disaster in the South Hills, but if I didn't want to wind up facedown on the pavement again, my options were limited. After a while, I found my rhythm and made better progress.

It was obvious the city works people hadn't visited South Hills in years. If I was complaining about the sidewalks, the few cars that drove past me were suffering even worse with the potholes. And, whoever laid out the street map for this district must have loved snakes. Greenbriar Drive, the road I was currently walking along, took me the better part of a half hour to climb with all its switchbacks and curves.

About the time I reached my destination, I felt more than saw a presence behind me. I stopped in a darkened doorway, but whoever was trailing me spotted my little maneuver. After a while, the sense of passing time forced me to move on. Someone was interested in what I was doing, which wasn't a good sign.

My exertions led me to an old, abandoned hotel near the top of Greenbriar. The main floor was boarded up, but I wasn't worried about that. The harpies in town used the upper levels. They'd turned it into a tent city and only moved indoors when the weather was bad. Tonight the sky was clear so they shouldn't be hard to find. Whether they'd want to see me was another matter.

Around back, I found what might have been the hotel's only working fire escape ladder. It was a little out of reach so with a little exertion, and a rather ingenious use of my belt, I snagged the lowest rung and tugged. With a sound that deserved to be the star of its own horror movie, the sliding ladder broke loose from the rust holding it in place and descended low enough for me to climb aboard. I began making my way up the rickety metal stairway.

About the second landing, I thought I saw something

moving in the shadows, but as before, I couldn't confirm it. I chalked it up to an overactive imagination or the lump on my head, and pressed onward.

As I climbed, the city noises faded and were replaced by more natural sounds—the wind, the cry of the seagulls circling, the sound of a foghorn calling out of the darkness to the south. I watched the fog roll in, covering the warehouse district of South Point with a blanket of white. It was as if the fog cut South Hills off from the rest of Calasia.

That's poetic, Chase, but it's not getting you any closer to the answers you need. Keep moving.

By the time I'd reached the fourth floor, I heard the slow thud of footsteps on the metallic fire escape below me. Apparently, my shadow wasn't as imaginary as I'd thought. I considered turning around and challenging him, but one glance at the fire escape's quality—or lack thereof—and how far it was to the ground changed my mind. A confrontation on the roof might not be safer, but the roof was less likely to collapse under the strain of our combined weight.

It's amazing how quickly aching muscles quit complaining when adrenaline is flowing. Reaching the roof, I was struck by the poles, wires, and tents stretching from one side of the hotel to the other. The harpies had turned the roof into a maze of cloth alleyways and homes. With my shadow gaining on me, I decided I'd take the ten-cent tour later.

I moved quickly into the interior and found a hiding spot, trying not to trip on the debris or clothesline myself on the supports. There were too many innocents around to risk using my .45, so I tugged on the sleeve of my coat and my head knocker, a nice thick piece of black oak, slid into my hand. The familiar weight brought a smile to my face and I waited for my playmate.

My turn.

The footsteps were faint, but steady. I could see a shadow

apparently moving on two feet against a tent across the way, but whoever had been following me was cagey. From the way the shadowy head moved from side to side, it could tell I'd gone to ground and was in no hurry to become the hunted. I held my breath and tightened my grip on the head knocker.

The shadow took one more step, bringing it within reach. I don't know how he did it, but as I stepped forward and swung, he brought up his arm and blocked me. I heard his gun skitter across the roof, but that was about all the time I had before we hit the rooftop together. I felt him shift and went for his neck but his knee caught me in a very sensitive place first. My stomach churned and my breath came out in an odd wheeze as I rolled over on my back. I caught him with a kick in the chest before he could take advantage of it, sending him stumbling back into one of the tents.

The tent collapsed amid a chorus of shrieks, curses, and a flurry of feathers. Before either of us could react, a dozen harpies took to the air and circled the rooftop. The shadow broke away from me and bolted toward the roof's edge, but a net came spinning out of the sky, enveloping the figure.

Deciding discretion was the better part of valor, I slipped my head knocker back into its sheath and stepped into the open with my hands over my head. Three harpies landed on tent poles near me—two armed with spears and one wielding a nasty-looking revolver. I did my statue imitation when a harpy with the fanciest hat I'd ever seen landed in front of me.

"Not many humans would sneak around the Aerie after dark, but I guess if any would, it would have to be you, Mr. Chase."

It was never a good sign when they knew your name.

"I'm afraid you have me at a disadvantage, Miss . . . ?" I let the sentence trail off, hoping she would fill in the gap. She looked a little familiar, though.

"You may call me Madame Xathria. Know your presence

here does not fill me with pleasure, fancy-pants detective Theron Chase."

"Madame, while I admit this visit isn't a social call, this is the first time I've ever visited the Aerie. I don't understand why you're so upset with me in particular."

She ignored my question. "So, why are you here, Mister Righter-of-Wrongs? Someone missing a bauble they left on their nightstand? Obviously, that means a harpy stole it. Face it, Mr. Detective, we get blamed for everything in this town."

This could have gone on all night, but I didn't have the time. I decided to take a chance and just level with her. Either it would get results or I'd get tossed off the roof. And given how little time we had until dawn, the roof-tossing might be a more pleasant way to go.

"Look, Madame, if I didn't have reasons to question a harpy, I wouldn't be here. I came here specifically to speak to—speak to, not arrest—Kova Illisi. A rather exotic pet was stolen earlier today. Harpy prints were found next to the cage. I'm not saying a harpy did it, but one was there around the time the theft took place."

When no one stopped me, I took another breath and continued. "I'd intended to announce myself, but as you noticed someone followed me up here. Why? I don't have a clue. But if I don't find this creature, it's going to be bad because the spell keeping it small and cute is going to wear off. When that happens, it will get *very* big and *very* hungry."

There was a lot of murmuring from the crowd. Finally a male harpy—Kova Illisi—pushed his way through the crowd, approached Madame Xathria, and bowed.

She waved a hand at him. "Speak, Kova."

"Madame, I know you are aware of Chase's reputation. He has always dealt with the harpies fairly. He's never arrested a harpy who has not broken a city law. He's disliked because he is good at his job, but he also risked his life to clear me. I humbly ask you to hear him out."

"Of course I *know* his reputation . . ." she said sternly.

Despite the situation, I smiled a little. Like I'd told Kyra, the word around town about me was pretty good.

". . . he sent two of my boys to prison," Madame Xathria continued as she glared at me.

Damn. *That's* why she looked so familiar—I'd been getting that same evil eye from the back of the courtroom every day of the trial.

"So, why shouldn't I toss him off the roof? We'll see how well he flies without feathers."

I shot a glance at the rickety fire escape ladder, but knew I'd never make it more than two steps before she tossed me into space.

"Were your sons guilty?" Kova asked.

"Guilty? Guilty of securing enough money to feed their families, maybe."

Maybe I should've kept my mouth shut, but I couldn't help myself. "Guilty of working for smugglers and slavers. The smuggling I might've overlooked, but they were helping steal people from the docks and selling them overseas."

I thought for a second she'd follow through on her threat to launch me, but the murderous light in her eyes faded and she lowered her gaze. "What they did was wrong, but it doesn't make me like you any better."

"I understand, Madame. However, if we do not find this bin chicken, it might be too late for anything, much less revenge. If I don't find it by morning, there may not be anyone left in Calasia by week's end."

A voice in the crowd spoke up. "A bin chicken? You mean Stymph?" The crowd parted, revealing a young harpy looking self-conscious.

"And you are . . . ?"

"Rani, Mr. Chase. Stymph, Winks, and I are friends. I visit him a couple of times a week. He gets lonely when Winks isn't around, so I take him snacks and sit and talk with him."

"Rani, were you there earlier today?"

"Yes, I was. I brought him some rats I'd caught. We visited for a while and then I left so I could get home before dark. Mom worries if I'm gone too long."

I wiped the sudden sweat off my forehead and pushed on. "Rani, I need to ask you a couple of questions. You're not in trouble, but I have to have the truth. Did you let Strymph out of his cage?"

"Oh, no, Mr. Chase. Winks's dad said I wasn't ever supposed to do that. He even made a slot so I could put food into Strymph's cage without opening the door. Winks and I like to watch him eat. He pounces on things like lightning! Two snaps and it's gone."

I tried to put that image out of my mind. "Did you see anyone else in the area, either before you arrived or afterward?"

Rani thought hard and then smiled. "There was someone. I didn't get a good look at him, but he looked human. He was standing in a doorway across the street when I arrived. After I left, I flew around a bit and then I saw him getting into a car with a blanket. I think the blanket was moving, too. The car headed downtown. I didn't think anything about it until you mentioned Strymph was missing."

Great, there are only a couple thousand buildings downtown. I'm certain I can search them all by morning.

There was a commotion over beyond the tents and I remembered my playmate. Several harpies were pinning a large man still wrapped in netting. I motioned for them to let him sit up and they grudgingly did, although several kept their weapons trained on him. After he finished cursing and thrashing about, I knelt down in front of him. A bola was still wrapped around his legs and a pair of odd-looking goggles hung crookedly from his face. He definitely was sporting some serious bruises on his face from fighting with the harpies.

Once we got some light on him, a smile crept across my face. "Mick Brewster. Fancy meeting you up here in the penthouse. I always thought you were more the back-alley kind of guy."

Mick's eyes narrowed as he stared at me. "You'll be talking out of a hole in your throat if I ever get out of this net, Shamus."

I reached out and tapped the goggles. "New toys?"

"What do you care?"

"Those look like sniper goggles, Mick. Those aren't for sale on the civilian market. In fact, you can get in trouble just having them in your possession."

He let out a bitter laugh. "Cry me a river, shamus. You got me with stolen property—who cares? A fine, a couple months in jail, and bang, I'm out on the street again."

"Mick, last I heard you were still working for Sammy Taylor. How is ol' Sammy?"

A cruel smile spread across his face before he answered me. "He's better off than you. He ain't behind on his rent and taking cases from creeps like these."

I shook my head. "Mick, while I'm flattered you've taken such an interest in my bank account, I suggest you keep your opinions about our hosts to yourself. Especially since there's a whole lot more of them than there are of you."

"I ain't talkin' to you, Chase. Until I see my mouthpiece, I got nothing to say."

"Now, Mick, that's rather short-sighted. From my point of view, talking to me might be the only thing keeping you from a very short flight."

He spat on the roof beside my foot and sneered. "Yeah, Mr. Goody Two-shoes, like you'd let anything happen to me."

I stood up. "I've tried to be reasonable, Mick. But, given how important this is, I think it's time to be unreasonable . . ."

Fifteen minutes later, I walked down to the first landing. Over to the right, Mick looked quite green from hanging upside down, a rope tied around his feet leading back to the roof. The harpies had done a great job hanging him there. He was in no real danger, but he didn't know that, so now that the cursing and screaming had stopped, I figured he might answer a few questions.

"Look, Chase, you gotta get me down. I can't take this anymore. I think I'd rather fall than stay here."

I moved to where we were eye to eye before speaking. "Not my call, Mick. But, if you answer my questions, I'll put in a good word with the harpies. Maybe they won't leave you here until they get good and hungry."

"Chase, that ain't human. You can't do that."

I gently pushed on his shoulder, sending him swinging like a pendulum. "Now, Mick, someone slugged me with a blackjack earlier tonight. I might have a concussion or worse, amnesia. I might not remember seeing you up here like a holiday ornament." The smile left my face and I hoped he wouldn't question the sincerity in my voice. "Who's got the bin chicken and where is it?"

The first two times I swung him, he just cussed at me, but after the third time he turned green again and finally broke. "All right, all right, just stop it. I'll tell you what you want to know." I grabbed him and he paused to catch his breath.

"It was Mr. Taylor's idea. He's been awful sick lately. He thought if he stole the damn bird, he could bargain with the Reaper—you know, the bird in exchange for a few more years. He's in no hurry to check out."

"Didn't he think the Reaper might want to get revenge once he'd gotten the bird back?"

I threatened to push him again, but Mick swallowed hard

and started talking faster. "Yeah, but he's got a couple of necro-mancers setting wards against ol' skullface. Once he had the Reaper under control, he was going to extract a promise to leave him alone for another twenty years. You know how things are with creatures like the Reaper; if they make a vow, they have to keep it."

"So, did you swipe the bird?"

"Are you kidding? I want nothing to do with no bird that can eat me. My job was to keep an eye on the place and see what the Reaper did. We hadn't even delivered the ransom note yet. No one expected him to hire someone like you this quick. Still, if he did, I was supposed to follow and discourage you." He paused and continued with a rueful tone in his voice. "Trouble is, you don't *discourage* very easily. That's why I followed you here."

"To finish the job?"

"Nothing personal, Chase. I was just gonna bop you and tie you up until things blew over."

I felt the lump on my head. "We'll discuss bopping another time. So, where's the bird?"

"All I heard was they was taking the bird back to Mr. Taylor's place. But even if it's there, *you* ain't gonna get it."

"And why not?"

"Unless you're bulletproof or can turn invisible, you're not going to get through the small army he's got guarding that damn bird. And even if you did, the necromancers brought a few 'friends' along for backup. Hard to kill what's already dead, if you catch my drift. The Imperial treasury is probably less well defended."

"Thanks, Mick. I think that'll do it."

A visible shudder of relief flowed through his body. "So, you gonna cut me down?"

I smiled before responding. "Something like that."

I signaled and the harpies began hauling Mick up. He began

screaming at me, "Chase you promised! You said you'd put in a good word with them."

"Don't worry, Mick. There are some things even harpies won't eat. You definitely fit that category."

He cursed all the way to the rooftop then there was a thud and blissful silence. Kova flew down and landed on the rail beside me. The frame creaked with the added weight, but somehow the old bolts held the fire escape to the brick wall.

"So, what will you do now?"

"I'm not sure." I checked my watch and saw it was after midnight. The enormity of what I had ahead hit me like a sledgehammer. "It's going to be tight, Kova. I'm not sure I have enough time to get downtown, infiltrate that building, slip past all the guards, swipe a demonic ibis without it raising a racket, *and* get back to the Reaper's before dawn. I mean, I'm good, but I'm not sure I'm *that* good."

"Is there anything we can do to help?"

"Rani, the young harpy who visits Strymph, would be useful. If she's nearby, she might be able to keep Strymph calm long enough for me to get it back to the Reaper's on time."

"I'll ask Madame Xathria for permission to have the girl accompany you. She still bears a great grudge, but your behavior tonight mollified her a bit. Do not presume this is the last you'll hear of it though."

"I'm sorry for her loss"—well, not really, but I wasn't going to get into that now—"but I won't look the other way for anyone, not even you, Kova."

"I know, Theron Chase, which is why I offer to work with you."

While Kova flew back up, a cold wind whistled up the hill, sending debris bouncing around in the alley below. The fog had climbed even higher up the hill, making the scene even more surreal. I heard the noise above me rise in volume. Apparently the harpies were having quite the debate about my proposal, but there was no time for me to wait for their decision. Besides, most of them fly faster than I can walk—they'd catch up if they decided to help me.

By the time I reached the bottom of Greenbriar, Kova swooped down. I could tell from the look on his face what the answer was. He apologized profusely and agreed to keep Mick under wraps for me, but I was on my own from here on out.

A n hour and a half later, I was standing at the entrance to an ordinary-looking office building. The only light I could see through the door was from the night elevator across the lobby. An old guy sat in there dozing. It took a dozen raps on the glass before he heard me and an eternity for him to shuffle over to the door.

His muffled voice came through the glass. "Building's closed, son. No one's here. Go home."

"Can't do it. Got an appointment with Mr. Taylor and I know he's in."

The old guy cocked his head to one side and scanned me from head to toe before fishing out a ring of keys and unlocking the door. "Mr. Taylor, eh? Didn't mention anything to me, but come on, I'll take you up to his floor."

He shut the door behind me and lifted the handle to make the elevator rise. I pretended not to notice him push a small button on the end of the handle, so I wasn't surprised four gunsels were waiting when the elevator stopped at the twenty-seventh floor. They hustled me out of the elevator, frisked me none to friendly-like, confiscated both my pistol and my head knocker, and then the youngest of the group stepped forward.

"So, you had an appointment with Mr. Taylor. Strange. I'm his personal secretary and I didn't book you."

"My apologies, I may have misspoken. I have information for

Mr. Taylor and it won't wait until normal business hours. It's in regard to a certain feathered item that's recently come into his possession. I represent its rightful owner."

"Oh, you do? Curiouser and curiouser. Whom should I say is calling?"

"Theron Chase."

"Ah-ha. So you're Chase. I've heard of you." That reputation of mine, again. "Bring him along, boys, this oughtta be good."

The three other thugs half-dragged, half-pushed me down the corridor to a corner office where I was none-to-pleasantly led inside and shoved down into a chair. My toys were deposited on a desk in front of a nondescript middle-aged man. If you didn't know Samuel R. Taylor, Entrepreneur—as the sign on his desk read—was one of the four biggest crime bosses in the city, you'd walk past him and probably never notice him. That's probably helped his long and prosperous career.

He leaned back in his chair and gave me the once-over before speaking. His voice sounded like velvet rubbed on silk, but there was no questioning the steel hidden beneath. "So, Mr. Chase, I understand you have a client who has expressed interest in an item I possess."

"If you mean the bin chicken, then yes."

"Short and to the point, I see. I want certain terms and conditions met before I return said item."

I glanced at my watch and decided there was nothing to lose by laying my cards on the table; otherwise, we could do the polite talk until we were all eaten. "Sammy, you're making a horrible mistake. The threat to you is not my client. The package you've got is what's gonna kill you. The spell keeping the ibis small and peaceful is wearing off as we speak. In a few hours, you're going to have a huge, carnivorous bird on your hands, one I doubt you can control—hell, I doubt the Imperial Marines will be able to subdue it. So unless you want to die, along with most of Calasia, I need to return the bird now."

The room fell silent for a moment after my rant and then laughter rang out around the room. Sammy wiped a few tears from his eyes. "Whooo boy, Chase. Whatever the Reaper is paying you, it ain't enough. You almost had me believing you." After a few more chuckles, the smile vanished from his face and his features hardened. At that moment, I had no problem believing Sammy Taylor was one of the most dangerous men I'd ever faced. "You go back and tell the Reaper to come himself. I need guarantees and I need vows or the bird is going to make some back-alley punk a great dinner. Get him outta here."

The ride back downstairs was a bit more crowded with the four extra thugs who rode down with me. We stopped by the front door just long enough for three of the guys to play bounce-the-detective before ignominiously tossing me out on my face. Junior strolled over and surprisingly handed me back my .45 and head knocker before leaving me in the street.

Well, at least I tried to warn him. My conscience is clear, but that doesn't get me any closer to getting Strymph and time's running out.

The night winds were as cold as my mood. I walked around into an alley to see if there was another way in I'd missed, but I couldn't find anything. I stuck my hands deep into my pockets to warm them and felt something . . . something that might just ensure this evening ended on a good note. I pulled the oddly-shaped copper coin out of my pocket and carefully placed it on my tongue.

Instantly, I felt hot and cold and I doubled over like something was ripping my guts out. When I finally opened my eyes, I saw my own body lying in the alley. *Wow, I must've hit my head again.* It took me several seconds to realize I *was* seeing my body. I was floating a few feet away from *me*. After I finished panicking, I realized the Reaper wouldn't go to all the trouble to hire me just to kill me with this coin. This must be what it's supposed to do.

Did I happen to mention I hate magic?

Since I was already floating, I turned in the direction of the Reaper's home and decided to try flying there. Well, I *thought* I was going to fly there, but the next thing I knew, I was at his front door. I can't even describe how I got there. It was as if I decided to go and there I was.

Before I could knock, it opened and he was standing there, hood flipped back and a cup of something in his hand. "Ah, Mr. Chase, I see you have news."

I guess if you're a reaper, you get used to apparitions just showing up on your front stoop. I gathered my thoughts and related the events of the evening to him. He shook his head sadly before speaking.

"Poor Samuel Taylor, always so worried about his health and how long he's going to live. Trade secret, Mr. Chase, Mr. Taylor wasn't due to kick the bucket for another twenty years. *Actually*, he was going to die peacefully in his sleep."

"Was?"

If I thought Samuel Taylor was dangerous, I was premature. If I never see a smile like the Reaper's again, I'll die a very happy man. "*Was*. You see, Mr. Chase, one of the perks of this job is I can adjust anyone's timeline in either direction if they deserve it." He flipped up his hood and his voice dropped two octaves and about forty degrees, "And stealing my daughter's favorite pet and making her cry . . . well, I would say his timeline deserves to be tweaked."

He flicked his hand; the cup disappeared and his scythe took its place. As he started moving toward the door, he spoke again in the voice I was used to hearing from him. "Oh, Mr. Chase, it might be a good idea to return to your body while you can. The coin's magic only lasts so long and I'd hate for you to be trapped without a body."

There was a sudden rush, as if I had been snatched up in a huge windstorm, and when I had my thoughts back together, I was lying in the alleyway, looking up at the office building. I felt a presence beside me and spun around to see Winks standing beside me. Somehow, seeing her without her dad looming around made her slightly less frightening, until I noticed the scythe with her. Yep, still sparkly and still very, very sharp.

"You found Strymph?"

"I know where he is and told your dad. I didn't actually see him, but I suspect he's fine."

As fast as she was nodding her head, I kept waiting for her cowl to fly off. "Oh, I'm sure he's fine. Besides, unless they had the right weapons, I don't think they can hurt him. Do you humans usually carry magical iron weapons?"

"Uh, no, usually lead and steel."

"Oh, that won't do. It's probably a good thing Dad went to get him, then."

I tried to envision a nine-foot-tall, ravenous, demonic bird rampaging through the city—who, by the way, was invulnerable to most weapons—and felt little cold feet running up and down my spine. Changing the subject, I pointed in the direction of South Hills. "I understand you have a friend, Rani, who comes over to help you feed him."

"Oh yes, she brings over the best rats and pigeons. Strymph really likes those."

I swallowed down a bit of bile imagining that scene. "By the way, Winks, was there a reason you followed me here?"

"Sure, Mr. Chase. I wanted to make sure you got back into your body."

I gave myself a quick patdown and frowned at her. "Was there a reason I should have been worried?"

"Well, it's no big secret magic and you don't get along well. I had to make sure the coin's spell worked. It wouldn't be much fun floating around as a spirit, especially if your body got buried and *then* you were put back in."

Now, there's a cheery thought.

"I appreciate your concern. Were you going to put me back into my body if I didn't get there in time?"

"Oh no, Mr. Chase, I was going to be sure your spirit died too. That way, you couldn't wind up buried alive by mistake. Better if you're all-the-way dead if that happened. Okay, I'm going to go visit Rani. I think Strymph deserves some treats after the night he's had."

After the night he's *had?* "Yeah, kid. You do that."

I shuddered all the way back to my apartment after that conversation.

The next morning, I grabbed the paper from the kid on the corner. The headlines blared about a gangland massacre last night. According to the article, Mr. Samuel R. Taylor and his associates were mysteriously killed last night. Seems they all just dropped dead in Sam's office. The constables had no witnesses, no motive, and no apparent cause of death. The constables had quarantined the building until they could rule out magical curses or plagues in the building.

Reading a bit further, apparently Mick Bradshaw was the only known surviving associate, but he was missing. The constables were searching for him as a "person of interest." I wondered how long the harpies would keep him.

I tucked the paper under my arm and headed upstairs to the office. Just as I put my hand on the knob, I heard Kyra's voice through the door and the sound of the receiver going back on the hook. I pushed the door open and strode across the office, poured myself a fresh cup of coffee, and took a seat on the corner of her desk.

"More bad news, Kyra?"

She looked at the phone, shook her head, and then turned to

me. "Boss! You look like hell. Did something happen last night after I went home?"

I took a sip of my coffee before answering. "Oh, nothing serious. A client approached me on the way home and I spent the night looking for a missing pet."

"Must have been *some* pet."

"Well, it was *some* client. I had a few playmates who didn't want to take no for an answer. I take it that call has something to do with this line of questioning?"

"That was the bank. They called to confirm the check they received this morning was accurate."

"Wow, he didn't waste any time paying off. But we get checks all the time. What was the problem?"

"The bank manager was trying to verify that Mortis Thanatos actually deposited a thousand-crown check into your account overnight."

In spite of everything that had happened last night, I nearly choked on my coffee. "Wow, Mort is a great tipper. I figured I'd get maybe a hundred for my efforts."

"Theron, I *know* who Mort is. What were you *doing* working for him?"

I smiled. "Well, he didn't seem to be the kind of guy you say no to, Kyra. Besides, it was a simple matter. I just had to find his daughter's bin chicken."

"His daugh—? Oh. Maybe that explains it."

"Explains what?"

Kyra smiled made a brushing motion with her hand. "The bank was concerned about the check. Apparently it was covered in sparkles that burst into flames when you brush them off."

Luckily, I had refrained from taking another sip, or I'd have probably choked again. "I'd tell them to process the check and not worry. I'm pretty sure Mort's good for it. And soon as it clears, be sure to pay off our creditors—and give yourself a nice bonus with the leftovers."

"Theron, shouldn't we put some of that away for later?"

"No, I have a feeling we should spend this as soon as possible. What's that quote—'eat, drink, and be merry because tomorrow we may meet the Reaper'?"

"That doesn't sound quite right, boss."

I closed my eyes and saw two hooded figures standing behind me. "Close enough, Kyra, close enough."

www.ingramcontent.com/pod-product-compliance
Lightning Source LLC
Chambersburg PA
CBHW070222260626
47160CB00002B/654